CROW'S ROW

JULIE HOCKLEY

iUniverse LLC
Bloomington

Crow's Row

iUniverse books may be ordered through booksellers or by contacting:

iUniverse
1663 Liberty Drive
Bloomington, IN 47403
www.iuniverse.com
1-800-Authors (1-800-288-4677)

Because of the dynamic nature of the Internet, any web addresses or links contained in this book may have changed since publication and may no longer be valid. The views expressed in this work are solely those of the author and do not necessarily reflect the views of the publisher, and the publisher hereby disclaims any responsibility for them.

Any people depicted in stock imagery provided by Thinkstock are models, and such images are being used for illustrative purposes only.
Certain stock imagery © Thinkstock.

ISBN: 978-1-4917-2874-1 (sc)
ISBN: 978-1-4917-2875-8 (e)
ISBN: 978-1-4917-2932-8 (hc)

Library of Congress Control Number: 2014904976

Printed in the United States of America.

iUniverse rev. date: 3/13/2014

For my husband

Thank you for your love, support, and enthusiasm ... and for finally convincing me to let you read this before I destroyed it. I couldn't have written it without you.

The man who desires something desires what is not available to him, and what he doesn't already have in his possession. And what he neither has nor himself is—that which he lacks—that is what he wants and desires.

—Plato, *Symposium*

PROLOGUE

The motor of my 1989 Chevrolet Caprice was thumping against the hood, making the whole car jitter. We sat in silence, stuck at another red light while the oversized muffler gurgled.

For the sixth time in the last five minutes, I checked my watch and sighed, aware that my left leg was impatiently shaking with the rest of the car. I stepped on the gas about a half second before the light turned green, trying to coerce the old lady in front of me to react a little faster—honking, swearing when she didn't react at all. The old lady woke up and finally stepped on it.

My bumper practically rubbed hers, but I had only one thing on my mind: colors. Would it be green or blue today? Maybe white—my favorite. A dark voice in the back of my mind offered no color at all as an alternative. I smothered that voice. The days of no color were simply too hard to bear. I needed color today. My cohort in the backseat echoed my edginess with a whine.

When the traffic came to Finch Road, the old lady veered off with everyone else. Finch was the line that separated city life from no man's land, which good people like the old lady ahead of me pretended didn't exist and steered away from as quickly as possible, lest it suck them in to the point where they would be forced to acknowledge its existence. I couldn't blame them—I wouldn't want my loved ones to come near this hellhole. Just the thought made my knuckles strangle the steering wheel.

As soon as I passed the Finch threshold, I switched on the music and turned up the volume until the tinted windows of the Caprice were vibrating. I was definitely in the projects now. Rusty, souped-up beaters lined the street, some half-parked on the crumbling sidewalks, others sitting tireless on cement blocks. Men and boys amassed in the doorways of decrepit apartment buildings, watching as I drove by. This was a place even the police avoided, and one of our best moneymakers when it came to drug traffic. I had nothing to fear here as long as I paid my respects before disappearing into the crowd.

I drove up to the last building at the end of the street, where a small group of choice gangbangers were waiting for me—a reminder that I was on their turf. This building was their headquarters, providing them with a full view of the business and goings-on of the street. I parked next to a fire hydrant, threw my baseball cap on, and pulled my hood up. I took a revolver out of the glove box and tucked it into the back of my jeans, making sure that just enough of the handle could be seen by those who would be looking for it.

Then I slipped out of the car, and Meatball jumped from the backseat. I had just enough time to grab the leash hanging from his thick neck before he followed me out.

In a motion that had become second nature, I scanned the area, gathering an infinite amount of information in a few short seconds: the shadowed doorways, the quick exit points, the thugs with guns who were staring at me, the ones who were avoiding my gaze. Basically, I spent my life with my stomach in a fist and my teeth clenched like I was already locked away, looking at the world through the steel bars of my cell.

But all was well in the projects today—as well as the projects could be.

The leader of the pack strutted over to me. He ordered his men to stand down, away from us, before he leaned in with a voice that only he and I could hear. "Afternoon, sir."

He was known as Grill—homage to his fully gold-plated smile, financed with his illegal fortunes. I nodded. Though Grill was a low-ranker—a much lower ranker—I was required to acknowledge him before entering his turf. This would ensure my safety, reassure him that my presence didn't mean that the leaders were trying to oust him.

"Out for a stroll?" he asked, and then he hopped back when Meatball stepped forward.

I tugged Meatball back and looked around us … I didn't need any trouble today.

Grill finally relaxed and cocked his head to the side. "You alone again today, sir?"

I checked my watch again and started to walk away, noting the look of indignation that crossed his face: he didn't appreciate being dismissed that way in front of his troops. But I had no time for ego stroking.

Meatball shepherded us through hordes of families that had gathered in a nearby clearing to enjoy the rest of the sunny May afternoon. The poor slobs had nowhere to go but here, and most of them would never leave the projects, nor would any of their gangbanger progeny. Stay. Procreate. Die. Repeat. That was the way of the projects.

Today it seemed as though they had all come out of their microscopic apartments into the clearing that kept them separated from the civilized world. With their apartment buildings looming in the background like human roach nests, the projects' colony was gathered in the field, the adults passing weed around makeshift barbecues while the little kids ran wild. I knew there was a pathway in the middle of the clearing, but you could hardly see it through the mob.

Meatball tugged ahead, and we quickly worked our way deeper into the crowd. I recognized some of the faces we passed. Judging from their stares, they recognized me too. There was no love lost there—I was the face of their problems; I couldn't hide the blood that stained my hands. But I wasn't trying to, either. All I wanted, needed, today was a few seconds of peace.

Meatball and I approached the picnic table that was farthest from the pathway. It was covered in cigarette burns, bird shit, and gum. The gangbangers who were gathered around it—their small piece of turf—vacated it as soon as they noticed me.

I pulled my shirt down over my jeans to hide my gun and leaned back against the dirty table.

After a few minutes, Meatball's head shot up, and his ears flattened to his skull. My breath quickened, the fist inside me loosened a quarter of an inch, and the dark voice inside my head was quiet, for now.

Chapter One

Forever Freakish

By the time the instructor called time, I had already meticulously gone over my exam paper five times. It must have been two hundred degrees in that auditorium, as if the school needed to make sure that absolutely no one would be spared the sweat of exam week. The steady trickle of sweat down the back of my neck was proof that I too hadn't been spared.

Callister University was not an Ivy League school. It had probably never even been in the running for a top one hundred, top one thousand, or any list of schools in the country. Still, I needed to maintain an A average to keep my full scholarship. So I took an extra second to check the dotted line at the right-hand corner of my paper, on the off chance that Professor Vernon was one of those profs who still gave students an extra point just for spelling their names correctly. *Emily Sheppard*. My name was spelled right, though I cringed, just a little. The Sheppard name was enough to make anyone squirm.

Then I put my pencil down, turned my exam paper over, and let a very small sigh escape me. I had officially survived one year of college. That milestone would have made most students gleeful. But for me, school was just an excellent way to kill time. Four months without school: I would be counting the days until it started again, the way kids count the days until Christmas.

I made it back to the house and stepped into complete chaos—then again, when you share a three-bedroom hole with six other students, every day is chaotic. You just learn to measure in degrees of chaos. In our house, chaos ranged anywhere from the morning run through the obstacle course of empty beer cases to get into the one bathroom, to the hope that using the toaster and the microwave at the same time wouldn't blow another fuse and send a disgruntled household back into the Dark Ages.

Today fell into the range of controlled anarchy. All my roommates were moving out for the summer. There were hampers and garbage bags bunched at the door, most of them filled to the brim with dirty laundry (a common end-of-term gift for parents). Everything was being packed—thrown, really—into whatever container my roommates could find, while their parents were shouting orders, trying to get out of our hole as quickly as possible.

Everyone who could escape Callister did so at the earliest opportunity. I was the only one of the seven of us who wasn't going home for the summer break. Burt and Isabelle, my parents, were spending the summer in France, where Isabelle had been born and overbred. Europe was a regular retreat for the Sheppard family. Like every other Sheppard pastime, I had put an end to that one: even a hot summer in a dead city was better than that torture.

My roommates were rushed with their good-byes and have-a-great-summers. And then they were gone, and I was left standing in the living room, alone with the abandoned schoolbooks and empty pizza boxes.

The house had been dubbed a dump by some—mostly the parents. I loved it. New and interesting stains regularly appeared on the living room carpet, unrecognizable smells emanated from the basement, the kitchen housed a family of ants, the sole bathroom (with the tub that often doubled as a beer bucket) was booby trapped with rotting plywood. These were but a few of the marvels of this jewel of student housing. And I would have it all to myself for four glorious months.

I basked in silence for a few minutes more and then ran upstairs to my bedroom before I ran out of daylight.

My bedroom was the one at the end of the hall. Except that it wasn't really a bedroom, but a broom closet that had been converted into a "rentable" space. In other words, if it was big enough for a semigrown person to lie down in, the landlord could charge student rent for it. It had no windows, no lights, and no electrical outlets, and a curtain hung in place of a door because my single bed took up all the floor space. I'd had to run a frayed extension cord from Hunter and Vincent's room into mine just to have a working lamp and alarm clock.

I considered myself pretty lucky to have my own cubbyhole—with five guys under one roof, the cards had been stacked against me, and it could have been a lot worse. Cassie, the only other girl in the house, found this out the hard way. She pulled the short straw and ended up having to share a room with Logan, who was a sleepwalker and slept in the nude.

What my room lacked in square footage it made up for in character. My doll-sized bed, squeezed by three walls, stood on three-foot-high stilts made of milk crates that had been secretly borrowed from the corner store. My clothes, shoes, and schoolbooks were stacked in Rubbermaid bins under the bed, and two-dollar Van Goghs hid most of the holes in the walls. The best part: it only cost me a hundred bucks a month—all-inclusive.

I switched my jeans for sweatpants and went back downstairs.

After hiding the house key under the front mat, I hit the ground running, literally, and zipped down the streets. I dodged people and the heaps of garbage that were piling up on the sidewalks—remnants of the lives of the students who were gradually abandoning the city. By nightfall, the city would be bare of the students that gave it life, the heaps would have been well looted, and only the real garbage would remain.

This part of Callister was considered the slums—a stark contrast to the manicured lawns I had grown up with. What had been, probably a million years ago, a nice, middle-class neighborhood was now another dilapidated (though affordable) blemish on the face of the city. With its proximity to the university, it accommodated a weird mix of college students, underprivileged families, and drug dealers. Still, it had a certain charm. Most of the houses were small, war-era frame homes built about three feet from the street and barely two feet apart from each other.

I was sure that the neighborhood must have been pretty at some point. Now most of the paint on the houses was chipping away. Multicolored layers showed through in spots like scars left by the previous owners before the houses were abandoned for good.

I slogged up one of the busier drags—my least favorite part of the run. Too many cars were driving by with practically everyone turning their eyes in my direction, as if this were the first time they had ever seen someone run. I told myself that it was because of where I was—in this city, someone who ran was usually running away from something, like the cops or the barrel of a shopkeeper's gun.

But somehow I knew it had nothing to do with the bad neighborhood and everything to do with me—I was a beacon for curious stares. My hair was red. "Not so much like a rusty car," as someone had once nicely put it, "but red like spaghetti sauce." (The gourmet kind, not the canned stuff that I could afford.) I once read in *National Geographic* that the red hair gene was becoming extinct. That made me the human version of the polar bear. One day, my kind would be seen only in a zoo, forced to procreate in order to save the redhead race. For now, however, mankind was satisfied with staring at me while I ran down the street.

Though my dying-breed red hair merited me the most attention, there were other impediments to my blending in with the crowd. For one thing, I was skinny. Not the "you-should-be-a-model" kind of skinny, but the skeletal, awkward kind. I still held out hope that I would someday add something, anything, to my bones. I was also on the pale side of the human complexion spectrum, but at least the reddish-brown freckles that speckled every inch of my skin gave me some color. That was good. Right?

My looks didn't really bother me as much as they seemed to distract other people. Overall, I just tried to fit into the normal world—the non-Sheppard world, that is—and remain positive about those things that I could not change. But that was difficult, I suppose, because every time I looked in the mirror, all I could see was my mother's reflection, her hand-me-down features.

I wasn't paranoid; maybe people weren't really staring at me, even though their heads turned as I ran past them, as though a fishing line were joining their noses with my backside. Okay, maybe I was a little paranoid. So I turned up the sound on my Walkman, because it's easier to ignore people's stares when you've got music blasting in your ears.

Contrary to my housemate Cassie's theory, I wasn't trying to be retro with my ancient Walkman. I'd discovered it in our basement when I moved into the house. It was free, and free was all I could afford. Yes, the Bob Marley tape that was already in there had melted in place. And so yes, I was forced to listen to the same tape over and over again. But it didn't matter—it was all I needed to quiet the (paranoid) voice in my head long enough to put one foot in front of the other without tripping.

I ran up the hill and took a right into an alley almost hidden between two brick buildings.

Behind the buildings there was a small patch of trees that towered overhead, shedding a springtime carpet of little white beans all over the street. It was one of the few areas in the ghetto that had anything green still living. I veered onto a pathway that led through a cemetery. Like the rest of the neighborhood, the cemetery had been neglected; there were weeds growing everywhere, around and within the slow cracks in the tombstones. Graffiti covered almost every surface of the graveyard, including some of the stones.

There among the broken beer bottles, cigarette butts, and fast-food wrappers stood the only tombstone that had been maintained by the caretaker—he must have been paid handsomely by my parents to keep the weeds and garbage away from my brother

Bill's grave. My parents could have afforded to bury Bill in his own underground palace, if they had wanted. But this place was better, for them. It was hidden. Bill was hidden. Finally. Forever. They could breathe a sigh of relief and hope their world would forget—though I'd never understood why they bothered to have it kept orderly. Merciless habits don't die with the dead, I suppose.

I ran this same route almost every day after school. Some days I would stop and sit to talk to Bill or just stare at his headstone. But today I kept running, trying to make the most of the lingering daylight. I'd gotten a late start, and a graveyard was definitely not where I wanted to be after dark. I had watched too many movies for that.

The pathway snaked through the cemetery and eventually led through a fence of overgrowth and trees. I ran through the opening into a field of weeds and then into the projects. The projects were a city within the city, a cluster of apartment buildings built by the good people of Callister. What they really were was ugly and, as far as I could tell, barely habitable. They'd been built quite hastily by the city in the middle of a large piece of land—an unusually large brownfield on the outskirts of the city. The plan was to keep the poor off the streets, or away from and out of sight of the rest of the city. Entering the projects was like entering another world.

While the cemetery had been virtually deserted, the field around the buildings was swarming with people—probably because it was the first really warm day of the year. The sun was shining, and the city, even the city within the city, was suddenly coming out of hibernation. Hard-up kids played and screamed in the tall grass, families were grouped around tiny barbeques, rap music was blaring, and people hung around, obstructing the walkways. So I made my way through the crowd, weaving in and out of the foot traffic to the beat of my breath and Bob Marley.

But as I ran through the crowd, I started to realize that something was different today, wrong somehow. People were staring at me, even more than usual. I looked straight ahead and tried to keep my mind on my pace, on my breath.

Except that I wasn't being paranoid this time. People were definitely staring. And then they were moving—away from me. Parting like the Red Sea as I ran past, although nothing about this felt biblical. It was infuriating that no matter how hard I tried to fit in, to become just another stranger in the crowd, the crowd moved away from me as though I had suddenly transformed into a cloud of sulfur.

But then I noticed a lady a few yards in front of me. The fact that she was wearing a yellow hat and had a plastic yellow purse made me notice her more than the fact that she was looking right at me. She was mouthing something, but all I could hear was Bob's voice. Something was clearly wrong.

I slowed my pace and pulled at my earbuds, simultaneously trying to read the woman's lips. The noise of the crowd became static in my ears as I focused on her lips and tried to grasp what was happening. Then something hard and heavy rammed into me from behind, and I crashed face-first into the pebbled walkway with barely enough time to put my hands out to break my fall. And that was where I lay, pinned.

The heavy thing bounced off my back, and I felt something hot, wet, and sticky on my face. It smelled too foul to be my blood.

Dazed, I saw the cow-sized head of a dog, a mammoth Rottweiler, too close to my face—very big teeth, leash hanging freely from its neck. I heard a winded voice but I didn't think that I could respond. Even if I could, I wouldn't—I was afraid the dog's tongue would slip into my mouth if I tried to open it to speak. Someone grabbed the massive beast's leash and pulled it away from my now-licked-clean face.

I saw my prized Walkman on the ground, its shattered pieces strewn all the way down the walkway.

I got up as quickly as I could and dusted myself off, embarrassed to now be the center of the large crowd's attention. "I'm okay," I answered, though I wasn't sure if anyone had asked.

As I looked down at my body and did a rapid once-over—my hands were pretty scraped up, and though I couldn't see any tears in my sweatpants, I knew that I would have plum-sized bruises on my knees tomorrow— an odd hush went through the crowd. I could sense some mothers reeling their children in and moving them away while rap music continued to blast in the background. When I glanced around, I noticed that everyone's heads had suddenly turned, and then, just as suddenly, conversations picked up, but in an unnatural fashion. Forced conversation.

I could feel people were trying hard not to stare. And I could feel someone behind me. Whoever was holding onto the heavy-breathing attack dog was still there.

Something primal was tingling at my extremities. For once, even though I had just given them all the ammo they needed to stare, or at least point and laugh, people were avoiding even looking at me.

Every person but one.

I forced myself to turn around. I was facing the setting sun and had to bring my hand to my forehead to shade my eyes from the blinding light. What I could see was the dog's owner, a guy in a gray hoodie. He was tall, and his face was hidden by the shadow of his hood and the ball cap that was pulled down to his eyebrows.

We stood there, studying each other the way boxers do after they step into the ring. I was waiting for what would generally come next after a dog attack, like an apology. But the guy remained silent, fingering his watch and swiftly scanning the scene before returning his darkened eyes to me.

I shook my head, half disbelieving, half aggressive. "Hi," I said sarcastically, because he still hadn't said anything at all.

"Your shoelace is untied," was the first thing that came out of his mouth.

"My shoelace?"

"It's untied."

My mouth went slightly slack-jawed; he shifted on his feet.

As I congratulated myself for not being the most socially inept person in the world after all and considered what I should say next, I crouched down to tie my shoelace, provoking the dog to bark and lunge to the end of its leash. I jumped back, fell on my behind, and wondered how long it would be before the leash snapped and the dog was back on me again.

"He's not going to hurt you." The owner had said this with irritation.

I tugged on my thread of a shoelace—it snapped.

"You need new shoes," was the next brilliant thing that came out of his mouth.

"My shoes were fine till your dog used me as a springboard."

It felt like he was actually trying to make small talk, in a fish-out-of-water kind of way.

While I struggled to tie what was left of my shoelace into a knot and make sense of this guy's social awkwardness, I glared up and watched as his hands clenched into fists and his shadowed jaw tightened. We were interrupted just as the hairs on my arms stiffened.

"Hey, girl," said a voice behind me. "Think you dropped this."

I got to my feet and spun around. A man in a baggy track suit handed me my Bob Marley tape: it had finally dislodged itself, taking pieces of the Walkman with it. I knew enough about the gang colors and teardrop tattoos that this man was showing off to understand that I should stay as far away from him as possible. It was clear to me that I was slowly being surrounded, outnumbered.

"Thanks," I said, trying to sound nonchalant.

"What is this thing, anyway?" he asked me.

When I extended my hand to grab the tape, the Rottweiler went wild again, barking, growling, almost snapping its leash.

I became very still.

The gangbanger stepped back, but his frightened gaze was directed not to the hostile dog, but to the dog's owner. "Sorry, man," he stuttered, taking a few short steps back before turning around.

I was perturbed by the reaction of this thug, who looked far more dangerous to me than the dog owner. I turned back to the man and confirmed that he looked quite ordinary—no signs of any gang affiliations.

"You shouldn't be running by yourself in this neighborhood. It's a really stupid thing to do."

I took a moment to wait for further enlightenment. But nothing else came from him.

"You're not seriously blaming this on me? *Your* dog attacked me, and *your* dog broke my Walkman."

The guy once again scanned the grounds and then looked at me without any retort.

"Am I keeping you from something more important?" I asked.

He continued to stare at me from under his hood.

I was at a loss for words. I thrust my broken tape into his chest and let it drop in front of him. He caught it before it fell to the ground.

Thwarted by his lack of response, I spun on my heels and started running again.

I didn't look back, but I could sense that he was still standing there, watching me run off. I waited until I was sure that he couldn't see me anymore before I slowed down to a walk, limping the rest of the way home.

****

By the time I got back to the house, it was getting dark. The streetlights were on, and Skylar was lounging on the front steps.

"Where were you? I've been waiting for almost half an hour."

I was limping. My knees were really starting to throb after my run-in with the attack dog and my subsequent angry jog.

"Are you okay?" he asked with genuine concern.

"Fine," I answered woodenly. My mood had apparently not been improved by the jog.

As I limped past him on my way to the door, I caught a whiff of something—cheap cologne. Skylar was my boyfriend of two months. He was a pretty boy—the sandy-blond, tanned kind of pretty. But he was also a really big granola; he wore Birkenstock sandals with socks, and corduroy pants year-round.

He was a strict vegan and refused to put anything in his body that wasn't natural—whatever that meant. So for him to wear a smelly chemical substance on his skin ... something was definitely up. And I had a hunch what that might be.

I avoided his stare and lifted the rubber mat, revealing the hidden key.

"Since when do you guys bother to lock the door?" he asked, standing way too close to me while I jiggled the key in the lock.

"I'm by myself for the summer," I confessed. This was information that I had been keeping from him. I glanced over and saw his wide smile turn wider as I said this, confirming my suspicions.

I left Skylar on the couch and went upstairs to have a shower.

Normally I would have been in and out of the shower in ten minutes, tops. Our communal bathroom was the most disgusting room in the house, plus there was almost always someone banging on the door, yelling at you to hurry up. Today, though, I took my sweet time detangling my wet hair and brushing my teeth. I got dressed and patted my hair with a towel until not a drop fell from the ends. I thoroughly examined my knees; they were already turning a dark shade of purple. Then I looked at my reflection in the mirror for half a second longer than usual or necessary. If I had owned makeup or a hair dryer, I could have extended my bathroom stay for five, maybe even ten minutes more, but even after searching the bathroom I came up with nothing else to do. So I put my hair up in the standard wet bun, unlocked the door, and stepped out of my hiding hole.

When I got back to my room, Skylar was lying on my canary-yellow bedspread with his legs dangling over the edge. It was a good thing I didn't make a habit of prancing around in a wet towel.

I threw my running clothes in the hamper; it was overflowing. I would have to do laundry soon or run out of socks again.

While my mind was distracted, Skylar had flipped onto his side. "So, what do you want to do tonight, E?"

I was named after my grandmother, Burt's mother; this was the same grandmother who to this day could never remember my name. Since I was not born a boy—one who could have carried on the family name—naming me after the matriarch of the family was, in Isabelle's mind, a way to legitimize her affair with Burt. My big brother, Bill, used to call me Emmy ... mostly because it irritated the hell out of Isabelle, his stepmother. I liked the nickname, mostly for the same reason.

I didn't really care that Skylar called me E. Anything was better than Emily. But I had a feeling that his reason for doing so had nothing to do with any kind of special attachment he might have had to me; it was just easier to keep girls' names straight if he only had to remember first initials. Maybe I could teach that trick to my grandmother.

I took my time dragging one of the Rubbermaid bins from under my bed and pulling out clothes for work.

"We could go see a movie," I finally offered. "I think the one you were talking about the other day is out."

"Or we could just stay here. Spend a quiet night in—"

I was past the curtain door before he had even finished his sentence.

The kitchen was a disaster zone. The counters were crusted with a year's worth of grime, and dirty dishes were, as always, piled in and around the sink. The only way to get a clean dish was to wash it right before using it—which I did before filling the freshly cleaned pot with water and putting it on the stove to boil. Then I filled the sink with soapy water and started doing dishes, almost excited by the fact that the dishes I cleaned would actually stay clean for longer than a minute.

Skylar just loitered by the fridge.

"You know I'm leaving in a few days," he reminded me for the thousandth time. "I don't even know yet if my student visa will be renewed next year."

"Yeah, I remember you telling me that. Hope they'll let you come back," I said, pouring the contents of a box of Kraft macaroni and cheese into the pot of boiling water.

"Ew. I don't know how you can eat that stuff."

I just smiled and stirred, thankful that I didn't have to cook for the both of us. Otherwise I would have been eating twigs and blades of grass for supper.

Skylar wandered back to the television in the living room while I finished up in the kitchen. I sat next to him on the couch, taking more joy than I should have in watching his face turn a nice shade of green while I poured ketchup over my orange pasta.

Unfortunately his aversion didn't last—as soon as I set my empty bowl on the coffee table, his arm was around my shoulders.

Two months of dating in college was like a lifetime in the rest of the world, or so my roommates had educated me. There were things that you were supposed to, just had to, experience in college. After two months of dating, I knew that Skylar and I should definitely have had sex by now. There had been a few close calls, times when superficial groping became more serious exploration. But I would get nervous and shy away, find excuses, or ensure that my housemates were around so we had no privacy.

I really did like Skylar, and I knew he liked me a lot too. But as time rolled by, I could tell that he was getting frustrated with me. Or desperate. Definitely on the verge of breaking up with me.

Now we were alone. Completely alone. Before long, Skylar's free hand had crossed over and made its way to my thigh. And he kept turning his face to mine, trying to catch my eye.

"Do you think you did okay on your exams?" I asked him, riveted by the *Seinfeld* rerun we were watching.

"Why wouldn't I?" he asked. (He was an A student.)

"Then why do you think your visa won't be renewed? I thought the school's only condition was that you maintain your grades."

"Nothing's ever guaranteed, I guess. There's always a chance that they could deny my visa. I'll definitely be away all summer."

This was something I couldn't argue with. I got up to get a glass of water and stood at the kitchen sink.

I made a list in my head of everything that was right about Skylar. For all intents and purposes, he was perfect for that college-required experience. He was a nice enough guy. He was pretty smart. He showered somewhat regularly. These things must have meant something, right? And then my mind wandered, and making its way to the top of the list was the fact that Skylar's forehead was too big—something I'd just happened to notice a minute before. His nose was too straight too—he must have had a nose job, I decided. I couldn't be with someone who'd had a nose job.

I rushed back to the couch before I could talk myself out of him entirely.

As if he could sense my fickleness, Skylar didn't miss a beat. "It'll be hard to be away from you for four months. I'll miss you like crazy."

His blue eyes—a dull blue, I'd noticed just now—were unblinking.

He took my faint smile as a green light, and his lips were on mine before I could think of anything else to say to distract him. He tasted like strawberry Starbursts. I wondered what I tasted like to him—probably like fluorescent-orange powdered cheese.

Skylar always seemed to know what he was doing. His hands made their way to my back, and with a quick, barely discernible flutter of his fingers over my shirt, he unclasped my bra. He then unceremoniously threw himself on top of me.

Giving myself to someone I knew, someone I liked, should have felt right. But none of this did. Something deep inside me was stopping me from giving myself over. I was like the present you shake excitedly, only to hear broken pieces rattling around inside. On the outside I might have appeared normal—at least, I tried to look as normal as possible. But on the inside there were just damaged goods, a darkness which had become innate. Something that I could not explain or understand. Something that prevented me from ever letting anyone completely in.

Skylar kissed my neck, and that was when it happened, as it always did when it came down to moments like this: I made sure that he broke up with me. Adrenaline rushed to my arms, the arms pushed out, and Skylar tumbled backward onto the carpet, hitting his blond head against the coffee table on his way down.

****

Skylar stayed long enough for the shock to wear off his face, long enough to tell me—a bunch of times, while he rubbed the bruise on his head—that he wasn't mad, that he could wait for me to be ready.

I wasn't dumb enough to think that in order to have sex you had to be in love with someone in that all-encompassing, skin-to-skin way. So why couldn't I bring myself to sleep with a guy I liked a lot, the way any other hormonal college girl would?

At the end of the night, I sat on the stairs and watched Skylar leave like the well-liked guys before him. I should have found our break-up more painful. Instead, I actually felt better, lighter, as though I had just punched a bully in the face.

I was definitely a freak.

And I was going to remain a virgin, even after a whole year away at college. I was now past being a minority and entering the realm of historic figure. I imagined a grade school class in the future *oohing* and *ahhing* while their teacher told the tale of Emily, the eternal virgin.

One more year and I would become a Greek myth.

CHAPTER TWO

THE SECRET TO MY EXCESS

I was running so unbelievably late. I got out of the shower, slipped my feet into flip-flops, and squeaked down the hall to my room. And then I just stood there for a long while, seriously considering skipping work and going back to bed. Would anyone notice if I didn't show up today?

There were days when I wished my bank account would just fill itself up without any effort from me. Today was one of those days. My bagel got stuck in the toaster and burned to a crisp. I barely hit my glass against the kitchen sink and it shattered into a million jagged gems. The sole pair of clean socks that I could find were mismatched, and one of them had a hole that kept cutting off the circulation to my big toe.

I hadn't slept a wink—not even a little bit. I could sleep through music blaring in the room next to mine. I could even sleep through a spontaneous game of dirty underwear football erupting on the other side of my curtain. But I couldn't block out the sound of police sirens going off in the distant city night. Go figure.

I ran the four blocks to school. My kneecaps were still throbbing from yesterday's incident with the dog, and they were slowing me down.

You wouldn't know it was a university if you drove past it. From the road, it looked more like a detention center without the barbed wire and the guards. The academic buildings were windowless on the back and arranged into a tight quadrangle so that there was only one way to access the university grounds. The cobblestone entrance was on the southeastern corner of the campus, across the street from the sole university parking lot. No cars were allowed past this point. If you wanted in, you had to walk or ride your bike. But once you made it past the windowless outside walls, the grounds felt less like a prison; there were real trees, real green grass, and dirt beds with real flowers. Sometimes you could even hear birds singing over the sound of the honking traffic outside the compound.

I followed the cobblestone path up to the school library. All the school's buildings were linked in some way or another, through underground tunnels or covered walkways; you never needed to leave the compound unless you really wanted to. The library was still by far the biggest and nicest building on campus, although I couldn't understand why the university would spend the most money on something they were trying to empty.

The campus was usually bustling with students and teachers and staff. Now it was more like a black hole had sucked out all signs of human life overnight. It would be a long, empty summer.

I pushed through the library's revolving doors.

Inside, it was cool—air conditioning was a luxury. I went through the metal detectors and grabbed my backpack off the conveyer belt. A long counter flanked one side of the library's main floor, and rows of vacant computer stations and metal chairs with burgundy pleather seats took up the rest of the space. There were no books left on this floor—and I was a conspirator in this tragedy. My job was to scan all the books in sections 341 to 471 in the library archives, four floors underground. Once I did this, the books were boxed and allegedly donated to charity—though the cynical part of me assumed they were simply destroyed. The horror of the digital age was too much for me to bear. I was selling my soul for minimum wage.

The lady at the reserve counter looked at the big clock on the wall and peered at me over her glasses as I rushed to the elevators. My kind, the soul-sellers, weren't exactly hailed in these parts. I hit the button to call the elevator—my ride into the depths of hell.

There were five elevators that ferried students among the seven floors of the library, but only one went down to the basement archives. That one was slow and temperamental.

I knew that I should have gone back to bed when, while impatiently waiting for the elevator, I saw Jeremy stroll through the revolving entrance doors. I knew it for sure when I saw another girl walk in with him. I had dated Jeremy for about a month at the beginning of the school year and for another two-week round over the Christmas break. He had helped me get a job in the library. And I'd needed all the help I could get—there was only so much creative writing I could note on my resume without having to admit that I had never actually held a job in my life.

I pressed the stupid elevator button twice more—too late.

"Hi, Emily," Jeremy said, flat-toned.

I pasted a smile on my face. "Hey, Jeremy, how are you?"

"Fine," he quickly said, throwing his arm around the girl. She was everything I wasn't: she was cute, she was blonde, she was big-breasted, and she probably put out.

"That's good," I said curtly.

I pressed the button once more and the elevator finally arrived. We got in and let the ding of the lighted floor numbers do the talking. Jeremy and the girl got off on the second underground floor. He looked back at me just as the doors closed, his arm never leaving her shoulders.

Jeremy was about an inch shorter than me, and he was viciously competitive—something I'd really liked about him. I beat him at poker once and he accused me of cheating; I made a point of beating him every time after that. When we broke up, he left with the same look of frustration that Skylar had had the night before, but no bumps on his head (that I knew of). At least I got to keep the job.

I didn't really miss Jeremy, nor did I want him back, but seeing him with another girl was just another reminder that I would never be that normal, blonde college girl. I would definitely have to remember to take the creepy, but vacant, archive stairs next time.

Luckily, I had the underground fourth floor all to myself. There were times when I craved being alone. When I was alone, I didn't have to try so hard to be that normal girl. I didn't have to try at all; I could just be. Being alone on the fourth floor underground was peaceful, but nothing new. Sometimes weeks would go by before someone other than me walked through the stacks there. Mathematics and obsolete statistics might have been some weird author's work of art, but they were not the most riveting (or popular) subjects. I spent my days alone, flipping through the pages of old books, scanning to the hum of the dingy lights encased in the thick cement walls.

I set my bag down on the butcher-block table. It looked like it could have been an antique, but it had been scratched, engraved, and penned beyond repair. Apparently, Stacey H. was here, Jessica & Naomi were BFFs 4Eva, and someone wished K. P. a gruesome death.

I yawned one of those tear-inducing yawns and picked up where I had left off a few weeks ago, before exams had taken over my life. My workstation: a computer and an oversized scanner that took up half the table.

I grabbed the next book on the shelf, opened it to the first page, and placed it face-down on the scanner. I typed the book's title, author, and publication date into the computer and pressed the green scan button. The lime-green light sped from one side of the scanner to the other, and my work day had officially started.

It was a boring and mindless job, scanning each book one page at a time, but all things considered it was a pretty sweet gig for a student. Of the few students who had been hired—one per floor to do this same job—most spent their paid hours either napping on the bottom of an empty shelf or making out behind the book carts, which Jeremy was probably doing by now. There was no adult supervision of the almost-adult students. The first week I started working there, I got in trouble with the other students for scanning the books too quickly—apparently this not only made the rest of them look bad, but it meant that the electronic library project would get done faster, taking jobs away from poverty-stricken students. I certainly didn't want to be responsible for that, so I slowed down and used my free time to study and catch up on my homework. Like I said, it was a sweet gig.

But with school being out, I didn't have any homework to do, and it was way too quiet to sleep. I could have brought a book to read, but my eyes were stinging from sleeplessness. With nothing but my brain waves to distract me, I had to break the golden rule: I started feverishly scanning books.

How do you know when you're There? I asked myself between the eight hundred pages of *Algorithms: An Annotated History. Do you just get up one morning, pour juice into a glass without breaking it, take a bite of your nicely grilled bagel and … boom! There is right there, staring you in the face—that moment when you realize you have everything that you've worked for, waited for, and you finally find yourself utterly fulfilled. What happens after that? Do you enter a new world of "What Else Is There?", or do you just finish your bagel and live happily ever after?* My There was not what I'd thought it would be.

For some people, probably most people, their ultimate goal had a dollar sign attached to it. They'd work their whole lives to build their There money. The biggest secret that I had kept from everyone in my new life was the fact that I came from money, a lot of it. I came from a world of privilege and excess—of a house full of people who were paid to be nice to me, of being forced to go to stupid private schools where I had to wear the stupid uniforms and go to the stupid parties. Burt was in his sixties, Isabelle in her fifties, and they were still working on their There money.

I was embarrassed by the fact that my parents had money, or rather by how they behaved because they had money. Money, in their minds, turned them into gods; they expected the world to celebrate them, bend to their every whim, be grateful just to be in their presence. My mother had been appalled when one of the maids asked if her eleven-year-old daughter could live with her in the staff quarters. "I pay them. I pull them off the dirty streets of third-world countries and give them a place to live. In a mansion, nonetheless. And they want more." My mother fired the maid, who went back home to Connecticut.

My embarrassment was only exacerbated when I listened to my roommates make fun of the kids with money, the ones who paid for parking spots, the ones who bought five-dollar coffees. Somehow I knew that normal people wouldn't understand my decision to leave it all behind. Some days, like today, I even questioned it myself.

I could normally scan up to three books a day without getting into trouble. Today I was on a roll and did over a week's worth of work, and it made the day fly by. I would have to figure out how to hide the evidence later.

When my paid workday ended, I rolled my cart filled with evidence to the farthest end of the room, behind the last bookshelf, and walked home. Then I did what I should have done first thing that morning: I climbed under the covers.

And I tossed around in my bed for more than an hour. The house was infuriatingly quiet.

Frustrated, I flung the covers off and dug some clothes out of the dirty laundry basket. I threw on whatever passed the smell test and ran out of the house into the peopled world. It was another beautiful evening. The days were already getting longer and hotter. A summer sleeping in a windowless room without air conditioning would be … interesting.

I noticed the absence of my Walkman as soon as I reached the sidewalk, but I didn't dwell on it too long. After being cooped up alone in the library basement all day, it was kind of nice to listen to the sounds of the city, of life. I made it to the cemetery in pretty good time and said a quiet hello to Bill as I passed his grave.

When I reached the clearing in the projects, I immediately noticed the guy sitting alone on top of the picnic table closest to the cemetery. I recognized him by his gray hoodie, the same one he had been wearing the day before when his dog mowed me down. But he wasn't wearing his ball cap this time, and his face was clearly visible in the lowering sun.

When he saw me, he got up and quickly intercepted me at the walkway. He pulled the hood off his head, tousling his brown hair in the process.

Yes, I could definitely see him now, and my already flushed cheeks were turning a new shade of red. He was handsome. I couldn't decide how old he was. Early twenties? Early thirties? Too old for me? His eyes were striking, almost black. I was immediately aware that I was sweaty and gross.

"Hello," he said quietly. He seemed like a different person today.

I was still trying to catch my breath.

His eyes scanned the grounds and stopped at me. "It's getting late. I was starting to think you weren't going to come today."

"My bruised knees were slowing me down." I stopped and narrowed my eyes. "Wait … you were waiting for me?"

He just looked at me for a second. "Yes," he finally said. "Does that surprise you?"

"You were really rude to me yesterday."

"I'm sorry, I didn't mean to hurt you. What I did, said … It was totally uncalled for."

"You didn't hurt me, really. Your dog did, though."

He glanced around us again. Then a careful smile crept onto his face as his eyes made their way back to mine. "Meatball was sorry too."

"Meatball?"

He paused; the smile vaporized. "Meatball is my dog's name."

His sudden change in demeanor made me remember the beast—or more specifically, his massive jaws and teeth. I could have easily become his late-afternoon snack. I looked around, expecting to be tackled at any moment.

"No worries, I didn't bring him," he said.

I must not have looked convinced.

"Really, he likes you."

"I don't think he knows me well enough to make such a crucial split-second decision." It was meant as a joke, but his eyes narrowed.

"Right," he said. "Anyway, I wanted to make sure you were okay and apologize for yesterday."

"I'm fine, and apology accepted."

I tucked an errant hair behind my ear. The minute I touched my head, I realized that most of the hair from my ponytail had fallen out in a sweaty mess. I immediately fingered it back into a snug ponytail.

His lips twitched as if he were suppressing a smile.

This time I was the one who glanced away. The projects were teeming with people again today, but no one seemed to notice that we even existed. Or maybe they were still avoiding us.

"So do you live around here?" I asked, a veiled attempt at changing the subject.

"Not really."

Was that a yes or a no?

"I live a couple of blocks away from here," I offered, leading by example—this was how normal people conversed.

His eyes shot back to my face. "You shouldn't tell people where you live. What if I was some kind of psycho?" I felt a chill run down my bare legs. "You need to be more careful is all I'm trying to say."

"I've managed to keep myself out of trouble so far."

"This isn't a good place for you to test your courage. You shouldn't be coming here. Find somewhere else to run."

I squared m shoulders. "It's a free country."

His face darkened again.

I sucked a breath through my teeth. "It's getting late," I said, taking a step backward. "I better go."

When I turned sideways to leave, his arm reached out to mine to stop me.

"Wait," he said, "I forgot something." He pulled his hand abruptly away. The warmth in my arm still tingled while he dug a small box out of his pocket and shoved it toward me, avoiding touching me again. "To replace the one Meatball broke."

I opened the clear plastic box and a silver iPod fell out. I turned it over in my hands. "Umm ... thanks. You didn't have to do that. My Walkman was pretty worthless."

"Yeah, it was. But this is brand-new and it actually fits in your pocket." He looked a little smug as he said this. "I even downloaded Bob Marley on there for you." I must have looked confused, because he tapped his chest with one finger and said, "You gave me the broken tape, remember?"

"Oh ... right," was all I could say, my cheeks afire.

"I can get you new running shoes too, if you want. Better than the ones you're wearing." He smiled, but then his eyes darted around us again.

I looked down at my feet. "What's wrong with my sneakers?"

I heard him mumble something and I glanced back up. His face was ashen and he was backing away from me. He had turned back into the menacing guy I had encountered the day before.

"I gotta go," he said. Just like that, he spun around and left.

Confused, I stood there for a second, took a few breaths. Then I proceeded to turn around too.

I heard a whistle. My heart jumped, and I looked back to find that he had stopped in his tracks a few yards away. "I meant what I said. Don't come back here."

"I meant what I said too," was what I wanted to counter with, but he had already disappeared. I stuffed his gift inside my pocket—it did fit in there nicely, I noticed a little resentfully—and turned back on my heels.

I finished my run, more befuddled than ever ... and realized that I had no idea what his name was. He was the strangest person I had ever met.

When I got home, I made myself a peanut butter sandwich—the bread was stale, but at least it filled one of the holes in my stomach. I took chokingly huge bites while I cleaned the broken glass in the sink that I hadn't had time to get to that morning. I found a pair of sweatpants that hadn't seen the light of day since ninth grade, and then I threw a box of laundry detergent on top of my dirty clothes, stuffed a roll of quarters in my pocket, lugged the overflowing basket down the stairs, and headed out the door.

The laundromat was a good block and a half down our street, so carrying the heavy load of clothes was not an option. But my roommates and I had already devised a first-rate system to solve that problem. I unlocked the padlock that kept our permanently borrowed grocery cart chained to the front porch; the stolen cart kept getting stolen on us, so we had to keep it under lock. I heaved the laundry basket into the cart and rolled it down the street, fitting in nicely with the rest of the neighborhood.

It was remarkable to me how far I had come in less than a year's time, since I had escaped to Callister. I had gone from having no idea how to do anything without hired help to being completely self-sufficient—well, most days, anyway. There were initial signs of my posh upbringing, of course, like the time I tried to make hardboiled eggs and found out the hard way that you needed to add water to the pot. The house reeked of burned eggshells for a week. I learned through observation and a lot of trial and error.

Inside, the laundromat was bright, with blue plastic chairs lined against the white walls and tumbleweeds of lint rolling on the checkered floor. I loved the smell of the laundromat—to me it smelled of fresh starts, possibilities, independence.

I started by going through all my pockets—good thing I did, or I would have washed my new iPod—before stuffing two machines with as many clothes as they could take and throwing half a roll of quarters in. Then I sat on one of the machines, swung my legs onto the top of the other one, and waited. The most important rule of the laundromat: never leave your clothes unattended, not even for a second, not even when the place seems completely deserted. If you do, you'll see some local flavor walking around the next day, wearing your tweed pants as a scarf and your underwear as a hat ... another lesson I learned the hard way.

I wasted my idle time playing with my new toy. Bob Marley was there, along with every one of his albums that was ever made or remade. Who knew there were so many remakes of "One Love"?

I scrolled down to the next name on the artists list: this obscure band called Purple Faced Ragamuffins. I didn't even know they had recorded an actual album. I had seen them play once in this dingy bar in Soho when I was still totally underage. I had sneaked out of school with a girl from my soccer team. She was stalking the drummer.

The iPod must have had more than a thousand songs, most of which I recognized—surprising, given my limited knowledge of music. But, in the end, I settled for what was safe and familiar and finished laundry night with Bob.

When I got back from the laundromat, I realized I had a message on my cheap cell phone. Skylar had called from an airport phone—he'd made it quick, like he was afraid that I might pick up and he would be forced to actually talk to me. I could hear his flight being called in the background (nothing like waiting till the very last minute). He said all the right things: that he wasn't mad, that he would miss me, that he would call me as soon as he got settled at home. "See ya" was how he ended it.

CHAPTER THREE

HAUNTED

Day two of my four-month escape from civilization, and another sleepless night. Insomnia was becoming a bad habit.

My brain was cluttered with things I didn't need: fear of boredom, anxiety about being alone with my thoughts, Skylar's effortless desertion … the guy in the gray hoodie. I spent more time thinking about the latter.

This guy was odd and beautiful—a dangerous combination, no question in my mind. Something about his guardedness, something about the way others in the projects had looked at him with fear, made me think that if I ever ran into him again I should probably run the other way.

At midnight I gave up trying to sleep, stuck my new earbuds in, and cleaned the house. By five a.m., the house was museum spotless, but I had exhausted the sole source of entertainment I'd originally saved for the now-looming lonely weekend.

At work I was a speed demon with my new music blaring in my ears. By the time lunchtime came around, I looked at the cart of scanned books in horror—it was already full. I would have a hard time trying to explain away that much evidence. I decided to take an extra-long lunch to think about what I'd done.

Lunch bag in hand, I walked out of the library. It was humid outside. The sun was beating down on the abandoned university grounds; the smart people were hiding in the air-conditioned cafeteria. I considered doing the same thing myself but remembered that Jeremy might be there. I was too tired to be pleasant today, even if it was just a matter of putting a smile on my face and saying hi. Or perhaps after only two days without housemates, I was already becoming a recluse.

I settled on a table that sat in the shade of a maple tree, took out my peanut butter and stale bread sandwich, and opened the book that I had borrowed from my scanned stack: *Dummy Variables for Stata*. It turned out to be less interesting than it sounded, and my mind wandered from the pages.

My life had been marred by events of turmoil and self-destruction. When I was five, I played hairdresser with Barbie before turning the scissors on myself. When I was done, Barbie looked like a model walking into rehab after a couple of months of hard partying. I looked like the lopsided top of a carrot muffin.

When I was eight, Tyler Brown convinced me that everyone had freckles but that they hid them with Wite-Out. (It made perfect sense to an eight-year-old.) So I spackled some on before I went to bed to make sure that it was well embedded before my big reveal in the morning. At least I got to stay hidden for a week while my skin recovered from the paint thinner the maid had to use to scrub it off.

It was hard being the kid who just wanted to get lost in the crowd, when my head was like a flare set off in an ocean of blonds and brunettes. People are always drawn to the girl with the fire-engine hair in the same way that they can't keep from slowing down to stare at car accidents on the side of the road—hoping that it's as bad as it looks, wanting to witness some shocking thing that only an elite few have ever seen up-close.

I also wasn't blind to the attention that I reaped from the opposite sex. It had started with the boys in grade school who would dare each other to run up to me and pull my hair; those boys would later grow up to be frat boys who were looking to do more than pull my hair. I was a rite of passage for most of the male species, at any age.

Now, as an almost adult, I was getting a little better at singling out the guys who were looking for the red-headed experience. So when a man with red-rimmed glasses approached me, my red radar was up right away.

"Excuse me," he said, standing across the table from me.

I sighed through my nose, looking up. He was tall and rail-thin. His spiked hairstyle made it obvious that his hair was thinning at the crown and that he was trying very hard to hide the fact.

"Would you mind if I sat here?" he asked, pointing to the bench across from me. "There are no other tables in the shade."

I nodded and went back to my dumb variables while he sat down.

He didn't pick up on my cues.

"I'm Anthony Francesco," he started, though it sounded more like a question.

I glanced over the edge my book. He was staring expectantly at me, obviously waiting for a response.

"Emily," I said without emotion and tried to go back to my book, but I somehow knew that he wasn't done. I instantly regretted my decision not to bring my iPod.

"No last name, Emily?" he said, nervously chuckling. "Are you like Madonna or something?"

I flipped a page of my book, even though I hadn't finished reading it.

"So ... do you go to school here, Emily?"

"Uh-huh."

"Are you from around here?" he asked.

I started to eat my sandwich faster, just in case I needed a quick exit.

"Yeah ... I'm not really from around here either," he said.

There was another blissful moment of silence, and then he continued, "Do you live close to school?"

"Kind of," I answered, my eyes never leaving the page, my lips never more than an inch away from my sandwich.

"I've got my own place a couple of blocks from here," he said. "Do you still live with your parents?"

"Yep," I lied.

"Do you have any siblings?" he hurriedly asked, likely noticing that I was shoveling the food into my mouth as quickly as possible. But he was too late. I was done eating, and for the first time I gladly offered more than a few syllables.

"Sorry, my break is over," I said with a mouthful. "I've got to go before my boss freaks out."

I picked up my stuff and left before he had a chance to find something else to question me about. I would have run, but that would have made it a little too obvious.

"What a freak," I whispered to myself as I walked back into the library—though he was probably thinking the same thing about me.

I was back at work half an hour early. And my fake boss didn't freak out.

By the time I strolled out of the library at the end of my workday, the weather had changed dramatically: the sky was dark, and black clouds were rolling in like a tsunami. With all the humidity of the past few days, I expected that I didn't have much time to get in a run before the rain came crashing down hard.

Back at the house, I spent more time than I had squinting into the mirror, fixing my devastatingly frizzed hair, trying to find something to wear. And when I reached the cemetery's entrance, black clouds were already threatening overhead. With only two or three people idling under the trees, the cemetery was almost desolate—the smart people were indoors again.

But when I took a quick right at the decaying mausoleum, I stopped dead in my tracks.

Someone had thrown a crushed pop can and a candy wrapper on top of my brother's grave. I knew it was unfair of me to be upset that Bill's grave had been desecrated—especially when the rest of the cemetery had never been anything but disrespected. But when it came to Bill, I couldn't help myself.

I took out my earbuds and crouched down to brush the garbage away, and then I grabbed the bottom of my T-shirt and wiped away the soda that had spilled onto the headstone. I took my hands out of my T-shirt and let my fingers trace the engraved lines of his name as though the headstone were his face.

You're supposed to hold your breath when going past a cemetery, or, as the superstition goes, you'll breathe in the spirits of the dead. You're also supposed to stick your thumbs into your fists to protect your parents. I did neither. In fact I ran through the cemetery almost every day. If only that were enough to explain why I was so haunted, and why my parents were … the way they were. I missed Bill—every second, every breath.

I had little recollection of my life before things started to go so wrong in my family. Burt and Isabelle had had an affair when Burt was still married to someone else and Bill was just a baby. When Burt left Bill's mother and married my mom, Bill's mother committed suicide. And I was born in the middle of all of this, a soap opera that my big brother had tried to shield me from. Through all of this, and despite the fact that I came into this world as the result of an affair, he was my biggest, my only, ally

Most of my family memories were of the heated arguments between Burt and my brother. Bill getting into fights, Bill selling drugs, Bill getting kicked out of eight different private schools, Bill the Shame of the Sheppard Family. The last argument was on the night that Bill was brought home in a police cruiser when my parents were having a dinner party, and there were too many witnesses to the shame. Burt shipped my brother off to Callister to live with his Uncle Victor—his mother's brother, and a police officer. A few months later, Victor called Burt to say that Bill had run away.

But Bill still came to visit me, secretly. He'd climb into my room in the middle of the night on my birthday, on Christmas, whenever he felt like it, just to check up on me and make sure that I was doing whatever he thought I should be doing—going to school, not doing drugs … according to my brother, what was good for the goose wasn't good enough for the gander.

Then when I was thirteen, a police officer came to our front door. Bill's body had been found in an empty apartment in Callister, the needle still hanging off his arm. There was an autopsy—Bill had died of a drug overdose. Heroin, I overheard.

I was awakened from my daze by a loud clap of thunder that seemed to come from just above the trees overhanging the cemetery. I pressed my hand hard against the cold stone and took one last glance at the grave site until, satisfied, I sped off, returning to my purpose. I quickly rounded the chestnut tree, and by the time I reached the clearing in the projects, the sky was pitch-black and the thunder was now belching steadily.

Unlike the previous few days, the clearing was completely desolate. My shoulders sank when I saw he wasn't there waiting for me at the picnic table, even though, logically, I knew that he wouldn't be there and that I shouldn't be looking for him.

I reluctantly kept running until I heard a bark.

I slowed down to a near-walk and looked back. He was there in his gray hoodie, leaning against the fence at the farthest point where the cemetery and the projects met, about two hundred feet from the cemetery entrance I had just run through.

Alerted by his leashed dog's warning, he brought his eyes to me. But he wasn't alone this time. There was another man at his side—a man with a shaved head and scary-looking tattoos.

While the guy in the gray hoodie was pulling on the leash, struggling to keep Meatball from running off to greet (attack?) me, the other man looked with confusion at his friend and his suddenly misbehaving dog, eventually following his friend's quick glances at me. He looked from me back to his friend twice more, and his confusion seemed to have turned to anger. The guy in the gray hoodie turned his body away from me, toward the tattooed man.

In that instant I decided that today was a good day to start avoiding him. Pretending to have slowed down for a stretch, I extended my arms and bent them over my head, very quickly grabbing by elbows. And then I picked up my running pace again.

I followed the pathway through the field that surrounded the projects, and as it slowly veered to the right, I finally felt it was safe enough for me to look back. At a far distance, I could still see him standing there with the other man. They seemed deep in conversation, possibly arguing. Another runner came through the clearing of the cemetery, and I saw Meatball feverishly tugging on his leash once again. As I made my way down the hill and out of sight, I smiled to myself, glad that I wasn't the only one that Meatball liked so much.

I was almost through the first third of my run when I realized that I didn't have my iPod. I searched my pockets but they were empty. It must have fallen out of my pocket when I pulled my earbuds out at Bill's grave site. Lightning split the sky a few yards ahead of me, thunder exploded, and the rain suddenly started to pour. I turned around and went back the way I came, praying that my new iPod wouldn't be ruined by the rain.

I was getting soaked. I ran faster, hoping that my iPod would be sheltered somewhat by the trees in the cemetery. I ran back up the small hill into the field by the projects, seeing through the gravel-sized raindrops that the guy in the gray hoodie and the other scary man had left.

I finally made it through the entrance back into the cemetery. Just as I had hoped, the lofty trees had managed to keep most of the rain out. I slowed my pace a bit to shake off the water. My sneakers were submerged canoes.

With the sun out of sight, the cemetery was dark. I could barely make out the contours of the winding pathway. I squeezed some of the water out of the bottom of my T-shirt and sloshed forward. I had run this route so many times—I knew every curve, every bump in the road.

I picked up a jogging pace, came around to the big chestnut tree … and heard a bone-chilling cry, as if an animal were being tortured.

I was used to Bob's voice here, not this.

I stopped immediately, wondering if my horror-movie-infected brain was playing tricks on me. Then there was another cry, even more piercing this time.

Too afraid to move, and beating myself up for having stupidly decided to run through a dark cemetery alone, I stood there like one of the tombstones. I could hear muffled voices, and then more cries of pain. Unsure where the sounds were coming from or what was making them, I didn't know whether to stay put or run away, or which way to run if I did.

My body decided for me, and I started to move quietly on the uneven footpath. Something, instinct or impulse, was leading me toward the quickest way home. I made it to the massive tree—a familiar mark. I didn't have much farther to go before I was on the street again.

I took a few more steps and heard a scream again. This time it was much closer—I had picked the wrong direction. Then I heard a bark I recognized and I froze. Was the guy in the gray hoodier getting mauled by his dog? If he was, what could I do except offer myself as a new chew toy?

There were growls, snarls, and then more cries. I had to do something. I took a breath of courage and quickly looked around the tree to get a better sense of the situation before throwing myself out there.

That was when I saw him, standing there with his dog still on a leash, the gray hoodie giving him away in the gloom. His back was to me, and the tattooed man that I had seen with him earlier was next to him—there was another tattoo on the back of his neck … maybe a spider web? Two other men were flanking them.

Meatball looked vicious and rabid. He was slobbering madly and trying to crunch into something that I could not see.

When one of the men shifted his stance slightly, I saw what all four of them were looking at and what Meatball had been trying to sink his teeth into. There, crouched on the ground, was a man; he was groaning. His pants were ripped and blood-spattered. From the bloody wounds on his arms and legs, I could tell that Meatball had already had a taste.

The guy I had obsessed over was murmuring to the crouched man. I couldn't hear what he said, but whatever the crouched man said in response displeased the group. The tattooed man proceeded to punch and kick him. The others stood around silently, calmly watching him do this, while the man on the ground curled into a ball, wailing, his arms covering his head. With each punch and kick came a disgusting thudding sound, like meat being pulverized. My ears were drumming, and I thought I was going to be sick, but I could not move away, could not look away. I wanted to yell, beg them to stop, but even if I'd had the guts to say anything, my mouth wouldn't work.

At last the beating stopped.

The man slowly peered up through the protection of his arms, and I was taken aback: although he was bleeding profusely, I still recognized him. He was the runner who had come out of the cemetery shortly after I did, right before I had disappeared down the hill.

My hands flew to my mouth to suppress the cry that was building in my throat. And the man on the ground immediately turned his bloodied eyes to me, as though he had seen me move in the darkness. I withdrew further into the gloom for fear that he would betray my presence and present the attackers with an alternate prey. When he turned to his aggressors and said something that I couldn't hear, my heart dropped. Whatever he whispered to the guy in the gray hoodie sent him over the edge. His arms started shaking. He reached behind his back and pulled a gun from the waist of his jeans. Shots rang out, each leading an echo across the cemetery.

When my eyes refocused, the man on the ground had stopped moving. Rain-washed blood spattered the ground, and the three other men who were flanking the shooter had spun around and were looking at me, stunned.

Without realizing it, I had been screaming, and I was still screaming and shaking and I couldn't stop or move any other part of my body—like my legs, to run away from them.

"Cameron," the tattooed man yelled breathlessly, grabbing the shooter by the shoulder and forcing him to turn around.

The guy in the gray hoodie spun. Our eyes met again. His face turned pale.

A twig snapped behind me.

Everything went dark.

Chapter Four

Chow Mein

There was a flash of light and distant noises. My head felt like someone was taking an ice pick and chipping away at my skull with sadistic blows. I decided that death couldn't be this painful, so I was probably not dead … or was this what hell felt like?

My eyes were pried open, and the light was flashing again. This was followed by an animalistic groan, like a bear cub—was that me?

I managed to flutter my eyes open without anyone's help. Inches away from my face, someone was holding a pen-sized flashlight. I couldn't focus enough to see him, but I could definitely smell him: cigarettes, booze, dirt, and possibly manure.

The ceiling was swimming. I thought I was going to vomit, and I had to let my eyelids drop to stop the spinning. Slowly, the muffled sounds became words.

"What's your name, sweetheart?" yelled the man with the flashlight. His voice was raspy, and I could smell the nicotine on his breath.

"None of your business," I managed, my voice bouncing like a rock against the walls of my skull. I could hear snickering in the background. I tried to get up but barely managed to lift my head off the pillow before it fell back with a thump.

"Whoa there, sweetheart. Not so fast. You've got a pretty big bump on that little noggin of yours," said the raspy voice.

That would explain the blinding pain. "My name is definitely not sweetheart." I tried to push him away, but my hand was clumsy and my push was more of a drunken swipe.

"Of course it isn't, honey. But that's all I've got to work with right now." He gently brought my hand back to my side.

It's not honey, either, I thought, but I was in too much pain to argue with him.

"She's probably got a mild concussion," said the man with the nicotine breath. "Just make sure she gets plenty of rest and wake her up every couple of hours overnight. Give me a call if she gets any worse."

"She looks like she's in pain. Can she take anything?" asked a deep voice that I instantly recognized.

"Not for the next twelve hours. But I'll leave you something for tomorrow," replied the foul-smelling doctor, his voice hurried.

I forced my eyes open. The guy in the gray hoodie was standing at the foot of the bed I was lying in. His name. What was his name? I knew this. I had heard someone shout it, right after. Right after what?

In the cemetery. There had been another man there. Dear God, there had been another man there and there were shots fired. The guy in the hoodie had murdered another man. He took the life of another human being.

Cameron.

His name was Cameron.

I had spoken to him, to Cameron. I had chatted it up with a murderer. At times daydreaming about the guy like a schoolgirl, like a senseless rich girl. Forgetting that even good-looking guys could be psychos.

And the killer was here at the foot of this bed. Did he bring me here?

With my head pounding and my eyes watering from the pain, I tried to take in as many details as I could.

The doctor's stink matched his appearance, as if he had just crawled out of a cardboard box in a back alley. His dress shirt, which might have once been white, was untucked and had dark yellow and brown stains, particularly under the arms and around the collar. His dress pants were extremely wrinkled and equally stained.

"Thanks, doc." Cameron, the murderer, glanced in my direction. His glance seemed sympathetic somehow. I was shaking. I wanted to scream. But I was too terrified to even accomplish that much.

There was another man there. A bald man—the one, I suddenly remembered, who had a spider web tattooed on the back of his neck, and who was now standing behind Cameron in a soldier-like stance. And next to him there was a young guy leaning against the white wall. Judging from the grin on his face, I decided that he was the instigator of the earlier giggling at my expense. He was a big kid, at least six feet tall and built like he should be throwing bales of hay around. He reminded me of an oversized Chucky doll, except with disheveled brown hair instead of red.

With a nod from Cameron, the tattooed man dug into his pocket and pulled out a wad of rolled-up bills. Not missing a beat, the doctor grabbed the cash and dashed out of the room without taking one more look at his patient. He was not there to save me from them.

The tattooed man followed the doctor out the door, shooting me a frosty glare on his way out. Cameron turned his focus to the tall guy.

"Get out of here, Kid," he ordered. I watched as the guy walked out the door without saying a word, but with the same stupid grin on his face.

And then we were alone. Cameron and I. I clenched the bedsheets. *How bad are things about to get?*

I stared at him—stared him down.

He just stared back, his gaze calm but wary.

It was as though we were seeing each other for the first time. Uncloaked. At least, I was seeing *him* for the first time.

He was still wearing his gray hoodie, although it was speckled with blood. His hood was off, so I could fully assess his face now. And I tried hard to find the demonic features that a killer ought to have had and that I had missed when we had first met. His features were dark, but not in a menacing way: ill-kempt, dark-brown hair and dark-brown eyes. Despite his five o'clock shadow, I could see that his face was youthful, fresh, almost rosy-cheeked, and yet lines had started to etch themselves into his forehead, as though he were aging prematurely. He was broad-shouldered and tall ("Well over six feet," I visualized myself telling a police detective someday soon, I hoped). The whole package was—despite what I knew about him—attractive. Inviting.

While I was evaluating him, I had started to loosen up a bit, my fingers releasing their death grip on the bedsheets.

When I realized this, I became terrified once again, but terrified of me, of my nonsensical response to him. I forced myself to remember what was real, to reconcile the image of the stranger standing in front of me with that of the murderer named Cameron, but it was becoming more and more difficult. He stood before me, and his eyes … they seemed worried now, almost gentle.

There was something familiar about this guy.

I immediately stopped this wobbly train of thought. What Cameron looked like, whatever he was trying to make me believe now—it had to be a show. Reality was his bloodied sweatshirt. This man was a killer.

I was glad when he finally turned away and walked out, closing the door and simultaneously breaking my trance, allowing me to work through the war between my new dual personalities: my yin versus my yang.

I lay there massaging my temples with my fingers and trying hard to remember what had happened. The last thing I remembered was Cameron's empty stare after I had watched him kill an innocent man in cold blood. But his demeanor now seemed more inquisitive than aggressive. I forced myself to remember every detail from my day leading to the murder in the cemetery, but I couldn't remember anything after Cameron spotted me witnessing the murder. How I had gotten wherever I was was still a total blur. Panic was starting to creep up my spine, but I forced it back down. Panic was useless right now—it wouldn't get me anywhere, and it wouldn't get me out of here.

So I started with what I did know. I was still alive—that was a good thing. And the name of the guy in the hoodie was Cameron. He had murdered someone, and he knew that I had seen him murder someone. Why I was still alive, why he had called a doctor to make sure that I lived when he could have just killed me in the cemetery, these were added to the list of things that I didn't know. Making a mental list of "What I Know" and "What I Don't Know but Will Find Out" helped me focus.

Now that I was allowing myself to calm down, the throbbing pain at the back of my head became noticeable again. I brought my fingers to it. The mere pressure of one of my fingertips against it cut my breath short. I had been hit on the back of the head—this explained why I couldn't remember anything after the murder. While the pain in my head was excruciating, this tidbit of knowledge fueled me, clearing up some of my confusion. Cameron might have been handsome on the outside, but he was not averse to hurting me. The large bump on my head would be my reminder of how much danger I was in.

Turning my stiff neck, I scanned my surroundings, looking for anything that would help me answer any of my questions. There wasn't much to decipher. I was in a small room. There was a lamp on the table next to my bed and an armchair with a rose velvet cushion in one corner. (I made a mental note to find an opportune time to try to break a leg off the chair or smash the lamp—anything that could be used as a weapon. New list: "Weapons.") Three of the walls were pristine white and unornamented. The other wall was made up of four floor-to-ceiling undraped windows.

I could try to throw the pretty armchair through one of the windows.

I struggled to sit up and flip my legs over the edge of the bed. My eyelids were heavy.

My feet hit the cool wooden floor—and I suddenly noticed that I didn't have my sneakers on anymore. I once again pushed down the instinct to panic, and instead I looked to see if anything else was missing or different with me, with my body. Except for the grass stains on my knees, the rubber band that was missing from my hair, and the immense throbbing against my skull, everything else on my body was the way I had left it.

After waiting for another bout of nausea to pass, I went to the window, holding on to the small table as support for my shaky frame. Outside, the sun was setting, a brilliant palette of orange, red, and pink; I was peering over the shadows of endless rooftops. Wherever I was, it was high above a city, at least thirty stories high. I couldn't decide if I was still in Callister—I thought I recognized the clock tower that stood at the center of the city square, but it was too distant for me to be sure. If that was the clock tower, then we were on the east end of the city, on the outskirts. I didn't know much about this part of the city except that it was an industrial zone.

I did a once-over of the windows, looking for an opening, but they were single-paned and did not open. There was also no ledge for me to hang off of. So while the windows were not immediate escape routes, they gave me a clue that I was probably in some kind of office building, because apartment buildings usually had windows that opened. This reaffirmed my suspicion that I was not in a residential area. My hand pressed against the glass; I closed my eyes until the dizziness passed.

When I pried my eyes open, I looked down and saw a yellow cab waiting at a red light on an otherwise empty street. Maybe the driver would happen to look up at this exact spot and see me. Out of desperation or instinct, I pounded my fist in three quick sequences against the window and then jumped and waved as though I were on fire. Then I heard something stir somewhere within the building and I stopped, every muscle in my body becoming rigid, like a field mouse hearing the cry of a hawk.

I listened and counted. One. Two. Three. Four. Five. Nothing. Six. Seven. Eight. Nine. Ten. Still nothing.

When I was sure no one was coming, I looked back down. The cab was gone.

I moved away from the window, for now.

I slowly, painfully trudged to the bedroom door and leaned in, placing my ear against its smooth white surface, listening for anything I could use. I was hoping, "maybe-ing," again. Maybe they forgot to lock the door. Maybe they were dumb enough to think that I wasn't strong enough to try to escape. Maybe, just maybe, I could escape right now through this simple door before they had time to plan anything worse for me or lock me up in a dungeon.

I could hear hushed voices, a TV echoing in the background. There were people somewhere, but as far as I could tell they were not too close.

My heart was pounding.

I was about to do something that could be very smart or very dumb. Something that could save me or end me.

I twisted the doorknob slowly, as though with each inch that turned, the knob might explode. I expected it to be locked. It wasn't. Without making a sound I cracked the door open, just enough that if someone were standing there, I could probably close it again without being noticed.

With one eye, I peered through the crack. All I could see was a blank white wall.

I opened the door just a little bit more so that I could quickly poke my head out and see what was out there beyond the bedroom. Then a sound from the floor startled me. Meatball, who apparently had been keeping guard and just seen me, quickly stood up.

I got spooked and slammed the door.

On the other side, the dog was betraying me with his whine. And then there were hurried footsteps.

Adrenaline kicked in and my pain vanished. I rushed back to the bed, got under the covers, and shut my eyes.

I heard the door open. Blood was roaring through my veins, but I did not move.

Nothing happened. Nothing yet.

I went back to counting to ten.

Once again, nothing. No blows. Not even screaming.

What if I screamed now? Would anyone hear me? Would anyone come rescue me before he put a bullet between my eyes?

I forced myself to take indiscernible, calming breaths and focus on what I could hear. There was someone standing in the doorway—I couldn't hear him, but I could feel him watching me. The distant voices I had heard earlier were silent, but the television was still on. I tried to figure out what they were watching based on the noise. From the constant jibber-jabber, it was some sort of sportscast, possibly football. I kept my eyes closed, waiting to hear him leave.

The problem with pretending to be asleep when your adrenaline is drained, your brain is broken, and your eyelids feel as though they are magnetized to the floor: you fall asleep, whether you want to or not.

****

I heard someone clearing his throat, and I startled awake. The room was completely dark except for the light that was pouring in from the hallway. Cameron was standing by the open door. I looked up at him through a sleepy, confused haze.

Adrenaline kicked in as soon as I realized that I wasn't dreaming, that I wasn't in my own bed or in my own bedroom. I remembered that I had been taken by this murderer.

Cameron stood there, watching me in this calculating kind of way. It was unnerving. He seemed to leave me alone when I slept, so I closed my eyes and pretended to sleep again.

I fell back asleep almost immediately.

****

The same thing happened three or four more times. Cameron would walk into the room, make some small noise, wake me up. Then I'd look up and he would simply stand there. I would close my eyes and let the seconds roll by while memories of my horror flooded back like low tide turning to high tide. He apparently had taken on the task of ensuring that I didn't die in my sleep. So far he had decided to keep me alive, for whatever reason.

Once I was awakened, I tried to keep myself awake, occupying my mind by going through my lists or singing Christmas songs or replaying old *Friends* episodes. But Cameron seemed to know what I was trying to do. He would wait me out and wouldn't leave until I really fell back asleep. And high tide went back to low tide.

****

In the morning I woke up to the sound of Meatball whining at the closed bedroom door and the blinding pain that had localized to the top of my head. The grayish light of dawn was coming in through the wall of windows.

I sat up in bed, letting my tired head fall against the cold wall behind me. It wasn't until I saw Cameron that I remembered where I was again—well, at least I recognized the room I was in. (I was being tortured by being forced to recall my nightmare over and over.) He was sleeping, uncomfortably sprawled on the too-small armchair. I had heard him sit down the last time he came to wake me, and I had been particularly stubborn about falling back asleep. He must have fallen asleep himself while waiting me out.

He was still fully dressed but had changed out of his bloody gray hoodie—I couldn't remember at what point his clothes had changed when he came to wake me in the night. Was it the third time or the fourth time?

His head was rolled back and resting on the wall, and he had one hand half-fallen over his eyes, an unconscious effort to block out the rising sun. His brown hair was scruffy, like he'd raked his hand through it a thousand times. The dark circles under his eyes told the story of someone who hadn't been sleeping much, probably for many days.

I watched him like this for a while, adding to my list of details. His square jaw. His straight nose. The sculpted features of his face. His hands—the hands of a killer. As I considered whether I would have enough time to smash the bedside lamp and grab a sharp piece before he woke up, Cameron's watch beeped and he jumped awake, momentarily disoriented. His eyes quickly found me.

"How long have you been awake?" he asked hoarsely, squinting down at his watch.

I pulled the covers up to my chin. What were the magic words? What could I say that would help me survive?

He passed both hands over his entire face, rubbing his skin awake. "How are you feeling?"

I knew I had to answer him, but I couldn't come up with something that would keep me noncommittal until I could hash out a strategy.

Cameron got up, walked to the side of the bed, and stopped short, deliberating. Was he debating whether to shoot me now or later? I looked for signs of trouble, like a dog going on the attack, like a gun being pulled out from the back of his jeans.

With a movement that was too fast for my bruised brain to analyze, Cameron sat next to me and rushed his hand to my face. I gasped and recoiled from him. His eyes widened, and he snapped his hand away like he'd just been burned. The features of his face were washed with … Guilt? Worry? Anger? Disappointment? I couldn't be sure.

"I'm sorry," he said, his voice notably softer. "I was just going to check the bump on your head. I won't hurt you."

His concern was unreserved, which made my throat immediately squeeze shut. Was I really that desperate for human compassion? It was too late—tears, spearheaded by the bolt of terror, had sprung to my eyes. I hadn't planned on the tears coming, not without some calculation. But now that they had come, I had no choice. I decided to go with it, perhaps play on his apparent sympathy.

"I'm fine ... really," I said in answer to the increased concern on his face.

"You don't look fine."

I made a show of wiping the tears from my eyes and glanced up at him, doe-eyed. But when our eyes met, when he started assessing me (as he seemed to do a lot), he frowned and I found myself cowering. I looked away.

"Can I check your head? Even if you say you're fine?"

I quickly weighed my options—I didn't have any—and very slowly bent my head forward.

My heart pumped hard in my chest as his fingers parted the hair at the crown of my head and pressed lightly on the bump. I winced, my face hidden by my hair.

"Does this hurt?"

"No," I lied, the strain in my voice betraying me.

"I didn't think so," he said. "I'll get you something for the pain."

Before I could refuse, he was out the door, and Meatball had found his way in. In an instant, he was on the bed.

I didn't move an inch.

He'd started to soldier-crawl his way closer, like a snake in the grass, when Cameron came back in. "Meatball. Out. Now." Cameron's authoritative voice startled both Meatball and me.

Like the big kid the night before, Meatball immediately obeyed.

"Does everyone just jump like that when you give orders?" I blurted.

"Not everyone," he said dryly. He walked over to my bedside and handed me two little white pills and a large glass of water. The water was liquid gold to my eyes: my mouth tasted like I'd been licking the chalk off a blackboard all night. As for the mystery pills, they continued the nightmare.

He stood and he waited. This was becoming his trademark with me. "You need to get more rest. The meds will help with the pain so you can get some sleep."

I looked at the pills in my hand as though they were mountains in my way. Cameron had just openly admitted that the pills were going to make me sleep. I needed to get out of there, not go back to sleep. Did he really just want me to get rest, or did he want to keep me drugged up? If he wanted me drugged up, why? To keep me quiet? Then why hadn't he just stuck a needle in my arm while I was sleeping? Why hadn't he just killed me in the first place instead of paying a back-alley doctor too much money?

What I chose to do with these pills, I knew, would be the key to my survival or my ultimate demise. Perhaps he was trying to drug me, or perhaps he was testing me, trying to see if he could trust me to do as I was told. The problem was that I didn't know his plan for me.

So right now, the decision was mine to make.

At least I had something to barter with: the pills he wanted me to consume. This was my leverage into his brain.

I raised the glass to my lips. "Your name is Cameron," I mused carefully, my voice echoing inside the glass.

Cameron's body stiffened. "Uh-huh."

We watched each other while I took two large gulps of water.

"What else do you remember?" he asked me.

"Is this where I tell you that I don't remember anything?" Immediately I felt color rushing to my face. I needed to be more careful with my words. I put a pill in my mouth, hoping this would undo my blunder, but I kept it under my tongue.

"No," he said without blinking. "This is where you tell me the truth."

"That man, in the cemetery, he deserved what you did to him." I had said this matter-of-factly, as a show that I understood him, although what I really needed him to tell me was that the man hadn't been just some random runner who was in the wrong place at the wrong time—that only bad people got killed. That girls like me didn't get killed just because they witnessed a murder.

Cameron's face hardened. "You assume that the man was blameless." This wasn't a question—he knew what I was thinking. "What if I told you that justice really was served?"

There was eye-for-an-eye type of justice, and then there was the American justice system that wasn't justice at all. I didn't know what kind of justice Cameron believed in That man was dead; he was still alive. "Justice means different things to different people, I guess."

"What does it matter?" he said. "It's not like you knew him."

He narrowed his eyes and put a finger on my chin. I was forced to swallow the mountain of a pill before he caught me. As I swallowed and opened my mouth for him to check, I knew I had just sealed my fate. The words came drooling out before I had time to process them: "His family will never know what happened to him, and they'll spend the rest of their lives wondering what they could have done to change things. There doesn't seem to be much justice in that." I braced myself for the blow that would come next.

When I felt his fingers quickly brush my damp cheek, I opened my eyes. There was no anger on Cameron's face—but his eyes were appraising. I shouldn't have felt comfort from his touch. I should have been repulsed, terrified. But the feel of his hand against my face made me want to burrow my face into his shoulder and cry. Was it something he was doing? Was I that easily brainwashed?

I cleared my throat to cut through the pain in my chest, and I swallowed my second pill. My fingers tingled—the first pill was already working its magic. Whatever I was chugging down, it was potent.

"Cameron," I said, hoping that repeating his name would make both of us seem more human, "what am I doing here?"

"You're resting, Emily."

Had I told him my name? I couldn't remember. I must have when I was semiconscious. My head was getting so heavy. "Who were all those people in the room yesterday?"

"My colleagues."

"How long are you going to keep me here?"

Cameron pulled the glass out of my numb hands and set it on the table next to me. "For as long as it takes."

"What are you going to do with me?" This came out as a whisper. My eyes were barely open.

Cameron paused for a moment. "I don't know," he finally said.

It was the last thing I heard him say before I fell asleep.

****

When I woke up, the sun was setting again.

I was feeling better, rested at least, though my joints and muscles ached from the lack of movement. Had I been out all day, or even longer? As for the bump on my head, it was only sensitive to the touch of my fingers—there was no more throbbing. My hair, on the other hand, was a tangled mess; my head felt naked when my hair was down, as though I were letting all the ginger hang out for the world to judge. I searched my pockets and then the barren room for anything that I could use to tie it back. The only thing I found was the glass of water that had been refilled, and which I greedily gulped down.

The bedroom door had been left open. This was very odd.

Perhaps I had made the right decision by taking the sleeping pills. Perhaps I had gained his trust.

I wasn't smiling, but the thought of having finally made a good decision reenergized me. It made me feel like I could still win my survival. I was back in the game.

I let my senses kick back in.

Hollow sounds from a TV could still be heard. And now I could smell food. The last meal I had eaten was the stale peanut butter sandwich I'd gobbled down on my lunch break from work; how long ago was that? My brain was still too foggy to count back the hours—or the days. The thought of this, my real life, made the grumbling in my stomach turn into a nauseous lurch.

I got up and went to the door. An open door: it was either an invitation or a mistake.

Either way, I wasn't staying in that room one more second.

I stepped into a hallway that was as blank as the room I had just stepped out of. More white paint on the walls but no furniture, no devil dog, and no people, dead or alive. To my left there were three doors that were identical to mine—to the room I was being held captive in. I surmised that these three doors probably led to more bedrooms, but who knew?

On my right, the hall ended into another space that I couldn't see because it was around the corner. The hallway was dark, with the only light coming from this place beyond.

I stood there, knowing that I had to make a decision. Going back to my cell was not an option. I could go to the light or creep into the dark hallway toward one of the bedrooms doors.

What was behind those doors? My captors? More prisoners like me? Or perhaps there were weapons, real or fabricated? Anything would be better than a rose-colored bedside lamp or a gaudy chair that I couldn't even lift, let alone rip apart.

In the end, I couldn't bring myself to go into a darker place than the one I had just walked out of. I chose the light and went right. I stopped at the corner and poked my head around.

I saw it, only a few feet away. Where the wood floor became the tiled floor.

A front door ... or a back door. A door that led out of there. An escape door.

There was no doubt in my mind that this was what it was. It was far thicker than any of the other doors, and it had a peephole in the middle. It also had five different locks—I had quickly counted them. It was definitely some kind of exit.

There was a torn entry carpet next to the door with several pairs of men's shoes on it.

Wait—not all of them were men's shoes. There was another pair there. They were much smaller, though dirtier. My sneakers. The ones that went missing after I did. While the men's shoes were mostly piled all over each other, my shoes were neatly placed in their midst. As though they had always been there. As though they had found their rightful place. I wanted to scream. I wanted to run and snatch them up like a mother would a child who was being lured away by a stranger.

I took a step into the light, pulled by wrath and desperation. When I got to the front door, I forgot about my sneakers and reached for the door handle.

I don't know how long Cameron had been there—whether he had just walked in or had been waiting for me. Another test. One that I had failed.

"Hi," he said, his tone cool.

I froze, a deer in the headlights.

He was holding onto a takeout carton and stuffed a heap of chow mein noodles in his mouth. His dog was at his feet, slobbering. After chewing a bit, he asked me, "Are you hungry?"

My mind was racing. My hands were shaking. I had just been caught red-handed trying to run away, and Cameron was acting like we'd met up for a lunch date. No normal human being could be this calm.

Was I hungry? No. I was not hungry. I was petrified.

When I didn't answer, he shrugged. "Come with me," he said.

He could have dragged me away kicking and screaming. I should have tried to scream. What if there was someone outside the door who could hear me? What if there wasn't? Cameron was unruffled after catching me trying to escape. If I screamed now, while I was well within his grasp, perhaps I would send him over the edge.

I went with him.

We entered a living room furnished with couches and a television.

The big kid, the one who looked like a big Chucky doll, was sprawled on one of the couches, remote control in hand, looking utterly bored.

The tattooed man was sitting erect on the edge of an armchair. He stood up as soon as he saw me, his venomous stare unimproved.

The kid mirrored his colleague's scrutiny, narrowing his eyes as he scanned me head to toe. "You look like crap," he said to me. Then his lethargic gaze returned to the TV.

Farther ahead, in the corner, I could see a small kitchen and a table. I was in a small, open-concept apartment. An apartment, not an office building as I had previously assumed. This small discrepancy rattled me. What else had I been wrong about? I was starting to doubt everything I knew—or thought I knew.

While I was taking in these new details, I realized that Cameron had already gone ahead of me. He appeared at the table with a plate of chow mein noodles. He placed the plate on the table, pulled out the empty chair. "Sit," he said and went back to the kitchen.

I sat and stared at the plate like a sunflower would stare at a hamburger. There were a million feelings and thoughts bouncing around inside me, but none of them had anything to do with hunger. There was no way I was going to be able to choke down anything. But Cameron was now leaning against the kitchen doorway and surveying me, having once again picked up his depleted carton of noodles.

With a trembling hand, I brought my fork to my mouth and chewed and chewed and chewed and forced the food down my throat. I had to breathe deeply to keep it down. Then I took another bite and repeated the effort. While I did this, I kept Cameron in my peripheral vision. Something had changed; I could feel it. He was more relaxed. The worried creases on his forehead and around his eyes were lessened, his movements less strained.

I didn't know how to take this.

I glanced around the room and into the adjoining living room, where my eyes met those of the tattooed man. He was now sitting on the edge of the couch, his head turned in my direction. Had he been glaring at me like this the whole time? I quickly brought my eyes back down to my plate, which still had an insurmountable amount of food on it.

Feeling the weight of the tattooed man's stare, I tucked my hair behind my ears. When I checked on Cameron again, I saw that he was smiling, a smile that almost reached his eyes. Sticking his chopsticks into the carton, he fished something out of his pocket and handed it to me. It was my rubber band.

"Do you feel better today?" he asked.

My face flushed as he watched me put my hair up.

His eyes narrowed. "How's your head?"

I doubted he knew what a loaded question that was. "My skull is fine."

"Any dizzyness?"

"Not right now."

"Throbbing?"

He had been watching me as I answered. I wasn't sure whether he was actually concerned or just wanted to see how I responded.

"Just a little bit," I admitted quickly, before he chose to poke and prod my head to catch me in a lie again.

He paused.

"Good," he said finally.

I breathed a small sigh of relief; I felt as though I had passed his assessment.

"Kid's going to take you for a drive," he announced.

My curdling stomach dropped to my knees, and Kid's head snapped up. At last he'd found something interesting besides the TV.

"I am?" he asked. *He is?* I had simultaneously thought—though my inner voice was more a horrified gasp than a question. The tattooed man also looked surprised; apparently Cameron hadn't shared his plan with anyone else.

"You're taking Emily to the farm tonight."

At this announcement, Kid let his head fall back in annoyance, like a ten-year-old who's been asked to clean his room. "Tonight? Are you kidding? It's already getting dark! It'll take forever!"

I still had hope: Kid—with the now-noticeable strangler-sized hands—was too lazy to kill me today. But Cameron offered an incentive: he grabbed a set of keys from the kitchen counter and tossed them across the room to Kid, who adeptly caught them with his monster hands, which were attached to his humongous arms. His eyes lit up.

"Seriously? You're letting me take your car?"

The tattooed man stared at Cameron in disapproval, but kept silent.

Not needing further encouragement, Kid shot up, glanced in my general direction, and headed for the door. "Let's go, Red."

My stomach had fallen down to my toes. Was taking someone "to the farm" some kind of code, along the same lines as making someone "sleep with the fishes"?

I turned to Cameron, incredulous. What had been the point? Keeping me alive, forcing me to rest, feeding me … only to kill me? Was it just a sick game?

I didn't want to believe it. But Cameron was decidedly stoic as he gave further direction: "No stops, Kid. As fast as you can go." Kid couldn't hide his excitement.

Had I been kept alive for Kid, like cattle being raised for slaughter? Was I his initiation into this murderous fraternity?

Cameron pulled a gun from his waistband and tendered it to Kid, who almost ran to him and greedily reached for it. Cameron held on and looked him in the eye. "Only if you absolutely need it. Use your judgment. Absolutely no stops."

"Absolutely no stops."

My breath was getting caught up in my throat. My world was spinning as though I had vertigo. I looked at the faces around the room, one after another. "Don't do this. I won't talk … I'll do whatever you want. It doesn't have to be like this. I have a family and friends …" My lips were quivering. Kid looked surprised by my reaction. He glanced from me to Cameron. But my beautiful abductor's easy mood turned to ice; his mouth was a thin line.

"Your shoes are at the door."

I turned my face away and closed my eyes. "Please."

Cameron took my plate off the table and went back to the kitchen.

All went quiet.

I opened my eyes. The man with the spider web tattoo was gone. I could see Cameron in the kitchen, holding on to the counter, his head down.

I felt a hand on my shoulder. It was Kid. "We should go," he said, his voice uncertain.

I got up and went with him. *He's just a kid,* I told myself. He didn't have his own gun. He was excitable, but he was green. If I were going to make something happen, it would be on his inexperienced watch. Not with Cameron, whose mood was unpredictable.

I went to the front door, slid into my still-soaked sneakers, and laced them up as tightly as I could—ready to run. Running was something I was good at. Running was my weapon.

The hallway was bright, with brick walls painted white and plush carpeting—not the kind of carpet you would expect to find in the hallway of an apartment building, but the expensive kind that your feet sink into and leave footprints in when you walk on it barefoot. By the time I made it out of the apartment, Kid was already down the hallway, holding the elevator door open. I looked back once—Cameron's back was still turned, his body rigid—and then I closed the door.

There were only two doors on this floor: the door I had just exited and the door to the elevator I was about to enter. The apartment must have been the penthouse. There were cameras at each end of the windowless hallway.

Screaming was of no use. Running was of no use ... not yet.

I got into the elevator with Kid.

The elevator had no buttons and no emergency phone, and it automatically went down as soon as the doors closed. The apartment had its own elevator, I surmised.

As we descended, Kid was silent, squirmy, eagerly spinning the key ring around his index finger, clearly indifferent that I would be joining him, even if it would only be for a little while—until I escaped or until I was dead.

The elevator doors opened and we stepped out into a garage. In front of us there was a garage door with just enough room for cars to enter and exit.

There were four vehicles in the garage: a newer-model black pickup, two rusted-out beaters, and an Audi, sleek black with tinted windows.

The Audi beeped as we came closer. Kid jumped right in and started it up. I hesitated, still searching for an exit that I might have missed. There were four more cameras hanging from the ceiling. Who was watching?

He rolled down the window and stuck his head out. "Are you coming or not?"

I wasn't dumb enough to assume that he was really giving me the choice. My heart pumping through my ears, I climbed into the passenger side. The Audi's locks clicked as soon as I closed the door.

Kid gripped the steering wheel and side-eyed me. "Put your seat belt on—this is going to be fun." He backed up and drove to the garage door, which opened as soon as we neared it. It either had a sensor or someone had indeed been watching us through the cameras.

As soon as we were on the street and out of sight, and while Kid was distracted with the joystick, I sneaked my hand to the door handle and pulled. Nothing happened. There must have been a safety feature preventing the door from opening while the car moved. I was stuck inside.

I looked out the window. I had been right: we were in Callister, on the outskirts, in the industrial zone. It was dark and the streets were empty. Kid held to his word. He didn't stop for anything, not stop signs or red lights. We were out of the city in a matter of minutes. From the side mirror, I watched the lights of the city—the place that was my home—recede and give way to darkness.

My sense of panic rose. It filled the inside of the car, front to back, side to side, squeezing me in.

"Where are you taking me?"

"You were right there, weren't you? We're going to the farm."

I glanced around for something I could use against him. The car was spotless. It still had a new car smell, mixed with a smell of dog.

Kid didn't let up on the gas pedal until we were driving well above the speed limit on a country road. Darkened street signs flashed by. What was the point of making me wear my seat belt if he was going to kill us both by crashing the car? I had a stranglehold on the security bar over the door; I was using my shoulder to wipe my nose.

With few distractions and the car's novelty having worn off, Kid remembered that I was sitting next to him.

"Sorry about hitting you on the head like that yesterday," he said, his eyes still on the road. "I didn't think I hit you that hard."

Unprepared for this revelation, I kept quiet. *So Cameron wasn't the one who hit me after all.* Though getting hit on the head was insignificant compared to what was coming.

"How did you manage to sneak right by me?" he asked.

"I was just trying to get home."

"Who runs alone in a dark cemetery, toward danger? That's the stupidest thing I've ever heard."

I needed a plan. I could outsmart this guy. I knew I could outsmart this guy.

When I was in high school, one of our teachers fell ill after consuming the glue that had mysteriously found its way into her morning coffee. We spent the rest of the day sitting in front of the TV while the principal scurried to find a substitute teacher at the last minute. Of the multitude of educational videos we were forced to watch that day, one had been a bad reenactment of an attempted abduction. I didn't have to rack my brain too long to remember the first rule: never get in the car with a stranger.

I started to panic when I noticed the yellow road signs flashing by us, pictures of crumbling rocks. We were heading into the mountains … the largely uninhabited mountains. And then my panic triggered something, a hazy survival tip from one of those crime shows: make the attacker see that you're a real person, not just a nameless witness to a murder, or something like that.

"My name is Emily," I announced.

He looked at me like I was crazy.

Right. I'd forgotten that Cameron had already mentioned my name.

"What's your name?" My stomach lurched as the Audi sped into a curve.

He considered the question while I gulped the takeout back down my throat. "You can call me Sexy Bull."

My head was buzzing, and a bead of sweat lined my forehead.

We were going to bond whether or not he wanted to.

"My mom's name is Isabelle and my dad's name is Burt; it's short for Bernard. And I had a teddy bear called Booger when I was a kid—he lost an eye after I tried to flat-iron his fur. And my middle toe on my left foot is longer than my big toe. And when I was four—"

"What's wrong with you? Are you still high?" There was incredulity mixed with an edge of worry in his voice.

"And when I was four—" The Audi was rushing through curves and up and down hills. The shadowed landscape was flashing by. Suddenly, as the car aggressively looped around a cliff, I felt a knot in my throat, my heart started racing, and my body temperature went up a thousand degrees. I didn't need to come up with a plan. My body made one for me.

"Oh god!"

"What now?"

"You need to stop."

"No stops. You heard what—"

"I'm going to be sick."

"What? We're in the middle of the mountains. There's nowhere to stop!"

I started heaving, my hand in front of my mouth.

"Hold on! Keep it in!" In a flailing panic, Kid blindly fiddled in the backseat with his free hand, his eyes never leaving the road.

He pulled out a plastic bag, emptying its contents before throwing it at me.

I pulled the bag open and threw up immediately, repeatedly.

"That's so gross!" he gasped, opening his window and sticking his head out. "It still smells like chow mein."

The fresh air rushing in from his open window made me feel better—and I had nothing left in my stomach to puke up anyway. After a few minutes, I pulled my face away from the bag and glanced up.

He was glaring at me, holding his nose and wincing. His face had gone from rosy-cheeked to pale and sickly.

"Throw the bag out the window," he ordered.

"I can't do that," I said. "It's a plastic bag. It will take over a hundred years to disintegrate. I don't want to pollute."

"Emily," he said, carefully enunciating every syllable, "if you don't throw that bag out the window in the next second, I'm going to be sick too."

I sighed and threw the bag out my window. So much for stopping to find a garbage can and running away.

He looked at me with revulsion. "That's the grossest thing I've ever seen. Now I'm kinda glad we didn't take my car. Who knew one girl could be such a pain …" His voice trailed off. "Ugh!" he groaned dramatically a few seconds later. "It really stinks in here." And he stuck his head out his window again.

I've never had an iron stomach. Once a guy on his bike crashed next to me, and a broken bone in his right shin pierced through his skin. As any Good Samaritan would do, I insisted on waiting with him until the paramedics showed up. He spent the next twenty minutes holding my hair back while I puked on the side of the road. I don't remember if he ever thanked me for waiting with him.

I thought about telling Kid about this life event to further solidify our captor-captive bond, but I was simply worn out.

Chapter Five

The Farm

There was the sound of gravel crushing against the Audi's tires.

We had turned off the country road onto a narrow gravel side road where the blackened branches of trees hovered too close, as though they were trying to grab hold of the car, trying to consume us. Kid was absentmindedly drumming his fingers on the steering wheel to a Britney Spears tune that was crackling through the radio in broken waves. The darkness beyond the headlights besieged us.

We had been driving for hours. I had stopped trying to make conversation with Kid. It was pointless, and I had no imagination left; all of it had been sucked dry with thoughts of what was going to happen to me. How I was going to die. I was exhausted. Given that I had nowhere to go, I had tried to close my eyes and get some rest. But every time he braked, even if it was ever so slightly, my heart rate jacked up as I expected that this was the end of the road.

And now we were, literally, at the end of a road.

"Where are we?" I croaked.

Kid stretched his arms, pushing against the steering wheel, and sighed. "Almost there, thank god. Cam totally owes me for this."

My throat was raw, and my body entirely consumed by fear. I could feel the dark isolation seeping into the car like a deep depression. I just wanted this to be over—to let things happen as they were intended to—but Kid seemed to be going to great lengths to drag out the inevitable. Maybe breaking my spirit first was part of the preparation.

After we bounced around on the road awhile, the trees gave way and Kid slowed down. My eyes were beyond tired; I was even starting to see man-sized shadows stirring in the woods. I focused on the speck of light that shone ahead. I couldn't have imagined that—it grew bigger as we drove closer.

The car came to a stop. Kid turned off the ignition and was out in a flash, breathing in the fresh air repeatedly, overdramatically. I waited, rubbing my eyes, forcing them to adjust to the light that had come on inside the Audi.

Kid eventually came back and leaned into the car, resting his hand against the frame of the open door. "I don't know how you can stand being in this car one more second. It really reeks in here."

I glanced up through weary eyes. Was I supposed to get out?

Kid wrinkled his nose as he observed me. I climbed out of the vehicle and my numbed legs failed me. I tumbled to the ground on all fours.

"You're so weird," he mumbled, shaking his head and walking away.

The air outside the car was crisp and clean—too clean; I wasn't sure my city-infected lungs could handle the pure stuff. The night sky was unbelievably clear, which I guessed was how it must always look when the city lights weren't there to distort it. Of course, I had seen stars before, but not like this. It seemed like every imaginable constellation was shining above. It took me a while to find the dippers—big and little were the only ones I knew—but in this perfect sky, they weren't the only superstars. If I was going to die soon, I wanted to die looking at that sky. *Please let it be quick and painless,* I thought.

Kid.

He was walking away.

His back was turned. I was still at the car, holding on to the open car door while my legs steadied. There were just a few feet between us, but he wasn't looking. And I could run fast. I knew above all that I could run fast.

It was so dark; I had no idea where I was. There were sounds in the darkness. Murmurs. I was drained. But running into the unknown was better than staying and waiting for more unknowns. Flooding my chest with as much as air as it would allow, I took a step back into the darkness.

The sound of a door creaking open and the flood of light that followed stopped me. A man walked through the earlier, guiding light—which, as it turned out, was a door with an etched-glass window. He was carrying a rifle over his shoulder, as though he were going hunting.

I stood motionless.

Kid greeted the armed man nonchalantly as they met in the middle.

"Why are you back so early?" the gunman demanded.

Kid shrugged and tilted his head in my direction. "Pain-in-the-butt delivery."

The gunman gave me a once-over. Then he made his way toward me.

I held my breath and closed my eyes, listening to the shuffling of his feet against the loose gravel—I didn't want to see the bullet coming. I pictured the open sky, the stars, tranquility. I thought of my brother, Bill. The footsteps approached and shuffled on past me. I opened one eye in time to see him disappear into the darkness of the surrounding woods. I heard his footsteps in the grass; the sound faded until I couldn't hear anything but the same murmur, which could have been the wind in trees but which to my city ears sounded rather humanoid.

I turned my eyes to the sky again. I was looking for them—my lucky stars—but it was early still, and there were just too many stars to find mine.

As I went through this rush of emotions, Kid had been watching me from the open doorway. With the same look of mystification on his face, he hollered, "Hey, freak, are you just going to stand there all night—or do you plan on coming in?"

The doorway where he was standing was set into a large building that, in the darkness, looked like a barn. Moonlight reflected off the tin roof, and tall cedars lined the front of the edifice, with the door being the only shrub-free space; I couldn't tell if the building had any windows because the cedars hid its exterior walls.

Knowing what awaited in the darkness, I chugged ahead to the slightly less-armed Kid.

Inside the barn was a foyer with a vaulted ceiling. The beige-marble-tiled floor of the foyer merged with dark, ancient-looking hardwood floor. Half-moon stairs led to a second-level hallway with a plain white wall and wood rail. Through a side doorway, another set of stairs led down to a lower floor. I could see the flickering lights from an unseen downstairs TV bouncing off the bare stairwell walls.

Kid kicked his shoes off onto the pile of huge shoes that were strewn by the front door and disappeared through an arched doorway at the far end of the foyer, next to the curved staircase. "Come on in," I heard him yell to me.

I didn't understand any of this. Why was I even there? I couldn't stand the unknowns. I wanted to slump to the floor and cry, or turn around and let the armed man make a decision. Kid's informality was too hard to decipher.

I could feel myself slipping. Giving in. Breaking all the promises I had made to myself to survive this.

I took my shoes off and marched ahead through the arched doorway.

By the time I made it down the two steps that led to a living area, Kid was already sprawled in front of the TV on one of the two couches, remote control in hand. It was like we had never left the apartment in the city.

I glanced around, waiting for his next move.

"You can sit, ya know," he said.

I sat on the edge of the other couch and waited, examining my newest surroundings.

It was one big open space that connected a living room to a kitchen to a dining area with a large, pine-colored table. I could see now that the barn was a home. The living room had brown leather furniture—the soft kind that seemed to conform to your body as you sank into it. There was a fireplace made of stones stacked to the high ceiling, and hanging over the mantel there was an oversized flat-screen television, which Kid hadn't taken his eyes off of. No phone anywhere that I could see.

A humongous open kitchen adjoined the dining area. It had two of almost every appliance: two restaurant-sized refrigerators, two microwaves, two toasters, two dishwashers, but only one oven. There were knives in there. I could see them from where I was sitting, a heap of them sticking into wooden blocks. They were the sharp kind, similar to the ones we had in the kitchen back home.

I turned my attention back to Kid, trying to decide which one was worse: not knowing how I was going to die, or not knowing when it was going to happen. I felt as though I was going to lose the only control I had left: control of myself.

Kid settled on cartoons, pulled out the gun that Cameron had given him, and began playing with it: flipping it over in his hands, putting his finger on the trigger while muttering sounds that were better suited for Batman comic books. Boom! Pow! Kapow! Bam!

He ignored me but I kept my eyes on him, expecting the gun to be pointed at me the second I stopped looking. After a few minutes of my stare, Kid sighed loudly. "Are you always this uptight, or are you just like that with me?"

"No, I'm usually a lot more fun when I get taken and brought to the middle of nowhere against my will," I snapped. His indifference was maddening.

"Hey, don't get upset with me. I'm just following orders."

"What are your orders, exactly?" I took the chance of asking, just in case he obliged me with an actual answer.

"Weren't you right there when I got them?"

"All I heard was that you were taking me for a drive to the farm. I don't know what that means, but this place doesn't look much like a farm to me."

"It does when you know the animals who live here."

My gaze swept the room again and rested back on his face. "This place is what Cameron meant by *taking me to the farm*?" I noticed that his face flinched when I said Cameron's name.

"What else could it mean?"

I frowned. Was he kidding or was he messing with me?

Kid seemed to consider this nonanswer; it took him a while to understand. "You mean you thought that Cameron would send *me* to kill *you*?"

I remained still.

"Really?" he insisted, his voice pitching on the last syllable. "Wow. Thanks!"

I let my face fall into my hands. I wanted to cry, but I was too tired to even accomplish that.

"Whoa! Hey! What's that all about?" Kid asked. "You're not doing that crying thing again, are you?"

I pulled my hands away, tears hanging at the corner of my eyes. "Please be honest with me. I know you don't know me. You don't owe me anything. You are obviously trying to impress this Cameron guy. Please do me this small kindness and tell me if and when you are going to kill me."

Kid was wide-eyed. "Please don't cry. I don't know what to do with that."

I lost it and screamed, "Are you going to kill me?"

Kid jumped. "No! Not that I know of."

"Why am I here then? Why did you bring me here? What do you people want from me?"

"Beats me! Nobody ever tells me anything around here!"

He was getting worked up. I needed him relaxed.

I forced myself to breathe deeply. *He said he isn't going to kill me. He said he isn't going to kill me.* I had to repeat this sentence in my head before it started to take shape, before it started to make sense, become something real rather than just more words bouncing around in my head.

Could I believe him? Could I let myself believe him?

"If you're not planning on killing me, then can you please put the gun away?"

He looked down at the gun and swiftly put it to his side where I couldn't see it any more.

I had nothing else to go on but his word and his demeanor. Kid was big and built, but he didn't come off as a killer. Then again, neither had Cameron.

I'm not going to die, was the story I decided to tell myself. *Not right now*, I added, just in case I forgot.

"Well," I began very slowly, "what do *you* think they might want with me?"

"No clue."

"Do you think they are planning to sell me?" I asked, my voice faltering. This worry too had been lingering in my mind. I had seen a documentary on this. Girls getting taken and sold for prostitution. It had given me nightmares. Forcing back the horrifying images that were trying to get in the way of my thoughts, I focused on getting answers, careful not to put any ideas into Kid's head.

"Sell you? Why would anyone want to buy you?"

I stared at him. Did I really have to spell it out?

He stared back at me and shrugged.

I felt as though I were trying to cut a block of wood with a butter knife. I consoled myself with the fact that at least he seemed willing to help me. "They must have told you something," I insisted. "Maybe you overheard them talking? Anything at all? Even if you think it wasn't important?"

A quizzical look came over his face—how a puppy would look if it were trying to think. "My brother is into a lot of stuff, but I don't think he's into selling people."

His brother. "Remind me. Which one is your brother again?"

His cheeks reddened.

"Is it Cameron? Is Cameron your brother?"

"No more questions, okay?" He slumped back into the couch. His hair flopped into his eyes and he blew it away with a sigh. Dark hair. Dark eyes. Paws for hands. Now that I looked at him, I could see the resemblance I had missed earlier. This kid was definitely Cameron's younger brother.

"What kind of business is your brother in, exactly?"

He kept his eyes trained ahead.

"Is his business legal or perhaps not so legal?"

Nothing.

"What about the other guy? The one with the spider web tattooed on the back of his neck? What's his name?"

He kind of chuckled at this question.

"Is that funny?" I asked.

"Yeah. It's kind of one of those rhetorical questions."

"Rhetorical?" I repeated.

"You know. Rhetorical. When you answer your own question."

I knew what *rhetorical* meant. Clearly this kid did not. While I didn't know what he was talking about, I now had a clue about his age and education, or lack thereof on both fronts. "Right. Rhetorical," I said.

It was quite possible that Cameron's brother knew absolutely nothing about anything. When it came to getting answers, I decided, I was on my own once again.

Someone taking an unbiased glance around the room would have thought it was part of a ski chalet. On one side of the room there were large windows that might have been overlooking ski slopes. The stone fireplace and the wooden beams, furniture, and floors gave the room a warm, earthy feel that made you want to leave your ski boots at the door and curl up with a blanket and a good book.

Unfortunately, I wasn't unbiased. I was being held there against my will, for reasons that were unknown to either of the two people in the room. And I sure as hell knew that I wasn't in a ski chalet. There was nothing in the room that I could use to fill in the blanks, and the total normalcy of it made me want to scream.

While I was casting my eyes about the room, Kid leaned forward, his grin picking up again.

"Were you scared of me? Ya know, when you thought I was going to kill you?"

I was awed by this guy. This was indeed just a game to him. Was he a product of too many video games and not enough school? Or was he just a complete psychopath? I felt I should be angered, or at least shocked, by his utter disregard for my plight. But I was starting to think nothing could shock me anymore when it came to these people. And I honestly didn't think this kid was a psychopath.

"What scared you the most? Was it my voice?" he asked, his tone noticeably lowering as he said this.

"Your driving skills." My mouth still had the aftertaste to remind me of this.

His smile faded. "I guess that explains why you were acting like such a freak. I was beginning to think Cameron was bringing home mental patients." There was some empathy, finally.

His eyes veered back to the TV screen.

Now that I understood that this kid was called Kid because he was, indeed, just a kid, I felt a little braver. Yes, he was a big boy who could probably crush me with one hand (and he also had a gun), but he was not going to be the one to kill me if I managed to keep my cool.

Yet I didn't take more than a little comfort in that fact, given that there was some man outside with a very large gun. I could also hear other sounds coming from somewhere in the house—another television and deep voices talking, answering each other. At least for now, in this room, we were alone. And as far as Kid and I were concerned, there were—currently—no plans to kill me.

With the threat of imminent death temporarily at bay, the rest of my senses kicked in—like the taste of regurgitated takeout in my mouth and the feel of the crusted tears that had dried on my face. And god, I really needed to pee. This made me think about Kid. How far I could take his benevolence and immaturity?

Suddenly, getting to a bathroom was bumped up to first place on my mental survival list.

"I need to use the bathroom," I announced.

"Down the hall. First door to your right."

That was a lot easier than I'd thought. I had expected to have to make a plea. Perhaps pee my pants a little for full effect. I had expected him to take me to the bathroom and keep watch while I did what I had to do. But he just kept watching television.

I made my way down the hall, my feet treading lightly on the wide-planked floor. The bathroom was the only door on my right and the only open door—it was easy to find—yet I hesitated. Because there were more doors in this hallway—four more, to be exact. Three on the left and double doors at the end of the hall. Back in the high-rise apartment in Callister, I'd chosen to ignore the other doors in the hallway. What would have happened if I'd chosen to go down the dark hallway instead of toward the light?

I heard a door slam somewhere in the house. I got spooked and bounded into the bathroom, shutting the door behind me. After struggling in the dark to find a light switch and finally switching it on, I felt like I was back in my rooming house in Callister. Dried soap splatters across the mirror. Remnants of beard shavings in the sink. Piles of dirty clothes and towels that littered every surface of the bathroom and the adjacent laundry room.

I went searching, first for an escape point. It was quick: no window.

Second, a weapon. The bathroom had a lot of stuff. A couple of sinks, a couple of mirrors that I supposed could be smashed for shards. I opened cupboard doors. Headache medication. Toothpaste. Shaving cream. Razors. I grabbed a fresh one out of a plastic pack and jammed it in the back of my pants. I found an unopened bottle of mouthwash. I tore it open and gargled.

I looked at the pile of clothes on the floor. These people treated guns like accessories. Maybe they had forgotten one in there? All men's clothes, from what I could tell. And really dirty, from what I could smell. I glanced at myself in the mirror. I hadn't showered in days. I looked like I'd been flying through a wind tunnel. I wasn't in much better condition than those dirty clothes on the floor.

I dug in, both hands deep. I looked through pockets, tried to avoid touching underwear as much as possible.

In the end, I came up with some tissues and a stick of gum.

After doing a full inventory of the bathroom—to my frustration, finding only normal bathroom things, my only weapon being a razor—I worked on myself. I was tired, and I needed to be alert and ready. I splashed water on my face. I found what seemed to be a clean washcloth, soaked it with freezing water, and washed up as best I could with my clothes on. It didn't improve the smell, but it did wake me up. My hair looked like I had stuck a finger in an electrical outlet; I could have tried watering it down to keep the frizzed locks flat against my head, but I knew that the baby spirals that framed my forehead would be back as soon as they dried. Besides, making myself look better didn't seem like the right thing to do right now. I needed to keep people away, not attract them.

Looking as rough as when I'd entered the bathroom, and ready to explore before Kid came looking for me, I opened the door without a sound and stepped out into the hallway, where someone was waiting for me. A slight young woman in red flannel pajamas.

The girl stood for a long second, her hazel stare refusing to release my face. She was the first woman I had seen in days. I wanted to throw myself at her, have her tell me that everything would be okay. But the girl was not happy. Her fists were tight by her side, and her jaw was so strained she was practically growling. With a swift move, she grasped my bony arm and pulled hard, dragging me back toward the living room, her dark hair flying wildly around her shoulders. She was stronger than she looked.

"Rocco!" she shouted, her eyes ablaze. "What is she doing here?" She dragged me to center stage and released my arm.

Kid sprang from the couch. "Hey! You're not supposed to be using my real name around other people—Carly!"

71

"I don't care—Rocco!" the one called Carly huffed. "What is she doing here?"

"Oh, right. That's Emily."

"I didn't ask you *who* she was, I asked you what she's doing—here," she shrilly corrected, her diminutive finger pointing down to the floor for further amplification.

"Right now, I bet she's wishing she didn't go wandering off and meet up with you."

He was very right.

"Stop fooling around, Rocco, and answer my question. What—is she—doing—here?"

"Why does everybody keep asking me that? I don't know what she's doing here, okay?"

"Where's Cameron?" she asked, glancing around. "Does he know you did this?"

"Cameron's the one who sent her here," he smugly replied.

Her face lost color. "What?"

"He's the one who—"

"I heard you, but I don't believe you."

She sighed, then she took another breath. "Tell me what happened out there."

"Someone," he explained, pointing accusingly at me, "thought it would be a good idea to run toward the angry guys with the guns."

I shuddered. I could only remember one guy with a gun—Cameron—but "angry" didn't fully describe how he'd looked. "Possessed" was more appropriate. I pushed myself to keep track of all the valuable information that was being offered by the people I now knew were named Rocco and Carly.

"And where were you when this happened?" she asked, her eyes narrowing. "Weren't you supposed to be keeping watch?"

"I was there, but I didn't see her! She's like a mouse. It was so dark in there. She snuck right by me."

In my head I was interjecting, defending myself. Rocco acted as though I were to blame for everything. For what? For going for a run? For going back into a public cemetery in the middle of the day to retrieve my iPod? For running into whatever he had bonked me on the head with?

"Anyway," he sulked, "I'm sick of being the stupid lookout. It's not even a real ranking position."

"It's a real position when you actually do the looking, like you were supposed to," Carly said, her voice picking up speed again. "You think Cam's gonna let you move up the ranks if you can't concentrate on one simple job for longer than three seconds?"

"Cam *wants* me to move up! Spider's the one who's keeping me back and won't let me do anything important!"

Carly stood there for a few seconds, shaking her head. "Your brother's the boss, Rocco. If he had wanted you to move up, believe me, it would've happened." Then she glanced at me and winced. "Still though, he must be losing his mind ..." As swiftly as she had come, she turned on her heels and stomped away, shaking her head and urgently digging something out of the frilly front pocket of her flannel pajamas. A phone! I watched the phone leave the room.

After she had disappeared through the archway, Rocco fell back against the couch, dejected.

He turned to me. "Sit down. Don't move. Don't talk. Don't do anything else," he ordered with a grumble. He made a show of grabbing the gun and putting it back on his lap.

In this short encounter between Carly and Rocco, I had gained more information than I had in the last few days, since I had first met the guy in the gray hoodie. For one thing, Cameron and Rocco were brothers, and the tattooed man was probably Spider, which would explain the spider web on his neck. Rocco had been right: I had answered my own question, though perhaps not in a "rhetorical" kind of way.

I also understood that Cameron was the boss—though of what or whom, I didn't know. And Carly was likely Cameron's girlfriend. His very angry, very scary girlfriend.

I forced myself to suppress a sudden twinge of jealousy and focus instead on the facts that should terrify me: I had witnessed a murder; I had been taken against my will; I was being held at this "farm" with some gunman walking around; and, until a few minutes ago, I believed that Cameron was sending me to my immediate death. These were the things that I had to remember in order to survive.

I was aware that there was a gun (like an elephant) in the room. It wasn't being pointed directly at me, but it was meant for me. And Rocco was now in a bad mood. Kids do crazy things when they're in a bad mood.

I settled in my seat, thinking it better not to push my luck any further until Rocco calmed down. Unfortunately, in my hurry to go exploring the other rooms for an escape, I had completely forgotten to go pee.

Rocco didn't utter another word to me. He got up once to fetch a bag of chips from the kitchen. He ate the entire bag, watching me from the corner of his eye, without offering me any. Making sure I knew that he was still angry.

When he got up again later to get a drink, he thumped a can on the table in front of me as though he were remorseful for not sharing the chips.

The night rolled by.

My eyes did eventually close in the wee hours of the morning. Rocco was still wide-awake, fuming.

When I opened my eyes, the house was quiet. No voices could be heard. There was an infomercial for back braces on TV. Rocco was snoring on the couch. The gun had fallen from his lap to his side.

I stood. I did not think. I refused to think because I was afraid of overthinking it, of chickening out. I went to Rocco and grabbed the gun. I was shaking but made no sound. I went to the windows. One of them was a patio door; I had already spotted it while Rocco was ignoring me. At the time it had been too dark to see anything, to see what was out there, and I was sitting too far away. *It doesn't matter,* I had told myself. *It's a way out of here. Out of this.*

I had thought about going to the kitchen, taking a knife, and making a run for it. That had been the plan. But the light was already coming through the windows, and I knew it was only a matter of time before Rocco woke up. Grabbing the gun had been a spur-of-the-moment decision. A godsend, I thought.

I should have shot him. Rocco. He was sleeping. It would have been easy for some people. It would have bought me extra time to run and hide. But I couldn't; I liked him. No matter what, I liked the kid too much to even think about doing something like that. I was still me.

I put my hand on the door handle and pushed to the side, enough for me to fit through. The door slid so smoothly, so easily. Until that moment I hadn't considered the fact that a security alarm might go off—not that I cared. I was already out on the deck. I scanned my surroundings quickly, checking for people and building a plan as I went, based on the quick details my mind could take in. I could see that there was some greenery ahead, but I was focused on my immediate surroundings. The deck was on a second floor. There was a pool on the ground floor. No people in sight. But also no stairs down.

I looked down. The deck was at least thirty feet off the ground. I would have to jump and try to forget the fact that I was terrified of heights. I thought I could hear the sound of motors, cars, somewhere in the distance. This thought fired me up. I put a leg over the edge and then another. I was holding onto the gun, and this made things difficult. I couldn't climb down with only one free hand, and the elastic of my pants wasn't strong enough to keep the gun secure. Throwing the gun down would make too much noise.

I jumped.

I landed on my feet on the concrete and immediately felt pain shoot up my right leg before I tumbled backward. I managed to keep my head from bouncing off the concrete. Earlier in the evening I had removed the plastic security cover from the razor while Rocco wasn't looking so it would be ready to use when the time came. Turning it blade out would prevent me from getting cut, I had assumed. Now the razor had broken from the force of the fall and sliced into my lower back. I got up and ran.

I ran ahead. I didn't look around. Straight ahead was the fastest way out: simple mathematics. I heard car doors being slammed somewhere. Somewhere close. I ran faster despite the pain in my leg. There was a line of trees. I would be out of sight soon.

As I got close, someone came out of the trees—a man. I could see him in my peripheral vision. I kept running but turned my head and saw that he was holding a rifle.

He yelled for me to stop.

I still had the gun in my hands. My arms were moving in tandem with my legs, the way they knew how to do. Running, I knew.

I could hear other people now; they were around somewhere. I was so close. I heard a shot go off and then a searing pain in my arm. It knocked me off my feet and forced me to drop the gun.

I was on the ground, surrounded by men. And their guns. One of them kicked my gun—the gun I had stolen—away from me.

Rocco shoved through the men, winded. And then Cameron.

My head was spinning. I couldn't breathe. Cameron's dog ran to my side.

"Are you fucking crazy," Cameron said. But he didn't say this to me. He was looking at the guard who shot me.

"My orders were to not let the girl leave," the shooter said. He sounded like he was going to cry. He was shaking.

Cameron bent down, looked me in the eyes, and then looked down at my arm. "You shot her. You could have killed her, you stupid son of a bitch."

"She pointed a gun at me. I just wanted to stop her. Scare her into stopping. The bullet ricocheted."

Rocco picked up the gun that I had stolen from him and sheepishly handed it back to Cameron. Cameron had that look— the demonically possessed look that haunted my thoughts— which was directed at the shooter. And now he had just been handed a gun. Spider, the tattooed man, came forward. "I'll take care of this," he said, putting his hand on Cameron's shoulder. An obese man came and took the shooter by the shoulders and led him away.

Strangers' faces were spinning around me as though I were taking a ride on a merry-go-round. I thought I was going to be sick. Cameron helped me to my feet. I stood, put weight on my right leg, and passed out.

****

I stirred, glanced up. Cameron glanced down. He was carrying me through the front door of a house. The Farm. I recognized it. We were in the foyer and then up the half-moon staircase. There was a lot of noise around. A lot of people going about. Hustle and bustle. We entered a room. Cameron sat me on a bed, pushed up my sleeve, and checked my arm. He got up and closed the door, shutting out the hustle and bustle. Then he disappeared into an adjoining room. I heard water running and cupboard doors opening and closing.

Things were still hazy in my head. I hadn't eaten anything for days. My escape had sucked out whatever energy I'd had left in me.

Cameron came back with supplies and set them on the floor by the bed. Someone knocked at the door. Cameron opened it a crack and took a bag of ice from an unseen hand. Then he came back and kneeled at my feet, placing a couple pillows under my right foot and removing my sock and shoe. He laid the ice bag on my ankle, which was already starting to swell up, and then went to work on my arm.

"He's lucky the bullet just barely grazed you," he muttered as he pulled up the sleeve of my T-shirt.

"You mean I'm lucky," I said.

He used a washcloth to wipe the blood off my arm and held it against my wound to stop the bleeding. Then he looked up. To my ultimate defeat, he was wearing blue jeans and a red T-shirt that only served to accentuate the dark features of his face. Adding insult to injury, he ran his free hand through his perfectly untidy hair. He was regrettably striking. Hadn't I *just* seen it again, the killer in him, as he was about to kill the shooter? This was a rhetorical question. A *real* rhetorical question. I knew this man was a killer. I knew he had hunted down another human and taken his life. Yet it took every inch of my being to keep my heart from doing somersaults.

There was something seriously wrong with me.

I looked down. There was blood on Cameron's forearm. He followed my eyes and noticed it too. A puzzled look came over his face.

Keeping the cloth pressed tight to my arm, he got up and leaned into me to look over my shoulder. I felt his breath against the skin of my neck. I closed my eyes, afraid of myself, my own emotions.

Then he lifted the back of my shirt. I was shaking from the drop in adrenaline and the ice that was cooling my body temperature. Cameron pulled out the handle of the razor, and then the blade that had broken off. His hand and the blade were covered in blood. A smiled played around the corners of his mouth, then vanished.

"You're a mess," he said solemnly.

He removed the cloth from my arm and checked it. Satisfied, he pulled a square bandage from the heap at my feet and taped up my arm. He went to rinse out the washcloth, sat next to me, close to me, and placed the cloth against my back.

His eyes caught mine.

Those same dark eyes that seemed to be constantly calculating.

The tears came, as though they had been lingering around the corner, near the surface. I put my head down and squeezed my eyes shut, but my shaking shoulders betrayed me. Cameron looped his free arm around my shoulder and pulled me to him.

He held me and said nothing.

I forced myself to pull away from him as soon as I could.

"I know that you don't understand any of this," he said. "It's going to be confusing for a while, I know. You have to trust me when I tell you that I have your best intentions at heart. Above all, I promise I won't hurt you. Okay?"

He lifted my chin so that I had no choice but to look at him. "Okay?"

"Okay," I heard myself saying, even though I wasn't.

He released my chin and checked the bloody washcloth on my back. I took a breath. I had witnessed him murder someone, I had stolen a gun from his brother, I had tried to escape from him, and he had just held me while I cried. To say I was confused would have been an understatement. I was in the Twilight Zone.

"Did you get any sleep last night?" he asked.

I couldn't even remember what that felt like: real, soothing sleep. "Do you live here? In this house?" I countered.

He turned to me. "Sometimes."

There was an awkward silence.

"Did Kid show you around?"

The kid. His brother, Rocco. What was I supposed to say? To admit to? "We watched TV."

"All night?"

From the distress in his tone, I knew I had given the wrong answer.

"So you didn't sleep," he said matter-of-factly and sighed. "I'll show you around later."

He's going to show me around? I repeated to myself. *Like I'm just visiting?*

When he went back to the bathroom, I took a glance around the room, which was either a really large bedroom or a small apartment. There was a king-sized, four-poster bed against the wall nearest the door and a small living area on the other side of the room. With its floor-to-ceiling windows, the room had the same open feeling as the main floor, but the walls were much darker, with shoulder-high mahogany paneling and, above it, dark-gray paint up to the high ceiling. The room definitely had a masculine touch. If this was Cameron's house, I gathered this was his room.

There was another knock. Cameron opened the door a crack again, someone mumbled something, and he opened the door fully. A beefy man moved through as Cameron walked over and stood in front of me. A couple more people came and went.

"Is that the rest of it?" Cameron demanded of the last man to come. His voice was different—cold, commanding. I peeked around him.

"Yes, sir. That's all of it." The man avoided looking at us and scurried away, closing the door behind him.

When Cameron stepped aside, I saw what the men had carried in: Rubbermaid bins that looked too familiar.

When I turned back to Cameron, I realized that he was waiting for me to notice them.

"You can stay here," he said. "This room can be yours."

"I don't understand."

"While you're here. This room is yours. To sleep in and whatnot."

My body went rigid. "This is your room."

"Yeah," he said nonchalantly. "I picked up your stuff so that you'd be more comfortable while you stay here."

I wasn't crazy after all. They were my bins. He had obviously broken into my house. He had obviously been through my stuff. He had obviously stolen my stuff. But that wasn't the worst of it. Was he delusional? I knew I was; my emotions were giving me whiplash, vacillating between fear and disdain for this man and an inexplicable pull toward him. But if he thought I was going to be staying in his room as his—as his what? His concubine? His "red-headed experience" slave? No matter what confusing feelings were at war within me, that was not going to happen. Over my dead body.

Cameron had used the words "while you stay here." He definitely saw this as a social call. He seemed to like having me as the agreeable, demure girl, as opposed to the screaming banshee that was raging inside me. I had to tread carefully.

"So while I'm in this room, your room, where will you be? Where will you be sleeping ... and whatnot?" I asked.

He turned his eyes to me. I held my breath.

Then a grin slowly made its way across his lips, and he chuckled. I detested his laugh because hearing it just made me want to smile and perhaps laugh too.

"Don't worry. I'm going to get my stuff out. I won't be sleeping anywhere near here. This room is all yours. By yourself."

I had no idea if he was being truthful. But it was better than the alternative. Better than him saying outright that he intended to keep me there as a sex slave.

He seemed sincere, albeit amused.

I let out a sigh.

He looked at his watch. "Why don't you go have a shower? Alone. Then we can meet up in the kitchen." He got up, glanced down at my sprained ankle, and then tendered his hand to me. "Do you need help getting up and into the bathroom?"

I shook my head.

This made him grin again. He turned around and left me. By myself. In his room. Which was now my room.

CHAPTER SIX

COOL KIDS

It was an ocean of green beyond Cameron's bedroom windows—
one of those views that you find captured in the pages of a
calendar, images that people use as wallpaper on their computers
at work as if they need to be reminded of something—perhaps a
primeval memory.

I had hopped on one foot, and my nose was now nearly
pressed against the patio doors that led to a small balcony outside
Cameron's bedroom. I was two floors up from the ground,
overlooking an egg-shaped, inground pool and a yard of thick,
golf-course-grade grass. Grass that I had just run through in a
botched escape. At the end of the pool area, where the interlocking
terra-cotta stones touched the lawn, there was a pink pool house
with crimson flowers bunched at the windowsills. Fifty feet from
the house, the grass stopped and was overcome by an infinite
forest of evergreens and maples and, on the horizon, jade hills that
divided the treetops from the expanse of blue sky.

As far as I could tell, we were somewhere within a densely
forested valley. The view from the second floor was at once
breathtakingly beautiful and terrifying. I had no idea where I
was, and the fact that I couldn't see any roads or signs of human
life beyond the border of trees hadn't escaped me. There was a part

of me—a big part—that wanted to breathe it all in, take a mental picture, and frame it in my mind so that I would never forget it; the other part was mutely horrified by the first part. The conflict that was building inside of me was tearing me apart. I hadn't forgotten—couldn't let myself forget—how I had ended up here.

Kidnapped, I said to myself. I had to force myself to say the real word. To say that I'd been "taken against my will" seemed like a watered-down version of the truth. Criminals were taken against their will and imprisoned. Even mental patients were taken against their will and placed in hospitals. I had been kidnapped, and the image of the murder in the cemetery was tattooed on my brain. But there was something else about this place—about Cameron—that was luring me in. It was as if my head and my heart were slowly choosing different paths, dragging me in opposite directions until I chose one over the other, or until I snapped in two.

I eventually peeled myself away from the glass and hopped over to my Rubbermaid bins. Everything was there—clothes, schoolbooks, bathroom necessities, even the indigo ballerina lamp that had been next to my bed and the ragged copy of *Rumble Fish* that I kept under my pillow. My cell phone, which I had so carelessly flung onto my bed before rushing out the door, was nowhere to be found. Cameron had really been through all my personal belongings. This realization was too alarming for me to deal with right then.

I found something quick to wear—after I'd worn my running clothes for however many days, even a potato sack would have done the trick—and hopped to the bathroom to shower and brush my teeth. I scrubbed hard, every inch, as though I could wash away the nightmare I was ensnared in. I was careful with the bandage on my arm, but I forgot about the one on my back and when I dried myself I reopened the wound. I could feel that it was just a nick at the top of my buttocks, but it bled enough to leave a large bloodstain on the heavy towel. Like the rest of the house, the bathroom was a showpiece that easily could have graced the cover of one of those snooty architectural magazines. It was cleaner than the main-floor bathroom; in fact, it was pristine.

I emerged from Cameron's bathroom looking, feeling, and smelling a little more like myself again. Cameron had either asked me or ordered me—I wished I knew which—to meet him in the kitchen. Being alone in this enclosed space, without guns being pointed at me or strange men within arm's reach, was almost nice. Too nice. I wasn't going to accomplish anything by holding myself prisoner. If Cameron wanted me or was allowing me (again, I wished I knew which one) to walk around the house, I would take it. The more information I had, the better I could plan.

I hopped out of the shelter of his room and grabbed hold of the banister. Then I heard roaring laughter from below and came to an abrupt halt at the top of the stairs.

Rocco's voice, high-pitched with excitement, echoed through the house: "It smelled like chow mein!" This was quickly followed by another wave of laughter.

There was an audience.

I stood, deliberating whether to go back into the hidden comfort of Cameron's bedroom or face the music. I would have to face it all, eventually. Cameron was giving me leeway to walk about the house unsupervised, and he was meeting me in the kitchen. I wasn't about to screw this up: the kitchen was where I was going, no matter what.

It took every fiber of my being not to hop to the front door as I passed it downstairs. But my injured ankle wouldn't have gotten me very far.

I took a deep breath and then slowly walked through the archway into the common room. With all the hefty men sitting around it, shoulder to tight shoulder, the extra-large dining table looked like a child's craft table. Rocco was standing at the head, emceeing for the breakfast crowd, while Carly and Spider had their heads bent together at the other end, engrossed in a whispered conversation. Their eyes glazed over the papers that were stacked in front of them.

Cameron wasn't there. I told myself that this was a good thing: at least I wouldn't have to be in the same room as him, trying to hide my neurotic stares while his angry girlfriend sat a few measly feet away from me, along with a tattooed man who glared at me like I was the fly that had flown under his flyswatter—it would take only one small motion of the hand to annihilate me.

"The girl thought the boss had sent me to take care of her," Rocco proudly recounted for the crowd. Another roar ensued. Rocco looked fleetingly insulted this time.

Cameron was also missing his kid brother's great tale—an added bonus, I thought.

I continued bravely to the table. Rocco was the first to see me and took it upon himself to announce my arrival.

"Hey, puke-breath, your ears must be burning."

All massive heads followed Rocco's gaze. Spider and Carly's communal head shot up too: Carly grimaced when she saw me; Spider resigned himself to his nasty glare. The whole room had gone tensely quiet.

Yes, my ears were burning … like I was wearing hot coals for earmuffs.

In an instant, Carly and Spider were out of their seats. With an added faint whistle and nod of the head from Spider, the rest of the men rose with them, rushing to grab last morsels from their breakfast plates.

Everyone except Rocco and me trudged out the common room with Carly and Spider. Apparently no one was to talk to me.

Rocco whistled. "That was fast. You sure know how to clear out a room. Do you have rabies or some other kind of contagious disease that I don't know about?"

I shrugged and chewed on the side of my lip while he started stacking dirty plates.

"I wouldn't worry about it too much," he said, his head bent over his task. "They're a tough crowd to break. It took them a while to get used to me too."

I clasped a few of the dirty cups and glasses between my fingers and followed him into the kitchen. "How long have you been here?"

"I got here over a year ago, I think. I'm not really sure. Time seems to stand still around here."

"Where are your parents?"

"My parents? I don't know. They're somewhere out in the world, I guess. Who cares?" He grabbed a frying pan from the stove; it was filled with what looked like canned beans fried in ketchup. "Are you gonna want any of this?"

"No."

"Suit yourself." He scraped the remnants into the garbage and flung the pan into the dishwasher without rinsing it first. "Help yourself to some food if you're hungry. That's the way it works around here—you grab what you want. Just don't expect to be served. I may have to clean up after these guys, but I don't serve anyone."

"Where's Cameron?" I tried to keep my voice indifferent.

"I don't know." Rocco's hand quieted over the dishwasher. "Why?"

"He's your brother, isn't he?"

"Doesn't mean I keep a leash on him," he said, taking his frustrations out on the plates that refused to fit into the fully loaded dishwasher.

In the meantime, I was pulling at invisible straws. "You left your parents and came here—on ... purpose?"

"I left my mom; never knew my dad. There wasn't much to leave behind. My mom got a new boyfriend," he said, as if that explained it all.

"So you came to live with your brother?"

"No. I came to work for my brother."

We were getting somewhere. "What kind of work do you do for your brother?"

"Right now, I look after the administration of the house." He looked over at me as though he'd guessed what I was going to ask next. "Meaning I do whatever Spider tells me to do, like cleaning the stupid kitchen. And driving Miss Daisy."

"Did you get into a lot of trouble because of me?" I really did feel bad about that. The escape attempt had probably made things worse for him; I didn't want him to pay for my bad decision. Then again, he was still alive, even after everything that had happened. Being Cameron's brother must have its advantages.

"No worries," he said, scowling. "I knew you were going to do that all along. I was just pretending to sleep to see what you were going to do."

I decided to change the subject instead of further hurting his pride. I remembered the argument between him and Carly the night before. "This work, this administration work, isn't the work that you want to do?"

"Do you know anyone who wants to spend his time cleaning up after a bunch of jerks? It's not work a man should be doing. No offense."

"None taken." I closed the dishwasher door and searched for the start button, letting him vent.

"I mean, this was supposed to be temporary so that I could prove myself. I've proven myself and should be working for Cam now."

He pushed me aside and started the dishwasher.

"What kind of work does Cam—"

Spider came into the kitchen and interrupted us. "Kid, if you're done in here, go air out the boss's car. It smells like death in there."

Rocco winked at me, and with a salute and an "Aye-aye, sir" to Spider, marched out of the kitchen.

Spider ignored me as though I were a fly in the kitchen and walked out too.

I was left alone. With the blocks of knives. Three blocks full of sharp blades. I was tempted, grabbing hold of the counter behind me, trying to resist the temptation.

What use would a knife be against a house full of armed men? Where would I even hide it? That last time I tried to hide a sharp object, I ended up getting it dug out of my backside. And Cameron could show up any minute.

My head buzzed and I felt faint. I wasn't hungry, but without food I was not going to regain my strength. Getting my strength back was probably something I could work on without getting killed. A box of Cap'n Crunch was still sitting on the counter. I fetched milk from the fridge. It was weird being there, helping myself as though I were at home. I was definitely not anywhere near home.

I waited awhile. Cameron didn't come. The knives were calling me.

When I'd finished my second bowl of cereal, I rinsed out the bowl and tucked my dishes away in the second dishwasher. *Screw it,* I thought. I hopped to the front door and outside into the warm May sun, looking for more answers rather than weapons I couldn't use.

Cameron's car was parked at the top of the circular driveway. All four doors of the Audi were open, and Rocco was crouched over the passenger seat with a spray bottle.

There was so much happening outside and so many big people walking around that it took a while for my brain to fully consider what my eyes were seeing. Four white, boxy minivans with darkened windows were lined up at the far end of the driveway. Men were buzzing around the property, some leaning against the vans, basking in the sunshine, and others walking about, intent on some mysterious task. Then there were the men who were far away from the driveway, past the grass clearing, all the way down at the edge of the woods; these men stood in a row along the property line, about thirty feet from each other, watching the scene from the shadows of the trees—their rifles either in hand or slung over their shoulders.

I figured that as long as I kept close to Cameron's brother, I wouldn't get in trouble.

Rocco was muttering and shaking his head, absorbed in an intense discussion with himself.

"Need any help?" I offered smartly, suppressing my rising sense of the alarm. I shouldn't have been out there. I should have stayed and waited for Cameron in the kitchen, as he'd asked me to do.

Rocco glanced up and chewed on my proposal for a minute. "Better not. I don't want to get in trouble again."

I was all kinds of trouble for this kid. That made me feel worse about using him again. But right now he was the only person I knew who didn't have plans for me. And he was willing to talk to me, despite probably having been told not to.

While he sprayed some kind of deodorizer on the front passenger seat, I sat on the backseat with my legs swinging out the side. I leaned my face forward into the outside air—it was really stinky inside the car.

"Who are all those people?" I asked him.

He didn't look up. "What people?"

I pointed my thumb in the direction of the gunners. "The men with the guns," I said, to start with.

"Guards," Cameron answered as he approached the car with Meatball at his heels. I noticed that he had showered. His hair was still dripping, and he had changed from jeans and red T-shirt … to jeans and gray T-shirt.

"I waited in the kitchen like you asked," I immediately confessed. "But when you didn't come, I thought maybe I had misheard and that you wanted me to meet you outside."

"I had some stuff to take care of. It took me longer than I anticipated." Cameron was a better liar than I was; he didn't seem the least bit upset by my inability to follow simple orders. "Let's go get something to eat."

I pushed myself into a one-legged standing position.

"I already ate," I admitted. "Rocco said it was okay if I grabbed something to eat."

"Kid finally has some good sense."

Rocco looked up and beamed at his brother's approval. I had finally found a way to not make things worse for him.

Without warning and without asking, Cameron looped his arm around my waist to help me walk. "I'll show you around then."

This gesture seemed to have come naturally to him. I was aware that his hands, one of which was holding on to my waist, were sullied with the blood of another. I was also aware that my heart thudded when he touched me.

"The guards. What are they guarding?" I asked, trying to keep my head winning the pull over my treacherous heart.

"Precious cargo."

With his help, I made it back to the front door of the Farm. Meatball was following us so closely that I almost tripped over him twice. Cameron had answered my question without further expanding, but readily nonetheless. I wondered how far his so-called openness would go.

"Where are we ... exactly?" I probed, testing the waters.

"Vermont."

"We're not in New York anymore?" I said before I had time to take the shock out of my voice.

He peered at me out of the corner of his eye. "Vermont is a different state, yes."

"Okay," I said slowly. I took a breath. "And what is this place? This Farm, as you call it?"

"It used to be a shelter for forest firefighters back in the day. I bought it a couple of years ago. It was basically just a barn, but I had it fixed up. I kept the tin roof and restored the façade. Everything else is new."

This was *his* house. A house that he'd designed himself. I filed this information away and kept going.

He led me through the front door, past the archway, and through the now-familiar kitchen, toward the hallway where I had been accosted by Carly the night before. We stopped in front of the bathroom.

"I never realized how filthy it was until I actually had to shower in it," he said, his lips curled in disgust. He quickly closed the door and we kept moving. I didn't understand why he was showing me around or answering my questions. Wasn't he just giving me more information that I could use against him? Wasn't he just giving me more ways to escape? Whatever his reasons, for now I would take what little information I was afforded.

"Spider … Tiny … Rocco," he pointed out as we passed each of the three doors on the left. Spider's room looked untouched. The bed was made up so tight you could bounce a dime off it. Rocco's room was a pigsty: the bed unmade, clothes piled on the floor.

"Who's Tiny?"

"You can't miss him. He's the fat guy who usually hangs close to Spider or me."

My eyebrows drew together. "Why call him Tiny if he obviously isn't?"

"That's what makes it funny, don't you think?" I thought I saw him roll his eyes as he said this. "Besides," he added as he opened one of the double doors at the end of the hall, "would you be willing to call that guy fat to his face?"

He had a point.

When we walked through the double doors, my chin dropped. It was a room with tall bookshelves and pale suede couch and chairs. The high ceiling had exposed dark-wood beams running across it. There was a fireplace between the two long windows that faced the back of the property, and the opposite wall was made of stacked stones in soft gray and rose.

"It's gorgeous," I whispered, unthinkingly letting my hand slide over the stones as I moved deeper into the room.

"Nobody ever uses this room," he said after a barely audible clearing of his throat.

I folded my arms and investigated the book titles on the shelves, rising up and down on my tiptoes, while Cameron stood by.

"There's a piano in the corner. You can come here and play whenever you want," he told me. I played piano. Not well, but I played.

I noticed something different about Cameron—something that had been there since he had arrived that morning, something that had only intensified since he met Rocco and me by his car. His cheeks were slightly flushed, and the lines around his eyes were almost gone. He looked decidedly younger.

It was as if a mask had been taken off—or put on ... I couldn't be sure—but I liked it more than I should have. It wasn't making me forget what had happened in the cemetery; it was making me forget that Cameron had been the one holding the gun, as though the monster were somewhere else far away from this place. As though this place and Cameron could protect me from that monster. I had to shake off that feeling. Concentrate.

We headed back through the foyer and down the stairs to the lower level.

"How old are you, Cameron?" I wondered aloud as we walked into a den.

"This is where the guys hang out when they're not working," he explained. The space had everything to keep overgrown children entertained: a stocked kitchen, Ping-Pong and pool tables, a big-screen TV, and a wall of movies and video games. It also had patio doors that opened up to the pool outside.

"Your age. Is that a question I shouldn't be asking you?"

"What? Oh, I'm twenty-six," he answered, distracted.

While my mind was trying to process how this twenty-six-year-old could afford the mansion I was touring, we made our way down another hallway.

"Some of the night guards sleep in here," he whispered, pointing at the bedroom doors that were closed. I could hear off-tempo snoring and wheezing through the doors.

This seemed like monumental information: information about his security. Where they were. Where they slept. Why was he telling me, showing me all this? It was just confusing me more.

At the end of the hall was a pumpkin-orange, fully equipped gym with windows that looked out onto the pool.

There were also two men in the middle of the room and a large, open box next to them.

"It's a high-speed treadmill for you. You know, so that you can still do the same stuff you normally do," Cameron announced.

"A treadmill. For me. You got this just for me?"

"Sure. When your ankle is better, of course."

I could feel it in the pit of my stomach: the more information he gave me, the less I knew. He was buying me gifts? How would he even know what I normally do?

Something was wrong. Everything was wrong.

We paused to watch the confused men arguing over the instruction manual, surrounded by pieces.

"Well," Cameron added, "it will eventually be a treadmill."

"Thank you," I said, with what I hoped looked like a genuine smile.

He helped me hop outside to the pool, where we rolled up our jeans and plunged our feet into the cool water. It felt amazing on my ankle.

"You have that troubled look on your face again," he said. "You probably have a million questions still."

My smile was not so unadulterated after all.

"How long are you planning on keeping me here?"

"Awhile," he admitted.

I took a breath, "I don't know what happened in the cemetery or why you killed that man. I'm sure you had your reasons." His brown eyes were still locked on mine. I was felt my nerve fading. "You have to know that I would never tell anyone what I saw. You don't need to keep me here to keep me quiet, because I'm not going to talk."

"Things are a lot more complicated than that. It's not just up to me. There are other people who have an interest in this."

"Spider?" I asked, remembering his furious glances at my expense.

"No, it's not Spider."

I must not have looked convinced, because he added, "I know that Spider comes off as a bit intimidating, but he's a good guy who's just trying to do his job of keeping us safe. And believe me, sometimes I make his job very difficult."

Cameron was watching me. I felt safe with him. Jesus, why did I feel safe with him? There were too many reasons not to feel safe with him, and not enough reasons for me not to want to run right now.

"This place isn't so bad, is it?"

"This is your home, Cameron. Not mine."

"I know," he said.

"You broke into my house. You went through my stuff. How did you even know where I live?"

"A guy like me has ways, Emily."

The way my name sprung from his lips sent tremors through me, as though I were being awakened, brought to life, like a seedling breaking through the earth in the spring.

I was looking at the water, but I could feel Cameron examining me again. "So your favorite book is *Rumble Fish*," he said. "I would have never guessed. Isn't it a bit childish for you?"

"I don't know. I've never read it."

"It looked pretty used."

"You mean the copy that you found hidden under my pillow in my room?" I said, glaring up at him. "I keep trying to read it, but I never get past the front cover."

His brow furrowed.

I had just finished reading the first chapter when my brother died. Now I couldn't seem to pick up where I left off and move on to the next chapter. Once in a while I would pick it back up, thinking I was ready. But I never was.

"It's complicated," I said. "Something that happened a long time ago." I could feel the golf ball rolling around in my throat as I said this.

A moment of quiet came, and we dangled our feet in the water. He smelled like shaving cream—I took a long breath, and I carefully started watching him from the corner of my eye. When he pressed his hand against the ground to slightly adjust his seating, the muscles of his forearm tightened and shifted with him. I also noticed some marking peeking out from below the sleeve of his T-shirt.

Without warning, he turned his head and caught me staring. "What?"

Words briefly escaped me.

I reached past his chest and touched his arm where he had a tattoo of a cross. This seemed to have caught him off guard. He didn't pull away, but he didn't move an inch, either.

Why was I touching him? I yanked my hand back, but it was like pulling magnets apart. I was once again astonished by my pull to him, but I filed this feeling away. I could handle only so much at once.

"You have a scar in the middle of the cross," I said.

He watched my expression before he explained, "Bullet wound."

I tried to hide my shock. He was a shooter and a victim. "Did the tattoo come before or after the bullet?"

"After," he replied, never taking his eyes off my face. He seemed to debate something before pulling down on the collar of his shirt. In the middle of his upper chest was another cross, with another mark—bullet wound—in the middle.

"This one came close," he explained, his voice guarded.

I took my time with this new information.

"You mark the spots where you've been shot. Why?"

His lips thinned. "Reminds me to be thankful that I'm alive."

"You need to be reminded?"

"Some days are easier than others."

"Does it happen a lot? You getting shot at?" I was trying to collect rational information to push out the horrifying images that were crowding my brain.

"On occasion. But the bullets rarely reach their target."

By *target*, he had meant him? "How many of these crosses do you have?"

"Three more." He lifted up his shirt and showed me the cross tattooed on his muscled stomach. "I have another one on my leg and on my back."

The door to the pool house opened all of a sudden, and I flinched. I hadn't noticed how tense my body was, like a rubber band on the verge of snapping.

Carly walked out of the pool house carrying a stack of papers. She was wearing a pretty sundress, her silky black hair falling down her back. With her olive skin and petite frame, she looked like a doll, almost breakable. She threw a disapproving glance in our direction as she pursued a path around the other side of the pool and went into the house without a word, banging the door behind her.

I was suddenly conscious of the fact that I was leaning into Cameron and that Cameron's girlfriend had caught me staring at her boyfriend's stomach. My cheeks burned.

"You're blushing," Cameron said.

"I don't think your girlfriend likes me very much," I said, trying to will away the rising color in my cheeks.

His eyes widened. "My what?"

"Your girlfriend. Carly."

He burst out laughing. "I can't wait to tell her that. It might actually make her feel better, or at least make her laugh a bit." He shook his head in amazement. "Carly's not my girlfriend, and you probably shouldn't tell anyone else about your theory or I'll need another cross to hide the new bullet wound."

I tried to stay indifferent about this news.

While I pulled myself together, Cameron explained that Carly lived in the pool house.

"She works for you, right?"

"Where did you get that from?"

I recounted my first meeting with Carly and her argument with Rocco about working for Cameron, the boss.

He sighed, clearly displeased. "Yes, Carly works for me."

"What does she do?"

"She's a whiz with numbers. She keeps track of all the money coming in and going out."

"So she's your accountant."

"Yeah, I guess she's my accountant. Or she's my accountants' accountant. Nothing goes through without her okay."

In the distance, I could hear the pulsation of car stereo systems resonating in the distance. The sound was becoming louder and louder.

"And Spider works for you too?"

He nodded and, anticipating my next question, added, "Spider deals with all of the security issues."

"And the guards?"

"Yes, Emily, they all work for me. Everyone here works for me."

"Rocco doesn't work for you."

"No, I guess you're right. Rocco is the exception. He's my brother. He can live here as long as he wants, but he doesn't need to work for me."

"But he wants to work for you."

"Rocco is young and has the chance to do anything he wants. Anything," he repeated and looked me in the eyes. "I won't let him make the same mistakes I made." The desperation on his face reminded me of that day in the cemetery when he had turned around to find that I had witnessed his crime.

By now I had so many questions for Cameron that I didn't even know where to start. My confusion was only worsened by his closeness to me, which clouded my judgment.

Spider came through the doors of the main floor and walked to the edge of the balcony, peering down at us.

"We gotta go," he said to Cameron, tossing a harsh glance in my direction.

"I'll be right there," Cameron replied, waving him away. Spider reluctantly turned around and went back into the house.

Cameron pressed his hand on mine, leaned in. "No more running away, okay? You can walk around the house as much as you want, as much as your ankle will allow you, but you need to stay on the property. If you feel the need to run again, use the treadmill."

His hand was on mine. His hand was touching mine. My head told me to jerk my hand out from under it. My heart was beating too fast to chime in.

I couldn't answer him. I just stared.

Cameron looked down at our hands and pulled his away.

I could think again. "Am going to be able to leave?"

"Yes."

"When?"

"I don't know. But you won't be here forever. You'll be back to your life as soon as possible," he said, his tone adamant.

He got up, rolled the legs of his jeans back down, stuck his feet back into his sandals. "I know you have more questions. And I know that this is hard for you to understand. I promise you that this house is the safest place for you to be right now."

"I don't know what that means, Cameron."

"You'll just have to trust me on that."

He took a few steps and stopped. "One more thing. Don't use my real name when there are other people around—I mean when there are people other than Rocco, Carly, and Spider around."

Then he walked away and, with Meatball at his heels, followed the cobblestone pathway that led around the corner of the house. They both disappeared.

Chapter Seven

Sandcastles

What I remembered was that Bill's sandcastles were always bigger and better than mine. I was six years old, and my brother and I were sitting on a beach in Martha's Vineyard. Our nanny, Maria, was standing on her tiptoes, batting her eyelashes at the bronzed lifeguard who sat in his high chair, savoring the attention. Bill had already stacked three buckets of sand perfectly, one over the other, and stuck a leafed branch on top as a flagpole.

There was no competition: my first attempt had crumbled as soon as I overturned the bucket; my second, less-crumbled attempt was washed away by a wave.

Bill had a knack for showing up just as I was ready to give up, or throw a tantrum. Leaving his castle unguarded, he rushed to my rescue and made a princess palace built to his baby sister's specs. In the end, my sandcastle had roads, bridges over a circling saltwater moat and a princess made of candy wrappers waiting in the tower.

His castle had long disappeared, crushed by the waves.

A gray-haired couple strolling by had dared to compliment him on his flair for castle building. My brother's eyes immediately darted to Maria. The last thing he needed was to get in trouble—again—for doing everything for me; he had already missed two consecutive nights of TV time because of that.

"It's not mine, it's my sister's. She made it—all by herself," he huffed at the couple.

Maria didn't catch him ... not that day.

When Bill died, my whole life fell apart. It was as if my crutches had suddenly been ripped from me and I had to run a marathon without ever having learned how to walk on my own. Thanks to my big brother, whom I loved more than anyone, I had no idea how to do anything for myself. Nothing could fill the overwhelming space that my brother had left in my life, and just the thought of letting anyone else do anything for me was, to me, an out-and-out betrayal to Bill.

Without a crutch, my legs eventually grew stronger, and I figured out how to take care of myself.

While my feet dangled in the crystal water of the pool, I wondered, as I often did, what my life would have been like if Bill hadn't died. Would I have left my parents, their money, their big plans, and moved to Callister?

I was used to repelling people. Keeping perfectly nice guys at bay. Ninety-nine percent of the time, being uncomfortable around them. Then along came Cameron, a perfectly horrible kind of guy. A murderer. A kidnapper. A criminal. If I were going to feel tense with anyone, it should have been with him. Yet in the very short time I had known him, I found myself becoming less and less uneasy with him. Like I was finding, seeing a glimpse of something else with him. Something I hadn't seen in a long time, since Bill had died. Perhaps this was the reason I was letting my guard down with him.

If Bill hadn't died, would I have found myself in this militarized mansion owned by a tattooed, bullet-holed, twenty-something guy who made me feel so different?

Only over Bill's dead body would this have happened. Of that I was positive.

Eventually I got up and walked back into the house.

In the kitchen, Rocco was making himself some lunch: baloney and a puddle of mustard slapped between two pieces of white bread, ten times over, stacked on a plate. He was bantering with a guy who was sitting at the table.

I kept my head down and pulled a can of pop out of one of the fridges. I turned around just as the carbon bubbles exploding in my throat made my eyes water. When the bubbles cleared up, I saw bright blue eyes—and a shot of carrot-orange hair spiked into a short mohawk—eagerly waiting for me. The guy was built like a linebacker and had a sleeve of tattoos and a metal bar through his lower lip.

He pulled out the heavy wooden chair next to him. "Why don't you come sit by me for a bit so that I can take a better look at you?" He spoke with a thick English accent. I glanced at Rocco, but he was too preoccupied with choking down bear-sized bites to be of any assistance.

I held my pop can in both hands, sat down as far away from the guy as possible, and leaned my elbows on the table. He came to sit next to me; his tree-trunk arm was around my shoulder as soon as his bum hit the seat. I flinched, but he didn't seem to notice or care. Either he was extremely warm, or I was extremely cold. I looked at Rocco again for help; he was still submerged in his stack. I was rolling my shoulder, trying to gently shove this perfectly huge stranger off me, but he was persistent.

"Well!" he boomed, "You are a real ginger! Just like me." He tapped his speared red hair and turned to Rocco. "This was meant to be. Not letting this one get too far away was the best mistake you ever made, Kid."

Rocco had, amazingly, already hit the bottom of his sandwich stack.

"I didn't make any mistakes," he countered through a mouthful. "Emily's just really sneaky."

I was thinking of interjecting into Rocco's subjective account but was beaten to the punch.

"Aye," he said and winked at me. "You definitely have to watch us gingers. We'll get you every time."

Rocco grumbled and strolled back to the kitchen.

"Emily." The big guy rolled the name off his tongue. "That's your name?"

I smiled dimly.

He extended his free hand and shook mine. "I'm Griff."

After a good squeeze, he took his hand back and glimpsed at his watch. "Geez! I gotta get back to work."

He pushed away from the table; everything on the main floor shook. He walked around me, placed his large hand on the back of my chair, and extended the other to me. "Come keep me company?"

This Griff guy was kind of friendly. Why?

Rocco had brought back a new loaf of bread, a butter knife, and an unopened jar of peanut butter ... dessert. I trusted Rocco. If he didn't see any harm in me going with Griff, and if Griff didn't see any harm in associating with me, then I would take the opportunity.

I didn't grab his hand, but I did let him pull the chair out for me. I hopped along next to him. He was beaming.

When we got to the front door, Griff shouldered the shotgun that was leaning against the wall, waiting for him.

"Is it loaded?" I croaked.

He raised one eyebrow. "What do you think?"

We were going outside, I realized. Cameron had said that I could walk around the property, but he hadn't said anything about actually talking to people. I glanced around before moving forward. No Cameron. I let Griff loop his arm around mine so that we would move faster. Wherever we were going.

We crossed the lawn and reached the tree line—Griff swaggering as we neared an armed guard standing next to a tree. I recognized this guard; he had been sitting with, and had left with, with the rest of the cool crowd that morning. From the look of disdain on his face, he recognized me too: the troublemaker who had tried to run.

Griff switched spots with him and dragged a tree stump out of the woods for me to sit on. The other guard glanced at Griff and looked like he was about to say something, but then he just shook his head and walked away.

I was pushing the limits by being there, right on the very edge of the property.

Griff lit a cigarette and took a few puffs, still beaming. We were a foot inside the tree line, half-hidden by dense green stuff. Deeper in, the forest was quiet, dark, and I couldn't see more than a few feet in before the brush blocked any further view. There were other guards lined up in the trees; I saw a head pop through the brush every once in a while.

"Is this what you do all day? Stand here?" I asked, swatting mosquitoes away and then rubbing my arms. I looked at the warm, bug-free house with longing now. I was afraid of being there alone with this newest man. That thing at the bottom of my stomach that I had grown to recognize as fear was constant now. Sometimes it rose above surface. Right now it lingered, not quite dormant. But I wasn't ready to go back. If he was willing to talk, I was willing to listen to this new perspective on the mess that was now my world. I would will myself to be brave and push down the twisting in my belly.

He pointed at another guard about thirty feet away. "Sometimes I get to stand over there too."

In my head, I was trying to exercise my math skills: the approximate size of the property divided by the thirty feet that separated each guard would equal the number of big men with guns that I had to worry about. And then I remembered that my math skills were fictional. "How many of you are there?"

"There's just one of me, love," he replied, wiggling his eyebrows. "But if you mean other guards, I don't know. It varies from day to day, from week to week. Since this morning, probably thirty or forty, maybe more. This is the most that I've seen here so far."

"Wouldn't it be better to stand in the sun?" I suggested casually, after another chill or bug tickled the hair on the back of my neck.

"Sure it would, but we're not supposed to." He pointed at the sky. "Too many guys, too many guns, attracts too much attention if someone were to fly above us. You never know who might be watching. These blokes are real paranoid about stuff like that."

"What exactly are the guns for?"

"Keep people out, keep things in. Not really sure. I just know to point and shoot when I'm ordered to." Griff took another puff of his cigarette.

"You don't know what you're guarding?"

He glanced down the line of trees. "Nope. And I don't want to know."

I had a hard time believing this. "Aren't you curious to know why you have to stand here all day with a very big gun over your shoulder?"

Griff was starting to look uneasy.

"Love," he said as he bent closer to me, "don't ask any questions about what goes on around here. I've gotten some pretty nasty stares for doing just that. Whatever these guys are up to, it isn't kosher, and they don't react well when people meddle in their business."

He leaned further in, his voice becoming barely audible, chilling. "Listen, from what Kid told me, you're very lucky to still be alive. They could've just finished you off when they realized what you saw. Count your blessings and do what you need to do to stay alive—play the game, keep quiet, and pretend you don't see anything."

The tension in my stomach mounted. I couldn't let it rest, I reminded myself. Ever.

He took a second and finally forced his lips into a smile. "Just stick by me, and you'll be all right."

"Thanks," I replied in a whisper. Griff's affability seemed to seep through him.

I was taking prolonged breaths to slow my drumming pulse. Griff finished his cigarette, and eventually his smile relaxed.

"How did you come to be here?" I asked carefully, keeping my voice low.

"I knew a guy who knew a guy."

"And now you work for Cameron."

He looked puzzled. "Cameron? Who's Cameron?"

I really hated lying to Griff, who had already been so forthcoming, but disappointing Cameron seemed like an even worse alternative. "I thought I heard someone mention that name. I must have been wrong."

"Nah, I work for Tiny."

"Do you actually get paid for standing around all day?"

"I wouldn't do this unless I got paid. I've never been without booze or women for this long. Hanging with these idiots all day only makes this job worse, and I thought I was going to go crazy until I saw your face this morning." He gave me a warm smile.

"Have you been doing this ... job for very long?"

"Couple months."

"What were you doing before this?"

"I was ... I am ... a mixed martial arts fighter."

Griff and I spent the rest of the afternoon shooting the breeze, staying away from the taboo topics. I found out that he grew up in London, fought his way into professional cage fighting. He made money by getting locked in a cage and pulverizing whoever they put in front of him until one of them—usually the other guy, from what he told me—called uncle or passed out or worse.

The best thing about Griff was that he talked enough for both of us. It was great to listen to him and block out all the other stuff. I didn't notice how cold and hungry I was until the sun lowered and we were approached by another guard, who switched spots with Griff and ignored me.

"Wow!" Griff bellowed as we walked back to the house. "That was the fastest shift I've put in yet. You should keep me company more often." I hadn't done much else but sit there while he talked.

We kicked off our shoes at the door. He stood by the basement staircase, his eyes hopeful. "See you tomorrow?"

"Maybe," I answered. Who knew what tomorrow was going to bring?

More guards started filtering in through the front door, their shoes quickly piling up on the tiled floor. The incoming guards wouldn't allow themselves more than a furtive glimpse in my general direction. Griff had already disappeared downstairs.

I went to the living area. No one was there. Cameron wasn't there.

I explored the kitchen. What I found were cupboards stacked with easy fixes: canned goods, frozen dinners, fluorescent orange pasta—it was like being back in student housing. I took out a can of peas and a can of whole tomatoes. I discovered a fully stocked spice rack hidden behind a George Foreman Grill in the bottom cupboard and placed it on the counter. Though the fridges were mostly filled with juice and pop, I was able to find some onions and green and red peppers. I also found a package of frozen chicken thighs, only slightly freezer burned.

Within minutes, I had a pot of rice boiling and a quick chicken paella steaming in a pan.

Carly appeared, quietly, like a pixie, around the corner. While I stirred, she opened and closed the cupboard doors, rummaged in the fridges, coming up empty-handed. Keeping my eyes on the hot stove, I felt her stop and look over my shoulder.

"It smells great, Emily," she said in an almost whisper.

I looked up—she smiled. A peace flag or a trap? She was really pretty when she wasn't yelling or glaring at me.

"My mom used to make paella all the time," she said.

"My mom doesn't know where the kitchen is."

Carly started pulling miscellaneous spices out of the spice rack.

"May I?" she asked. I stepped aside. When she was done, the paella was extra spicy and tasted absolutely amazing. Then, a bit reluctantly, she turned and started walking back out the way she had come in.

I wasn't sure what to do next. I found myself wanting to like her. Maybe because she was the only other girl around for miles and miles and miles?

"Um, there's more than I can eat ... do you want some? Share?"

She stopped but stayed silent. I wondered whether she had heard me. Just as I thought about repeating my question, she turned and went to grab two plates.

Before we had even set our filled plates on the table, Rocco came sniffing in.

"Hey, what's that?" he asked as he followed his nose into the kitchen. Not waiting for a response, he helped himself to the rest of the paella and came to the table with a heaping bowlful.

Carly threw him a nasty glare.

"You guys weren't planning on eating all of that were you?" he asked as he stuffed in a huge mouthful and sat down.

"We're not used to eating *real* food around here," Carly said to me.

Eventually, the rest of the crew I had briefly encountered that morning made their way in, with the exception of Spider. Cameron didn't come back, either. The full-sized man at the lead, the one who had dragged away the guard shot me—*This must be Tiny,* I told myself—stopped when he saw me at the table. Then he halted the incoming guards at the kitchen threshold.

I saw Carly give him a nod of approval. Satisfied, he trudged to the table, and the rest of the guards followed him in. I took in this small detail. Carly was at the top of this food chain. A boss. Or one of the bosses.

With Carly there, no one left because of me and there were no nasty glares thrown my way. I was comfortable with just being ignored.

After their self-prepared suppers, the group of men dissipated outside or downstairs. Carly and I helped Rocco clean up the mess. And then, with a hushed goodnight, Carly left as quietly as she had arrived. Rocco and I went back to the couch in the living room, where he commenced his endless channel surfing.

I looked at the clock every two minutes. I twisted a strand of hair around my finger until it turned blue. I fidgeted in my seat and jumped every time the front door opened, only to sit back in disappointment when I heard one of the troops come in or go out.

"Cameron's not going to be back till late," Rocco groaned, never taking his finger off the remote trigger. "So stop moving around, it's annoying."

He'd caught me off guard.

"I wasn't …" I started to object, but the quick look that he shot me told me that he wouldn't buy any excuse that I came up with, anyway.

I scampered upstairs before he could observe anything else.

Cameron had a long, hip-level dresser in his room, against the wall near the doorway. I opened the top drawer slowly, as if something might shoot out and pull me in. I became braver as I pulled open each drawer, one by one, and found them all empty. Cameron had said he was going to empty them so that I could put my stuff away. He had kept his word, his promise. Was he going to keep all his promises?

I looked over at my Rubbermaid bins. My stuff had been squashed inside them since I moved to the university. I considered what it would feel like to have my things, my life possessions, properly put away in drawers. After all, that's what Cameron wanted me to do—make myself at home. Could I? Pretend that I was home? Wouldn't that just make this all easier, pretending that everything was totally normal?

I could compromise, to keep Cameron pleasant. I dragged my bins close to the dresser (as best I could with an injured foot). I put my toiletries in the bathroom and my tattered *Rumble Fish* copy back under my pillow (which Cameron had also taken from my room and placed on his bed). Everything else stayed in the bins. I left my tacky ballerina lamp lying on its side on top of one of them.

Being in Cameron's bedroom gave me that feeling again. That feeling of not wanting to leave because out there, it was too hard. I went to the windows, watched a guard pacing the property. I wondered what his story was. We all had a story, mistakes that had brought us here. I hopped around, looking in more drawers, finding nothing of use and nothing interesting. My gut told me that Cameron—or one of his minions—had probably already gone through every inch of the room.

Hopping around all day, everywhere, was exhausting. I looked at Cameron's large, comfy bed. I could nap. I badly wanted to close my eyes, just for a few minutes. Napping was a totally normal thing. Something that normal people would do in normal circumstances when they had been up for more than twenty-four hours. I missed normal.

I went to the television, to Cameron's movie selection. *The Godfather* seemed fitting somehow. I tucked myself under the fleece blanket that had been thrown over the couch and settled in, resting my foot atop the coffee table.

By the time Vito Corleone saw the Statue of Liberty for the first time, I was asleep, numbed.

****

When I awoke in the morning, I was in Cameron's bed. My ballerina lamp was on the table next to me—it looked even tackier in this luxurious room.

Cameron's room was where I was. Things were coming to me more quickly now, as they forced their way into my short-term memory, forming part of my history. Or perhaps these memories would be my last.

I took an extra minute lying there, pretending I was simply in a hotel room somewhere—an illusory cocoon—before I had to face another day of unknowns. I flexed my ankle up and down, side to side. I could feel that the swelling had gone down. It still hurt to move it, but I was encouraged by the fact that I could move it at all.

Then I noticed the snoring.

I lifted my head, saw the dog, Meatball, asleep close to my feet. This explained why my feet were boiling hot. I wasn't sure what to do. Lie still until he woke up and wandered off on his own?

I tried to peel myself away, tucking up my legs in an inch at a time. His head popped up. He wagged his tail and let his steak-sized tongue hang loose. I knew what he was capable of. Why was he here? I tried to avoid eye contact and roll out of bed, toward the door, but Meatball jumped over to the side of the bed, hemming me in. Then he flipped over with all four paws in the air, like a turtle stuck on its back. Even capsized, he still managed to wag his tail, and he was nudging my hand with his sticky nose. Nudging, not trying to take a bite out of it. I tendered my hand over his exposed belly and slowly lowered it to his fur. He grunted and closed his eyes. I dug my fingers into his fur and scratched. He didn't move an inch, unless I happened to stop moving my fingers.

I must have fallen asleep while rubbing his ears. When I woke up, we were spooning. I decided that until he tried to chew my face off, we would be friends.

I got up and hobbled to my bins while Meatball lay stretched out next to the bed. The bins were empty. I opened the drawers. My stuff was there.

Cameron. He was persistent. Did he have no boundaries at all, or was he just like that with me?

I threw on some clothes and headed downstairs with Meatball at my heels. When we reached the foyer, Meatball sped ahead of me to the top of the lower-level stairs and waited there. For me?

When I went the other way, toward the kitchen, he barked. I stopped, turned around, and went toward him. He wagged his tail, which I now recognized as his sign of approval.

It was like playing a game of hot or cold, canine version.

The house echoed with the heavy breathing and snoring of all the men who filled the rooms. I followed Meatball, tiptoeing down the basement hallway to the orange gym.

And there was Cameron, lifting dumbbells.

It felt like I was suddenly breathing differently, breathing air that was touching, enlivening every cell in my body.

Cameron smiled at me but looked tired.

"You're up early," he said.

"What time is it?" I asked, trying to keep my voice even.

"Seven-thirty."

"I guess that means you're up early too."

"I don't sleep much," he admitted. His eyes swept over my face. "Did you sleep well?"

"I think I slept for almost ten hours straight. I don't usually sleep that much either."

The treadmill was now all in one piece and faced the windows near the pool. All the windows were open, and a warm wind filled the room. Outside, the sun was shining. I was longing to run, outside especially. In many ways, running on a treadmill was a lot easier than running the streets of Callister—I didn't have to worry about tripping on the cracked sidewalk, or diverting around garbage, or keeping an eye out for the weirdo in the trench coat who liked to linger in the bushes. In other ways, running on a treadmill was a lot harder—I had no cracks, garbage, or weirdoes to distract me from myself.

I looked down at my ankle and flexed it again. It was painful just to do that, but I was antsy to have full mobility. I started walking toward the treadmill—maybe I could walk, stretch the injury out a bit. Cameron grabbed my hand.

"That's a really bad idea. Why don't we go for a dip in the pool instead? Rest your ankle?" he murmured in his deep voice that made it impossible for me to say anything without betraying myself, my confused feelings.

"Sure," was all I could manage.

"Go get your swimsuit on and I'll meet you back at the pool. I have to go feed Meatball before he takes a bite out of one of my guards."

As though he understood what Cameron had just said, Meatball darted out of the gym. Cameron jogged after him while I stood in horror.

"Bathing suit?" I whispered as I finally trudged out behind them. I hadn't really realized until now that by "dip in the pool" Cameron had meant "swim." The thought of being seen half-clad by him, by anyone, petrified me—because the skin under my clothes was just as freckled and ghostly as my face, because bones tended to protrude around my clavicle and shoulder blades, because I had barely graduated from a training bra.

I met Cameron in the pool, throwing my towel off and sliding in as quickly as my ankle would allow. Meatball, who had followed me, lay down by the side of the pool.

Cameron was bare-chested. He was skinnier than I'd imagined, than I thought he might be, and he had a farmer's tan. He spent too much time dressed.

I avoided glancing in his direction while we swam around. The water was nice on my ankle, better than running would have been, but I had to go slow and try not to move it too much.

"Where did you go yesterday?" I asked, forcing conversation, bringing Cameron out of his daze.

"Just work stuff," he replied with firm vagueness.

"Boss stuff?"

A smile reached his eyes. "Boss stuff."

"You looked pretty tired this morning," I observed, mentally noting that he was starting to look less tired.

"Yesterday was a long day."

"You should get more sleep. You can have your room back if you want; I can sleep on the couch." Or go home and sleep in my own bed.

"If only that was all it took to make a difference. You'll make more use of that room than I ever did." He paused. "How was *your* day yesterday?"

My stomach clenched. This question, standard fare between people who had known each other longer than a couple of days, brought me back to the reality of my situation. This was not a vacation, and it wasn't a normal day. I had to choose every word of my answer carefully. What did Cameron know? Did he realize that I had been interrogating one of his friendlier guards?

"Uneventful," I replied.

His brow furrowed. "You don't like it here?"

"It was just a bit lonely, that's all," I said, happy he didn't seem to know about Griff. "This place is a palace compared to where I came from."

"You mean your place. In Callister."

"Where else?"

"Why do you live in that dump?" He was swimming around, but not really. His eyes never left me, or my unclad body. I had trouble taking my eyes off him. He was gorgeous. I wondered if he knew that already.

"I don't know," I answered, feeling heat rising up my chest. "It's cheap and close to school. The house has tons of character, and my roommates are decent, for the most part. It's a really great place." It wasn't the first time that someone had criticized my choice of housing. I smiled to myself, remembering the day my mother was in Callister for a conference and decided to stop in for a surprise visit. She stayed less than a minute, just long enough to get gum on the heel of her Manolo Blahniks.

"I guess I just like to keep my parents guessing," I found myself saying aloud.

Why was I telling him this? Owning up to these things that he didn't, shouldn't, know anything about?

"Your parents don't approve," he summed up.

I noticed that his question had become statement of fact. It was unnerving. As though he knew me, could see right through me.

"No. Not really," I answered as I started swimming away to escape his scrutiny. I pushed too hard and a shot of pain in my ankle sent me under momentarily, but Cameron immediately pulled me back to the surface and tugged me to the shallow end, where he grabbed me by the waist and hoisted me up onto the side of the pool. He lifted my ankle, pressed it against his chest, and held it there with both hands, rubbing it with his thumbs.

Beyond what we saw, beyond what we'd admitted to each other, Cameron and I didn't know one another. Yet this felt effortless, as though he had always done this, taken care of me. I hated it—how good it felt, how good he felt to me. I wanted him to let go and at the same time never let go.

"You don't get along with your parents," he said, continuing his questioning.

"I never said that I don't get along with them."

"Do you? Get along with them?"

"We're just very different," I snapped.

He stopped and looked up.

This startled me. My heart thumped and started speaking before my head could catch up. "When I was a kid, I was in the car with my mother, my father, and my brother. My father stopped at a gas station, and I begged my mom to let me get a soda, but she wouldn't. I wasn't allowed to have sugar. Bill went inside and stole one for me, but he got caught and the store clerk started going around from car to car, dragging him by the shirt, asking if anyone knew him. My father just drove away and left Bill in the middle of nowhere. They didn't send anyone for him for three days, after Bill had spent a night in juvie and was put in a group home by the police." I left out the fact that my parents had sent one of the maids to get him. "Bill never even cried or said a word about it after he got home."

Cameron remained silent, looking at me. I had that feeling like I was going to cry, like I wanted to cry on his shoulder again, like I was going to say something that I had never said to anyone else. "Bill. My brother. He died of a drug overdose when I was thirteen. I blamed my parents." My foot was still nestled in Cameron's hands. "He's buried in the same cemetery where ..." I glanced up through my eyelashes. "Well, you know which one. I guess that's the real reason I live in that dump, as you call it—it was the best place I could find, that I could afford, that was close to school and Bill."

My mind was going in so many directions now that I could hardly breathe. I refocused while Cameron took his time before answering.

"I can see that your brother's death was ... difficult for you."

My brother had been my best friend, but I didn't admit this to Cameron. I shrugged. "Toward the end, I would only see him a few times a year. He changed so quickly. Then he was gone." I pulled my foot away from him and got up. I could feel Cameron's stare boring into the back of my neck as I limped away.

"Hey!" said a voice from above. Rocco was standing on the balcony of the main floor. From the indentations on his face, he had clearly just rolled out of bed. "Don't move! I'm going to grab my trunks!" He dashed back into the house.

I found my towel and a long patio chair to sit on. "How old is your brother?" I asked.

"I think about sixteen. I don't really know; he won't tell me. Rocco and I didn't grow up together. Hell, until about a year ago when he knocked on my door, I didn't even know that he existed ... though I think he's forgiven me for that by now."

Rocco came running toward us, cannonballing into the water and spraying a disgruntled Meatball, who ran off. I curled up under my towel.

I watched the two brothers splashing and wrestling in the water. When they stood next to each other, it was so easy to see the similarities that I still couldn't believe I had missed them earlier. Like Cameron, Rocco had shaggy dark curls that hung around his face and looked like they had never seen a comb. They both did this thing where they would rake their hands through their hair and then shake their heads like dogs to get the rest of the water out. They also had the same broad grin and infectious laugh—something that I hadn't heard much of, but that now seemed natural. And both of them were tall and lean, although Rocco still had a bit of baby fat in his rosy cheeks and stomach. Cameron was solid. Rocco was already almost as tall as Cameron, and I supposed that within a year he would probably be slightly taller.

When Carly walked out of the pool house, balancing a stack of papers in one hand as she closed the door behind her with the other, the brothers furtively glimpsed at each other. They grinned conspiratorially as Carly coolly walked too close to the battleground. Then they wound up their arms like paddles and showered her with half the water in the pool.

With a shriek followed by prolonged cursing, Carly, who was completely drenched, shook herself and her soaked paperwork. I shuddered, suddenly reminded of my first encounter with Carly's wrath. Rocco and Cameron just high-fived each other and snickered as she stomped away, still swearing under her breath. She was powerless against their lapse in maturity.

She disappeared into the house, but to my utter amazement, she walked back out after a few minutes and came to share my long chair.

I hadn't noticed until that moment that Spider had been standing on the threshold of the basement doors, watching all of us with a confused look on his face. Then he practically tiptoed over and sat next to Carly. I scooted down to give them some room and me some distance from Spider. As usual, he sat nervously on the edge of his seat, unable to relax. However, after significant taunting from Rocco and Cameron, he went to join them in the pool.

It was strange to see all of them together, playing around. It was as if they were acting their own age—and I didn't feel like a kid among adults. Even Carly seemed to be enjoying the scene.

"You realize this never happens. Them, acting like this," she muttered.

"Like what?"

"Like normal human beings."

Eventually Cameron gazed down at his water-pruned hands, climbed out of the pool, and came to sit next to me, letting Rocco fend for himself.

Carly smiled and went to watch Rocco and Spider from the side of the pool.

"How is it that you and your brother only just met?" I wondered.

"Technically, he's my half brother—same mother, different father. My dad and mom had me when they were teens. When I was six, I was sent to live with my dad. Our mom had a bunch of kids with different guys, from what Rocco tells me. The only times I saw her were when she managed to track my dad down to get some money."

"Why didn't you stay with your mom?"

"She's a drunk and had enough problems of her own without having to worry about another mouth to feed," he said. "My dad was forced to take me in when the social worker threatened to put me in a foster home."

"So you lived with your father." I mulled it over. "Where did you grow up?"

"Everywhere, I guess. We moved around a lot." He continued to watch Spider and Rocco play in the pool, but his mind seemed to be a hundred miles away.

And then he snapped out of it and looked at me with his wide, overwhelming grin. "Any more questions?"

"At least a thousand more."

He put his arm around my shoulder and squeezed me in a half hug. "You're exhausting, you know."

I could feel myself molding around him, into him. I should have been pushing him away, as I normally would have with a guy. At the very least, I should have knocked him over. There were no coffee tables to speak of, nothing I could push him into as I had Skylar. I knew enough bad things about Cameron that I should have been trying everything I could to keep him away from me.

But everything inside and outside me was tranquil, lulling me. Within Cameron's arms, it was just easier.

I jumped when a little boy with blond curls came bounding into the pool. I was surprised even more by the person who trailed him.

Chapter Eight

Unclothed

She was a tanned, blonde beauty. Like a girl from those hair-removal cream commercials: long legs, cutoffs, high heels—I was expecting her to break into a song any minute. In the few seconds it took her to glide a few steps, the climate around the pool went from warm and cozy to below freezing. I watched Carly's smile turn tortured. I watched Spider's eyes circle over to Carly, his face turn to ice; he lunged out of the pool and met the blonde. I watched Rocco gawk dreamily at her. He was apparently in charge of keeping the pool water from turning to snow.

And I watched her as she watched me; her gaze fell on Cameron and then back to me. I noticed all these things, but not before noticing that Cameron's arm shot away from me as soon as she materialized. His jaw had clenched, transforming the beautiful, youthful features of his face. When I met his eyes, I was frightened by the impassive man who had taken his place once again—the creature that had been haunting my nightmares, lingering under the surface of Cameron's beauty. It was like getting a door slammed in my face and falling back into the abyss, the reality of my screwed-up existence.

Spider had—somewhat gently—grabbed the girl by the arm, rerouting her back into the house. Cameron chased after them, without a word or backward glance. When they had vanished, Carly was still, her head bent forward, her hair hiding her face.

I hugged myself around my wet towel, sitting ramrod straight on the side of the chair, and took a moment to get my voice back.

"Who was that?" I managed. There was panic in my voice, and I didn't know why.

"That," Rocco told me, "was Frances." He said this with admiration. He said this as if it were enough to satisfy all the questions that were running through my head.

Rocco squinted while the little boy splashed water at him. "Superman," the boy commanded in his tiny voice, arms spread-eagle. Rocco picked him up by the torso and flew him over his head with a whoosh. The curly blond kid looked more like a cherub or a clip-winged Gabriel than like Clark Kent. There was something familiar in his triumphant, devilish grin.

"And who's this?" I tried to sound noncreepy and aimed my forced smile in the child's general direction. I'd always been awkward around kids, especially when I was one. The only kid I had ever known well was my brother, who was seven when I was born and already more of a grownup than any of the adults I knew. I tended to stay away from other kids when I was forced to assimilate, positive that they could smell fear. They pounced on carrot-haired oddballs like me all the time.

"This little guy is Daniel," Rocco said to me. He fell backward, letting Superman plunge into the water. Daniel's head popped back out, and he giggled while Rocco remained submerged.

"How old are you, Daniel?" There was that awkwardness again.

The kid did the other thing that kids tended to do around me: he completely ignored me. He busied himself with dogpaddling around the pool, trying to sink Rocco's submarine body. I readjusted my towel and peeked at Carly. She hadn't moved a muscle.

"He's six," she said flatly. She then stood up and walked into the pool house. A few seconds later, Spider emerged from the patio doors, sneaked a quick look around the pool, and then went to the pool house, banging the door so violently that one of the flower boxes on the windowsill tumbled to the pavers below—petals, earth, and roots spilling everywhere.

Rocco was heavily engaged in a new game of water wrestling, having finally found a partner he could beat.

I waited two long minutes for Cameron to reappear. He didn't.

Curiosity heated up my impatience, but jealousy made it boil over. Cameron was in the house with the blonde mannequin, sans his arachnid chaperone. It was silly to be jealous. I barely knew the girl. I barely knew Cameron. I had no claim or cause to hope for anything good to come my way. So I sneaked back into the house when Rocco was submerged, armed with the excuse of needing a fresh towel if I was discovered.

Inside, the house was hushed. I could hear the wheezing of the night guards, who were sleeping in one of the basement rooms. Floorboards were slightly creaking upstairs, and voices were moving about. Through the kitchen, down the upstairs hallway, the strained voices became strained words. The door to the library was ajar. I crept toward it, the bottom of my naked feet sticking to the hardwood floor.

"How much is it this time?" I heard Cameron coldly ask. I peeked in and saw him facing the high shelves against the wall. Books were stacked at his feet. He was crouched in front of the emptied third shelf and fiddling with the combination lock on a small metal door.

The safe opened, revealing a heap of bills inside. The woman— Frances—was waiting behind him.

"Um, five thousand should do it." Frances's voice was seductive and unaffected. "Rent is due next week."

Cameron grabbed a stack of cash and very swiftly leafed through the bills. He stopped midway through the stack, split it, and put the uncounted bills back in the safe. He slammed the metal door shut and abruptly turned around with the remaining bills in hand. I threw myself—in a one-legged, Indiana Jones style—into Rocco's room, landing on a pile of dirty clothes. I ducked behind his door and sat on a mass of socks, underwear, and shirts, as well as a plate and a Victoria's Secret catalog.

"Seems like the amounts get bigger every time I see you," Cameron was saying.

"I have a growing child to raise. Or have you forgotten that?"

There was a deep sigh. "Are you going to tell me why you're really here?"

"What do you mean? Money. Like I said. Like always."

"You could have just called Spider. He would have made arrangements to have it delivered to you. It would have been more convenient."

"More convenient for who?" she shot back. "I couldn't wait for Spider to make his arrangements. I need the money now."

"You don't look like you need money, Frances." I wondered if he was referring to the designer purse that had been hanging off her arm.

"How dare you!"

"Keep your voice down," Cameron hissed.

Frances's voice was hushed. "Daniel has been and will always be my priority. You, of all people, are in no position to judge me."

"This isn't a place for kids. You shouldn't be bringing him here."

"I wouldn't say that ... you seem to be surrounding yourself with children these days."

"You have your money. Take the boy and leave immediately." Cameron's tone was calm and businesslike.

"What's the hurry? Are Daniel and I getting in the way of your latest sexual exploit?"

"It's time to go, Frances."

"I saw the way you were looking at that girl. For God's sake, Cameron, she looks barely fourteen years old."

"Frances—"

Frances ignored the warning in his voice. "Then again, purebreds like her tend to be well preserved. I guess that's what happens when a girl spends her life being kept away from the likes of you. She's a little out of your league, don't you think?"

"I'll have Tiny escort you out."

"Don't you touch me!"

"You have what you came for. The rest is none of your business."

"This has everything to do with me!" she yelled. "You will damage that poor girl. Good girls like Emily aren't equipped to deal with guys like you."

Severe silence swept into the library and the room where I was hiding. A slight whimper escaped my lips; I had just been thrown onto a roller coaster, mid-plunge.

"Do you really think that I wouldn't recognize the red hair?" Frances pushed. "How old is she now? Seventeen, eighteen?"

"You can leave, or I can make you leave. It's your choice." Cameron's voice was tight now.

"You don't scare me, Cameron—even though I know what you're capable of. Question is … does she know what you're capable of? Does little Emily know the monster that you are?"

"Enough, Frances!"

"Yes, it is enough, isn't it?" she spat. "Bill would've had you by the throat if he saw her here, saw you looking at her like that."

I had heard enough. My ears shut out all sound, as if my body had turned on the autopilot to stop the crash-landing that would have come if I had kept listening. My knees tucked themselves into my chest. My hand clasped the chain around my neck—the one my brother had given me, the one I never took off—so tightly that the angel pendant that hung on it was leaving a bright-red indentation in the palm of my hand. I felt like I had been caught in a tornado that had sucked the air out of me.

Frances knew Bill. Cameron knew Bill. After years of yearning for answers, searching for any glimpses of that other life, the one my brother had lived away from me; after desperately sitting by as traces of my brother slowly disappeared with every moment, day, month, year that passed, until it started to feel like he had never really existed; I had discovered that someone other than me had known Bill—and knew who I was.

How could I have missed this? I tried to go back through all the events of the past few days, but all I could remember was my conversation with Cameron that morning. He had listened to me while I had told him about my big brother's premature death, something I had never told anyone else about because it was too painful. And yet he had never said a word.

How well had they known Bill? From the way they spoke about him, I sensed they'd known him well, well enough to know that I was his sister. Had they been friends?

Or worse, had they been enemies? My brother had a lot of those, including almost his entire family. As this thought flew into my head, I hated Cameron. I even hated poor, defenseless Rocco. If they had been my brother's enemies, I hated all of them. Being an enemy of my brother was a mortal sin to me.

I'm not sure how long I parked in Rocco's room like that. Frances and Danny were long gone when I peeled off the front cover of the catalog, which had stuck to my half-clad behind, and let my limbs carry me back toward the front hallway.

Cameron intercepted me as he was running down the steps.

His eyes canvassed my face, and he halted on the second-to-last step. My face was hot and sweaty.

"What's up …?" he asked slowly, carefully.

I considered side-stepping him and continuing up to his room, where I could get a moment's solace. I considered spitting in his face and running out the front door, screaming until I got shot down. But something in his expression told me that he wasn't going to let me through without an explanation. My throat was constricted.

"Bill …" was how I started. Cameron's face went white. "You knew me too … I needed a clean towel … how could you?" In my head, these were fully structured sentences with nouns, conjugated verbs, and all that stuff that made sense to other people.

Cameron and I just stared at each other. I looked at him through a veil of gathering tears. Cameron blinked, but his face remained otherwise expressionless.

This made me furious.

"You knew Bill," I spit out, my thoughts clearer now. "All this time, you knew exactly who I was. You never said anything."

Cameron's breathing was perfectly normal. "Yes," he said, after a pause.

"Yes, you knew Bill, or yes, you lied to me?"

"I didn't lie to you."

"You omitted vital information."

"That's not the same as lying."

"Spare me the semantics."

He sat down on the stairs. "This isn't what you think."

"Oh? Tell me—what am I thinking?" Because I had no idea—jumbled words were all I could manage to think about. "You seem to have all the answers."

"Em—" he started, but I wasn't finished.

"Were you ever going to tell me?"

"No," he admitted. There was no pause, and he looked straight at me. "There are some things that you're better off not knowing."

"Do not make decisions for me! You might know who I am, but you don't know me well enough to know what's good for me."

"Listen, Emmy, I know that you're mad at me—"

I took a step forward. He put an arm out to block my way. I shoved him. He didn't budge. "Get out of my way!" I screamed.

"Fine," he said, holding onto my arms, forcing me to look at him. "You're beyond mad, but I swear to you that I'm just trying to keep you safe."

I shrugged out of his grasp. "No thank you. I've seen what you do with the people you should be keeping safe. You can't even manage to care about your own kid."

Cameron opened his mouth as if he were going to say something, and then stopped. He frowned; I could see him trying to digest what I was saying. "Wait ... what?"

"Throwing money at your children, at your son, won't make him safer. It'll just make him resent you more." I had intimate experience with this.

"Ah. I understand what you're saying now. You're talking about Daniel." There was a barely audible tremble in his voice. I had obviously hit a nerve. I decided to press it.

"What kind of man would leave a child to be raised without a father? Paying off your son's mother doesn't make you less of a deadbeat."

Cameron flinched faintly. He slid his hand down the banister as he stepped around me and down the stairs, and calmly, too calmly, walked out the front door.

I had meant for my words to hurt him.

The door gently clicked behind him, and I heard someone clamoring up the basement stairs. When I turned around, Carly and Spider were standing at the top of the stairs and Rocco was rushing up behind them. The grim look on Carly's and Spider's faces told me that they had seen enough of the show.

"Did you know all along too?" I demanded.

"Know what?" Rocco replied, popping his head between Carly and Spider and dripping pool water everywhere. Carly and Spider simply stared back at me in response. That was enough for me to understand how deep the treachery had run.

I did what I knew best: I dashed off to hide.

"What's going on?" I heard Rocco ask in a loud whisper as I reached the second floor. This was followed by the sound of a slap on wet skin. "Ow! Carly! That hurt! What was that for?"

I was quaking. The world around me was a dark shade of gray. I spotted my stupid, tacky indigo lamp. I grabbed it and threw it against the wall. Part of me noticed that it had smashed, but I had already moved on to the next defenseless thing that happened to be within my grasp. The drawer from the bedside table went flying across the room. Then the bedside table was sent tumbling to the ground. The blankets, the pillows, the bedsheets were yanked off the bed. I knew I was screaming, I could feel the heated escape that rose up my throat, but I couldn't hear anything outside myself. My hair was sticking to my face. I wanted to chop it all off.

I spun and went to Cameron's dresser, where he had put all my stuff. I grabbed an empty bin and started putting my clothes in it, but I couldn't manage. I was crying. I wanted to rip them all apart. When I couldn't make a dent there, I just threw them down. Threw all my worldly possessions on the floor. And I fell in their midst, sobbing with my head between my knees.

Eventually, my fists became my hands again. My breathing normalized. Tears were still streaking down my cheeks, but they were no longer gushing. I wiped my eyes with my fingers and glanced around at the mess I had made. My lips were quivering as my body temperature dropped back down.

All I could think about was how much I missed Bill, missed talking about him with someone outside myself.

Losing my brother so suddenly, without any information from my useless parents, was like waking up one morning with a missing limb and having no idea where it went. What happened before he died? How did he get to that point?

Was he alone when he died? Was he afraid? Did he know it was going to happen?

So many things were going through my head. Most of all, I felt I'd betrayed myself. After spending so much time shutting people out, how could I have let Cameron in so easily? This man had purposely kept critical knowledge from me. Why? What was he hiding? Did he have anything to do with Bill's death? What about Carly? What about Spider?

I was suddenly freezing and realized I was still in my bathing suit.

I grabbed a pair of sweatpants and a sweatshirt, put them on, and limped to the windows. My ankle was throbbing badly now. I opened the patio door and stepped out onto the deck off Cameron's room. It was dark; another day had rolled by without me. *I could try to climb down,* I thought. *I've done it once; I could probably do it again.* Somewhere in the darkness, there was an army of guards.

But they weren't the reason that I didn't try to escape—I was. I stopped myself.

I had too many unanswered questions, and the possibility of spending another lifetime not knowing, when I was so close to answers, so close to the people who knew something, forced me back into my captor's room. Whether they were Bill's friends or his enemies, I was going to find out and deal with it.

I shut the patio door and turned around to find Cameron standing there in the darkness of his room.

"I knocked, but you didn't answer," he said.

CHAPTER NINE

MISERY

Cameron had shooed Rocco away from the television and into his room and was now in the kitchen; pots were clanking in his wake. I was sitting at the kitchen table where he had bidden me to park myself, trying to blink through the pain in the back of my eyes from the very bright overhanging lights.

"I can't stand it, Cameron. If you don't tell me right now what you know about Bill, I swear I'm going to scream."

Cameron set two ibuprofen and a glass of chocolate milk on the table in front of me. "I know. I need a minute to figure out what to tell you."

"What to tell me? Just tell me everything. It's that simple."

"Believe me. It's not that simple."

"Start by telling me how you knew him. That seems pretty simple."

"That's the hard part," he muttered and went to the stove. "How much did your brother tell you—about what he was up to when he was gone, away from you?"

I swallowed the pills because I was having trouble concentrating with the splitting headache that had taken my brain hostage. "He didn't need to say much," I replied, rubbing my temples with two fingers. "The police reports and school records spoke for themselves." There were also all the rumors that were floating around, things that were being whispered, things that I had heard my father scream at my brother behind the closed mahogany door of his study. I didn't feel the need to tell Cameron this.

"What about when the police reports stopped after he left school? Did he ever talk to you about what he was doing?"

"Not much," I admitted. "I didn't see him very much after he ran away. He would sneak back into the house mostly to just boss me around, tell me what not to do." I exhaled. "We argued a lot toward the end." This I regretted more than anything.

Cameron was busy over the sizzle of the frying pan.

I was gripping the edge of the table, trying hard to keep it together. "Earlier, you called me Emmy, you know."

He brought grilled cheese sandwiches and a bottle of ketchup to the table. He sat down facing me and raised his eyebrows. "I did?"

I nodded and watched him while he watched me.

"Your brother used to call you that," he said.

"You knew him well enough to know that."

He took a bite of his grilled cheese. Though my stomach was grumbling, I left the sandwich there and waited. "Well?"

He shifted in his seat. "I'm honestly not sure where to start."

"Starting from the beginning seems to work for most people."

"Starting from the beginning would take a very long time."

"Apparently I'm not going anywhere for a while, so talk as long as you need," I said.

"I don't need to talk. I'm doing this for you," he stalled.

I crossed my arms over my chest, not giving him any other opportunity to delay what I needed to hear.

"Fine," he said, shaking his head. "If you eat, I'll talk."

I squeezed ketchup on my plate, picked up half the grilled cheese and dunked it in my pond of ketchup. I brought it to my mouth and waited to see if he was going to keep his end of the bargain.

"Let's see," he said with his eyes turned to the ceiling. His gaze then came back to me. "The first time I met Bill Sheppard, he beat the crap out of me."

I took a bite of my sandwich and almost choked. Bill had beaten the crap out of Cameron, not the other way around? I had to keep my composure and keep Cameron talking.

"Your brother had just been transferred to my school—"

"Which school?" I interrupted with a mouthful.

"Saint Emmanuel."

Saint Emmanuel was the last private school my brother had attended before being shipped off to live with his uncle. "That's one of the most expensive schools in the Northeast."

Cameron's stare bore into me. "What shocks you more—the fact that I went to a private school, or that I went to school at all?"

"Neither," I told him. "I just didn't peg you for the snooty type."

His smile returned. "What's your problem with rich people, anyway?"

This was obviously another stall tactic—and even if it wasn't, I wasn't going there. "So you met my brother at Saint Emmanuel, and he beat you up. Why?"

"Bill had decided that he was going start selling to the kids at school. One day he caught me selling on what he thought was his turf, so he beat me up to teach me a lesson. I was just a kid myself," he clarified, "and I thought for sure that Spider was going to kill him for giving me a black eye—"

"How long have you known Spider?"

"A long time." He hesitated before he added, "We were roommates in juvie. Spider had come up with the same plan as your brother a couple of years before."

"You were in juvenile detention?"

"Yeah, for a little while." His face flushed slightly, and he hurriedly continued, "By the time your brother came along, Spider and I already had the school as our turf. We'd spent a lot of time building business with the rich kids—"

"What were you selling, exactly?"

Cameron sighed. "Emmy, the only way I'm going to tell you this is if it's a one-way conversation. That means no more questions." He waited for my acknowledgment, so I nodded. It hadn't escaped me that he was now calling me Emmy, and that I really liked it when he did. It had been years since anyone called me that—since Bill died.

"The people Bill had planned to sell to had actually been my customers for a couple of years. And my customers were a paranoid bunch of kids who were always looking over their shoulder, afraid that people would know their dirty little secrets, embarrass their families. They never bought from anyone they didn't know, or didn't trust, even a persuasive guy like your brother."

I could picture my big-headed brother among these privileged kids. This was the world Bill and I knew too well—the hiding, the lying, the sham.

"When Bill finally figured out why he wasn't getting any business, he decided that he was going to become my partner. At first I told him to get lost." Cameron grinned. "But when he told me about his new plan, it made a lot of sense. So I finally convinced Spider, which wasn't easy. And your brother, Spider, and I became business partners. Spider kept the product coming in; I kept the school kids well supplied; Bill expanded the business to the parents, aunts, uncles, cousins, et cetera." He paused to take another bite. "You know, Bill had a way of making people feel like they were untouchable. Spider said it was the smell of money, that it was engrained in his skin. Whatever it was, your brother was a great salesman, and for a while, with our customers' deep pockets, we had so much business that we had a hard time keeping up. But your brother had one major weakness: women—the kind that came with a lot of baggage. He always had to come to some girl's rescue."

Our gazes collided.

"Seemed like he had a different girl hanging off his arm every other week. But once the excitement was over and he decided that he was done saving them, he'd move on to the next train wreck, leaving a bigger wreck behind. He got caught up with this one girl whose boyfriend liked to use her as a punching bag. Bill came to her rescue and beat up the boyfriend. Turned out that the boyfriend wasn't just one of my regular customers, but he was also the dean's nephew. Just a string of bad luck," he said, shaking his head. "Bill's dorm room was searched, and they found the stash that was hidden under the floorboards. Bill got arrested and kicked out of school."

I remembered this. Bill had been sent home in a police cruiser. Of course, no charges were ever filed—the Sheppards were too well connected for that to ever happen. But not even the Sheppard name could stop the gossip. Bill had to be sent to live with a distant relative, cut off from the family, for the family name's sake.

"You know, I had bigger stashes in my room, so Bill could have used me as a scapegoat to save himself. But he never did. Spider and I kept the business going after your brother got kicked out. We kept it lower key, though, selling only to the students I knew. When I finished high school, your brother came to find me. He had whopping plans to expand the business, beyond rich kids and their families, and he needed a partner. I brought Spider in, and we spent the next couple of years getting new suppliers and building more contacts. Your brother had big dreams, and the business kept growing, so much so that we had trouble keeping track of all the money. So Spider brought Carly in, and soon we had the competition working for us. No one made a move unless your brother approved it."

Cameron paused. The smile left his face. "When you're on top like that, things get a lot more ... complicated." He spoke carefully. "Everywhere you look, there's someone who wants to take you down so that he can get a piece of your action. You start having to look over your shoulder all the time because your friends can become your enemies overnight. Just trying to keep yourself ... trying to keep the people you love alive becomes a twenty-four hour job. It's exhausting. And your brother had started to ... change. He became ..." He was trying to find the right word. "Jittery. He started keeping secrets, disappearing from Spider, Carly, and me." Cameron took a breath here. "Things started to really fall apart when our clients and the other partners noticed the change and began second-guessing his decisions. Before we knew what was really going on, Bill was dead."

Cameron finally looked up; his gaze lingered on my face. "To answer your question, yes, I knew your brother very well, and yes, I knew him well enough to know who you are. Your brother was my best friend, and he talked about you all the time."

"Why didn't you tell me before now? Why did you say that you were never going to tell me about my brother?"

He pressed his lips together. "Because your brother wouldn't have wanted you to know."

"How would you know what Bill would have wanted?"

"If he'd wanted you to know, he would have told you, wouldn't he?"

"Maybe he just ran out of time."

"Believe me, Emmy," he insisted darkly, "Bill wouldn't want you to know this much about his life."

Cameron came to get my plate as I lifted it from the table. Our fingers brushed. My arms went slightly weak. He darted away.

"Okay …" I said, catching my breath, "Why are you telling me this now?"

He came back from the kitchen and leaned against the table. "I had no other choice. I know how close you and Bill were, and that it was difficult for you when he died." He forced a smile. "I also know that you wouldn't let up until you heard the truth. I wanted you to hear it from me and to stop harassing my kid brother for information that he doesn't have. He had no idea who Bill was or who you are. You're making it very hard for me to keep him away from all that stuff."

"Rocco wants to be part of all that stuff," I reminded him.

"That's not up to him."

"Spider and Carly—they know who I am, though."

"Yes. They do," he confessed. He came and sat down next to me. I could feel the heat off his arm. I wondered if he did this on purpose, to confound me.

"I have to leave for a little while," he said quietly. "I know that you have a lot of questions, but I meant what I said: the less you know, the safer you are." He gave me a crooked smile. "Please don't start any hunger strikes while I'm gone. Rocco will not feed you, and judging from the smells that come out of his room, I don't think he would even notice the smell of a decomposing body."

The more Cameron talked, the more I wanted him to keep talking. It was the way he talked to me, his voice reverberating through me. I wanted to touch him, just a little bit, to see if he was real, but instead I yawned a long, boorish yawn. He reached over and gently squeezed my shoulder. My heart was beating so quickly—he was very real. "It's late. You need to go to bed."

I squinted toward the clock in the living room. Though my eyes were burning and my neck felt like it was holding up a bowling ball, I couldn't go to bed. There were still so many unanswered questions.

"When will you be back?" I asked.

"I don't know. Could be a couple days, could be a week. It depends on how things progress. I have a lot of catching up to do. I have to finish the business that was interrupted last time I was in the city."

The business *I* had interrupted, was what he had meant to say. That man in the cemetery, had he been part of that business? Suddenly I found myself pushing the thought out of my head. Purposely forgetting reality. The cemetery. Cameron in the cemetery. The gun. I was refusing to let my brain go there because it changed Cameron in my eyes. And it changed Bill, the brother I had idolized. I was too tired to put this all together—this new picture that changed everything I thought I knew about Bill and therefore about myself. Cameron's revelations had transformed my whole history.

This time my yawn hit my eyes and made them tear up.

"Go to bed, Emmy. I promise we'll talk when I get back."

Cameron got up, hesitating before extending his hand to help me up. I slipped my hand into his. My hand entwined with his awakened something in me. It felt like I was touching water for the first time. Something that felt inborn, familiar, and yet strange, different from anything I had ever touched. I had the overwhelming desire to let myself fall in, completely immerse myself in it, knowing that I would drown if I did.

He had led me to his bedroom door. There was an awkward pause between us. *He's going to kiss me,* I thought. I wanted him to kiss me.

"Goodnight, Emmy," he whispered.

He turned and started to walk away.

"What made you think that Daniel was my son?" I heard him ask as I grabbed the door handle.

Daniel. The gorgeous little boy. I had forgotten about him. Or perhaps I had forced myself to forget about that too. "Why else would you be paying Frances?"

Cameron considered this for a moment. "He's not mine," he said.

And with my heart still hotly pounding, I closed the bedroom door and pushed Meatball over before crashing into bed, still fully clothed.

There was overwhelming desolation: I sensed it as soon as my eyes fluttered open, even before I noticed the string of light that was poking out from around the curtains, and before Meatball started whining at the door to be let out of our cave. Whatever place Cameron had come to occupy inside of me was now being wrenched by distance. Weirdly, I felt him far away, and the only way I could explain this to myself was that he had quickly become the only true tie I had left to Bill. It was the closest I had ever come to knowing about my brother's other life, and I was starved for more.

The fact that Bill had been involved in something most likely highly illegal wasn't all that surprising to me; he had spent most of his life trying to get into as much trouble as possible. How entrenched he had been in these extracurricular activities, and what part Cameron had played and might still be playing in them, I didn't know. Part of me wondered if the whole truth—and I was starting to have an idea what that truth might look like—would change the feelings that I had for Cameron. Feelings that were still so utterly bewildering, yet besieged me.

I had never been in love. I didn't even believe in love. I had watched too many people faking it. My mother fell in love with my father every time she got a new car, or jewelry that cost as much as one. She'd be affectionate for a week, maybe two if the car was expensive enough. That wasn't love. At the most it was lust. Lust was temporary, circumstantial.

Maybe that's what I was feeling: lust. That made more sense to me. I was only feeling like this because of this place, this world that my brother had known, and because of Cameron, who oozed masculinity.

My sixth sense was validated when I went outside to let Meatball get to his business and saw that Cameron's car was gone. I'd had a small hope that perhaps he hadn't left yet—perhaps he had changed his mind and decided to stay. A hope that was squashed like beetle against a windshield.

Rocco and Griff were on the front stoop, so I held back the deep sigh inflating my chest and resigned myself to pinching my lips together.

"Ginger!" Griff exclaimed, emitting a cloud of cigarette smoke. "Where have you been hiding, love?"

The place looked abandoned. The vans and cars were all gone, and there were just a few guards left along the property line.

I smiled meekly at Griff while Rocco watched poor Meatball dash for the first patch of green he could find. "What's Meatball doing here?" Rocco asked. "He should be with the chief."

"I guess he forgot to bring him," I said, feeling guilty for having forgotten to let him out at a decent time.

"Doubt it," Rocco muttered. He coughed out smoke signals, his lungs refusing to inhale the toxins from the cigarette he was trying to smoke. He quickly gave up the habit, putting out the cigarette with barely a puff's worth gone from it. Griff had already finished his and snuffed it out with his sneaker. He kept his twinkling eyes on me.

"Is everyone gone?" I asked, changing the subject and holding on to a miniscule glimmer of hope that my intuition was flawed.

"Yep," Rocco confirmed gloomily. "Everyone is gone."

The sun was blazing, but I was still cold. The melancholy had followed me outside and engulfed Rocco too. Griff, who was cheery enough for the three of us, put his hand on Rocco's head and shook it about, messing up Rocco's already messy hair. "Aw, cheer up, buddy. You'll get your chance to run with the big boys soon enough."

Rocco shoved Griff's hand away and stared dejectedly ahead.

Griff chuckled. "I don't know why you want to leave so bad, Kid. This place is great when they're not here to boss us around."

"It's boring here, and I'm not a damn babysitter," Rocco sulked.

I imagined that I was the baby he had to sit for. I didn't take it personally.

"I can do a lot more than this, but they won't let me," he said.

"Tell you what, Kid," Griff offered, his eyes narrowing, "I'll teach you how to fight, toughen you up a bit. And I'll talk to Tiny when he gets back. Maybe he'll let you tag along with them next time they go out."

Rocco's face lit up. "Really? You'll teach me some stuff? You think they'll let me go with them?"

"Sure thing." Griff got up, using his rifle as a stretch bar over his head. He then swung the gun strap over his shoulder and sighed. "I better get back to my spot before another fly escapes through the tree line." He gave me a wink and walked away.

Rocco went into the house, and I sat on the stoop and closed my eyes, soaking in some warmth. Griff hadn't taken two steps before I heard the crunch of gravel stop. "What are you up to today?" he asked me.

I opened my eyes and shrugged. My options were looking pretty bleak.

Griff had a mischievous smile. "Wanna help me play hooky?"

I couldn't help but smile back.

He strolled back and grabbed my hand, pulling me up like a string puppet.

"Won't you get in trouble if you don't go back to work?" I asked as we made our way down the driveway, Griff holding me by the elbow while I shuffled next to him.

Griff made an exaggerated show of scanning the landscape around us. "Tiny's gone. Spider's gone. There's no one here to tell me what to do."

"Couldn't they just call Tiny to get you in trouble?" I observed, my eyes on the other guards, who were glowering in our direction.

"Have you seen any phones around here? Because I haven't. All of our stuff, like our cell phones, was confiscated before we got here."

"What if something happens, like someone gets hurt, or there's some kind of emergency?" I was also assuming that 911 was an option in the middle of nowhere.

"Look at the guys with the big guns," he said, pointing at one of the guards. "Do you think anyone else can just waltz in here? If someone gets hurt here, they stay hurt ... or they disappear."

I could feel the blood draining from my face.

"Don't worry," he said forcing a smile. "I won't let anything happen to you." Griff put his arm around my shoulders and squeezed me in a one-armed, crushing hug.

We kept walking down the driveway until we reached the tree line where the driveway became the gravel road that continued into the forest—the same road that Rocco and I had driven up when we first got to the Farm. There were two burly men with machine guns standing on each side of the driveway, at the perimeter. They looked like twins in their identical black T-shirts and jeans and mirrored sunglasses.

As we attempted to walk past them, they swiftly blocked our way.

"The girl doesn't leave the property," said the bigger of the two.

"C'mon, man! We're not going far. I won't let anything happen to her. I've got my gun if something happens," said Griff.

"Sorry, Griff. Chief's orders. The girl stays here."

"No one's around. I won't tell anyone if you don't." Griff was laying on the charm.

The guard's tone became harsh. "Listen, man, if you want to break the rules and mess with the girl after you were told not to, that's your funeral. But I ain't gonna get shot for you. Now, you can turn around and we'll forget all about this, or you can keep going and I will make this your funeral."

I held my breath as Griff stood facing the two men, considering his next move. I felt like a dwarf among giants. Finally he turned back to me, slightly smiling. "I guess we're not gonna get anywhere here." He hooked his arm around mine and led me away.

We walked along the property line, passing an armed guard every once in a while. None of the guards spoke to either of us. Griff remained silent, sulking. When I was sure we were out of earshot of any of the guards, I asked, "Who ordered you to not mess with me?"

"Spider, who else?" he said.

I couldn't imagine that Spider would care who I hung out with. "Why?"

"Who knows why these thugs do anything. I don't think they know themselves half the time."

I glanced around. "What's out there? I mean, we're in the middle of nowhere. What could be so dangerous out on the road that we can't take a walk?"

"You're right, there's nothing out there. It's not so much them wanting to prevent you from getting hurt out there. It's more about them wanting to keep you in here."

"Why?"

"Beats me," Griff shrugged. "One thing I do know, though: eventually everything leads to money for them. So whatever their reasons for keeping you here alive, it probably has something to do with money."

A shiver went down the back of my legs. That lingering doubt about Cameron, that part of him that I was trying to dismiss, that I was downplaying, was climbing its way back, like a spider up my spine. No matter what Cameron told me about Bill, about himself, I was still a prisoner here. I was safe—as far as I knew—only as long as I didn't try to leave.

"Look around you, Ginger," Griff said. "The big house in the middle of nowhere, the brutes with the guns ... This isn't a vacation, and these guys are definitely not tour guides. They're crooks. All of them. Except for the kid, maybe—I think that Kid's too young to understand, but he'll eventually become like the rest of them. He has no chance of ever getting out." A light seemed to go on in Griff's head. "C'mon. I have to show you something."

We quickened our walk, with me managing something close to a one-legged jog, and made our way back up the driveway. We passed the front of the house and followed the driveway, which led us down and to the right, away from the house. As we neared a clump of bushes, I saw that the driveway kept going through the trees and down a small hill. At the bottom there was a large garage with another guard pacing back and forth by the tree line.

"What's this?" I asked as we approached the garage.

"This is where the no-rankers sleep." Griff sounded proud of this. We walked through the side door.

Inside, the garage was more like a showroom. Parked side by side was an array of cars. I had no idea what kind they were, but they were really shiny. As we walked past each car, Griff explained with passion and in great detail its particulars: make, model, horsepower, torque, engine. It was all beyond my understanding, but it sounded good.

I was told that the silver car parked nearest the door was a Ferrari; it gleamed under the fluorescent lights that hung above it. Next to it was a lime-green Lamborghini, followed by a red Porsche, a burgundy Rolls-Royce, a black Aston Martin, and a canary-yellow Maserati—a rainbow of expensive cars.

In some ways, Griff reminded me of my brother. Bill had also been a car aficionado. As a teenager, the walls of his bedroom had been plastered with pictures of cars, pages he'd ripped out of magazines. Of course, he also had pictures of half-naked women—though these women were usually straddling cars.

We reached the end of the showroom and walked through a doorway. Hanging off nails on the wall were masses of vanity plates from all the states and even a few from Canada and Mexico.

"This is what I mean. These guys are real good at hiding, and I'd venture a bet that none of those cars was bought off a car lot," Griff said.

Something hanging off the wall caught my attention. I moved in closer.

Stuffed in a clear plastic bag that hung off one of the nails were hundreds of driver's licenses. Stunned, I immediately recognized the grinning face on the top of the stack. It was Bill's face, though the ID indicated that the man in the picture was John Aldridge from Arkansas. I pulled the bag off the nail and unzipped it. There were more drivers' licenses that had my brother's face. I also found cards from other states and countries with Cameron's, Spider's, and Carly's pictures on them. Like my brother's cards, they had various names attached to the faces.

I pulled one of Bill's cards out of the bag and struggled to swallow. There were few photos of my brother. The last picture I had seen was taken when he was fourteen, one of those fake-looking school pictures—awkward smile, neatly gelled hair, green-and-yellow cardigan worn only once, for five seconds. That picture was stacked with the rest of the family stuff that my father strategically placed on a shelf in his office behind his desk—his clients could see the pretense of a family man, not noticing that my father's back was to the shelf.

The worst thing about this was that I couldn't remember what Bill looked like as a grownup. In my mind, he'd been fourteen forever. Now I had a picture of my brother ... as a man. He looked more tired as an adult, but at least he hadn't lost his curly blond locks.

Griff looked over my shoulder at the ID in my hands. "I wonder who that is? I haven't seen him around here." He stepped away and added in passing, "A thug like the rest of them, I'm sure."

I should have, could have, defended my brother—he had been so much more than what Griff pegged him to be—but the achy feeling in my chest was threatening to overtake me entirely if I didn't keep it under control.

Griff made his way to the back of the room and disappeared behind another wall, where a stairwell led to a second story. I stuffed Bill's—or rather Buzz Killington's—driver's license in my pocket, put the plastic bag back on the nail, and went after Griff, who was already waiting for me at the top of the stairs. As I climbed up to meet him, he smiled and, with a finger to his lips, motioned for me to be quiet.

The second story was one big open space covering the length of the garage. The space was dimly lit, with black garbage bags and bedsheets covering the six-foot windows that lined both the room's long walls. About a dozen cots were lined up in two rows, one row on each side of the room. Four of the cots were occupied by sleeping men, one of whom I recognized as a night guard. The sound of snoring and heavy breathing echoed eerily off the walls.

We tiptoed over to one of the cots in the middle of the room. "This one is mine," Griff whispered, color appearing on his cheeks.

Griff had things strewn everywhere under and around his cot. I sat on an empty cot nearby while he rummaged under his. I noticed a box of magazines on the floor; the one on top was called *Cage Fighters Weekly*, and it had a caption in large red letters that read, "Griffin 'The Grappler' Conan: Best Pound-for-Pound Fighter in the World?" Under the caption was a picture of a bruised, black-eyed, threatening-looking Griff, shot from the waist up. He had his gloved fists up and muscles seemed to bulge out of every part of his body, including his neck, which was the size of parking meter. One by one I picked up the other magazines that were stacked under it, most of which pictured Griff on the front taking a similar stance, or holding a huge gold belt.

Griff finally reappeared from under his bed, pulling out fighting gloves like the ones he was pictured wearing on the magazine covers.

"This is you," I murmured. Griff sat next to me on the bed and peered at the magazine in my hands.

"Yeah. It was me," he said somberly. "It'll be me again once I get back on my feet."

"Don't you need to be out there if you want to get back on your feet?"

Griff pressed his lips together. "There are a bunch of dodgy people who are waiting for me to pay them. I have to pay off all the bad debt before I can do anything else—otherwise I'll turn up dead before I ever get a chance to hit the gym."

"Don't fighters make a lot of money, especially those who win?" I asked, tapping on the cover of the magazine where he was holding up a title belt.

"They do, and I definitely did. But I also made a lot of stupid mistakes while I was on top. I got too used to people serving me wherever I went. You should have seen it, Ginger. I could walk into any hotel and they'd put me and my buddies up in the executive suite right away. Gambling. Unlimited booze. Chicks. Whatever I asked for. I thought that I could get away with anything and that the money would never run out. That was true, for a while," he said, his eyes distant. "I was spending more time partying and forgot all about fighting ... especially training for fights. I started showing up in the ring out of shape and hung over. Then I started borrowing money to keep up with the lifestyle. I lost all of it."

He took the magazine from my hands, threw it on top of the others, and kicked the box back under the bed. Then he straightened up and forced a smile. "Working for these crooks will get me the money I need to pay off what I owe. At least no one can come find me here, and I can stay alive long enough to get the dough."

We got up and tiptoed past the sleeping guards, making our way back downstairs and outside into the bright sunlight.

We walked up to the house and into the kitchen, where Rocco was sitting at the table, halfway through a loaf of bread. I fixed some lunch for Griff and me while Griff thrilled Rocco by handing over the black gloves that he had dug out from under his bed. Rocco tried them on, but they were one size too big.

"You'll grow into them," Griff reassured him.

****

It wasn't so bad at first. It took me a few days to clean up my ransacked room. When I was done, I realized that the pieces of the ballerina lamp I had smashed were missing.

I spent my time with Rocco and Griff. I watched from the sidelines while Griff taught Rocco how to fight and wrestle. Griff even let Rocco practice punching his face. Griff chuckled every time Rocco's fist connected; I hid my face in my hands.

"Iron jaw," he told Rocco and me, slapping his own cheek. "That's how I was able to keep my title so long. I let 'em hit me till they get too tired or too cocky. When they start making mistakes, I attack and finish them off."

Rocco was a captive audience to Griff's fighting tales.

I watched a lot of TV. My ankle finally healed, and I started to run on it again.

One afternoon we started up a game of football with some of the other guards. Griff kept finding ways to play opposite me so that he could tackle me, but I was able to outrun him (and most of the other guys). Rocco found this hilarious.

"You don't run like a girl," he said.

It was one of the nicest things anyone had ever said to me.

I was being well entertained, and it worked … for a short while. But I wasn't sleeping. I spent my nights rolling around in bed, annoying Meatball, or else wandering aimlessly around Cameron's room, looking out the window at the dark night or poring over my brother's fake ID.

Every day I waited, anxiously, and the more time that passed, the more I started withdrawing from Griff and Rocco. I didn't want to be entertained anymore. This place—this beautiful mansion without Cameron, without new information—was starting to feel like the prison it was. I felt as though the air were thinning. I felt lightheaded, like I might do something stupid. Griff and Rocco just wanted to goof around. I was not in the mood.

I started to go off by myself, trying to find a small space where I could be alone; that was what I was doing when Rocco found me in the library, curled up with a book. He lumbered in with a bag of Cheetos and plopped himself on the opposite couch. We sat in silence while he crinkled and crunched away. He got up, picked up a book, and leafed through it, leaving orange fingerprints behind. He threw the book down next to him, put his feet on the coffee table, sighed, took them back down, repeatedly tossed a pillow up in the air and caught it—more orange fingerprints.

Then all the noise stopped. When I glanced over my book, Rocco was looking at me. "What's going on between you and my brother?"

Heat rose up my neck. "Nothing," I stammered, caught off guard. "Why do you ask?"

"I have my reasons ... and you look like you're about to slit your wrists."

"Where's Griff?" I asked, looking for a change of subject.

"Dunno. Still sleeping, I guess."

I wasn't surprised. Griff had become a man of leisure; he'd taken well to life at the Farm without the bosses.

"He's too old for you," Rocco said.

"Who? Griff?" Griff had also taken to following me around, which made my quest to be alone very difficult.

"No. My brother."

"Cameron's not too old for me!" I tried to recover by adding, "Isn't he only twenty-six?"

He raised an eyebrow. "Yeah, and how old are you?"

Eighteen. No, nineteen. When was my birthday again? I had to trace back a few months to the day I had gotten a birthday card in the mail on the exact day—someone had planned it well. The card was signed "Love, Mom and Dad," in Maria's handwriting, and had a check stuffed in it. The check had been signed by my father—that was something, right? Except that the numbers were in Maria's handwriting too; she had been far too generous with the zeros. (It didn't matter in the end. I tore the check up and threw it away.)

"Nineteen," I said.

"Oh." Rocco looked deflated.

"How old are you?"

He seemed to think about this. "Eighteen."

"What year were you born?"

He was stymied and couldn't respond quickly enough. "Fine. I'm sixteen."

I couldn't tell if this was true or not. It didn't really matter. "Shouldn't you be in school right now?" I sounded like someone's mother. (Not like mine, though.)

He shrugged. "I can't go back."

"Why not?"

"I got in a fight because of a girl."

This was starting to sound familiar. "I thought you couldn't fight?"

"I didn't win," he said. "I won't go back until I know I can beat the other guy, one way or another."

I suddenly understood why Rocco was bent on growing up so fast. "What happened to the girl?"

He chuckled softly. "She felt sorry for me, so she stuck around for a while."

"That was nice of her."

He shook his head. "Not really—she hooked up with my mom's boyfriend. They stole our TV before they left."

I couldn't hide my shock. He chuckled again. "I couldn't wait to get rid of my mom's boyfriend. I just didn't think I would lose the TV too."

We slipped back into silence. I tried to go back to my book. There was another long exhalation.

"Watcha reading?"

I put my book down. "Philosophy." I'd found a whole shelf dedicated to ancient philosophers—worn books, many of which I had already read in my first-year philosophy class.

"What's that?"

"Philosophy? Aristotle. Plato. Descartes. Rousseau. Ethics. I think, therefore I am."

There was a blank look on his face.

"It's the rational investigation of existence, truth, beliefs, all that stuff."

He looked even more confused.

"It's supposed to help you understand why we are the way we are ... why we do the things we do ... why we think the way we think."

"Who's *we*?"

"Humans."

"Oh," he said and went back to his bag of Cheetos.

More days passed. Some days it seemed like tending to Meatball's needs was the only reason I ever left Cameron's room. Other days, I would just lounge around the house in my pajamas all day. The insomnia was getting to me.

In the middle of the night, I heard my door squeak open. I opened my eyes to see a tall figure in the moonlight leave the room, closing the door behind him.

Chapter Ten

About Taking Risks

"Cameron?" I was so confused, and I was so tired. I was sure my eyes were playing tricks on me, making me see what I wanted to see most.

After a dazed second, I started to turn the switch of my ballerina lamp but then remembered it wasn't there. It didn't matter. The moonlight coming in through the windows confirmed the apparition.

"I didn't mean to wake you," he whispered.

"I wasn't sleeping," I confessed.

A rush of joy—and relief—filled me. I was suddenly wide awake and energized.

Cameron stood on the threshold, debating. When he made up his mind, he walked to my bedside. He looked like he had been dragged to hell and back. His clothes were crumpled and he had dark circles under his eyes; he was his other, older self.

We stared at each other for an awkward while. His lips were pressed together tightly, and his face was hard, unreadable. It upset me to see him like that. Whatever he found in my face displeased him too.

"You haven't been sleeping," he said.

I shrugged and wiped my hair away from my face. A hint of warmth reached his eyes.

He brought his hands to his face and rubbed it with exhaustion. When he reappeared, the warmth had spread to the top of his cheeks and his shoulders seemed to have relaxed a bit, as though he were slowly defrosting. I exhaled.

"Is everyone back?" I asked, listening for the shuffles and banging of doors, but the house was dead quiet.

"No. I came back early," he admitted. "It's just me." He gave me a tired smile. The square line of his jaw and his dark eyes stood out in the dim light.

A radiant smile escaped me before I had time to scale it down to normal. Then I took a gamble … and scooted over so he could sit down. He took me up on my offer.

Silence fell upon us.

My head was propped up on my elbow, my eyes watching him; Cameron sat with his back to me, his head moving as he looked from one side of the room to the other, stopping as he looked with interest at my the bedside table. When he reached over, I followed his movement. My gaze reached my brother's ID just before his hand did.

It was too late to try to hide it. I anxiously awaited his reaction, expecting to get in trouble for snooping around.

He looked the picture over, chuckled, and shook his head as if he remembered some private joke. I exhaled again.

"I see you kept yourself busy while I was gone." His voice was calm. He put the card back where he had found it and turned to me.

"You were gone a long time," I reminded him.

"Yeah. Things took longer than I thought they would."

My arm was too tired to hold up my head. I grabbed the pillow from the other side of the bed and folded it under my head. "What kind of things?"

"Just business stuff," he said with a yawn.

"Like what?"

"Inventory, orders, negotiating prices …" He sighed. "You know … normal business stuff."

149

"I know that whatever stuff you're involved in, there's nothing normal about it," I blurted. "I mean, I know that your *business*," I amended with emphasis, "involves some or maybe a lot of illegal stuff." It didn't sound any better the second time around.

"Oh?" He raised his eyebrows. "How do you know this?"

In my mind, I replayed what Griff had told me. I tried to make it sound like I'd come up with my suspicions on my own. "I'm not blind. I see the armed men walking around."

"That just proves that I'm taking every measure possible to keep everyone safe."

"From what? Lions? Tigers?"

"And bears," he finished for me.

"What about your lineup of fancy cars in the garage?" I probed. "I imagine that most of those cars were probably stolen." Again, this was Griff talking through me.

"Actually, none of those cars is mine." His mouth smiled faintly, but his eyes did not.

"Whose are they then?"

He seemed to consider this. "Well, I guess they're your cars, now."

"Mine?" Maybe I had misheard.

"As next of kin. They used to belong to your brother. They're all yours now." He smiled again and added coldly, "Bill bought those cash, special order. Nothing here is stolen."

I flushed, realizing that my insinuation had insulted him, more than he was letting on. "So, you're saying that you're not involved in any illegitimate business."

His face became somber. "No, that's not what I'm saying."

"You deal with things like drugs, guns …" I prompted.

"Emmy," he said before I could get too carried away, "please don't take offense. But I really don't want to talk about that with you."

"Okay," I agreed gently. I wasn't offended. I was just happy that he had put a limit on that topic, and not everything. "How does one get into that … profession?"

I was treading lightly, unclear as to what was off-limits.

He closed his eyes and rolled his neck and shoulders. "You mean, why didn't I become a lawyer or a doctor?"

"Or an astronaut, or a philosopher," I assisted.

His dark eyes flashed to me. "Philosopher?"

"For example."

"Is philosophy even a profession?"

I frowned and glared.

"A lot of important people have made philosophy their life's work."

"Yeah, like ten thousand years ago," he chuckled, then stopped. "Aren't you pre-law?"

I didn't remember telling him that, although I tended to be too self-conscious around him to remember anything I said to him.

"It was just an example," I insisted.

"There isn't much money in that," he told me in a protective kind of way.

"Are you going to answer my question?"

"Don't philosophers spend their days sitting around and thinking about life while they starve to death?"

I sighed, waiting for the rant to be over. I couldn't expect him to understand. I was pre-law because it was the only full scholarship I could get at Callister. I didn't mind my law classes, and my grades were good, but my father was a lawyer, and so was his father before him, and his father's father before that. One way or another, I would be forced to follow the Sheppard path. But that didn't mean I had to like it.

Cameron kicked off his shoes, swung his legs onto the bed, and slid next to me. He laid his head on the pillow, lacing his hands behind his head and gazing at the ceiling. "Philosopher," he mused with a chuckle.

His closeness was enough for me to forget my aggravation. I took a deep breath, his scent so familiar to me now. I didn't know that someone's scent could stay with me like that, even after he had gone. His dark, dangerous eyes gleamed in the moonlight.

"Did you pick your profession solely based on money?" I asked.

"Yeah. I did."

"Do you like what you do?"

"What do you think?"

I was thrilled that he was taking part in the interrogation, but what I was thinking had nothing to do with words and everything to do with us being in his bed, just a few inches apart.

"Well, I suppose you make a lot of money doing it," I said.

"Money isn't everything."

He was full of contradictions. "I thought you said you chose to do this for the money?"

"I said I *did* pick my profession for money. Past tense. I think you and I both know that I have more money than I know what to do with. If it were still only about money, I would have quit a long time ago."

"So why don't you just stop doing it then? Take your money and get out?"

I took a breath.

"I'm just curious," I whispered.

"I know."

He sighed and stared at the ceiling. "I can't just run away from it. Once you're in, you're in it for life. If you try to leave, people become suspicious. They think that you're either talking to the cops or you're changing your affiliation."

"Who cares what people think?"

"People who talk, who leave, get hunted down and killed."

I tried as best I could to hide the shudder that was fermenting at the nape of my neck.

Cameron yawned and swept his hand over his face again. I wondered if his weariness made him more tolerant of my questions, made him answer them without editing or sugar-coating. I felt like I was taking advantage of him—it was a nice role reversal. My thirst for his words overpowered everything.

"Why don't you just run away? You have enough money to hide, to protect yourself, don't you?"

"Because they don't just kill you. They kill your family, your friends, everyone you know … then they kill you. There's no such thing as running away."

I gulped. "Who are *they*?"

"The people I work with." He turned his head and looked at me pleadingly. "Change of subject?"

Even I had to admit that it was too much information—more than I could immediately swallow. And what I really wanted to know was him. Everything about him. As though this would help me justify my strange pull to him, a pull that was intensified a million times over when he was here, so close to me. A pull that grew despite my knowing what he was capable of.

I *needed* him to be more human than monster.

I took a second. "Tell me about your family."

He smiled, but his eyes were cautious. "What do you want to know?"

Everything. "For starters, what does your mother do for a living?"

"She drinks," he answered promptly.

Okay. "What about your dad?"

"I don't like to talk about my father."

"Why not?"

"Because he's … not a very nice person."

"Neither are my parents," I said.

"It's not the same thing. My father's a con artist."

"Can you tell me about him?" I murmured. "Please?"

He closed his eyes. "When I lived with my mom, my dad would come strolling in every couple months with his expensive suits and big cars, while my mom and I lived in dumps. The small amount of cash my dad did give to my mom she drank away. When I went to live with my dad, I thought that things were finally going to get better. But my dad was … he wasn't who I thought he was. His money was not his own. He hung out with rich people, pretended he had money so that he could swindle old ladies out of their money …" His tired voice had started trailing.

"He must have had some money to put you through private school," I said, pressing for more.

"When I first came to live with him, he didn't know what to do with me. Eventually, though, he figured out that he could use me too. He put me in that private school and showed up once in a while with some woman who'd have money but no husband. Then he'd put on the rich, father-of-the-year act. It worked like a charm; they trusted him ... and he stole all their life savings and disappeared. The payments to the school would stop after that."

"What happened then?"

"The school sent me to live in a group home."

"Wow." I found myself instantly hating his father, a man I had never met. It was as though I were putting my own father's face on him. What Cameron's father had done to him, my father had done to Bill.

Cameron settled deeper into the pillow. "He always came back sooner or later, usually when he was getting low on cash. He'd put me back in school so that he could start the show all over again. When I got older, the cops assumed that I was his partner in crime, 'cause he kept coming back to find me, and I was the only one the women could identify. I turned fourteen, my dad disappeared again, and I got thrown in juvie when I couldn't tell the cops where he was hiding. That's when I met Spider and we cooked up a plan to sell drugs to the rich kids I went to school with. Within a month of getting back from juvie, I was making my own payments to the school and never had to depend on my dad's stolen money again."

"What happened to your dad?"

"I don't know. He came back once with some woman, but I didn't want to be associated with him and get thrown back into juvie, so I told him to stay away. I never saw him again after that."

His breathing became slower, deeper. I took another second.

"Cameron?" I said softly.

"Hmm ...?"

"Was my brother happy?"

He considered this. "Most days."

I held my breath.

"Do you think he knew he was going to die?"

There was a long pause.

"Cameron?"

He sighed. "I really wish I knew, Emmy."

After a minute, he was asleep.

He snored, just a little bit, like a subdued Darth Vader.

It was strange having him sleep next to me, so completely vulnerable that I could have killed him if I wanted to. I could have tiptoed to the kitchen and grabbed a knife. I could have plunged it into his chest. But all I wanted to do was lay my head against his chest and listen to his very human heart thump.

I lay there for a while, next to him, feeling the heat that radiated from his skin, listening to his calm, even breaths, watching his chest rise and fall in the shadows. I was exhausted. Having him there, so close, was strangely peaceful, but it didn't help me relax. I could feel every tired muscle in my body tingle. His lips seem to swell with the moonlight, as though inviting me to them. Would he notice if I pressed my lips against his?

The feeling that there was something wrong with me came back. I had to turn my back to him before I did something foolish.

But even then, his every movement made my breath quicken, as though his hand were about to cross over my hip.

When half an hour had gone by, I was wrestling with the sheets. I was afraid of waking him; I was afraid that if he awakened, he would leave.

I considered … decided, listened vigilantly. When I was sure he was in a deep sleep, I extended my hand … and very slowly slid it under his. I clasped our fingers. In an unconscious reflex, his hand squeezed mine. I felt whole, like I could let go of the bad things that had happened to me in the past, of the bad things that Cameron had done. I inhaled and I exhaled, and finally, finally I fell asleep.

****

We were awakened in the morning by the commotion of incoming guards downstairs. I woke up a few seconds before Cameron, carefully peeling my hand away from his before he could realize what I had done. My hand suddenly felt cold, unnatural, like it was missing a finger.

The front door slammed shut.

Cameron shot out of bed like a bullet and stood, disoriented and panting, every muscle of his body tightly clenched, like body armor.

"It's okay, Cameron," I gasped. I was scared of him, for him.

He turned abruptly toward my voice. His expression was ominous.

He kept his wild eyes on me. He blinked.

His fists loosened; his body drooped.

Then he sat on the edge of the bed, ran his fingers through his hair, and scratched his head, breathing with purpose. After a long second, he turned, a forced smile on his face.

"Good morning." My voice croaked a little.

"Mornin'," he answered gruffly. His cheeks were now flushed, and his hair went every which way. He was beautiful again.

"I thought you said that you don't sleep?"

"I don't ... usually," he replied with a sheepish smile.

The bedroom door was still ajar, the way Cameron had left it during the night. Meatball was already downstairs, probably checking his food bowl.

Cameron and I walked downstairs together just as Spider and Carly were walking in through the front door. Spider grimaced as soon as he saw us. Carly turned to him. "Told you he'd be here," she muttered loud enough for us to hear.

Spider turned to Cameron. "Is there a reason why you weren't answering your phone? You could've at least left us a note, man. We had no idea where you went."

Cameron cleared his throat, looked like he was about to respond, glanced at me, and flushed a little more. Guards carrying boxes were lining up at the doorway behind Spider and Carly, who were blocking their entrance. Carly moved ahead to let them through. Spider followed her, making sure to throw a glare at me before he disappeared into the kitchen.

Some of the guards shot a look in our direction as they walked through.

Cameron sent a small, discreet smile my way. Then he walked out the door, passing Griff on his way out.

"Hey, Ginger," Griff called out, sounding chipper. He peered at me over the box of frozen dinners he was carrying. He paused at the door to take off his shoes, balancing the box at the same time. As Cameron passed, his head momentarily turned toward Griff, but he kept walking across the yard to the waiting vans.

Griff eyed me top to bottom. "Did you just get up?" he asked in passing and continued into the kitchen. I realized, mortified, that I was still wearing my pajamas.

The second I was back in Cameron's room, I wanted to leave it and go find him, as if he'd stolen something of mine—something vital, like my ability to breathe, to think normally. What had happened last night? Nothing. I had held his hand. He had held it back. All night, nothing more than that had happened. And this left me wanting more, as though I had been given a taste of freedom after being locked inside myself since Bill's death.

I managed to grab a quick shower and get dressed with whatever clothes were within reach.

Then I bounced back down the stairs and into the kitchen, where Rocco was busy putting the groceries away. Cameron, Carly, and Spider were sitting at the kitchen table, murmuring over paperwork. Cameron, who was also freshly showered and dressed, sneaked a look as I walked into the kitchen. His eyes sparkled. His lips curved at the corners as he bent back over the documents in front of him before Spider and Carly ever noticed the momentary lapse of attention. My heart was exploding, and I felt a little lightheaded. My skin was tingling all over. With a face-splitting smile, I helped Rocco put the groceries away, tucking them into whatever free space we could find.

I fixed myself a bowl of cereal even though it was already past lunchtime. Then, not wanting to disturb the business meeting and feel Spider's resentment, I strolled to the back deck, where I sat to eat breakfast alone.

The sky was gray; the air was still and muggy. A storm was brewing.

I watched the dark clouds billowing above, threatening rain for the day. Underneath them, the far-reaching forest was resiliently calm, and a thin layer of fog draped the treetops. I closed my eyes and took a deep breath; the mossy, damp smell of the woods that surrounded me was a newfound reassurance, as if the blanket of greenery would keep the storm from ever really reaching me. *An uncanny reaction for a city girl,* I thought.

When Cameron came to sit next to me, he put his feet on the table, and we watched the dark sky while the clouds debated whether to burst or keep moving.

He was next to me, but he was far away.

I turned to look at him just as a raindrop splashed against his forehead.

"Why didn't you listen to me?" he asked, his voice distant. "When I told you to stay away from the projects, why did you come back anyway?"

If his eyes hadn't been locked with mine, if my brain worked when he was near me, if I were able to lie to him, I could have come up with a million plausible excuses. Except that I couldn't lie to him, and I couldn't tell him the truth, either. Was I even sure what the truth was, exactly? I broke the spell and started pulling on a thread that was unraveling from my shorts.

When I looked up, Cameron had turned his attention back to the sky. He was far away again. My lack of response had been enough of an answer for him?

After a short while, a steady rain started coming down.

CHAPTER ELEVEN

FUN AND GAMES

Cameron had announced to me that he wanted to do something fun. We headed down the driveway, with Tiny straggling behind. Rain pelted down on us, and we had to pick up speed.

When we came to the bend in the driveway, something at the back of the property caught my eye. Griff and Spider were standing near the tree line at Griff's usual spot. Spider's face and his shaking finger were very close to Griff's face. His chest was pumping; his face was beet red. His lips were moving rapidly, angrily. Griff had his back to me, with his head bent.

While I was quickly taking in all these things, I hadn't noticed that my pace had slowed and Cameron had come back to get me.

"You don't have to wait for Tiny," he told me, grinning.

Tiny had caught up to us, panting. He glanced knowingly at the back of the property before catching my eye, but remained silent.

When we got to the garage, Cameron stood by with an even larger grin on his face.

I smiled back. "What?"

"Which one?" he asked, waving his hand back and forth along the lineup of cars like a game-show host.

The smile was washed from my face. I shook my head in disbelief. Was this Cameron's idea of "fun"?

159

Cameron nodded as if he'd heard my thoughts. "They're your cars. You should know how to drive them."

I'd only had my driver's license for a few months. Getting a license was one of those Real World things that I had wanted to achieve. I celebrated my feat by buying a car from our landlord for a little less than $200. It was a baby-blue 1991 Buick Roadmaster station wagon with wood paneling and a sunroof that was covered with a garbage bag because it leaked when it rained. Sometimes I could even afford to put a little bit of gas in it. The car was made of real steel, which was crucial. The bent stop signs and crushed garbage cans on my street testified to my driving abilities.

I remembered the recently added dents on my Buick and looked at the shiny, fragile cars lined up next to me. I imagined the kind of damage I could do to them … I lost my breath and leaned against one of the colorful toys to steady myself.

"Ah!" Cameron said, waking me from my nightmarish trance. "The Maserati! A bold choice."

He went to grab the keys from the back wall.

"Cameron, I can't … I have no idea how to drive … this … thing …"

"It's amazingly easy," he reassured me. "I'll show you."

Cameron climbed into the driver's seat, while Tiny squeezed into the backseat, setting his handgun next to him. Cameron spent the next few minutes with his eyebrows raised, suppressing a laugh, as I attempted to close the trick door. When I gave up, he got out of the car and closed it for me.

Tiny was in on it. I was sure they were making faces when I turned my head to struggle with the stupid seat belt. Cameron ended up leaning over me to help me with that too. As he pulled the strap over my lap, our eyes locked briefly, and I let my smile reach my eyes. His cheeks colored a bit; he looked down and then away and fumbled to get the strap secured as quickly as possible.

Driving out of the garage, Cameron looked at everything and anything that wasn't in my general direction. At the end of the driveway, he decelerated just long enough for the soaking-wet armed guard to peer in and quickly step away. I realized that we weren't just driving—we were driving off the property, something I'd been fantasizing about the way a pregnant woman might crave fried chicken. I also realized that I was allowed to leave the property as long as Cameron was with me.

Within seconds, the car was racing at an incredible speed down the gravel road. I held on to the door handle and the middle console for dear life, while Cameron explained over the roar of the motor how the transmission worked. But I heard nothing. The trees by the side of the road were a big emerald blur, and I was seated so close to the ground, it was like sliding on a bobsled.

The rain was hitting the windshield hard. We raced through sharp curves, never slowing down.

Cameron was completely calm. And then he happened to look over at me. He slowed down a bit, and I was able to swallow again.

We had been driving for quite a while, at least fifteen miles, I thought. Though I wasn't sure, I didn't think that I had seen any other exits off the gravel road. I definitely had not seen any other houses. We were in the middle of nowhere.

When the gravel road turned onto the paved highway, Cameron turned the car around and stopped.

"Ready?"

He was already out of the car, making his way around to the passenger side. He opened the door and stood in the pouring rain. I scooted over to the driver's side, catching a glimpse of Tiny's reflection as I adjusted the rear-view mirror. His brow was knotted and his pupils were dilated, as though his life were already flashing before his eyes.

Even though Cameron coached me through, the car kept jerking forward and then it would stall; Tiny's head slammed into the seat in front of him every time the car came to a jolting stop. After a while I was able to make the car move more than a few inches at a time, and before long, we were coasting along the muddy road.

The car did corner curves effortlessly. It was—almost— exhilarating. Tiny's knuckles had gone white, never loosening their grip on the door handle. Cameron seemed to be looking on proudly, enjoying the ride.

And then it all went very wrong.

I got to a curve faster than I expected.

I turned the wheel, but nothing happened.

I braked hard; the car fishtailed in the mud.

Cameron was looking ahead, one hand on the dashboard, the other pushing me against my seat.

"Hold on … we're gonna crash," he said evenly.

We all held our breath.

I touched the brake again as a reflex. The car did a full circle in the mud and slid, picking up speed in the process.

The last thing I remembered was Cameron ordering me to cover my face, which I did without thinking. Next came a loud bang, swiftly followed by the screech of wood against metal and the sound of shattering glass. The engine ticked. And then all was silent—just the sound of the rain against the hood, which echoed our tandem breathing.

"Em … Are you hurt?" Cameron's voice was anxious, finally.

"No," I answered from behind my hands.

"Let's see." He tugged my hands away and turned my face to him. When my eyes flicked open, he was laughing. "You just crashed a three-hundred-thousand-dollar car!"

In the back, Tiny was giggling too, his large belly moving up and down. He was covered with shards of broken glass from the small back window, which had been pierced by the branch of an evergreen. The car was on its side, half in the thread of a ditch, half in the woods. Cameron, Tiny, and I were also hanging sideways, our seatbelts holding us to our seats. Outside my window I saw a lot of mud. Nothing about this was funny, or fun, to me.

After trying to push the car out, we all stood in the rain and watched the Maserati sink deeper into the mud. When realization set in, Tiny took out a short-wave radio and called for someone to come dig the car out. I recognized Spider's sharp voice on the other end.

My mood had improved after the rain ceased, and Cameron and I walked the rest of the way home. The road was flooded in parts, and my beloved sneakers were engorged with mud.

At Cameron's command, Tiny had stayed behind, watching uneasily as the boss left without armed defense.

Help drove past us in the form of a black pickup truck: Spider and four sodden guards, grimly holding onto shovels in the bed of the truck. After our bit of fun, Cameron was in an excellent mood. So when Spider's passing glower landed on me again, I decided to seize the moment.

"Spider doesn't … like me much," I mused.

"He's just being overprotective."

"Am I that much of a threat to you?"

Cameron grimaced and looked at the road ahead. "More than you know," he mumbled as he hopped over a large puddle. "I meant Carly, not me. Spider is trying to protect Carly." He turned around, extending his hand to help me jump over the puddle. The electricity that shot through me as our hands connected sent me heaving forward. I missed my jump, badly, and splashed both of us.

"Why would I want to hurt Carly?"

"It's not a matter of you wanting to hurt her. It's who you remind her of every time she sees you." Cameron had an intent look on his face, willing me to make the connection.

"My brother?"

"Bill and Carly used to date."

"But I don't look anything like him."

"Your hair might not be blonde," he said, "but you're very much like Bill."

This made me smile, despite the hair comment. "How long did they date?"

"Awhile. Longer than any of the other girls he dated." He waited until our eyes met. "Before Carly, Bill never let any girl stick around long enough to get to know him."

Part of me wondered if this remark had been added for my benefit, if Cameron was referring to himself … or if I was reading more into it than there was. The other part of me was trying not to ogle: Cameron's soaked T-shirt clung to him … it was very hard not to ogle.

I looked away.

"When it came to Carly, Bill was … different," he said with difficulty. "He told her everything, no matter how bad … and there was lots of bad stuff."

"He must have loved her very much," I said. "To feel like he could tell her everything without being afraid of what she might think. Takes a lot of guts and trust."

"Carly's a tough cookie. She can handle a lot more than most girls. Before Carly came around, your brother had been with lots of girls, and he left a path of destruction behind him. Spider tried to warn Carly about his … bad habits. She didn't listen." Cameron's voice turned sharp. "Spider was right."

I hoped with every fiber of my being that he would negate the next thing that came out of my mouth. "He cheated on her, didn't he?"

"Yeah. Except that it was much worse than that."

I couldn't imagine what was worse than cheating on someone you loved and who loved you.

"He got the other girl pregnant."

He was right: this was much worse.

"Who was she?" I demanded.

He gazed ahead. "You've already met her and her son. The kid is Bill's spitting image."

From a corner of my mind, I dredged up the picture I had of my brother as a child: blond, curly hair; sun-kissed skin; gray eyes. He had kept those traits as an adult … and I had seen those same traits very recently.

"Daniel," I gasped. "Bill fathered a child with Frances."

"Spider confronted him once," Cameron said. "When your brother was acting … weird, Spider accused him of cheating, right in front of Carly and me. Bill denied it, and Carly believed him. Hell, I even believed him—not that it had anything to do with me. Bill could be pretty convincing when he needed to be." It started drizzling again, but we kept our slow pace. "After he died, we found out about Frances when she came looking for money."

"Did Bill know she was pregnant?"

"He must've. Her belly was already out to here when he died," Cameron said, holding his arms out in front of his stomach.

"Spider must have felt vindicated," I guessed, unable to keep the irritation out of my voice.

"Not really—he was too busy with Carly, with bringing her back, to worry about being right. When Bill died, Carly was devastated. Then when Frances came around, she still wouldn't believe that Bill had cheated on her. But when the baby was born and he looked so much like Bill, Carly was ..." He took a second and brushed his hand over his face. "We didn't think she could take any more."

While my brain took a moment to recoup, my mouth asked, "Are Spider and Carly related?"

Cameron burst out laughing. "What? God no! It would be pretty sick if they were!" His eyes narrowed. "Why do you ask?"

"He seems very protective of her. I just thought ..."

"There's nothing platonic about Spider's need to protect Carly." His laugh cooled to a chuckle, and he explained, "Spider has been in love with Carly for at least as long as I've known him— probably longer. They don't like to talk about their childhood, so I don't know a whole lot. From the bits and pieces I've heard, they grew up together; Carly had a creep for a father, and Spider has been watching over her his whole life."

He leaned in and lowered his voice, in case the trees heard us. "When Bill and Carly started dating and they got really serious, I thought Spider was going to snap. I figured he was either going to kill Bill or himself. Instead, he spent his time trying to prove to Carly that Bill wasn't good enough for her."

Something didn't fit. "Bill has been gone a long time, and Carly seems okay with me now," I said. My interactions with Carly had grown from her shooting deathly glares and screaming profanities at me to something civilized, almost friendly.

165

Cameron grinned. "Spider and I are just as surprised as you are. We both thought she would have been mad longer than that."

My head shot up. "You talk to Spider about me?"

He kept his eyes trained ahead.

Thunder roared, and new rows of black clouds rolled in. The mist had dropped from the treetops to the ground, making the gravel road barely discernible just a few feet ahead of us. Cameron and I walked closely and silently for a while. Questions still colored my thoughts. For one, what did my brother's idiotic mistake have to do with me? For another, if Carly was okay with my being there, why did Spider still feel the need to scowl every time he saw me?

"There's more to this than what Bill did to Carly," I said, watching Cameron carefully. "There's some other reason Spider doesn't like me."

Cameron slowed our already-slow pace. When he looked up, I could see the struggle. "He doesn't trust you, and he definitely doesn't trust me with you."

"Why?"

"For the same reasons he never trusted your brother, even before Bill and Carly met."

All of a sudden, I had a sick sensation in the pit of my stomach—I somehow knew that I wouldn't like what Cameron was about to tell me.

And he took his time telling me, prolonging the agony.

"People like you, like your brother—people who come from money like you … will always have your family money, your family name, your family power to fall back on and protect you, cover you, when things get bad."

I tried to keep my voice normal, though a storm was raging inside me. "Bad as in getting caught. Arrested."

"Among other things," he said, refusing to look at me. "When people like Carly and Spider and me get into trouble, the only thing that people see is that we come from the streets. They're happy when we get caught, because we deserve whatever comes to us. There aren't any search parties when one of us goes missing. No one cares if we turn up dead—we're just another crime statistic. If the ship starts to sink, we go down with it. No one will be there with a life raft for us."

I couldn't imagine ever going to my parents for any kind of life raft. My family was more apt to stand on the luxury liner beside the sinking ship—entertaining, diverting the guests, so that no one would notice that one of us was drowning.

"Do you think the same way that Spider does? Do you see me as one of those people who skips town when things get hard?"

"I think that you have a lot more options than anyone else I know."

"You're judging me because of the amount of money my parents have in their bank account?"

Cameron finally looked at me through narrowed eyes. "I've been judged my whole life because of the money my parents didn't have."

"I am not my parents' money, and neither was my brother. I didn't get to choose who my parents were going to be or where I grew up."

"Neither did I," he snapped. "You can run away from your big house, pick the crappiest school you can find, and live in the ugliest house in the worst neighborhood ... none of that changes where you come from, Emmy. To the rest of the world, you and your brother will always look like two confused rich kids who are trying to slum it because of their issues with their parents. But when you're done slumming it, you get to go back to the big house and the bank accounts. I don't have that comfort. This is it for me," he said bitterly, throwing his arms out. "I have nowhere else to go. Fancy schools and rich friends didn't change the fact that I'm just another street kid."

The sky exploded and the rain poured. I hadn't realized that Cameron and I had stopped in the middle of the road, and that was where we stood, glaring at each other, getting drenched.

"So you don't trust me ... just because my parents have money."

"I didn't say that," he said through gritted teeth.

"What are you saying, Cameron? Why did you say that Spider doesn't trust you with me?"

"Because he's smarter than me. He knows that I like having you around too much when you shouldn't even be here in the first place. And I don't know if you've noticed, but I tend to spill my guts when I'm around you. I'm in a business where people who talk too much disappear. Permanently. And people like you get taken out even before they get the chance to snitch on people like me."

His body stiffened. His nostrils were flared, his lips a bare line. He stared fixedly at me as veins became visible on his temple, pulsating, warning. The darkness that still lay inside him, begging to come out.

I wanted to make myself small, cower at his feet like a beaten dog. I felt my face screw up and my hands start to tremble.

Cameron suddenly dropped his head. "Emmy … God, I'm sorry … I don't know what's wrong with me. I—" He took a deep breath, then blew it out slowly.

When he glanced up, the monster was gone.

"Emmy, I didn't mean to scare you. It's just so confusing for me to have you here." The rain dripped from his straggly hair into his eyes. He looked dismal and beautiful, all at once.

I stood a little straighter and tucked an errant hair behind my ear.

I found myself wanting nothing more than to make him happy again, wishing that I had never decided to clear the air about Spider. As though keeping the beast away was in my contract. And this realization scared me more than the words that had come out of his mouth. I couldn't resist him. The good. The bad.

I dangled a smile at the corner of my lips. It took him a while, but he forced a lackluster smile in return.

"Can we start over?" I asked.

"I don't know. Can we?"

I considered and smiled wider. "What's your last name, Cameron?"

He smiled a little wider too. "You know, no one has dared to ask me that question in a really long time. I don't think anyone here knows my real last name, except for Rocco and Spider."

I waited, tapping my foot in the puddle we had been standing in. I thought it must be odd to be surrounded by people who had no idea who you were. And then I realized that this wasn't much different from my own life in Callister.

Cameron looked pensive—another of his private debates. Finally he shook his head in defeat. "I can't believe I'm telling you this … My last name is Hillard."

My thoughts began engraving his name inside the walls of my head, like a student at a blackboard during detention. Repeating *Cameron Hillard* over and over again until it sunk in.

"Nice to meet you, Cameron Hillard. I'm Emily Sheppard."

Cameron just stood and watched me; his gaze was penetrating. I felt as though he wanted me to do something. I extended my sweaty hand to him so that he could shake it. So that we could start over.

He grabbed my hand and pulled me into him. He laced the fingers of his free hand into my hair and rested my head against his chest. I could hear it. His heart. It was in there, beating as fast as mine.

Thunder and lightning crashed. The fog was starting to lift, but the rain was still blinding.

"We should go," Cameron said, stepping back. He pulled me behind him and we jogged the rest of the way back to the mansion. I was startled by the two soaked guards who appeared out of the fog as we neared the property line. They quickly receded when they saw Cameron.

When we made it back to the house, we were breathless, covered in mud, and soaking wet. Puddles were rapidly forming around our feet on the marble floor.

I watched, my pupils wide, while Cameron stripped down to his boxer shorts.

"Wait here," he ordered with renewed energy and ran off through the kitchen. He came back with a bath towel in his hand and another around his waist. He draped the towel over my shoulders and held it so that I could get undressed under it. "I promise I won't look," he said.

Shivering, I removed my clothes while Cameron looked away. Part of me wanted him to look.

I relieved Cameron of his post and draped the towel tightly around my torso. My teeth chattering, I flew upstairs and stood under a scorching hot shower until I was sure I had accomplished my mission of getting a first-degree burn. Dressed and warm, I bounded back down the stairs and walked in on five nearly naked men standing at the front entrance.

Piles of wet, dirty clothes had been thrown on the floor. It seemed that, like Cameron and me, everyone had decided to peel off their clothes at the door rather than track water and mud all over the house. The foyer floor was now a brown lake.

I waited for them to move out of the way so I could get by. Clad only in their soaked underwear, the trembling men largely disregarded me and argued about who had the highest rank and therefore first dibs on a hot shower. They kept the argument going as they made their way downstairs.

A bare-chested Griff was left behind in the foyer, still struggling to get his soaking-wet socks off his feet. He had a sour look on his face, his mood matching the stormy weather.

"Hey, Griff," I said.

Griff lifted his head, acknowledged me with a grunt. He finally managed to pull one of his socks off and proceeded to kick it onto one of the piles of wet clothes, but he slipped and almost fell on his behind.

"I saw you with Spider earlier; he looked pretty upset," I said. "Did you get in trouble for slacking off while they were gone?"

"That and other stuff." After tugging for a while, Griff pulled off his wet jeans and stood unabashedly in his underwear. I looked away.

The uncommon smell of a home-cooked meal was coming from the kitchen. The prospect of food always cheered me up.

"Are you at least coming in for supper?" I offered, motioning toward the kitchen.

"No thanks. I think you've gotten me in enough trouble as it is. I'll be lucky if I live to see another day."

"What do you mean?"

Griff's eyes shot over my shoulder. "Never mind. I gotta go," he said, his voice low and panicked. He rushed past me and disappeared into the basement.

I spun around. Cameron was behind me, leaning against the doorway into the kitchen, his arms casually crossed over his chest. I went to him.

Carly was standing over the stove, vehemently stirring foodstuff in a large frying pan while barking orders at Spider, who was dutifully cutting vegetables. Cameron led me to a table set for five, where mismatched candles awaited us. Rocco was already sitting there, eagerly holding his plate over his heart with both hands.

"Where's everyone else?" I asked.

"It's just the family tonight," Cameron said.

Rocco glanced at his big brother with interest, momentarily loosening his grip on his plate while Carly and Spider filtered in with masses of food. Burritos, fajitas, guacamole.

****

Rocco was still picking at the crumbs on the counter when the first hand was being dealt out. After much debate between Carly and Cameron, we were playing poker—Texas Hold 'em. The stakes were extremely high: a week's worth of laundry duty.

Bill had taught me how to play poker when I was eight, and I'd always thought I was a pretty good bluffer, but after just a few hands I was out of chips. I didn't feel too bad, though—Carly and Rocco were in the same boat.

It was getting late. Cameron was sitting behind a fortress of chips and Spider was barely hanging on. Rocco had his head on the table, and I was leaning mine on my fist.

"Is it always like this?" I whispered to Carly.

"You mean, does Cameron always win?"

I thought about it and nodded.

She squinted in Cameron's direction. "He wins, but he cheats."

I heard a grumble from Cameron's chair.

"How?" I gasped, my attention fully on Carly.

"He counts cards and he reads people." She paused and watched my puzzled expression with enjoyment. "He knows what people are thinking just by looking at them. Cameron didn't brag about that to you?"

I shook my head.

Carly shrugged. "That's surprising."

I turned my eyes to Cameron. "Is that true? Can you really tell what people are thinking?"

"Not exactly," he answered with a sharp glance in Carly's direction. "Carly likes to embellish."

Spider pushed the rest of his chips into the pot and mumbled, "All in." Cameron immediately called. They overturned their cards on the table and waited for the dealer's cards to unfold. The first three cards gave Cameron a flush. Spider waited for the next two, hoping something would save him.

But the game was no longer of any interest to me. "What part of it is embellished?"

"I don't know what people are thinking," Cameron clarified. "All I can tell is if someone is nervous, or mad, or happy, or bluffing their brains out ..." He winked at me.

The fourth card was a nine of diamonds. Spider jumped a little. Another nine or a king would give him a full house to beat Cameron.

This made me wonder. "Are some people easier to read than others?"

"Everyone has their own quirks that give them away," he said. "Though, yes, some people are definitely easier to read than others."

"Well, do you count cards too? Because *that* is cheating."

"Poker is more about knowing your opponent than counting cards," he said, glancing at Carly again. "I do count the odds in my head. It's not a sure thing, but"—he smirked at Spider—"for example, I know that Spider has almost no chance of winning this hand."

"We'll see," Spider retorted.

Carly turned over a queen. Spider bent his head in defeat.

CHAPTER TWELVE

A DARK PLACE

It rained, for days on end. The front hall was mostly flooded—I only noticed because I had to trudge through the gathering water on my way to meeting Cameron in the kitchen in the morning. Otherwise, the rain went mostly unnoticed by me.

Early mornings were my favorite. They were the only time that I had alone with Cameron before the rest of the house awoke and Rocco started following us around.

Sometimes I found Cameron walking through the front door, carrying his clothes to the bathroom where he would shower, as though he'd slept outside. I didn't know where he slept. I wondered, but I didn't know.

Most of the questions floating around my brain went unanswered because I didn't ask them. After the car crash, after the brief emergence of Cameron's monstrous counterpart, I tried to keep him happy and keep his demons away. This wasn't an easy task. Rocco and I were a good team. We kept things light; we kept Cameron's light on. Cameron would laugh with us, sometimes.

After the crash, Cameron was distant with me. He was polite, I observed, but he didn't speak much, as though he were trying to push me away. He didn't hold my hand again, or hold me in his arms. He didn't touch me at all. Not at first.

Then there were the other, darker times, fleeting moments when his eyes would veer to an empty corner. A glaze would wash his face, and the premature wrinkles around his eyes resurfaced. I noticed that the monster seemed to seep through when Spider or Carly came to whisper something in his ear. Business, I assumed. But who knew? One more question I didn't ask.

I hated these moments.

Eventually, though, his eyes would find me, and he would come back. I'd wonder where he'd been—what dark corner he'd come out of. It scared me, that thing that lurked inside him. It scared me because of what it did to him: made him dissolve.

I also noticed Rocco's immeasurable attachment to his older brother. Wherever Cameron went, so did Rocco, eagerly. Cameron would flash me a smile as his brother tried to impress us with his newfound fighting skills, or tried to match whatever weights Cameron was lifting in the workout room. Carly and Spider would join us once in a while; one was never without the other. They mostly kept to themselves. I really liked Carly. Spider was tolerable.

With the torrential weather, I had expected the house to be bustling with people trying to get out of the rain. Yet the house was quieter than usual. Guards only came in for mealtimes, and some for sleep.

The third thing I noticed was that even the mid-rankers now ate in the basement kitchen. It seemed that when Cameron was around, the guards stayed away and all upstairs meals were eaten with just Cameron, Carly, Rocco, Spider, and me. With every day that passed, Cameron was getting better at keeping the devil away—and I was getting better at it too. Cameron's smiles became more tender and his eyes softer. I could feel him tilting toward me when we happened to be near one another.

I saw Griff briefly a few times, rushing in out of the wet weather for his meals. He'd glance at me but ignored me otherwise, as if I weren't there at all. I felt guilty, like I had abandoned him. He was obviously upset. But I couldn't confront him without making

Cameron wary or Spider unnecessarily suspicious. Although Spider had started to relax around me somewhat, which seemed to please Cameron and Carly, I didn't want to give him ammunition to speak against me further.

The last thing I noticed was that I was sleeping—dreamlessly and peacefully. Every night I dreaded leaving Cameron to get some shut-eye; he practically had to drag me off the couch. But as soon as my head hit the pillow, I was out; not even Meatball's snoring could wake me. Maybe it was the soothing way the rain pelted against the tin roof, like drops hitting a champagne glass. Maybe it was something else.

One evening, Rocco had fallen asleep on the couch with the remote control tightly clenched in his hand and the TV stuck on the Weather Channel. Cameron had disappeared, and I was considering going to look for him when he reappeared, soaking wet.

"Holy cow! What happened to you?"

"I had to run to my car," he told me breathlessly. "I have a surprise for you."

My heart dropped. The last time he had a surprise for me, it ended up costing him, or me, $300,000. The Maserati was still stuck in the mud.

"Don't worry," he said. "You can't crash this one."

Although Cameron claimed he couldn't read thoughts, I'd started to wonder if that was entirely true.

He pulled a box out and handed it to me. "Coppola," he said, like that would mean something to me.

I looked down, then up. "They made a movie of *Rumble Fish*?"

"Now you can finally find out how the story goes." Cameron put his finger to his lips and led me out of the living room.

Hanging out with Rocco was great, but for Cameron and me, finding time alone had become an art.

"Don't get too excited," he warned as we walked upstairs to his room (and he read my mind again). "The kid at the video store said it's pretty old and filmed entirely in black and white."

The thudding in my chest had nothing to do with the movie.

After Cameron stuck the disc in the player, we sat down, throwing our feet on the coffee table. As the opening credits rolled, Cameron did something I wasn't prepared for: his hand crawled over to mine. His fingers slipped between mine and squeezed. I looked straight ahead, feeling the wrecking ball pounding against my chest.

I peeked at him from the corner of my eye.

Holding Cameron's hand was much more nerve-racking when he was awake to witness it.

Then my eyes were drawn to a movement over Cameron's shoulder. Outside the wall of windows, I saw Carly and Spider by the pool. They were walking together very closely but not actually touching—something I had noticed them do. They walked to the pool house and closed the door behind them.

"Do you think that Carly and Spider are dating now?" I wondered aloud while I tried to persuade my heart to lighten up so that my head and hand would stop pulsating.

"I know they are," he said. "They try to hide it, but everyone around here knows. We just let them think we don't notice."

I couldn't understand why Spider would go to so much trouble trying to hide something he had waited his whole life for. "Why do they try to hide it?"

"They don't want the fact that they're ... together to be held against them."

"I don't understand," I confessed, as I often did around him.

He took a long, ragged breath. "In our line of business, if someone sees that you care for someone else, it's a weakness—something that people will use against you, or try to control you with."

"How?" I looked earnestly at Cameron while he fidgeted in his seat.

"Well, think about it. What if somebody threatened to hurt someone you cared about ... like your parents or your brother, for example? What would you do to keep them safe or prevent them from getting hurt?"

"Anything," I whispered with concentration. I had often lain in bed at night, asking myself what I would have done differently if I'd had a chance with Bill, a chance to save his life. The answer was always the same—anything and everything.

"Right," he agreed reluctantly. "So somebody who knows that—"

"Somebody like who?"

His face hardened. "A bad person."

"How bad?"

"The worst," he muttered.

I knew I ought to be scared, but that was no longer a feeling I had around Cameron. Despite everything, I felt safest when I was with him. "You were saying?"

He looked at me blankly.

"That the bad person who knows who you love—" I prompted.

"The very bad person will use that to control you." He squinted. "Can we stop here?"

"No. We can't."

I was unwavering. Cameron's world had once been my brother's world—I needed to know about it, however dire. I needed to know where Bill had been, where Cameron still went.

He sighed and paused the movie. He let go of my hand and rotated his body toward me, resting his elbow on the back of the couch and leaning his head against his fist. "Imagine what Spider would do if someone ever took Carly and threatened to hurt her if Spider didn't do what they wanted."

The image of a crazed Al Pacino brandishing a machine gun in *Scarface* came to mind. "Okay ..."

"Someone ... a bad person, who knows that Spider would do anything to keep Carly safe will use it to control him by threatening to hurt Carly and force Spider to do something that he doesn't want to do or can't do."

"So people use other people as leverage to get what they want."

Cameron slightly cleared his throat. "Right."

"People do that all the time, Cameron. It's not the end of the world. People can move past it." I had hoped to be proof of that ... someday. "It's not worth hiding your love away," I added, artfully.

"That's why I don't want to talk about this with you," he said with exasperation. "You've got this naive view of the world. You're beautifully naive, Emmy ... I don't want to change that."

"I'm not naive. What did I say that was so naive?"

"In my world," he admitted, watching my face, "when a loved one gets ... taken ... they don't come out of it unscathed ... if they're lucky enough to come out of it at all."

"They're killed?" I tried to keep my voice professional, non-scared, non-naive.

"Sometimes."

"How often?"

The look on his face was enough response.

"Why—" I had to adjust my tone again. "Why wouldn't they just let people go once they got what they wanted? Why does anyone need to get—"

"It's more complicated than that. Sometimes you can't do what they want you to do without getting a whole lot of other people killed. And sometimes the person you love is killed ... just because you love them."

"That doesn't make any sense," I said.

He leaned in and his eyes held mine. "What would you do if the person you loved was hurt? What would you do to the person who hurt them?"

"I would hunt them down and hurt them. Kill them." I was taken aback by the violence in my own voice.

"And then you would have gang war, which was probably what they wanted in the first place."

"Like street shootings and stuff like that?"

"That's the stuff you see on TV—the unorganized street gang stuff. In the real, organized world, no one sees gang wars. You don't hear about mass shootings. You might hear about weird disappearances or house fires or car accidents or robberies gone bad. Normal stuff that could happen to anyone on any day." He paused. His face was impenetrable. "What are you thinking about?"

179

"You tell me. Can't you just read my mind?"

"I don't know what you're thinking, but I know that every time I open my mouth you get a little more nervous and eager all at once ... I don't understand it." He shook his head and waited.

I hadn't realized that I was holding my breath. He was very observant.

I exhaled and swallowed. "Why would anyone want a gang war?"

He shrugged lightly. "For the same reasons that the rest of the world starts wars—because they want something. Territory, power, money, intimidation ... there are a lot of reasons that people start wars. But in our business, they're usually a bad idea— eventually they attract too much attention."

"Like when too many weird things start happening to too many people."

"Precisely." His expression was getting increasingly tense. "We wouldn't start a war unless everyone agreed."

"Who's everyone?"

"Let's just say it's a bunch of bosses who sit down and make all the decisions for the good of the business."

"Like a board of directors?"

He chewed on this. "Sure. The board of directors."

"Are Carly and Spider on this board?"

"No, they work directly for me."

"But you're on the board."

He smiled wryly. "Kind of."

"What happens if the directors don't agree?" I couldn't imagine that the vote would be put to the stockholders.

"Majority rules, usually. Otherwise, there's one person who runs the board and who has the right to make the final call."

I was amazed by how abnormally normal it seemed. "Kind of like a CEO?"

"CEO? That's a good way of putting it." His eyes lit up a bit. "You seem to know a lot about this stuff."

"Looks like I was born to do this. Maybe I could start working for you too."

Cameron's expression grew severe. "Don't ever joke about that, Emmy. That will never happen."

I decided to move away from the job hunt and continue the inquisition. "What happens if someone doesn't follow the rules? What if they don't follow the board's decision or they just do what they want without going through the board?"

"You mean, what happens when someone goes rogue? Then you have a big problem. The board has to decide what they want to do about it."

"Can they decide to kill that person?" I realized my voice was barely audible.

Cameron started fidgeting.

"Yes. They can."

"Have you ever had to make that kind of decision when you were on the board?"

Cameron pressed his lips together. "I don't want to lie to you."

"So don't. Just tell me the truth."

"I can't. There are some things that I can't talk to you about."

"I need to know," I admitted. Then I admitted more. "I need to understand you, Cameron."

"That's the problem, Emmy. You're trying to understand me, but what I do isn't who I am." The full power of his gaze was on me now. "The thought of you seeing me this way, of knowing this other side of my life that is so … it makes me feel sick." Cameron took both my hands in his.

I wanted to reach out, press the palm of my hand against his cheek.

He said, "I trust you, and you can ask me anything else you want. But please don't ask me that."

A moment of wordlessness passed between us. I inhaled, realizing that I already knew the answer, and that I wished I didn't. What did that mean? What did that say about me? That I could … that I could love him, despite what he did but *wasn't*? That I was prepared to blind myself to all the horrible things he probably did … from all the things he *did* do? What did it say about us if he would never be able to tell me everything?

181

Us.

I exhaled.

"The night I got here, Rocco told Carly she wasn't supposed to use real names."

"Carly's temper gets her in trouble a lot." Cameron gave a short sigh. "Nicknames are insurance. We come into contact with a lot of people every day. Any one of them could snitch on us, sell us out. It's a lot harder for cops to narrow their investigation on some guy called Bubba or Tiny or Kid."

I thought about this. "What's your nickname?"

He shrugged. "I never really got the chance to get one ... but your brother used to call me Kid."

A lump rose in my throat. I glanced away.

The sun had set behind the black clouds. Other than the eerie blue glow of the TV, the room was quite dark.

Cameron restarted the movie and, in another unexpected move, put his arm around me. In the almost-darkness, I wasn't as nervous anymore. But I wasn't paying attention to the movie, either.

He had killed someone before—I had witnessed it with my own eyes. But the fact that this man had not been Cameron's first ... kill ... was starting to sink in, like a drop of dye in a glass of water. I started wondering about those people—who they were, what they might have looked like—then I stopped myself. I couldn't think of Cameron in that way. Because it wasn't who he was but what he did, I reminded myself.

Or because it only accentuated the fact that I was accepting this as normal. The fact that I was letting go of myself, of everything I believed in, blurring my own line between what I thought was right and what I knew was wrong.

I closed my eyes and rested my head on Cameron's chest. I could hear his heart pound, quick beats at first; after a while, the booming in his chest steadied and sounded more like a lullaby.

The next time I opened my eyes, everything was dark. I couldn't see a thing, yet I felt surrounded. Slowly, as my eyes adjusted to the darkness, the half-moon shapes of tombstones appeared around me. I was in a graveyard, and Cameron was standing in front of me with his back turned. He was looking at something on the ground. I approached, putting my hands on his shoulders and standing on my tiptoes to peek over him and see what he was looking at. There was nothing there.

Cameron swiveled and faced me. He smiled. When I smiled back and reached out, his face started to change. It became deformed, evil. A gun materialized in the monster's hand. I could hear someone screaming behind me. *Run, Emily!* I couldn't move. My feet were stuck in the mud. I heard gunshots—and nearly fell off the couch.

I woke up gasping for air. Cameron was holding me by the shoulders, trying to prevent me from falling face-first into the coffee table. Hot tears were streaming down my cheeks.

I twisted—there were no monsters, just Cameron's panicked gaze. "Emmy … Jesus! You were screaming."

Apparently the person screaming behind me in my dream had been me. I looked at Cameron, and as the nightmare wore off, I could feel the flow of tears increasing. Cameron clasped his arms around me and held me while I buried my head in his chest.

"It was just a dream," he shushed, almost abrasively.

I recovered slowly and lifted my head. Embarrassment flushed my cheeks. Cameron looked ill.

"Sorry," I sniffled. "I didn't mean to scare you like that."

Cameron's lips were pressed together in an unconvincing smile. "Well, looks like we're good at scaring each other." There was no humor in his voice. "No more talking about what I do; otherwise you'll never sleep again, and you'll give Meatball a heart attack."

Meatball was stationed by the coffee table with his ears flat to his head. I called him, drumming my knee, and he pattered over. I reassured him with a rub behind the ears.

"It had nothing to do with you," I lied. "I dreamed I was falling out of an airplane."

"Don't worry about it," he said, the dark veil expanding over his face. He fingered his watch but didn't look at it. "It's getting late."

He stood up, hesitated, and listlessly grazed my shoulder. "Get some sleep," he ordered.

Without saying good-night, he left the room. I heard the door gently click behind him.

I rubbed Meatball's ears until he was well recovered, and then I sat in the darkness of Cameron's room.

Chapter Thirteen

Therapy

I saw a plane today. I happened to walk to the window and look up, and there it was—a little white dot spearing through the clouds. It triggered something that had been buried deep inside me: a fading memory of that other world, the one that must still have existed beyond the sweeping forest, beyond the hidden Farm, beyond Cameron. The house in the slums of Callister, the closet-sized bedroom, the cycles of school and work and surviving ... I wondered at what point that life had begun to feel like someone else's. I wondered how long it had been since I had left that other person's life—the days, the weeks were becoming blurry to me. I wondered if anyone from that life had even noticed that I was gone.

I slowly—very slowly—climbed down the stairs, attempting to drag out the inevitable. My dream had agitated me, penetrated my bones, reawakened me. Forgoing sleep, I had spent a good chunk of the dark hours concocting stories that would better explain my reaction to Cameron's confessions. The rest of the night was burned up searching for ways to make myself look and sound convincing when I would have to lie to Cameron's face. All I could hope for was that Cameron had forgotten; but from the wounded expression on his face before he ran out on me—a picture that was now cruelly ingrained in my brain—hope was fruitless.

I let Meatball out of the house. He raced away at full speed as music pulsated in the distance. Griff, who was standing guard at his usual spot on the property, looked as miserable as I did. I considered further delaying the inevitable, going out there and merging our gloom. But I didn't. It was too hot outside, I was entangled in enough turmoil, and Griff had glowered even more the second he had noticed me standing in the doorway.

The drama boiling in the kitchen only firmed up my decision not to deal with Griff (postponing another unavoidable). I closed the front door and followed Rocco's loud and agitated voice into the kitchen.

"This is stupid. I'm not doing it!" I heard him yell.

"As long as you stay here, you will do what you're told." Cameron's tone was unforgiving.

I shivered and stepped through the threshold just as Rocco went whizzing by, almost crashing into me.

He stopped in front of me, his eyes narrowed. "You put him up to this."

While the list of things that I could have done to wrong Rocco ran through my head, my eyes sought silent assistance from Cameron, who was sitting at the large table, absorbed in the paperwork in front of him.

He glanced up, barely looking in my direction, and went back to his papers. "Emily had nothing to do with this, Rocco. You will do this. End of discussion."

Rocco stood, affronted, and huffed. I stood recovering from Cameron's use of *Emily* versus *Emmy*.

Rocco stomped down the hall and slammed his bedroom door.

I gathered the papers strewn by Rocco's recently vacated seat—forms of some sort.

"Did I miss something?" I was surprised by how small my voice sounded.

"I did some research while I was gone. Rocco's fifteen years old and dropped out of school a month before coming here," Cameron said, his voice, his expression still bland.

"Yikes! You mean he's not even close to being full-grown yet? He'll be a monster by the time he's eighteen." I tried a little harder. "Are you sure you can afford to keep feeding him?"

I thought I had seen Cameron's lips twitch, but whatever semblance of a smile might have been coming, it was gone by the time he raised his eyes; in its place was a cold stare.

"He's getting his GED if he's going to stay here. I won't have him spend his days rotting in front of the TV and doing nothing good with his life."

I swallowed hard while he collected his papers.

"I could help him," I offered uneasily. "With homework and stuff."

He pushed his chair back. "Whatever keeps you busy."

I felt the sting.

"Cameron, about last night—" I started, making a split-second decision which story I would go with, but his dagger stare stopped me.

I lost my voice; he looked over my shoulder. Spider and Carly were in the kitchen doorway with files in their arms.

"What is it?" Cameron snapped.

"We're ready," Spider said to him, completely impervious to Cameron's mood—unlike me, and unlike Carly. Her eyes veered between Cameron and me, and she gave me a weighted smile. I couldn't manage to give her anything back.

"I've got a lot of work to do. This will have to wait," Cameron said to me in passing, never actually looking at me.

They left me standing in the middle of the kitchen. After an intense session of staring down my bowl of cereal, I fiercely pushed it down the table—it tipped over and spilled. I went to the kitchen to get a dishrag. When I got there, I kept walking.

Outside, the morning sun was already steaming the waterlogged lawn, making the air stifling. No wind blew through the trees. No birds chirped. I could see Griff's shape shimmering in the heat, like a mirage, and I was sweating before I even reached the halfway point between us, and soaked by the time I actually reached him. The scowl on his face hadn't improved since I'd last seen him.

"You're making it really difficult for me to ignore you," he grumbled.

"Oh? Were you trying to ignore me? I hadn't noticed."

Griff rolled his eyes and scanned the scene, a valiant effort to continue to ignore me.

This irritated me even more.

"It's not my fault you got in trouble with Spider for not doing your job while they were gone," I said. "You have no right to be angry at me."

"Who said I was angry at you?"

"You just admitted that you were trying to ignore me."

"Ignore, yes. Angry, no—never with you," he said with sincerity.

"Same difference," I snapped.

"Huge difference. I'm just trying to protect you." This seemed to be the common explanation for everything that aggravated me. "I've been told to stay away from you, or it's lights out for me." Griff put his hand to his throat and pretended to slice his neck from ear to ear; that feeling that had attached itself to my bones twisted. "I figure I can't keep you safe if I'm dead. So I'll stay away and keep an eye on you from here."

"I think the only way Spider can convince you to do your job is by threatening you," I reasoned, for both of us. "Anyway, I can protect myself. You don't need to protect me from anyone, and you definitely don't need to use me as your excuse for not working. There's no need to be overdramatic about this. Spider's just doing his job." I heard myself echoing Cameron's words.

"I'm being overdramatic?" Griff repeated incredulously. "What world do you live in? These guys have killed better people than me without even blinking. So far, they seem to like to have you around. But believe me, once they have what they want or they get sick of you, you'll be in big trouble too." He looked around and lightly grabbed my arm, leaning toward me and whispering, "I won't let them do anything to you. They'll all die before they hurt you."

He let go of my arm and took a step back, his eyes flicking over the grounds. Of the few guards that I could see through the heat waves, all of them seemed as preoccupied as I was with keeping cool.

"So you'll just keep ignoring me. And then what?" I asked, my irritation evaporating. Griff was genuinely scared. I couldn't be angry with him for that—though I was a little disappointed that I wouldn't get the chance to air out my frustrations with him anymore.

"I don't know," he admitted wearily. "I haven't figured that out yet. Do you know why they're keeping you alive?"

I wondered if Griff noticed that I didn't flinch when we discussed my life—and death; I had no reason to be scared. I wanted to tell him about Cameron, but I couldn't. I wanted to tell him about Bill, but I didn't. I was suddenly afraid that he would see me differently. So I simply shook my head in response.

"Do your parents have a lot of money?" he asked me.

"What does that have to do with anything?" I said, my irritation resurfacing.

He shrugged. "I thought maybe these guys were trying to collect ransom in exchange for you."

His voice trailed off. A silver Mercedes had driven up the road and was stopped at the entrance. One of the guards had his arm coolly resting on top of the car and was chatting with the driver through the open window. The other guard stood close behind him, at times standing on his toes, trying to catch a glimpse of the car's occupant.

From the stupid grins on the guards' faces, I guessed who was in the car—a guess that was confirmed as I glimpsed a flip of the driver's blonde hair.

Frances eventually drove through the male barriers and got out of her car.

"Looks like Long-Legs is back." Griff exhaled.

"Long-Legs?" Only a tinge of jealousy colored my tone.

Frances strolled toward Griff and me. She was wearing a short, white cotton dress and cowboy boots. The air was stifling and stagnant, but her golden hair seemed to have found imaginary wind, as it (along with other noticeable parts) bounced with her every step. She looked like she was walking out of a country music video.

"We didn't get the chance to meet last time I was here. I'm Frances. You're Emily, right?"

I smiled weakly.

Griff practically knocked me over extending his own hand to Frances. "I'm Griffin."

Griff-in? I mouthed to myself.

Frances shook his hand. "Where is everyone?"

Griff had forgotten how to speak.

"Working," I responded for both of us.

"Well, I guess it's just us then. Griffin, mind if I steal Emily for a bit?" Frances asked as she hooked her arm around mine. Griff just grinned and nodded.

"See you later, *Griff-in*," I said and threw him a glare.

He smiled back sheepishly, his cheeks glowing red.

Frances's Mercedes sparkled in the sunlight. I spotted an empty booster seat in the back.

"Where's my nephew?" I blurted.

She was a little shocked.

"Cameron told me about you and Bill," I explained.

She eyed me and shook her head in disbelief. "I'm very surprised he would have told you that."

"I overheard the two of you talking."

"Ah," she said. "My mom is watching Daniel."

We ended up sitting by the pool. Some of the guards who were supposed to keep watch over the clearing behind the pool house took turns promenading closer inland. The stupid grin outbreak had spread to them too—a pandemic was surging. While they were trying to catch Frances's attention, her eyes were partly fixed on me, though she kept an eye out for them too.

"It's weird finally meeting you. I've heard so much about you from Bill," she gushed. I was coming up smiling until she added, "You don't look anything like I thought you would."

While I busied myself with watching the pool water leak down my legs, I imagined her blue eyes making their way to my hair.

"You just don't look anything like your brother is what I meant …" She was trying to make small talk, and amends. Her voice was hushed and sweet, like a mourning dove cooing.

"How did you meet Bill?" I asked her, still looking at my wet feet.

"Gosh, that was such a long time ago." From the corner of my eye, I could see a smile coming to her lips. "We met in high school after he moved to Callister."

"How long were you together … dating?"

"The first time, just a few months."

I looked at her. "The first time?"

"We broke up in high school. He dropped out, and I didn't hear from him for a long time. Then I ran into him on the street a couple of years later." She stopped and took a breath. "I didn't know about Carly. Bill never told me he had a girlfriend … I had never met her. I thought … he told me they were just friends."

Although I felt another flash of extreme disappointment in my brother, I knew that this was really none of my business.

"Did he tell you he was taking drugs?" That was one of the questions that was bugging me most.

"He didn't need to tell me. Your brother was always using, Emily. He was using even when we were in high school. Everyone who knew him well enough knew that."

"Cameron didn't," I blurted. It wasn't that I didn't believe her … I just didn't want to believe her.

"Is that what he told you?" she hissed under her breath, her fingers clenching the side of the pool.

I noticed that she kept a distant eye on the loitering guards. She smiled at one of them, artificially; he looked elated with her attention.

"I guess Cameron is just trying to protect you. The truth is hard to swallow." Her voice was sweet again.

"It must be difficult for you to have to keep coming to Cameron for money," I said.

Frances sneered. "I don't *need* to come here and I certainly don't need their money ... Bill had opened a bank account for Daniel and me before he died." She half-turned to me, never fully taking her eyes off the guards. "You know how much money your brother had when he died." When I shrugged, she raised her eyebrows. "Didn't you get Bill's money after he died?"

I shook my head.

Frances became somber, pensive. The guards had finally gotten sunstroke from watching us and went back to rest in the shade of the trees along the property line.

"Why do you come all the way here if you don't really need—"

She interrupted me by turning her attention completely to me and leaning in very close. "We don't have a lot of time," she whispered. "Are you okay? Have they hurt you?"

"I'm fine," I answered awkwardly. "Has who hurt me?"

"Cameron, for one—"

"Of course not!"

She held out a hand to shush me and glanced around erratically. When she seemed reassured of our seclusion, she brought her blue eyes back to me.

"Cameron is ... very nice," I whispered, trying to find a descriptor that wouldn't make me blush. It was pointless. The blood was already climbing up my neck in a ladder of red blotches.

She paused long enough to catch sight of my ruddiness.

"Cameron is handsome ..." she ventured, watching my expression.

I went back to watching my feet splash in the water.

She exhaled very slowly. "Emily, you need to be extremely careful around Cameron. He's young ... too young to be a boss, too young to be doing what he's doing." There was a resentful edge to her voice. "He's charming and very smart, which is why he has managed to keep himself alive for so long, but he's immature. When he gets bored, or when things start to get too hard for him … bad things start to happen." She seemed rushed. "Am I making any sense?"

"He's not like that," I said confidently.

She put her hand on my shoulder, willing me to look at her.

"Your brother was a terrific boss," she cooed. "Cameron always looked up to him. They were like brothers. Spider was very jealous of Bill because of that. When Bill died, he tried to take over the business. But the other bosses wouldn't have it—they didn't trust him, didn't think that he was smart enough to manage the business for them and make them money. They picked Cameron." Her voice was bitter. She shifted in her seat. "Spider knows that Cameron is too young to make the tough decisions, and he uses that to get what he wants … to control the business. To control Cameron."

I shook my head, trying to find the words to explain to her that Cameron wasn't the fickle monster she was making him out to be, but she wasn't done.

"From what I saw the last time I was here, Cameron seems to be taken with you. You're like a new, expensive toy to him … but this won't last. I'll help you get out of here, but I have to find a safe place for Daniel and my mom, somewhere they can't find them. You need to keep Cameron happy until I can come get you out."

"Frances, really, I'm fine," I insisted. "Everyone has been nothing but nice to me—"

"There's nothing nice about these people—"

"Frances," interrupted a stern voice from behind us. We simultaneously wheeled around.

Spider was standing by the basement doorway, glaring.

Frances quickly regained her composure, a cheerful smile replacing the fear on her face. She got up and strolled toward Spider. Unlike the guards', Spider's mood did not improve as Frances approached.

"It was very nice to meet you, Emily," she called. She disappeared into the house, closely followed by Spider.

Frances was wrong. Griff was wrong. They didn't see what was under the mask. I knew what Cameron looked like to everyone else—cold, scary. I had unwillingly seen this side of him—this morning, for example—and I didn't like it either. But when the hard surface melted and Cameron reappeared, he was luminous and tender. He was full of life. It infuriated me that I couldn't let anyone else in on this secret. They were all wrong.

By the time I made it back to the front of the house, Frances was rushing out with a paper bag in her hand.

"Take care of yourself, Emily," she whispered intently as she passed me and hurried to her car.

Spider followed her out and stood in the driveway until her Mercedes was out of sight. After a fierce look at me, he made his way toward the garage.

Griff was still standing by the tree line. I purposefully ignored him and smugly walked into the cool, air-conditioned house.

Rocco was slouched at the kitchen table with two empty frozen dinner trays in front of him and a third one well on its way. I copied him and threw a frozen dinner in the microwave.

Out of everything happening, Rocco being upset with me, even if it was for absolutely no reason, seemed the worst thing of all.

"I didn't say anything to Cameron about your age. I didn't even know that he was going to make you do this," I told him as the microwave counted down.

"I know. I wasn't mad at you. Not really, anyway. I just really hate school," he said and shoveled rubberized meat into his mouth.

"Why?"

"I don't know. It's hard and too boring and it's a waste of time. I don't need school to work for Cameron."

"You know," I said, thinking out loud, "you could use this to your advantage."

Rocco looked up and listened. I continued my train of thought. "You could tell Cameron that you'll do the homework and get your GED *if* he takes you along when he goes to work."

"Like blackmail?" he asked hesitantly.

"Call it a negotiation tactic."

Rocco chewed this over and grinned to his ears. "Negotiation tactic ... I like it."

"I'll even help you do the homework, if you want. It'll be easy, you'll see. Before you know it, you'll have your GED and won't ever have to think about it again."

"Thanks, Emmy."

I peeled the lid off my steaming TV dinner and burned two fingers.

Rocco looked up questioningly. "Did you and Cameron have a fight or something?"

"Not really," I said with a mouthful of burnt fingers. Then I wondered if Cameron had said something to his kid brother. "Why do you ask?"

Rocco shrugged. "He was in a really bad mood this morning. I haven't seen him in a mood like that since you got here."

"How was he before I got here?"

"I don't know. Mad, I guess. I rarely saw him. He worked. All the time."

"Doing what?"

"Beats me," he muttered. "I never get to go along, remember?"

Rocco took his empty trays into the kitchen and sat back down at the table, watching me finish my cardboard meal and breathing loudly.

"I'm bored," he finally said. "Do you want to watch a movie or something?"

I looked over at the forms that were still on the table where I had neatly stacked them earlier that morning. Rocco let his head fall back in despair as he understood my meaning.

"No time like the present," I said brightly. And, to annoy him a little bit more, I added, "We should probably get started on the laundry too. Since we both lost at poker." Technically, he had lost two seconds before me—but who was keeping track?

I thought Rocco was going to start crying after my last suggestion.

It was a lovely afternoon of filling out forms, writing an essay on cage fighting (to attest to Rocco's ability to write), and washing and folding never-ending piles of laundry. Still, we had barely made a dent in the laundry room as it neared dinnertime. Music thumped in the distance again.

By the time the troops started making their way downstairs for dinner, Rocco and I were finishing up a load of bath towels. He kept eying the kitchen doorway, antsy to show his big brother the work that he had done and commence the negotiation round.

Dinner came and went, and Cameron never walked through the doorway. Disappointed, Rocco went to the couch. The two of us lounged in front of the TV for the rest of the night and eventually fell asleep there. We were awakened at midnight when Cameron finally dragged himself in and began rummaging through the kitchen cupboards.

Rocco drummed his finger on the arm of the couch, waiting for Cameron to make his way to the table. Then he got up, picking up the paperwork he had strategically laid next to him, and dropped it on the table in front of Cameron. I smiled after him—his unfettered excitement made me excited for him.

Cameron sighed, his eyes small and lifeless. "Not tonight, Rocco."

Rocco looked jittery as he willed his brother to look at the documents. "But I want to talk to you about this. Look, I've done all this work—"

"I said not tonight," Cameron snapped.

Rocco and I both jumped. He looked at me despairingly. I didn't know what to say.

He stomped back to his room and slammed the door behind him. It was déjà vu from this morning.

Cameron continued picking at his food.

I got up, having decided to let him brood in peace.

"You were talking to Frances today?" he called out as I reached the doorway.

"Yes."

"What did you talk about?"

I spun on my heels. "Why?" I asked, attempting to mimic his coldness.

"Because I have a right to know what goes on under my roof."

"We were outside."

Cameron fixed his stare, waiting for an answer.

"We talked about Bill," I finally conceded.

"Anything else?"

"Nope."

Cameron didn't answer and took a bite of his food as he stared me down.

The fact that he was still angry with me, and that he had taken his anger out on his little brother, suddenly made my jaw tighten.

"I know that you're still upset with me because of last night, but you have no right to take it out on Rocco. Rocco worked really hard today, and he was excited to show you what he did. You just blew him off like he's one of your foot soldiers. He's your *brother*. And your brother is a really great kid who deserves better than to be ordered around like a maid. And Frances and I didn't talk about much, but if I wanted to talk to her some more, I would. This might be your house, but you don't control me or what I do. I will talk to whoever I want, whenever I want."

Cameron sat frozen at the table.

I turned around and calmly walked upstairs.

I heard the fierce scrape of Cameron's chair on the floor and the clang of a bowl being pitched into the sink. I was afraid that he was going to come running after me. I was afraid that his monstrous equal was going to show up, that I had forced Cameron back into his shell.

Neither one came. After a few loud footsteps, the house was dead quiet once again.

The release of fury must have been therapeutic, because I slept quite well that night. I was awakened only once, by the usual sound of scratching and whining at my bedroom door. I drowsily got up and let Meatball in.

I had never had a dog growing up, so at first it had definitely been strange having Meatball sleep next to me. But I was surprised by how quickly I'd gotten accustomed to the brute being there. It was comforting, even if, deep down, I knew that whatever the reason he slept in my bed, it was not out of any sense of duty to me.

CHAPTER FOURTEEN

THE PROPER KIND OF DIVERSION

In the morning, a light knock at my door brought Rocco into my room. He lounged on my bed while I got dressed in the bathroom.

"I heard you and Cameron arguing last night," he said.

"As far as I know, it takes at least two people to have an argument. It was more like I talked loudly to myself while Cameron watched," I said back through the door.

"Yeah, that's usually how it goes with Cameron. It takes a lot for him to lose his cool, which is really annoying when all you want is to just have it out. Sometimes I wish he would just be like everyone else and fight back instead of acting like such an adult."

I pasted a smile on my face and walked out of the bathroom with a towel twisted on my head.

Rocco lay on his side, watching, while I towel-dried my hair. "I heard all the stuff you said about me to Cameron … It was really nice of you," he said. "But you should know that you're really not my type."

This made me smile, genuinely. "I didn't think that fifteen-year-olds even had a type. Don't you just go for anything with breasts?"

"Maybe that's why you're not my type. Besides, I'm much more mature than most fifteen-year-olds."

"Yes, I forgot that only real men throw tantrums in their rooms when they don't get their way."

"Well, thanks for sticking up for me. I've never heard anyone talk to my brother like that."

"Don't mention it. Not that it did either of us any good. I didn't get to fight it out, and you didn't get what you wanted."

"Actually, after you left last night, Cameron came into my room," Rocco said, breaking into a big grin. Something was up—he was getting eager and fidgety. I waited patiently, excited by his excitement. "Our plan worked. Cameron said that I could go with him next time. That I could be more than just a lookout."

I didn't know what being more than a lookout meant, but I was glad to see Rocco so happy again. "When do you leave?"

He scowled at the ceiling. "I don't know. I forgot to ask." He shrugged his shoulders, slumped onto his other side, and looked out the window.

When I turned around to go hang my towel in the bathroom, I saw Cameron standing in the bedroom doorway. I froze, and Cameron put on a wary smile. I wondered how long he had been standing there, how much he had heard.

"Can I come in?" he asked with his velvety voice. He was wearing a red T-shirt, which somehow made his beautiful features even more noticeable to me. I was now sure that he did these things on purpose.

Rocco looked at me, awaiting my response, but I just continued on to the bathroom. "Join the party," he responded for the both of us.

I came back out and fingered my hair into a wet bun while Cameron sat on the edge of the bed. He raised his eyebrows at his kid brother.

Rocco sat up and cleared his throat. "I better get going."

On his way out, he stopped and squeezed me in a bear hug until my feet were no longer touching the floor. "Thanks, Emmy," he murmured into my ear and then let me go so my lungs could suck air once again.

Cameron shook his head as Rocco closed the door. "Funny kid," he said.

I had decided that that exact moment was the perfect time for me to put away the clean laundry that had been sitting in laundry baskets on the bedroom floor. I had also decided that this chore required my complete and undivided attention.

The room was tensely silent as I folded laundry and opened and closed drawers.

"You're still angry with me," Cameron finally said after a few minutes.

I briefly lifted my eyes but otherwise ignored him and continued my imperative chore.

Defeated, he fell backward on the bed, his hands passing over his face and halting forked in his hair. "This is so much more complicated than I ever thought it would be."

"I'm sorry to be such an inconvenience to you," I snarled. Then I remembered that I wasn't talking to him and went back to the laundry.

He laughed and shook his head at the ceiling.

"I should be mad at you, you know," he said. "There's no way that Rocco could ever come up with a plan to blackmail me into letting him work for me."

"You wanted something; he wanted something. That's called bargaining, negotiation— not blackmail. Anyway, you don't give Rocco enough credit. He's a really smart kid."

"Are you saying that you didn't put the idea in his head?"

"He would have eventually found a way to get what he wants, whether or not I helped him."

Cameron turned his head to gaze at me. "Having Rocco follow in my footsteps could get him killed. That's not something that I can live with."

"You know," I said with a sigh, "for someone so smart, you can be really dense. None of this has to do with working for you. Rocco is just looking for a way to spend more time with you, his big brother. Since you work all the time and won't talk to him about your life, he probably thinks that working *for* you will get him more time *with* you."

I could feel Cameron's eyes on me while he considered this.

"You think so?"

"I know so," I said, rolling one sock into another. "This has everything to do with you and Rocco and nothing to do with me. I'm just trying to give Rocco something to look forward to for once. Something beyond channel surfing."

"This place isn't so bad, is it?" Cameron asked, an edge of concern in his voice.

"It's definitely one of the nicer prisons I've been in," I said. "You can be mad at me all you want for not following your rules, but Rocco is bored and lonely. You really need to keep his mind busy. Doing dishes and babysitting me just won't cut it."

"Rocco likes to be around you," he said. "I don't think he feels like he's babysitting you."

"Maybe. But I'm a very poor substitute for you."

Cameron sat back up, resting his elbows on his knees and clasping his hands together. I could sense that he was studying me, and I tried to ignore him.

"Emmy, can you look at me?" he asked. "Please?"

I finally let him see my eyes, since he had said please.

His lips curved into a little smile, but his eyes were still very tight. "I didn't come in here because I was mad at you," he said. "I came here to apologize. I didn't react very well after your nightmare because it was hard for me to see you afraid of me. The last thing I wanted was to make you fear me. It made me feel sick to my stomach. But I don't blame you for reacting like a normal person."

I exhaled. "Cameron, I had a bad dream. People have bad dreams all the time. They mean nothing."

"You *should* be scared of people like me, Emmy. We can hurt you."

I crossed my arms. "If you came here to order me to be scared of you, then you might as well just turn around, because I don't feel like being ordered around again today."

"I never order you around."

"What about yesterday, when you gave me the third degree for talking to Frances? I didn't do anything wrong."

"I'm trying to protect you," he reminded me, like a broken record.

"You use the words *protect* and *control* interchangeably." I shut the drawer with more force than necessary.

"You just need to trust my judgment," he said more softly. "You can do whatever you want here. Just think of this place as a long-deserved rest, like a spa or one of those places where girls like you pay a lot of money to be forced to relax."

"If I can't go anywhere or talk to anyone, then I am in a prison. This is no spa that girls like me pay a lot of money to go to." I felt my ears grow hot. He had put me in the box that I hated so much.

He seemed surprised by my change in demeanor. "I didn't say that you couldn't talk to anyone, and you can walk around as much as you want. I'm just asking you to stay away from Frances."

"But I can't leave the grounds, and I have to stay away from Griff too."

"Griff?" Cameron's face was impenetrable.

"Griff, one of your guards. The one who's been told to stay away from me, or else."

"You mean the big, tall guy with the red hair who keeps looking at you with goofy eyes?" His tone was light, but his expression had grown severe.

"So you've met," I said with torrential sarcasm.

"I didn't say anything to him. Why would I?"

"Maybe you didn't, but Spider sure did. Spider works for you, doesn't he?"

"Security is Spider's job. I don't mess with his business, and I certainly don't question how he manages the watchdogs," he scoffed. Then he bent forward slightly. "What's your interest in this Griff guy, anyway?"

I wasn't really sure what Cameron and I were doing. Were we fighting? Couples fought. Couples fought, kissed, made up. Didn't you have to be in a relationship to fight? Whatever Cameron and I had, whatever we were to each other, it was nothing traditional.

"We're just friends," I sighed. "You can't expect me to barricade myself in your room when you're gone all the time."

Cameron smiled ruefully. "Why not? You could sit here, counting the minutes till I came home after a hard day's work and made your wait worthwhile."

I threw a T-shirt at him. He caught it in midair, tried to fold it, and threw it back onto the pile.

"Fine. I get it. You need some diversion. But does it have to be with that guy? I mean, can't you just hang out with Rocco?"

"I can only watch so much television in one day." I properly folded the T-shirt and stacked it on top of the others.

"Well," he said, grinning broadly, "I guess I'll just have to stay here all the time and make sure to keep you really busy."

"That's quite an undertaking," I responded, barely managing to catch my breath. And then a thunderous splash hit the window—and another, and another. We could hear jeering coming from outside. I didn't have to get up to know that Rocco, and maybe a few followers, were throwing water balloons at the bedroom window.

"When do you have to leave next?"

"Tomorrow."

My shoulders drooped a little. "So much for staying here and keeping me busy."

"I wish I could stay," he started softly, then seemed to recompose and continued in a more officious tone. "I wish I could do all my work from here, but I can't. There are some things that I have to be there in person to do."

Another water balloon assault started, and Cameron sighed. "We better go down there before they break a window or kill themselves trying."

The day was well wasted at the pool with the rest of the family. Cameron laughed at the appropriate times and had a near-constant smile on his face, but something was different, particularly when he was near me. He was detached—like someone else was artfully playing the role of Cameron Hillard—and he definitely never came closer than a few feet from me. This I noticed more than anything else, though I ought to have been used to it by then.

But it was different this time. This was not something innate; he was doing this on purpose. He wanted to me to hurt.

It hurt. Like my skin was being pulled off, one layer at time.

In the evening, after dinner, Cameron, Spider, and Carly removed themselves from the table and headed out to talk business. Rocco and I headed to our station in front of the TV. But before we had a chance to settle in for the evening, Cameron halted at the threshold and called out to Rocco. "Well, you want to learn the business, don't you?" he said.

Rocco jumped off the couch and the family disappeared through the kitchen doorway.

Cameron had been so adamant about not letting Rocco partake in his business; I knew he wouldn't have changed his mind about that. Certainly there were alternatives, other ways to bribe a kid into going to school—unless there was an ulterior motive.

Cameron had taken Rocco away from me. He had ripped away the last layer of skin.

I was alone.

****

It was early in the morning when I heard the commotion downstairs; the house was too quickly emptying itself once again. This time, I let Meatball out so that he—at least—could join Cameron. Then I went back to bed to pine under the covers.

When the house was quiet again, Meatball came begging to be let back into our shared bedroom. We had both been left behind, on purpose.

I tried to go back to sleep, and the rolling around under the covers lasted for a good hour. I gave up, threw on an old T-shirt and shorts, and went outside to let Meatball out and find diversion.

But Griff wasn't at his station near the bottom of the property.

I ought to have known that with the bosses gone, Griff would start slacking off—immediately. I considered going to drag him out of bed but decided against it—one of the line guards was watching me, with persistence. Making a scene on the first day Cameron was away was probably a bad idea. After talking myself out of it, I bitterly went back into the house and tiptoed past the snoring night guards on my way to the gym.

I'd never been one for running on a treadmill; something about running for miles and never getting anywhere used to make me feel uneasy. I had forgotten about that, but now the memory resurfaced. Running in a room, a house void of people, staring at the unmoving water of the pool, the large windows … I was feeling claustrophobic, like a mouse stuck in a cage, getting nowhere fast on an exercise wheel.

With significant effort, I managed to run a few miles, then made it back upstairs to shower and dress.

I had given Griff enough time to sleep in. If he wasn't up, I was going to go wake him up—no matter what. I opened the front door just as the guard who was staring at me earlier was coming in.

The guard followed my gaze with delight as I looked for Griff outside.

"You're wasting your time," he sneered. "Griff already left."

I saw another guard standing at Griff's usual post. "Where did he go?"

"Don't know. He left with the rest of the crew this morning."

"What? Why?" I asked with slight panic.

"For some reason, the chief all of a sudden decided that he couldn't leave without Griff going with them. Griff got woken up late last night and told to get ready to leave this morning."

We stood facing each other for a moment, and I immediately regretted being alone with him. All of a sudden I was very afraid and felt very alone. The guard reached for the door, and Meatball flew in before the door could close on him.

Meatball stood between us while the guard kicked off his shoes and made his way downstairs, mumbling, "Go figure. The guy that screws off the most gets promoted first."

I breathed hard and kept my hand on Meatball's head, but neither of us moved for a little while. And then my mind started working again, and I started thinking. Cameron's sudden interest in Griff … a coincidence? The sick feeling at the pit of my stomach told me otherwise. Then another reality set in: Cameron and Rocco and Griff were gone; I had absolutely no human refuge until they all came back. I looked down at Meatball and decided to stay very close to him from now on.

When Meatball and I had taken a few deep breaths and our limbs had uncrystallized, we went into the kitchen. I started a load of laundry and fed the hungry dog. I crisped some bacon and fed that to him too. I got whatever I could find out of the fridge and cupboards and started measuring and mixing and frying and baking. I labored away until the kitchen table and counter were stacked with pancakes, French toast, muffins, cookies, and a couple loaves of bread. I knew I was done when I ran out of room and supplies.

I brought all the food downstairs to the guards' kitchen, with Meatball close at my heels. No one was there, thankfully. I left the food out and sped back upstairs, hoping that maybe feeding the guards would keep me in good stead. At least no one would starve while I was still alive.

Within minutes, I could hear cheering from the night guards, who had been awakened either by the smell of food or by the clamor of pots and pans from my cooking session. Either way, happy jostling sounds filled the house—in many ways, a small relief. But when I looked at the clock, dread struck again, because I had managed to kill only a few hours.

I took a box of dog biscuits out of the pantry and tried to lure Meatball to me so that I could entertain myself by teaching a guard dog to roll over. But Meatball had stationed himself by the threshold and would not move, no matter how much I begged.

So I threw the wash in the dryer and a new load in the washer and waited, walking aimlessly from the kitchen to the living room windows. I turned on the TV and then paced down the hall, pausing in front of Rocco's chaotic room. For a second I thought I might be desperate enough to clean his room; that is, until manifold, nauseating images of what I could uncover in a teenage boy's room suddenly popped into my head. I gently kicked some clothes out of the way so I could close his door and crept away as if the thought had never crossed my mind.

I eventually reached the end of the hallway and the house, and wandered into the library. My roving eye was drawn to the piano. Bill had been a natural at everything he touched, and music was no exception. Anything I produced in his shadow was a failure in comparison to what my brother could do. Eventually—with Bill's help, as always—I had been able to memorize sequences of keys, enough to fool my parents into thinking that I could play, enough for them to stop cycling piano teachers through the house.

Taking advantage of the fact that there was no one in the house to deride my triumphant musical comeback, I sat at the piano and made a brutal attempt to recall the theme song from *Cheers*. I almost fell backward off the bench when something moved toward me from the corner.

"That sounds really awful," said Carly, now standing by the couch.

I was never happier to see her. "I thought you were gone with the rest of them?"

"I decided to take a few days off and stay here instead." She approached and sat next to me on the bench.

"You mean you were told to stay back to babysit me."

"Something like that," she said, smiling, gliding her fingers over the piano keys. "I don't think anyone has played this thing since Bill died. He was a really good musician."

I was surprised to hear Carly talk about my brother in that way. "Don't you hate Bill for what he did?"

"No. I don't. I know I should, and it would probably be a lot easier if I did, but I don't."

"Do you hate me, then?"

"No, I don't hate you either. But it was definitely a shock to see you, here, after so many years." Her eyes met mine. "When you first got here, it was almost like having Bill here again. Seeing you, it just brought back a lot of the anger that I had when Bill died. I couldn't believe that Cameron would have brought you here, that he would do that to me. I understand why now."

"What do you mean you understand why?" I pressed.

Carly smiled wider. "That's something you need to talk to Cameron about, not me."

I made a mental note to remember to ask Cameron.

"Why do you think he did that to you? I mean Bill, and the whole Frances thing. I know that he would have loved you very much. Given my family's history, how angry he was, it doesn't make any sense to me that he would have ever done that."

Carly sighed and paused, her face slightly tensing. "I don't know. I never saw it coming, to tell you the truth. Even when Bill started getting weird and secretive, I never once thought he would do that. Of all the things that I imagined, that was never an alternative."

"Did you know he was taking drugs?" I asked.

"No ... I don't know ... maybe," Carly said, shaking her head. "If you'd asked me that question a year before he died, I would have said absolutely not. Bill hated drugs, which was pretty funny given our line of business. But then he started to change. A few months before he died, he started waking up in the middle of the night in a cold sweat—screaming, not making any sense. He was losing so much weight, and the way he was handling the business ... he was going to get all of us killed." Her eyes came back to me, and she held them there. "Emmy, this life that we lead, it's not for everyone. Most people can't handle it. Your brother was too sensitive ... he just couldn't handle it all anymore, it was killing him. I think that he wanted to get out before it killed him. The drugs, Frances—they were his way to escape it all." She took a ragged breath. "When he died, the business had been falling apart for a long time. Cameron brought it all back. If it wasn't for him, we might not ... we definitely wouldn't have survived."

She took another breath. I couldn't take my eyes off her.

"You know, Cameron's really brilliant. He spent some time in juvie but *still* managed to get into MIT."

I wasn't really shocked. "Why didn't he go?"

"Your brother called him with a better offer."

I wondered if he ever regretted that decision—and then realized I already knew the answer. "What were Cameron and my brother like when they were together?"

"I guess they were a lot like Cameron and Rocco, except that Bill was like the kid brother, even if he was older than Cameron. It was funny to watch sometimes. Your brother coming up with the quick moneymakers, as he called them, and Cameron the voice of reason, the one who brought him back to reality. I guess Cameron hasn't changed much in that way. I think if it wasn't for him, your brother would have gotten arrested a thousand times."

"What about Spider and Bill? What were they like together?"

"Exact opposites. Fire and water. Bill was charming and outgoing. Spider is, well, much quieter. They fought constantly, sometimes in front of customers. It was embarrassing."

"Spider hated my brother for what he did to you," I mused.

"Spider did hate Bill for cheating on me, but he had his own reasons for hating Bill too," Carly said, eyeing me. "You know, no matter how cool some guys think they are, when it comes to certain girls, it's like they lose their mind. They start saying and doing really stupid stuff."

I knew that this observation was directed at me.

"I don't like to be ordered around," I said, "and I definitely don't like to be told who I can and can't talk to. What if Spider told you that you couldn't talk to someone, for no good reason?"

"He did ... so I started dating Bill, just out of spite," she said, smiling. "Anyway, you shouldn't be so hard on Cameron. He's got a lot on his shoulders right now. This business isn't easy for any of us. Some days it feels like it sucks all the life out of you—whatever's left feels inhuman sometimes."

"Was my brother ever happy?"

Carly wasn't smiling anymore, and she hesitated before answering. "Yes, at one point he was really happy. We all were in the beginning. It was hard not to be."

"Was Bill ever suicidal? Do you think he wanted to overdose?"

"I don't know. Like I said, he wasn't the same person in the end." Carly looked at me searchingly and then exhaled. "Cameron was right. You are exhausting."

My heart leaped. "What else does he say about me?"

She titled her head sideways and put a hand on my shoulder. "Let's go downstairs before all the food is gone."

We made our way to the basement, picking up our guard dog on the way down, but we were already too late—not a morsel was left from the spread I had prepared. Two of the night guards were sugar-crashed on the couch, vacantly staring at the ceiling with their hands on their full bellies, stuck in a gluttonous daze. The scary guard wasn't there.

"Animals," Carly grumbled as we strolled past them. She motioned for me to follow her to the small pool house.

Carly's hideaway in the pool house was cozy, distinctly feminine, and very festive. Bright red, orange, and yellow and deep blue were splashed everywhere, from the walls to the curtains to the assorted furniture. Wooden dividers painted with purple and yellow flowers separated the small apartment into three rooms: bedroom, living room, and kitchenette. It all hurt my eyes a little bit.

While Carly fixed us some food, I asked her about her bold choice in décor.

"It reminds me of home," she explained.

She told me about her mother, who had emigrated from Mexico as a young girl. She told me about her five sisters and about the house she grew up in—a house that had been decorated in a similar bright fashion and was almost as small as Carly's cottage. She laughed when she talked about the trials of living in a one-bedroom house and sharing one tiny bathroom with six other women. She never mentioned her father. I didn't bring it up.

"Do you see your family very often?" I asked.

She glanced away, blinking, shook her head. "Not anymore," she said. "It's just too dangerous. I don't want them to get caught up in all this. My sisters have kids. I don't know what I would do if one of them ever got hurt because of me."

Then she looked at me, and her eyes lit up, a bit. She dashed into her bedroom. After searching through her dresser drawers, she rushed back.

"Spider had to go steal this from my mom's house for me last Christmas," she said, handing me a photo of her family. They were standing in front of a bright, ornate Christmas tree—a cluster of happy, smiling faces, young and old. "It's all of them—my family. The holidays are always the hardest for me."

"Do you ever regret choosing this life?"

Carly looked at me strangely, like I had just asked her if she regretted breathing.

"I didn't have any choice, Emmy. People like Spider, Cameron, and me are lucky just to survive for this long. If we weren't doing this here, we would be doing it from the street, where things are just as dangerous with little return. We've all had to make big sacrifices in order to get here, but at least we have some control over our lives now. I send money back to my family. I can keep them safe from here."

"I'm sorry," I said. "I didn't mean to suggest that you shouldn't be doing this."

"I know. It's hard to understand when you don't come from the streets, when you've always had everything you've ever wanted. Your brother always had that problem too."

That hurt.

We spent the rest of the day together. I found that I liked Carly more and more. In some ways she was very reserved—but her temper seemed to flare up easily. I thought that we were very similar in this way; yet it was clear to me that in her eyes we were very different.

In the evening, we popped some popcorn and settled in for a girls-only movie night—though our chick-flick choice probably had more explosions and gunfights than a movie most "normal" girls would have picked.

Carly even brought out a bottle of wine.

"I was able to sneak this past Spider last time we got back from the city," she said, a little shamefaced.

"Why would you have to sneak it in?" Dating the head of security should come with some perks.

"Spider doesn't allow booze anywhere on the property."

"That's ... unorthodox," I said, though *control freak* came to mind.

She cocked an eyebrow. "Would you want these boys carrying machine guns after they've been drinking?"

Touché.

Two bags of popcorn later, with plastic goblets and an almost-empty bottle of wine, Carly and I were thoroughly on our way to having a great time. But just when the main character got hit by a bus, Carly suddenly turned the volume down. The slam of a car door confirmed her suspicion that she had heard something.

I turned to Carly questioningly. Her face had blanched.

"Oh God," she gasped, bringing her hand to her mouth. "They're early. Something's happened."

She jumped off the couch just as the front door flew open. What we heard next stunned both of us.

"Is someone singing?" we asked simultaneously.

CHAPTER FIFTEEN

FLYING HIGH

Cameron and Spider slumped in together and were followed by Griff and Tiny, who were dragging Rocco in by the waist. Rocco's foot was heavily bandaged, but he looked very happy.

Carly, shocked, locked eyes with Spider, who shook his head at her meaningfully: now was not the time to ask questions.

Rocco was still singing like a drunken sailor as Griff and Tiny helped him to the couch. Griff was ashen. He glanced at me from the corner of his eye, and then he glanced at Cameron. He looked like he was about to say something to Cameron, but Tiny grabbed him by the arm and led him back out of the room.

While Carly and I wondered about Rocco's solo performance, Spider caught sight of the almost-empty bottle of wine on the coffee table. He picked it up and looked at us accusingly; our cheeks burned (wine red). Carly smiled, guiltily, and examined her fingernails. I immediately went searching for the remote control to turn the movie off.

Cameron smiled, but his eyes looked tired. "Did we interrupt your party?"

I found the remote too quickly and changed the subject. "What's wrong with Rocco?"

"He's heavily sedated," Cameron said.

Rocco suddenly took interest.

"I'm not sayne-dated. Dr. Lorne just gave me some happy pills," he said, shaking a plastic sandwich bag filled with multicolored pills. And then he grabbed the nearly empty popcorn bowl, and we all watched him try to bite through the unpopped kernels.

Carly piped up. "So are we supposed to guess what happened?"

There was a strained moment of silence between Cameron and Spider, punctuated by Rocco's tooth-splitting crunches.

"Rocco shot himself in the foot," Spider finally said, keeping his eye on Cameron.

Cameron's already treacherous mood exploded like a volcano. "He wouldn't have shot himself if my orders had been followed."

"It was an accident, Cameron," Spider reminded him, quickly, patiently.

"I said no guns! What part of my order wasn't clear?"

Rocco got up from the couch and limped toward the patio doors.

"Where are you going?" Cameron demanded, his voice ricocheting off the living room walls.

"To bed. It's too loud in here," Rocco responded groggily. He opened the patio door, limped through, and disappeared into the darkness outside. Carly and I watched Spider and Cameron stare each other down. The tension in the room was now thick and unnerving.

Carly smartly excused herself and left through the kitchen doorway. I followed her lead and went to check on the patient out on the deck.

It was pitch-black outside. At first I couldn't see where Rocco had gone, but as my eyes adjusted to the darkness, I saw his elongated shadow lying on a lounge chair. There was no moon; the sky was softly lit by a million twinkling stars. It was amazing how quickly it came—my sense of insignificance in the grand scheme of things.

I sat down next to him and watched the sky. It smelled like summer now, like the woods were breathing, too alive to sleep.

Rocco mumbled and shifted on his improvised bed, and after a few minutes he went silent. I assumed that he had finally fallen asleep.

"He loves you," he said, garbled.

At first I thought he was still mumbling to himself, but as I turned to look at him, I saw that he had twisted onto his side and had been staring at me. His hair was disheveled—one side was completely flattened while the other stood straight up on end.

"Who are you talking to?" I asked.

"You, stupid. Who do you think?" he grumbled and turned on his back and squinted, like he was trying to figure out what those twinkly things were doing on his bedroom ceiling. He gave up trying to focus on anything and sighed. "I think he has for a long time."

I couldn't remember how it went: drunk people always tell it like it is, or never trust what a drunk person tells you? Maybe the truth was, as always, somewhere in the middle. Either way, my heart thudded. I suddenly felt stronger yet lighter. There was so much air around me. I could feel crinkles forming at the corner of my eyes.

Rocco scratched his nose and then his ear. "That night, when I knocked you over the head, I seriously thought that Cameron was going to kill me … I screw stuff up all the time, so I guess that wasn't really weird … except that he made me bring you here; you were more than just some chick he picked up off the street. I think it's driving him nuts having you here. He must have called me a thousand times in the middle of the night to check up on you the last time he left to go to work."

"You should really get some sleep, Rocco," I suggested, unwillingly.

"Before you came here, Cameron used to work all the time and then left us whenever he wasn't working. We used to assume that he just wanted to be alone. Since you've been here, he doesn't disappear anymore. Don't you think it's strange that out of all the people in the park that day, Meatball ran after you?

I mean, I'm not really good at math, but it seems pretty slim odds that the dog would jump on the one girl whose brother just happened to be the dog owner's best friend. I think Meatball knew who you were a long time before you actually met. He likes you better than everyone else, that's for sure." Was Rocco still talking about the dog? He turned to me, keyed up. "You know what else?"

I shook my head.

"I overheard Tiny tell Spider that someone told Tiny"—I was having trouble keeping up with this, given my state of mind, and wondered how Rocco managed, given his state of mind—"that Cameron was in the projects a lot even when he wasn't working. After you came here, it all stopped ... *and*," he added like he was expecting a drumroll, "Tiny told me that when they went to get your stuff from your house, Cameron knew exactly where you lived and where your room was. Tiny was the only one Cameron even allowed in the house. And no one was allowed to go near your stuff. Cameron packed it all himself."

Images were running through my head—images of what had, might have, already happened; images of what could be ... it took me a while to remember how to speak.

"Why would Cameron send Meatball after me?" I asked, but there was no answer. While my brain and my heart were fighting, I hadn't noticed that Rocco had gone quiet. I looked over at him. He was asleep, saliva leaking down from the corner of his mouth.

Then a serene voice in the darkness did answer me. "I didn't."

Cameron had been standing in the doorway with his arms crossed, listening.

"Meatball got away from me after he spotted you running." His shadow moved past me to the far end of the deck. "Taking advantage of my brother's state to extort information?" He spoke from the darkness; I listened for traces of anger but deciphered nothing like that. I exhaled just a little.

"He offered," I said and moved a little closer to his voice. From what I could see, he was standing with his arms casually draped over the rail, looking toward the shadows of the trees. Other than the lights coming from Carly's house, the landscape was black, and I could barely make out Cameron's face—just his dark eyes.

"So what were you doing there in the first place? In the projects, I mean." I was trying to keep my voice casual.

"Checking up on you. Making sure you were safe," he answered, his voice mastering nonchalance.

"Did you do that ... often?"

Cameron didn't answer.

"How long have you been doing that?"

"Since Bill died."

I gasped. "That was six years ago, Cameron! You've been doing it for that long?"

"Bill made me promise a long time before he died that I would look after you if anything ever happened to him. I kept my promise."

I was trying to analyze his tone again. This was even more difficult when I had nothing but a darkened face to match the voice with. "Is that the only reason?"

He went silent again and kept his dark eyes fixed on the imperceptible landscape.

"If Meatball hadn't gotten away from you that day, would you have ever introduced ... shown yourself to me?"

"No," he said firmly. "You had your own life."

"Not much of a life," I mumbled.

"Better than this." His head bent low. "You would have never known the difference, Emmy. Your life would have gone on without ever knowing that I was there or that this ... life even existed. It's not like it was easy to do, especially after you moved into that hellhole in Callister."

"It must have been inconvenient for you to have to spy on me in a grubby part of town."

"That's not what I meant," he said. "At least if you had done what you were supposed to do and gone off to a good college, lived in a nice place, and eventually met a good guy, I would have felt a lot better about letting you live your life. But imagine what it was like for me to see you so miserable and not be able to do anything about it."

"So why didn't you do anything about it?"

"You and I are just too different for me to have any direct involvement in your life."

I didn't know if it was the wine that I had shared with Carly or the fact that Cameron and I stood in the darkness, hidden from the world and each other, but I suddenly felt very brave.

"So is Rocco right? Do you love me?" My voice sounded both brazen and disbelieving.

Cameron chose silence.

"Answer me," I demanded.

I wanted to cry. I wanted to scream at the top of my lungs. I wanted him to kiss me. More than anything, I wanted him to kiss me. Just this once, I wanted to know what that would feel like. I wanted him to want me instead of pushing me away. Just this once.

I felt Cameron's hand move tenderly over my cheek, where he found a strand of hair that had fallen out of my ponytail. He curled it between two fingers before pushing it back behind my ear.

I pressed my hand against his chest, which was rising and falling in quick sequences. I could feel him on the verge of imploding.

"Cameron," I exhaled, "do you love me?"

His hand lingered there, by my ear.

I was terrified that he would walk away again.

I couldn't live through that anymore. I searched in the darkness until my hand fell upon his hot cheek.

His hand slid under my ear and around to the back of my neck, lacing into my hair. He pulled me into the darkness. My breaths were short and my heart was beating recklessly. I could feel his burning breath blow against my lips. His lips touched mine, taking a gentle hold over my bottom lip. My tongue tasted his lips and his tasted mine. I let myself fall into him as he wrapped his arm around the small of my back and pressed me against him. I stood on my tiptoes, grabbed his head with both hands, and locked us in embrace.

He kissed me softly.

I could feel heat rising inside me, feverish for more of him. The muscles of his body began to stiffen. His embrace sharpened, becoming more impatient, as though he too could not get enough. The world beyond this, our need for each other, evaporated.

I was overwhelmed, too overwhelmed to notice the patio door open—but Cameron noticed. Footsteps approached; he grabbed my shoulders and pushed me away. He rushed past me. I was left blurry.

Griff was standing over Rocco. He was startled when Cameron emerged from the darkness and fleetingly glared at me as I followed Cameron, hurriedly attempting to fix my disheveled ponytail.

"Get away from him!" Cameron ordered.

Rocco, who had been awakened by Cameron's loud voice, sat up and looked confusedly from Griff to Cameron and me.

Griff looked terrified and angry. "I'm sorry, sir. I didn't see you … standing there. I just came to check on Kid."

"You've done enough for one day. Leave."

"Sir … I wanted to apologize for what happened earlier today …" Griff stammered.

Cameron's eyes looked crazed. "I said leave! Now!"

Rocco and I both jumped, and Griff gave me a furious look and quickly spun around, leaving just as Tiny and Spider came running through the doors.

"What's going on?" Rocco asked, dazed.

I looked through the group of panting, angry men. Instinct told me that I needed to get out of there—quickly.

So I turned to Rocco. "You need to go to bed. You can't sleep out here."

"Out where?"

I just grabbed Rocco's arm and helped him off the lounge chair, painstakingly holding him up as we dragged ourselves back into the house. I made sure to close the patio door behind us, sensing that the tension bubble between Cameron, Spider, and Tiny was about to burst.

After heaving Rocco into his bed, I hurried back to my room to be alone and let the men air out their differences. I was still quite high—though I wasn't sure whether to dance around my room or lock my bedroom door. I plummeted onto the bed, tracing my fingers over my lips over and over until I drifted off to sleep, before I could drift back to reality.

That night, the disfigured monster came back into my nightmares. I woke up screaming, but no sound came out of my mouth—and no air came into it, either. A large hand was covering my mouth and nose. I fought back, kicking and punching my unseen assailant. I forced my eyes to focus and saw that it was Griff standing over me with his hand over just my mouth now, anxiously scanning the room and shushing me.

"Emily! It's me! Chill out!"

When I could take a few breaths through my nose and my heart had finally slowed to an almost normal tempo, Griff let me push his hand from my face.

"Griff, what are you doing here? It's the middle of the night!" I demanded in a half whisper.

He got up and started pacing back and forth, looking at the floor while he collected his thoughts. "How could you do this to me?" He looked up, wretched. "When the boss asked me to go with them today, and then he kept glaring at me the whole time, I should have known that he meant something by it. I'm such an idiot. I've been racking my brain for weeks, trying to figure out what these mongrels want with you and how I was going to get you out of this place, when it turns out that you're the boss's hooker?"

I shot straight up in bed. "What did you call me?"

He moved over to me with a look of disgust on his face. "I've been putting my life in danger for you while you're messing with the boss like a call girl."

Before I knew it was happening, my hand was raised and I heard it smack Griff across the cheek. "I'm not messing with anyone, Griffin! Not that it's any of your business. I've already told you: I don't need to be saved, and I certainly didn't ask you to do anything for me. Don't pretend that your choice to slack off has been entirely for my benefit."

Griff rubbed his cheek and looked away, glaring.

I tried hard to calm myself down. "What on earth happened out there today?"

He sat on the bed, still rubbing his cheek like a child, like someone who wasn't used to getting paid to pummel or be pummeled by much bigger people than me. "It's like I said. I was told last night that your boyfriend insisted I go with them today. Apparently I was supposed to keep an eye on the kid while he learned the trade. Spider almost blew my head off when I said I didn't want to go. So I followed orders and went, like a good soldier. Your boyfriend stared at me the whole way down. It was getting creepy. Then we get to this house, and all the boys were told to hang back on the street while Spider, Tiny, and the boss went in to talk business. They were in there for almost an hour ... Kid was getting bored and asked to see my gun." He shrugged defensively. "I gave it to him. I didn't see any harm in it—it wasn't like he was going to shoot anyone. But one of the boys thought it would be funny to come up behind him and scare him, and Kid jumped and shot himself in the foot. Spider came out of the house, screaming at me, something about no guns. How was I supposed to know Kid would shoot himself?"

"Roc ... Kid is fine. So what's with the theatrics?" I said, falling back onto my pillow.

"You don't get it, do you? These guys have been looking for an excuse to whack me ever since you got here. Now I know it's because the boss wants you for himself. With Kid shooting himself today and Spider's warning last time, I'm done for sure. They're going to off me."

"Griff, don't be ridiculous. No one's going to do anything to you. I'll talk to them tomorrow if you want." I rubbed my burning eyes and yawned.

Griff leaned in to me. "I'm not blind," he hissed. "Even I can see that the boss is a great-looking guy. You probably imagine yourself spending your days at his beck and call, and I'm sure a pretty girl like you could definitely keep him busy for a while. You also probably think that because the boss wants a piece of you, you've got some kind of power over him and that you're safe." He grabbed me by the shoulders. "Wake up, Emily! The guy doesn't love you and never will. The minute he gets what he wants, you're done for too. I won't be here to save you when that happens."

His eyes were bloodshot and looked like they were about to bug out of his head. He was panting and still holding me by the shoulders.

"Griff, you're scaring me," I said.

He let go, stepped away from the bed, and started pacing back and forth again. "We have to leave tonight," he thought out loud.

I pulled the warm blankets up to my chin. "We're not going anywhere—"

"You need to pack a bag. We leave tonight. One of the night guards usually falls asleep against the tree. We'll sneak past him when he does and follow the road from the woods and flag someone down on the highway. We'll have to hitch a ride out of here."

"We're not going anywhere … tonight. This is ridiculous. You're upset and paranoid. Everything will be better in the morning. You'll see."

Griff sat back down on the bed and looked at me closely. "Emily, if you don't leave tonight, they will kill you. Maybe not tomorrow, but they will, eventually. There's a reason they don't want anyone to talk to you—makes for less witnesses when you suddenly disappear from the face of the earth. I've been looking on the news to see if anyone is looking for you. There's been nothing at all. I don't think anyone even knows you're missing. I didn't tell you that because I didn't want to scare you."

I suddenly realized that Griff was right. I had watched enough television with Rocco to know that my face hadn't appeared on any news bulletins. That realization upset me for reasons beyond Griff's grasp.

He took my hands into his. "I'll come back in three hours. Get your stuff together. Just the essentials. We have a long trek ahead of us."

I didn't know what to say to him, except that I wasn't leaving with him. I looked around for inspiration and noticed that something big was missing.

"Where's Meatball?" I asked him, when what I really meant was *How did you get in here without Meatball biting your arm off?*

He pointed to the patio door. My guard dog was lying on the deck outside, gnawing contentedly on the gigantic, meaty bone that was nestled between his paws.

Griff got up.

"Remember, three hours," he whispered again as he stepped out onto the balcony. Then he climbed down and out of sight.

I did set the alarm clock to go off in three hours. In three hours, I would have another chance to convince Griff that running away alone in a dark forest was a really bad idea. I had three more hours to sleep.

Three hours later, the alarm rang. I let Meatball back inside and waited.

But Griff never showed.

Chapter Sixteen

Scar Tissue

The next morning, the house was filled with people and yet unnaturally, densely quiet, like the woods right before a storm comes crashing down.

I could have sworn Cameron had seen me trotting down the stairs, but he kept walking as if he hadn't. When I called out to him, he paused at the front door without looking back. Carly did turn, and she glared ... at me?

Cameron murmured to Carly and Spider that he would catch up with them. They left, he finally turned around, and I was almost in tears. His face was impenetrable, robotic. He forced a smile—it was thin and bloodless. That only made it worse.

"What's wrong?" I managed to ask as I slowly walked toward him—I was sure he took a minute step back when I did.

"Nothing ... just work," he said with the same strained smile. "I'll be gone most of the day. Can you keep an eye on Rocco for me?"

"Are you sure everything's okay?"

"Everything's fine," he answered with an automatic tone. "Have a good day."

He turned and left the house. I stood in the foyer, bewildered.

I wondered how bad things had gotten the night before between Spider, Tiny, and Cameron for Cameron to still be so upset. I found myself being angry at Griff—for refusing to follow orders, for ruining my sleep and my perfect moment with Cameron, for causing a rift in the family.

Rocco was in his room, lying in bed, looking at the ceiling. His face was wrenched in pain.

"How are you feeling?"

"I'll be fine in a few minutes once these green pills kick in," he said through gritted teeth.

I noticed the bag of rainbow tablets next to his bed. "What does your prescription say?"

Rocco laughed, with difficulty. "Dr. Lorne isn't the type of doctor who gives prescriptions. Who knows what these pills are. I just know they make me feel a lot better … once they work."

"Can I get you anything?" Like a drug dictionary or a stomach pump …

"You can come keep me company," he said, still focused on the ceiling. "I'm getting really bored lying here by myself."

I scooted next to Rocco and we watched the ceiling together.

"You didn't have to shoot yourself in the foot just to get out of doing homework."

He inhaled sharply as the pain hit him again. I took his hand and he squeezed it hard.

"I think I told you some stuff about Cameron that I wasn't supposed to tell you last night," he said.

"You weren't making much sense. I didn't pay any attention."

"Just don't tell Cameron I told you, okay? He'll be really upset if he finds out."

I hated being the bearer of bad news. "Actually, you weren't exactly discreet about it." I downplayed it a bit. "I think Cameron might have overheard you."

He swore under his breath. "Was he mad?"

"I don't think so." I struggled to keep the burning localized to the back of my ears.

"What did he say?"

"Not much."

A wide grin formed on his face. "I guess he had a hard time talking when he was sticking his tongue down your throat."

"You saw?" I gasped in horror. "I thought you were sleeping!"

"Actually, I thought I had dreamt the whole thing," he narrowed his eyes, "which would have been really weird if I did dream about my brother kissing you, of all people … But you just confirmed that I'm not going nuts. Thanks."

I reached over and punched him hard on the arm. "How much did you watch, pervert?"

"I just saw a couple of arms thrashing around in the dark. And then of course there were the sounds." He puckered his lips and made exaggerated kissing noises near my face to remind me that he was definitely fifteen years old.

I pushed his face away. "You got Griff in a lot of trouble yesterday for shooting yourself."

Rocco's grin was replaced with a pout. I felt a little smug.

"Cameron promised me a rank position. I was the only one who didn't have a gun. How am I supposed to get any respect from the guys if he keeps treating me like I'm a kid?"

I was going to remind him that he was a kid, but changed my mind. "I think Cameron was just trying to keep you safe."

"I can take care of myself."

"Maybe. But you obviously can't take care of yourself when you have a gun in your hand."

He sulked for a while and then asked, "How much trouble is Griff in?"

"I don't know. Cameron was pretty upset last night. He still looked really angry this morning."

"I bet Griff is pretty upset with me too."

"I don't think so. But he's definitely scared."

"Scared? Why?" He looked as incredulous as I had been.

"I don't know. He came into my room last night and kept saying that they were going to kill him." I decided it was better not to tell Rocco everything that Griff said. It was too painful.

"He went into your room!"

"He climbed up the deck in the middle of the night."

"Wow! He must have been really freaked. Have you talked to Cameron about it? I mean, Griff is being pretty ridiculous about this. He's not going to get killed just because I shot myself in the foot."

I was glad to hear that I wasn't the only one who thought that Griff was being ridiculous—but at the same time I didn't want to tell Rocco about Griff's notion that he was going to get killed ... because of me. Had I led Griff to think that there had been something more than friendship between us?

"I haven't said anything to Cameron about this yet," I said. "He wasn't in a very good mood this morning."

"I'll talk to Cameron," Rocco said, stepping up. "This is my fault. Griff shouldn't get in trouble because of me."

The moment of maturity was short-lived ... Rocco started giggling.

"So you finally sucked face with my big brother. Hallelujah! I think I deserve a prize for that one."

"I wouldn't advertise the fact that you can't keep your mouth shut," I snapped.

"Looks like we have something in common, then."

I punched him in the arm, even harder this time, but he was quite numb now and didn't feel a thing.

"You're gross," I muttered. I stood up and stepped on something sticky on the floor. "And your room is gross." I thought about it and announced, "I think I'm actually going to clean it today."

"You wouldn't dare," he said, his eyes round.

I started picking up dirty clothes from the floor and throwing them out into the hallway. "You're going to be spending a lot of time in here, and you can't lie in this disgusting smell all day," I said. "You can watch me go through all your stuff, or you can tell me where I can and can't go, but either way, I'm cleaning your room today."

I fixed him a couple of sandwiches. With a full belly and incapacitated, Rocco agreed to guide me through his maze of a mess. It took us a long time to dig our way out; in the end, I had stacked three large bags of garbage on the front stoop and filled the dishwashers to the brim with newly discovered dirty dishes, and we had five more loads of laundry to do.

Suppertime came. Rocco's room was close to spotless, and I helped him limp into the living room to eat and watch TV—which, as he explained, was his treat for working so hard all day. (Talking while I slaved away had been exhausting for him.)

I knew that Rocco was feeling better when his needs became more extravagant. At some point, he complained that his voice was getting tired from having to make so many demands; he suggested that I get him a bell so he could just ring it instead of moving his mouth. I went to bed.

****

I still hadn't talked to Griff since the night he broke into my room. So I threw on a pair of jeans and a T-shirt and went to check on Rocco before going down to confront Griff. The kitchen was empty; the house was still hushed. I peeked into Rocco's room—he was snoring. I groaned quietly when I noticed clothes already piled on the floor.

It was sunny out and the guards were out and about, but Griff was not. I could feel their stares as I walked toward the garage, but I didn't care if they saw me. I was determined to clear the air.

I opened the side door to the stifling hot garage and walked past the lineup of cars. The Maserati had been dug out of the mud and dragged back in. It was hard to tell because of the extreme amount of mud, but it looked to be in pretty bad shape: clumps of grass were stuck under the crooked front wheels, the front fender was bent and scratched, and the driver's-side mirror was missing.

I tiptoed up the stairs and could feel the choking, humid air get worse as I climbed. Upstairs, there were half a dozen floor fans running in tandem, which caused the makeshift curtains to billow in and out of the windows, sporadically allowing rays of light into the room. A few night guards were sprawled on top of their beds, sleeping uncomfortably in the heat.

From my end of the room, I couldn't see Griff in his bed. I tiptoed over to be sure. What I found when I did get to his bed shocked me: not only was he not there, but his bed was completely empty—devoid of any pillow, sheets, or blankets. There was just a naked mattress. The areas around and under Griff's bed had been almost cleaned out. Griff had already left, but—I realized this in horror—he hadn't taken everything with him. Still tucked under his bed was his box of fighting magazines. The nonessentials.

I didn't care much that he had left me behind or that he had broken his promise to come and get me before he did leave, but the thought of him walking around in the woods by himself concerned me greatly.

I dejectedly sat on his bed and ruffled through a magazine, looking for an explanation, until something in my peripheral vision interrupted my train of thought. The garbage-bag curtain next to Griff's bed had moved with the wind of the oscillating fan, and from the second-story window, I noticed someone walking on the grass by the tree line below. I looked closer and saw Carly walking by herself, carrying her usual stack of files. She strolled toward the woods, turning onto a shoelace of a beaten dirt path and disappearing through the brush.

A booming voice abruptly raised me from my meditation. "What do you think you're doing in here, girl?"

It was one of the line guards, the same one who had informed me that Griff had left with Cameron a few days before, the same scary one who liked to glare at me. He was standing at the top of the stairwell—a tall, grossly skinny man with hair that looked like it hadn't been washed in a few days. Adding to my luck, all the night guards had been awakened by the man's roar.

In the moment it took the angry guard to stomp toward me, it occurred to me that coming here alone, without Griff, had been a really bad idea.

"I was just looking for Griff," I stammered.

The man approached the bed. "Your boyfriend's long gone, honey," he sneered. "Finally got what was coming to him. Acting like he was better than us … maybe if he hadn't been so high and mighty we would have told him to stay away from the boss's latest girl. Playing that game will always get you whacked."

"Griff ran away," I insisted, my shaking voice failing to convince either of us.

"The only place that guy is running to is hell."

He grabbed me by the arm and tried to pull me off the bed. "Girls like you come and go around here all the time, you ain't nothing special, and I ain't gonna get killed for some prissy little girl." He twisted my arm and yanked me from my seat. "Get the hell out of here before you get another one of us killed."

"You're hurting me!"

He twisted harder. I yelped.

"Roach! Let her go!" one of the bigger night guards commanded.

"Mind your own business, asshole." Roach was dragging me away from the bed.

Two night guards jumped off their beds and made their way toward us. Roach immediately released my arm.

"Go," the guard ordered me as he pushed Roach out of my way and fixed him with a stare.

I ran from the garage without protest, without looking back. Outside, nothing was different. The sun was still shining. The armed guards were still stalking the property, still doing their best to ignore me. But to me it was all a little different, as if Griff's absence had shaded everything in gray. I loved Cameron. And Cameron loved me. Of this I was sure—I couldn't have imagined that feeling. Everything else was now gray.

I didn't stop running until I was back in the house. My heart was pounding through my chest, and Rocco was shambling down the stairs.

"I was looking for you. Where were you?" he asked.

"Just walking around," I lied. I knew that I wasn't supposed to be hanging around Griff or even looking for him. My head was buzzing too much to give Rocco a better excuse.

I had to admit that Rocco looked funny standing in his swim trunks with a plastic bag over his injured foot.

"I'm going for a swim," he announced. "Coming?"

"You really shouldn't be going in the water with your foot injured like that. It'll get infected."

"No it won't," he said, pointing at the plastic bag. "My foot will stay dry in this." My expression was laden with doubt, but he ignored me. "So are you coming or not?"

I desperately needed to be with a friendly face while I cleared my head. When I got to the pool, Rocco was in the water, and the plastic bag had already been thrown to the side.

"It didn't work," he explained before I could ask him. I raised my eyebrows in a "told-you-so" way and plunged into the pool.

When I came back up for air, he was looking at me oddly.

"What's on your arm?"

I followed his gaze and looked at my upper arm—five finger-sized bruises were surfacing where Roach had grabbed me.

"I think I'm getting a rash," I said.

He swam away from me.

I tried to forget Roach, count my blessings, and focus on what Roach had said, not what he had done. I could tell that he wasn't the most reliable source, yet he had seemed so sure of himself that Griff was … I couldn't bring myself to believe him. Still, why would he lie to me about this? He had no motive for lying to me about this or anything else. What was I to him? But if I let myself believe this, believe this total stranger, then that would mean that Cameron had …

"Did you talk to Cameron about Griff yet?" I asked Rocco, trying to sound as cool as possible.

"Yeah. I talked to him about it last night."

"And?"

"And nothing. Cameron said the same thing I did. Griff is being stupid—no one's going to kill him or anything like that. I'm the one who screwed up, not Griff." His voice was slightly bitter.

"One of the guards told me he was gone," I said innocently, as if mentioning it in passing.

"I know. Griff was sent away yesterday."

I wondered if *sent away* was a code for something else. "Why would he be sent away if shooting yourself in the foot was your fault?"

"Because he doesn't follow anyone's orders. I guess him breaking into your room was kind of the last straw."

I was mortified. "You told Cameron that Griff climbed into my room!"

"No I didn't!" Rocco whimpered. "They already knew. Spider caught Griff climbing down."

I knew this couldn't be good.

"Where was Griff sent away to?" I asked, acting as casual as I could.

"Cameron found him another job with one of his distributors."

"And you believe him?"

He looked at me strangely. "Why wouldn't I believe him? That's a stupid question."

I left it alone because Rocco was getting upset, and so was I.

After a while, the patio door opened. Spider and Carly walked straight to the pool house, completely ignoring Rocco and me. A short while later, Cameron also appeared and tensely sat on the edge of the lounge chair.

He surveyed me.

"What's on your arm?" It sounded like an accusation.

"Rash," Rocco explained for me.

Cameron continued to stare at my arm. I swam away, grabbing the piece of bandage that floated by and throwing it at Rocco. He mumbled a curse, stumbled out of the pool, and hopped on one leg back into the house to fix his foot.

From the opposite end of the pool I was suddenly brave. "Why didn't you tell me Spider saw Griff climb out of my room?"

"Why didn't *you* tell me that Griff climbed into your room?"

"You weren't in a good mood, and I didn't want to get him in trouble. He was already pretty scared," I answered right away.

"He didn't follow orders. He had reason to be scared."

His voice chilled me, and I was less brave now. "You still haven't answered my question."

"I realize that you and this Griff fellow have grown ... close over the past few weeks. I can't have an employee who refuses to follow my orders."

"What? You think that Griff and I were having *sex* in your room?"

He flinched. "I still have a job to do, and that includes keeping you safe. We have rules for a reason around here, and someone who doesn't follow rules is a danger to you and the rest of us."

I tried to push my family's history of adultery out of my head. "Do you really think that I would kiss you and turn to someone else on the same night? What kind of person do you take me for?"

"That thing last night—"

"That *thing*?" I should have braced myself, but I never got the chance.

"The kiss was just a kiss. It didn't mean anything. I was really tired, and you were drinking ... It should have never happened. Let's forget about it."

He was stone-faced.

I took a long, ragged breath. "You told me you loved me."

"No. I never said that," he reminded me coldly.

The words had done their damage, each syllable leaving a crater-sized gash in its wake.

I could hardly breathe, could hardly hold on. I pulled myself out of the pool and wrapped a towel tight around me.

"Just so you know," I said, my voice shaking, "Griff and I didn't do anything. We talked. Well, he talked mostly, and I listened."

"What did he talk about?"

"He thought that you were going to kill him," I said, watching him to see if I could figure out the truth from his face.

He just looked at me.

"He also told me that I should be scared of you. That you were going to kill me too." I fired the words, hoping they would hurt someone else for once.

"And you believe that?"

I had no answer to give him.

I walked away.

I held on while I climbed the first staircase. I still held on as I made it up the second staircase. When I was safely concealed behind Cameron's bedroom door, I let it go, let myself fall apart. Cameron ... Griff ... Cameron ... it was all too much. I wasn't sure of anything anymore.

CHAPTER SEVENTEEN

DIFFERENT WORLDS

I didn't want to open my eyes. I could feel the warmth of the sun on my face—which was the last thing I wanted. Why couldn't it just rain today? Part of me wished that I would open my eyes and find myself back in my tiny room in Callister, living an ordinary life where people like Cameron remained unseen and definitely unfelt. But the other part, that bigger part again, knew that I didn't want to go back to my former life—a life without love, in a world where I didn't fit in—no matter what awful things Cameron Hillard found to say and do to me. I threw the blanket over my head, hoping that if I waited in the darkness long enough, clouds would come to match my mood. But now I could feel the bed shake; Meatball was wagging his tail wildly. He knew that I was awake.

"Not yet, Meatball, please." My stomach was hurting, and I felt drained.

"You're going to have to get up eventually." I didn't have to pull the blankets away to know that it was Cameron. I hadn't heard him come in, yet there he was. "Anyway, Meatball won't go back to sleep if he knows you're up."

His tone hadn't improved. It was going to be another one of those days.

"Don't you have anything better to do than watch me sleep?" I said from under the blankets, trying to keep my voice as cool as his, even though my somersaulting heart silently betrayed me. I hated that he had this kind of power.

Something thumped next to me. I peeked out—Cameron had thrown a black object at me. It was a cell phone—*my* cell phone.

"Call your mother," he ordered.

Call my mother? That was probably the last thing I felt like doing at that moment. And it was definitely not what I ever expected Cameron to say. "Why?"

"She left you three messages. Sounded urgent." His voice seemed unnecessarily guarded.

"You've been listening to my phone messages?" I didn't know what made me more upset: the fact that he had totally violated my privacy, or the fact that I had probably missed only three calls—from my mother, no less—since disappearing from the face of the earth, and that Cameron now knew how pathetic my other life was.

He lifted one eyebrow.

Sighing, I climbed out of hibernation and picked up the phone. I scrolled through the list of missed calls and found that my mother wasn't the only one who had called. I couldn't help but bring this to Cameron's attention.

"Looks like Jeremy called a bunch of times too. Did he leave any messages?"

He glowered; I took that as an affirmative response.

"And?"

"And nothing. He left a bunch of messages asking why you were mad at him. The guy sounds like a doorknob, if you ask me."

"I didn't know that doorknobs could talk."

"They don't. They just squeak and spin in a circle."

I tried to not dignify that response with a reply, but I couldn't contain myself. "So, I should probably call him back too, then. It might be urgent."

"No worries. He'll never call you again."

"Oh my god, Cameron! What did you do to him?"

Julie Hockley

Cameron frowned, understanding my meaning. "Definitely not what you apparently think I'm capable of."

I breathed a sigh of relief, and then immediately regretted my impulsive insinuation.

Cameron said, "I got Rocco to call this Jeremy guy last night and pretend to be calling from a hospital in … Sweden or Switzerland, I forget … I was laughing so hard … something about you having a highly contagious rash that made your ears swell up … that he should run to a hospital right away to get his ears checked."

I couldn't imagine Rocco pulling off any believable accent—but then again, Jeremy was pretty vain, and the mere possibility that his ears might swell would have certainly distracted, devastated him.

"And Jeremy bought it?"

Cameron shrugged. "Like I said, your boyfriend's a doorknob. Don't know what you see in that guy."

"He's a nice, normal guy," I emphasized, for Cameron's benefit. "Anyway, he's not my boyfriend."

"Well he *was*, wasn't he?" he insisted dryly.

I narrowed my eyes. "What difference does it make?"

"It doesn't," he responded abruptly. "Call your mother."

I dialed my mother's mobile number, and the line rang over and over. I hoped … and grimaced when she finally picked up. "Emily? Is that you, honey?" my mom asked, almost sweetly. *Honey?* There were so many things wrong with that question that I couldn't even begin to analyze it.

"Hi."

"Honey, where have you been? I've been trying to reach you for the last two weeks."

The fact that I'd been kidnapped by a gang of drug dealers in their million-dollar compound out in the middle of nowhere came to mind. "Er, sorry. I've been really busy. What's up?" was what I actually said.

I could hear the clink of dishes and silverware in the background. It was close to dinnertime in France.

238

"Well, you'll never guess who we ran into." Drumrolls played in my head as I paused for the incredible revelation. "Mr. and Mrs. Jacobson. You remember them, don't you?"

No. "Uh-huh," I lied, to keep things simple and quick.

"Well, imagine the coincidence of them meeting us … here! And guess what?" More drumrolls. "They brought their wonderful son Damien with them!"

"Is that what you wanted to talk to me about?"

"Yes, honey. What else is there?"

"Nothing," I grumbled. "So what were you saying about the Jacobsons?"

Cameron had settled himself by the couch, leaning back and watching me while my mom carried on about the Jacobsons and their son: they were such a good family, and Damien was absolutely delightful and well-bred … not to mention the fact that he was positioned to succeed his father in running the family empire. I was biting my tongue a lot.

"I've been talking to Damien, and he is just dying to see you. How quickly can you catch a plane to come meet us?"

There it was—the reason for the niceties. The only time Isabelle was ever motherly was when she wanted something; the only time my mother spoke English to me and didn't force me to speak French to her was when she was trying to impress someone who was listening. This time I assumed it was both. I couldn't imagine what embellishments my mom had told Damien for him to be just dying to meet me. The truth was that I remembered Damien Jacobson all too well. We were seven years old, and I had been forced to go to one of those stupid family picnics for one of my dad's clients. Damien had decided it would be good fun to play connect the dots with my freckles—and when I dared to protest, he stabbed me in the back of the arm with a pencil. I still had the scar to prove it. I doubted that someone like Damien Jacobson would remember that small fact, but unfortunately for him, I never forgot it—and I was really good at holding a grudge.

"Europe is just not an option right now and—"

Cameron raised an eyebrow curiously.

But Isabelle didn't let me finish. "Oh, here he comes now. He wants to talk to you."

"No! I don't want to talk to this Damien—"

"Hello? Emily?" A deep voice rang through the phone.

I cringed. "Yes. Hi. Damien." Cameron's interest appeared to pick up when I said Damien's name.

The clinking and chattering noises became more distant on the other end of the line. Damien had clearly walked away from the rest of the party. "So, did you ever grow out of your polka dots?"

So he remembered me—and apparently had not matured past the age of seven.

"No. I haven't—actually, it's gotten worse. Much worse. How about you? Are you still eating your snot when you think no one is looking?"

Cameron practically choked on his own saliva.

There was awkward silence on the other end of the phone. Damien then cleared his throat and continued the conversation, unfortunately. "So ... you should totally come meet us here. A bunch of us are spending the summer chill-axing in the Riviera. The whole gang is here—Chuck, Jimmy, Lance, Chrissy, Angela ..."

Images of the "whole gang" came into my head—each of them had, at one point or another, pulled my hair or taunted me in some horrible way when I was a kid. "Sorry, I'm really tied up right now."

Damien wasn't listening. "Dad had the yacht sailed to port in Monaco. I'll take you sailing—just you and me. Come on ... it'll be great!"

Nothing about being alone with him, where the only way to escape was to drown trying to swim to shore, sounded fun. I would have picked drowning any day. "Damien, sorry, my phone is about to die. I'll get back to you on the boat thing. Say—bye—to—my mother—for me ..." I hung up and threw the phone at the foot of the bed. Then I fell back onto my pillow.

"Emergency averted," I said. "Happy?"

"Yeah. I am," Cameron said with a grin that almost reached his eyes. "That was more entertaining than I thought it would be. I didn't know Europe could be an emergency."

When you've had everything handed to you on a silver platter, it was surprising the things that became a crisis. "Weren't you afraid that I would tell my mother where I was?" I asked. Not that I had any idea where I was.

"Would she have believed you?"

He had a point.

I heard music booming in the distance. "You're working today," I mused, surprised by my automatic connection.

He nodded, but he didn't look like he was in a big hurry to go. "So who is this Damien fellow you were talking to?"

I thought I glimpsed jealousy—or maybe it was just wishful thinking.

"His parents' money is friends with my parents' money," I explained, but Cameron looked lost. I sighed. "Just some boy my parents would love to see me settle down with." As I said this, another thought occurred to me. "You know, you and my parents would probably get along quite well."

"Oh?"

"You both try to control my life and seem to think I'm better off sticking with my own kind, whatever that is." I threw the blanket back over my head before he had time to respond. "Do you have any more orders, or can I go back to sleep?"

"I wasn't ordering you. I was just concerned that—"

"Whatever," I interrupted. Now I was in a *really* bad mood—a common side effect of my mother. "Can you let Meatball out when you leave?" I exhaled loudly, my indication that the conversation was over.

The room was silent; he remained still. I imagined that he was staring at the big bulge under the blanket, considering his next move. After a minute, I heard him walk with insistence past the bed, calling Meatball to follow him as he left the room.

As soon as I heard the door click and confirmed the noise of his steps down the stairs, I ripped the blanket off. I had an idea where Cameron was going—and I had a plan. With record speed, I was dressed and ready to execute. I crouched by the bedroom door and listened. After what seemed like forever, I heard what I was waiting for: the muffled voices of Cameron, Spider, and Carly as they walked out the front door. I waited a few more minutes after I heard the door close and then headed out to follow them. I opened the door a crack and peeking out first to make sure they were out of sight.

My encounter with Roach had taught me that wandering around the grounds was a dangerous thing, especially now that Griff was gone. I glanced around and didn't see Roach; I was safe enough—for a while, anyway. I made my way down to the garage, stopping as I neared the corner. There was a guard by the entrance of the pathway I had seen Carly use the day before, so I waited for my opportunity.

The guard was walking back and forth near the path's entrance, but after a few minutes of having nothing to look at but the back of the garage, he got bored and kept marching down the line until he disappeared around the corner. This was my chance. With as much speed as I could rally, I ran straight for the pathway and didn't look back until I was sure I was hidden in the trees.

I stopped and listened: just the rustling of leaves and creaking and cracking of branches, all above my head. I breathed again when I was sure no one was running into the woods after me.

I warily continued on the path. I had no idea how far it went, or how far I would be able to go before I was discovered—then who knew what would happen. I tried not to think about that, and focused on getting moving instead.

The dirt line seemed to go on forever. With every step I took, I was losing my nerve. I was starting to consider turning around when I reached a green brick wall. Strangely erected right up against the tree line was a windowless, one-story building. The dirt path ended right at its metal door, which had been left ajar.

I stood by the door and listened for voices—I heard nothing. I gulped and, with the speed of a snail, quietly crept inside.

Inside was a small office—or at least it looked like it was supposed to be an office. At the far end of the room was an oversized wooden desk with a sleek, black leather chair half-hidden behind it. In the middle of the room there was a burgundy rawhide couch with a ratty blanket thrown on it. There were two wood-burning stoves wedged in a corner, but no wood.

The floor and desk were spilling over with disarrayed piles of clothes. Recognizing some of Cameron's wrinkled T-shirts, I realized that this was where he had been sleeping since I had taken over his room. I glanced at the stiff-looking couch and the yellowed pillow and felt a bit guilty—I couldn't imagine having to sleep on that every night.

I moved toward the large desk. Apart from Cameron's improvised bedroom, there was something else that made this room seem like just the shell of an office—its emptiness. The floor-to-ceiling bookcases were, for the most part, bare of normal office stuff. There were no pictures, papers, pens, computers, files, or anything else that would make this office an office.

When I heard quick footsteps, I froze.

Next to Cameron's improvised sleeping quarters was a closed door. The footsteps seemed to be approaching from the other side of it, and getting closer quickly. I pushed the leather chair aside and hid under the desk, peering through the hairline cracks between the wood planks that made up the front of the desk.

There I held my breath and watched Carly speed across the room and exit outside, closing the heavy door behind her.

My heart was thumping wildly. I took a few seconds to calm myself and exhaled. That had been a close call. Too close. Ghastly thoughts of what Carly would have done had she discovered me went through my head. Somehow I knew that I was not welcome to snoop here.

I crawled out from under the desk and headed for the metal door. Whatever this place was, it wasn't worth getting in trouble for ... or worse.

But when I pushed on the heavy door, nothing happened.

I pulled and then I pushed, using my whole body, but the door did not budge.

It was stuck—and so was I. I thought I was going to vomit. I bent over, holding on to my stomach.

When I heard unrecognizable voices through the other door, I froze in place again, terrified, listening. There were several voices echoing in the distance, yet none seemed to be coming closer.

I tiptoed to this door—possibly a new, alternate exit—and peeked out. It opened onto a short, narrow passageway that led nowhere. A dead end. And oddly, there was no one there, though I could still hear the voices.

I walked to the dead end and noticed a door-shaped slit in the wall. At the bottom was a small pedal, which I assumed would open the hidden door. In the middle of the door was a dime-sized peephole. I slowly brought my face forward and peered through.

People were talking over each other in a room with harsh fluorescent lighting. In the middle of the room there was a large, rectangular glass table. Cameron was calmly seated at the head, engrossed in paperwork, while the others were slowly finding seats.

It was a mind-boggling assortment of people. Seated around the table were more than a dozen men and one woman who looked like extremes of each other, people of all shapes, sizes, and ages. Some were dressed in three-piece suits, while others wore sideways ball caps and gold chains or full leather outfits ... gang bosses, together in one room, acting like normal people.

The seated members, the bosses, were noisily talking among themselves, each with a man standing guard behind them, each guard looking fiercer than the next. Spider was standing behind Cameron.

When Cameron lifted his head, the table immediately went quiet. "We have several items on the agenda today. I thank you again for making the trip out to attend this meeting. I can assure you that we will pursue our meetings in the city as soon as it's feasible for me." The room stayed very quiet. "Let's try to keep on topic today so that everyone can get out of here at a decent time for once."

Cameron's voice was intimidating and very businesslike. Everyone inside—and outside—the room remained captivated. "The most pressing item is an apparent breach of territorial lines, which has led to hostilities between two of our branches and the loss of some of their members. This conflict has also attracted news coverage, and our suppliers have expressed concern over the media attention."

Cameron eyed one of the suited men sitting at the table, a guy with heavily gelled hair. "Johnny, I understand that this started after some of your boys tried to distribute product in California."

A man who was wearing a blue bandana around his head piped up. "They didn't just try to distribute. They were trying to undercut me and take over my territory."

Cameron calmly lifted his hand. "Viper, you will get your chance to speak. Johnny, my sources support what Viper just said. Can you explain?"

Johnny shifted in his seat. "Listen, some of my boys went on a road trip and got a little carried away. It was a misunderstanding. No disrespect was meant."

Cameron turned to Viper. "Viper, you heard the explanation. Do you have anything to say?"

"Just that it's total bull," he mumbled.

Cameron continued, "Johnny, I believe that a ten percent contribution of your branch's earnings last month should be sufficient to settle damages to Viper. Do you agree?"

Johnny nodded begrudgingly.

"Viper?"

Viper nodded, cheerfully.

Cameron glanced around the table. "Any objections?"

Everyone remained silent.

Cameron wrote something on a piece of paper and handed it to Spider. "Johnny, next time your boys want a road trip from Chicago to LA, make sure they leave the business at home, all right?"

Johnny sulked in response.

I was entranced as an officious Cameron led the meeting and methodically went through a list of agenda items: new products coming onto the market, competitors, price listings, FBI reports and sightings, and other bad blood that had developed between the participating gangs. Spider hung back and collected the paperwork that Cameron handed him as these topics were discussed. It didn't take me long to realize that Cameron didn't just sit on the crime bosses' board of directors—he was their CEO.

After two hours, my legs were like jelly, and Cameron finally stopped the meeting for a break. Everybody stretched out and slowly made their way out of the room while Cameron and Spider went through the collected paperwork. When the room was empty, Spider took the stacks of paper and walked straight for the hidden door, and me. I struggled to wake up my legs and ran back to the office like a baby deer taking its first steps. I barely had time to duck my head under the desk before Spider stepped through the doorway.

Just as Carly had, he walked straight through the room to the metal door. When he got there, he realized, as I had, that the door was stuck. He backed up and rammed his whole body into it. The door burst open and, cursing under his breath, Spider disappeared, leaving the door ajar.

My heart jumped: I was finally free.

I waited a few minutes more to make sure that Spider wasn't coming back right away. Then I crawled out, only to hear voices nearing from the passageway again. I banged my forehead on the desk as I hurried to crawl back underneath it.

"It seems like forever since I've been here," said a female voice.

Through the cracks in the wood, I saw Cameron approaching. I recognized the woman next to him as the only female who had been in the meeting room, sitting with the other crime bosses. She was tall and slim, with short, dark hair that was tucked behind her ears. She looked like one of those girls in my brother's car magazines—the girls that made any car look fabulous just by standing next to it.

As Cameron rummaged through a duffle bag on the floor, the woman glanced over the clothes that were stacked on surfaces.

"Are you sleeping in here?" she asked.

"Sometimes," he replied, distracted.

He found what he had been looking for and handed it to her—a small pink T-shirt.

"You left this here," he said to her as she took the shirt.

The woman kept her eyes on his face.

"She's still here, isn't she?"

"Who?"

"That girl who saw you killing one of Shield's boys in the projects," she responded.

Cameron squinted, arms crossed. "What makes you think I brought her here?"

"I heard from one of my guys that you took her home with you," she said, her voice steady.

"The board has already ruled on this, Manny. The girl will not be a problem for any of us. I don't intend to revisit this issue with you."

"The board was forced to make a decision without having all the facts. I think that they might be interested to know that the girl is alive and that you're keeping her here." Her voice had gone up an octave.

"What are you saying, exactly?" he snarled.

Manny immediately became sedate. "Nothing. I didn't mean anything by it." She raised her hand and stroked his cheek. I squirmed. "I'm just wondering what interest you have in her."

He didn't pull her hand away. "You know we can't have contact like this when there are other leaders around."

"Do you love her?"

"Of course I don't love her," Cameron told her without skipping a beat.

I felt the gash in my heart rip open again.

"Then why is she here? I thought I was the only one you would ever bring here."

247

Cameron sighed like I had heard him sigh so many times with me. "I'm just bored right now, Manny. I need something to play with, to keep me busy. When I'm done, I'll get rid of her."

"Well, hurry up and be done with her. I miss you. I want to be with you again." She leaned in and kissed him on the mouth. His body tensed, but he let her kiss him. I couldn't breathe, even after he finally pushed her away.

His voice was softer now. "That was a one-time mistake that will never happen again. I can't show bias for one boss over the other."

Spider came back inside, empty-handed, and patiently waited for Cameron by the closed trick door. With an indifferent nod, Cameron motioned to Manny to leave. Resigned, she walked out. After Spider looked through the peephole in the hidden door, all three stepped back through the passageway—and I was left hiding alone under a desk, shaking, beaten.

I fought back tears.

Then I ran out the door.

I followed the dirt path back through the woods, falling at least twice. I ran out into the clearing at the other end without stopping or looking to see if the guard was back at his post. In a split second, I decided that he probably wouldn't rat me out if he did see me—otherwise he would have to admit to Spider that he had let me through in the first place. Even if he did rat me out, I didn't care: either way, I was dead. Cameron had confirmed this himself. What I did, or didn't do, didn't matter anymore. It had never mattered. I was just a pawn in Cameron's twisted game.

I ran straight to my room and fell onto the bed. My teeth and my fists were tightly clenched, and a few tears started to escape.

Chapter Eighteen

Heated Moments

When Rocco came knocking on my door, I sat up and wiped the tears away with the back of my hand before he limped in and plopped down on my bed.

I leaned against the wall with my knees tucked into my chest, and we sat in uncomfortable silence. I didn't know who to trust any more. *No one*, answered the brooding voice of reason that I had been quashing for too long.

Rocco eyed me and finally asked, "Em, is everything okay? You look really awful."

Only Rocco could find a way to critique my appearance on the worst day of my life.

"I'm fine," I lied.

"Are you sure? Because you look really pale—even more than normal." He suddenly looked deathly afraid and pushed himself down to the foot of the bed, as far away from me as possible. "You're not going to throw up, are you?"

I did feel like I was going to throw up, but I didn't tell him this. "Really, I'm fine. I'm just a bit tired, that's all."

He exhaled. "Good, 'cause if you're going to puke again, I'm outta here."

He convinced me to watch a movie with him. I wanted to trust Rocco, despite his total loyalty to his brother, and figured that spending a little more time with him might help me decide, one way or another, whether I could still trust him. Whether there was anyone I could trust.

Even if Rocco spent most of the time under the influence of his rainbow-colored pills and sleeping with his head bent back and his mouth wide open, here—huddled head-to-toe on the couch in Cameron's room with Rocco's big feet stuck behind my back—it was easy to feel safe. Though the pain in my heart was still throbbing, the feelings of helplessness and isolation dissipated. He had no idea of the turmoil bubbling inside me, and I was thankful for that. His obliviousness, at least, would remain unspoiled. I imagined that I would have liked to have a little brother like Rocco, even if he was bigger than me and a total slob.

When my mind had quieted and I could think without interruptions from me, I pushed myself to concentrate on making sense of it all. Cameron wasn't just a drug dealer or a crime boss; he was the big boss and led most, if not all, crime bosses in the United States. And there was no doubt in my mind that I loved him, no matter who or what he was, no matter what he said. Why did I still love this monstrous man? I had overheard the truth: I was just a game to him. Cameron had broken my heart. I didn't know if he knew this. Maybe this had been his plan all along—to hurt me, to break me, to kill whatever small bit of hope I had left inside me after Bill died. It turned out that Cameron was not the tortured soul I had thought him to be. The monster was the man; the man was the monster. There was no separation.

And yet it was clear I still loved him because my heart was broken, because I wished that things were different, that he was the person I'd thought he was. I wanted him to be savable. Perhaps I had wanted to be the one to save him from himself.

I loved him despite myself.

That made it all the more painful.

I was still alive because Cameron wanted it that way, because he was bored, because he was looking for fun. Whether Griff was still alive … I had my doubts, though I couldn't be sure. Theories were too terrifying, too crippling right now.

How did I get myself into this situation?

I remembered the person I had been back in Callister. Cautious. Removed. Invisible. Parts of an armor that had taken me years to erect; parts of an armor that had too quickly fallen away the day I had met Cameron.

There was no point in trying to find an answer to the question—the damage was already done.

This led me to my next question—could I do anything about it? Could I fight back? Cameron hadn't let his guard down—everything he did was done with purpose. Earlier that day, I had halfheartedly accused him of being like my parents. That comparison had been more accurate than I'd realized, even though Cameron, like Carly, seemed to have some preconceived notion that his world was much different from mine. But our worlds were not so different. Yes, I could fight back … I had a lifetime of practice fighting my parents, fighting their attempts to control me. The controllers, I knew how to deal with their kind.

I didn't know if it was Rocco's allied presence—the sense of having someone in my corner—or the headache that had slowly grown into a massive migraine, but my grief had morphed into something different: anger and power. As the hours rolled by, I stewed in my thoughts and the tension in my body intensified, like a bull being held behind a gate, fueled by the goading of the crowd. I realized that my head was tilting forward. By the time the sun set and the sound of the board members' car stereos faded into the distance, I was seeing red. I spent the next minutes listening, half-hoping that Cameron would show his face, half-hoping that I would wake up and find that all of this had been a dream—some of it really good, some of it nightmarish.

One of my desires was realized when I heard the front door slam and someone stomping up the stairs. My heart and head pounded riotously. I immediately got up, marched to the bed, and rigidly sat. I faced the door, geared up for combat. Cameron thrust the door open and entered the battlefield. His eyes were fierce and wild, like those of a caged animal set loose—his war face looked much more daunting than mine.

I shrank back, realizing that my plan for an ambush had been crushed.

I attempted to regroup while Cameron flashed his eyes at me then around the room. He spied Rocco, who was sleeping on the couch. "Rocco, get out."

Rocco didn't move.

"Rocco!"

Rocco snapped up instinctively. "What?" he yelled back with annoyance.

"Get up and get out," Cameron repeated, regaining his calm voice. He was glaring at me, breathing through his nostrils.

Rocco turned to me, his eyes round. "Why? What's going on?" My heart was thumping through my ears, making the headache a thousand times worse. I wanted to tell him that I was okay, that he could leave without worry, but that would have been a colossal lie.

"Now!" Cameron ordered again. For the second time within the span of a few seconds, he had lost his composure. I knew that this wasn't good, and wondered what excuse the path guard had made for his own lack of attention when he squealed on me.

"Geez! Okay! I'm leaving," Rocco said. "You don't have to yell. I'm getting really sick of no one telling me what the hell is going on around here."

He hobbled out, and Cameron closed the door so quickly that he almost knocked Rocco over. Cameron then spun around and raced toward me. I flinched as he grabbed my arm; I had prepared for a battle ... but not the bloodshed that came with it. There was never any physical warfare when I fought with my parents, just a lot of yelling and crying.

He lifted the sleeve of my T-shirt with such force that I thought it would rip.

"Jesus," he gasped. "Why did you lie to me?"

I didn't know where to begin. I hadn't expected our combat to start in this fashion. The speech I had prepared in my head started with me accusing him of being a liar, not the other way around. My mouth was frozen shut.

What came next was not what I had expected him to say, either.

"One of the guards attacked you yesterday," he said. "Why didn't you tell me?" He held my arm out as evidence and waited.

I looked down and realized that he was looking at the bruises that Roach's fingers had left on my bicep. They now had a greenish-purple hue.

Though this wasn't what I'd thought I was being attacked for, it gave me the ammunition I needed to fight back. I mentally discarded my planned discourse and decided to improvise. "Why would you care?" I asked, yanking my arm away. "You'll just get rid of me when you're done with me. Why would it matter if one of your guards roughs me up before you do it yourself?"

He squinted. "What are you talking about? I would never hurt you or let anyone else hurt you. I would definitely not let one of my men do ... anything to you."

"Do not patronize me! You care about me the way people care about their pets. I'm just something for you to play with when you come home. Then you'll have me put down when you get sick of me."

"Emmy, if this is about the kiss thing, I shouldn't have—"

"Cameron, please don't insult my intelligence by pretending that you care about what happens to me. The game is over. I overheard you talking to Manny in your office."

The blood rushed from Cameron's face and his eyes widened. He turned his back and walked a few steps away.

My skin was on fire; I tried to steady myself by sitting on the bed.

When he came back, his face was completely composed.

"You shouldn't have gone wandering." His tone was acerbic. He sat next to me and glared.

I was getting extremely dizzy but stood back up anyway.

"I can't believe I fell for … all of this. I actually thought that you loved me. I thought …" I was shaking my head, pacing, winded, struggling with the tears and the heat. I didn't know what to think anymore.

When a very calm Cameron leaned over to take my hand— and I wanted him to take it more than anything—I panicked and jumped out of his reach. He flinched, and I caught a glimpse of something in his eyes.

Suddenly I remembered how to fight again. I stopped and narrowed my eyes at him. "I guess I should apologize to you because I haven't been much fun at all since I've been here. So, I'll make this really easy for you."

On a calculated whim, I furiously pulled off my T-shirt and unbuttoned my pants.

"Jesus! Emmy, what are you doing?"

I kicked my jeans off and stood in front of him in my underwear.

"Have you gone completely crazy?" he asked.

I put on a brave front, although I felt like I was going to throw up.

"This is what you told Manny you wanted, isn't it? Well, go ahead—have your fun with me. I'm not sure why you went through all this trouble in the first place—it's not like I have anywhere to go. Hell, you could have done this on the first day and gotten rid of me then instead of going through the effort of making me love you. Or is that your fun? Messing with my mind before … all of this," I said, rapidly waving my hands over my nearly-bare chest.

Cameron was up on his feet. He looked ill, but his expression remained otherwise even. He took a step toward me. Out of fear that I would let him calm me down, and in an act of devotion to the cause, I threw myself onto the bed and lay on my back, my body rigid as a soldier's.

When I glanced up, I saw that he had folded his arms and was waiting. His attempt at patience was disparaging.

"What are you waiting for?" My voice was pleading, almost begging.

He didn't move an inch and continued to watch me, his eyes concentrating on my face.

I didn't know which was worse: the fact that I had unclothed myself without much effect, or the fact that he wasn't even slightly interested in taking me up on my offer.

I took a breath and posed myself on my side. I looked him in the eyes. "I love you. There … I've admitted it. Now you can check that one off your list of things to do. Just know that I don't have any experience with the next part … but I'm getting pretty good at taking orders from you."

"Actually, you're not. If you were good at following my orders, we wouldn't be here. Now put your clothes on. Please. So that we can talk about this … rationally."

I turned on my stomach and buried my face in the mattress. My head was shaking from side to side. "I've been cooped up in this house, slowly going crazy, trying to figure you out … but you've just been using me. All this time. You treat people like they're your personal property. I don't even think that you can tell the difference between right and wrong anymore. Whatever makes you feel good is right. Everything else is wrong. You had Griff killed just because you thought that he and I might be more than just friends … or maybe because we were just friends …"

"I didn't kill this Griffin guy. I don't know why you would think that I did."

"The guard, Roach, told me," I said into the mattress.

I could feel the chill of the room climbing up the skin of my legs. I popped my head up.

Cameron's had lips thinned until all the color vanished from them.

"You would believe an idiot who takes his anger out on a girl, rather than believe me?" he asked, finally.

255

"This *idiot* had no reason to lie to me. But you haven't stopped lying since I got here. I just didn't know that you were still lying to me until I overheard you speak to that woman today."

He swallowed. "What you overheard me say to Manny wasn't true, Emmy. If I told the truth … I'm just trying to protect you."

I sprung from the bed and stood in front of him. "Protect me? You bring me here against my will, you order your guards not to talk to me or let me go anywhere, and you even leave your dog here to make sure that I don't run away when you're not looking. You're not protecting me—you're keeping me prisoner."

The pain was now fully visible on his face. "Meatball sleeps here because he wants to, and I thought you would like the company at night."

"Don't do me any more favors," I spat.

"You have to know that I would never hurt you …" He almost sounded sincere, but this was nothing new, and I was prepared for it.

"I don't believe you. You're a liar and I'm not buying it anymore." My whole body was aching and shaking—I was hot and cold, all at once. I looked up through my saturated eyelashes.

"Em …" he started again, slowly regaining control.

I covered my face. "Go away."

He just stood there.

"Get out!" I screamed.

Cameron left, slamming the door behind him.

I heard the thundering whack of his fist punching a hole through a nearby wall. Then the whole house shook as the front door slammed shut.

The room was spinning uncontrollably. My breathing was labored. And then my stomach lurched. I struggled out of bed as quickly as I could and sprinted to the bathroom. I made it to the toilet in time. Too bad the lid was closed.

When I woke up, I was still lying on the cold bathroom tiles. I crawled back to bed and shivered under the blankets, squeezing my eyes shut. I slept very badly—nonsensical voices talked over each other in my head.

The next time I awoke, the room was exceedingly bright, and Carly was standing over me with the back of her hand on my face. I tried to push her away, but none of my muscles were responding to my brain's orders.

"She's burning up. She must have picked up the same flu virus that the guards have. It's no wonder with her not sleeping, not eating. Going around, burning herself out, acting crazy like that. Go get Cameron," I heard her command.

"I did. He told me to go get you," Rocco moaned.

Carly cursed under her breath. "Neither one of us can carry her." She sighed. "Go fill the tub with cold water and I'll get him."

My throat felt like it was on fire. I closed my eyes when it became too much work to keep them open. When I forced them open again, I saw Cameron's strained face. I was floating, and we were in the bathroom. He placed me in the tub, and I cried out as my body hit icy-cold water. I flailed my arms, trying to get out, trying to grab hold of him, but he walked over to Carly.

"She doesn't want me here," he said to her in a low voice.

"Fine!" She waved him off. "Leave. You're just in my way anyway."

She spoke, or cursed, in Spanish while she poured buckets of freezing water over my head. My body was trembling, and my jaw quaked so hard I was sure my teeth were going to shatter.

Rocco came through the door with his hand covering his eyes.

"Here," he said as he blindly tendered a bucket over to Carly.

"Geez, Rocco! Have you never seen a girl in her underwear before?" Carly grabbed the bucket and poured its contents into the bathwater. It was ice, and I wrenched forward as the chill hit my skin once more.

"Please … stop …" I managed to say through my teeth.

"And she finally speaks! Must be a good sign." She poured another bucketful over my head. "I come from a family of six kids, remember? Too bad for you, a cold bath is the only thing that will bring the fever down. I'm afraid you'll have to suffer through it until your skin stops boiling."

257

My body had graduated from trembling to full-out convulsions. Carly looked worried, but she continued to soak me, over and over. After a short while, she dunked her hand in the bathwater to check the temperature. She cursed again. The ice was melting quickly from the heat of my skin. Rocco followed her shouted order and rushed back with another bucket of ice.

"I'm still mad at you, you know," she finally said softly. I was curled up in a ball and just stared at her while she continued to douse me. "Spider told Cameron that you would disappoint him—something about betrayal being in your blood. But I defended you. The whole time, I stuck up for you. Why you decided to mess with that Griffin guy is beyond me. I mean, the guy had nothing going for him. He looked at us like we were trash, even though we're the ones who put money in his pocket."

"Just ... friends," was all I could stutter between shivers to defend myself.

"Right. Like I've never heard that one before." Carly sneered. "I swear, people like you are way more trouble than you're worth. Now it looks like I'm stuck playing nurse Carly just because you and Cameron can't get along."

"Can ... take care ... of myself."

She rolled her eyes. "Yes, I can see that." She poured more water over me and placed the back of her palm over my forehead and cheeks, and then she hummed contentedly as she pulled the rubber plug. I watched the water drain out of the tub while she wrapped a thick towel around me. She walked out, and Cameron walked back in to carry me back to bed. I looked up at him. He kept his eyes straight ahead and left the room like a ghost. Carly helped me get changed into my pajamas and then threw all the blankets that Cameron had brought in over me. I gobbled down the pills and took a few sips from the tall glass of water she gave me. Every bone and muscle in my body ached. I closed my eyes and fell into a comatose sleep.

****

The smell of food hit my nostrils, and I thought I was going to be sick again. I opened my eyes. Carly had brought a bowl of soup in. It was dark outside, and the room was lit solely by the bedside lamp. I turned away in revulsion as Carly shoved the bowl under my nose.

"I'm not leaving until you eat all of this," she announced.

My hand struggled to bring the spoon to my mouth. My stomach heaved. I dropped the spoon back into the bowl.

Carly grumbled and picked up the spoon. "It's late, and I'm getting really tired of this babysitting thing. This won't be a pretty visit if you don't hurry up."

She fed me the soup, and I ate as quickly as my stomach could manage. She gave me another round of pills, which I took without argument, and then she left. I laid my head back on the pillow and closed my eyes, focused on keeping the soup down.

The door opened and clicked back closed. I opened my eyes.

Cameron was standing by the bed with his arms folded. My head was pounding from watching him stand there; I couldn't focus on him and on my stomach at the same time. I squeezed my eyes shut and after a moment felt him sit next to me on the bed.

When I slit my eyes open, I saw him leaning on his knees, looking at the ground.

He took a long, ragged breath. "I know you're not feeling well, so I'll try to keep this short. I have no excuse for what you heard me say to Manny, except that you weren't supposed to hear or see any of that. It was very dangerous what you did ... for you to be there. I don't know what I would have done ... if any of them had seen you, found you there ..." He shook his head and then paused.

"I know you don't believe anything I say, so there's no point in me trying to defend myself to you anymore, even if it kills me to see you so disgusted with me. But there's one thing I do need you to know: I love you, Emmy. I've loved you for a very long time." He turned his eyes to me for the briefest of moments, and I felt a crack in my newly erected armor. "To have you here, with me ... I guess in some sick way, for a while, I thought that this thing between us could work. Hurting you was the last thing I wanted to do, but it looks like I managed to do that anyway." He took another breath. "This place is where I have to be, but it's not a place where you can or should be. There's nothing that I can do to change that. I won't force this life on you."

He looked at me like he was waiting for some kind of response. But I wasn't lucid enough to come up with any response to what he had just hit me with.

Cameron sighed and continued his conversation with the carpet. "I'm leaving for work in a couple days. I'll speak to Spider and make arrangements while I'm in the city to have an armed guard watch over you from your house instead of here. When I get back, we'll plan for you to go back home. I'll make sure to stay out of your way until I leave."

He got up and hesitated over me.

I squeezed my eyes shut.

He kissed my burning forehead before walking out of the room.

I wanted to cry. I fell asleep instead, my mind in a state of shock.

In the night I heard Meatball whining at my door. Cameron shouted for him to come downstairs, but ended up having to come to the door to drag Meatball away by the collar. Sadly, in my battle with Cameron, I had also lost my bedfellow.

I fell asleep again. Cameron's face cruelly filled my dreams. But the monster never came back.

Chapter Nineteen

Expecting the Expected

Over the next few days, Cameron didn't have to put much effort into trying to avoid me, because I didn't leave the room or the bed. Rocco came to visit regularly, but he would quickly get bored watching me lie there; he'd drop onto the bed next to me and then venture to the couch to watch TV, or leave altogether. Carly sourly continued to bring me my meals, and I slowly got stronger as the days wore on. The virus that had gone through the house and through me was a powerful one.

By the third day, I was able to walk around my room without feeling like I was going to vomit or pass out, and I took a long-overdue shower. After I got dressed, I went to the open patio door to feel the fresh air on my face. There were voices coming from the deck below. I peeked around the curtain to see Spider and Carly lounging on patio chairs while Cameron slouched against the rail, facing away from them.

"Carly and I can't keep this up for much longer," Spider said.

"Carly and you? Did you really just admit that out loud?" Cameron's voice was bitter.

"We know that you're tired, but we need a decision to be made on this before things get too out of hand," Carly added in a near-whisper.

"I have enough to deal with right now without having to think about that," Cameron snapped.

Spider raised his voice. "We've waited long enough. All this time and things keep getting worse. She sneaks around here like she owns the place. She gets the guards on her side and they tell her whatever she wants to hear. I can't control them when she's around."

"Why can't we just order her to stay away from here, away from us?"

"She knows too much already, Cameron. Besides, we all know that she won't follow any orders you or anybody else gives her. She's proven that already."

Cameron spun around and glared. There were deep lines carved into his forehead and his eyes were coal black. "What about Bill? Have you thought about what this would do to him if he heard us talking about her in this way?"

"Bill is dead." Spider's tone was cold and to the point. "We're in this far because of him."

Cameron turned away from them. "You're letting your resentment of Bill affect your perspective on this."

Carly got up and put her hand on Cameron's shoulder. "Spider's right. Bill has been gone for a long time, and we have to protect ourselves now. We can't let someone who has this much information run loose like that. If it had been anyone else, she would have been dead by now. We've waited long enough to try to make this work, but it hasn't. It's time to get rid of her for good."

Cameron stood and looked out over the grounds. After a while, he let his head drop and sighed.

Spider stood. "We'll take care of it."

Just like that, my fate had been determined, finally. Carly and Spider walked back into the house, Cameron was left to ponder his decision alone, and I sank to the floor. I knew it had been coming, I knew I should be making a plan fast, but all I could think about was that I didn't want to leave Cameron. Where would I go? There was nothing for me in Callister or anywhere else. My life was with Cameron and Rocco and Carly. Spider could stay too—if he had to.

I loved Cameron; that hadn't changed. When Cameron had looked at me and told me he loved me, I'd believed him without a doubt; what he had also said to me and then to Manny, that he didn't love me, I'd decided was made up, like he told me it was. But he had also promised that I would live, that he would send me home with an armed guard. Even if I didn't want this to happen—the thought of being separated from him made me feel nauseated—and I had planned to convince him otherwise, this promise had proven to be a lie.

A chapter in one of my criminology books was dedicated to the story of this rich girl from California who had been kidnapped by a left-wing group. Two months later, she walked into a bank with a gun and helped her kidnappers rob it. After she was arrested, her attorneys later argued that she suffered from Stockholm syndrome, a condition in which hostages start having feelings, like loyalty and love, for their captors. The girl was convicted but then pardoned a few years later: apparently, there was such a thing as Stockholm syndrome.

Everything was different between Cameron and me. What I felt for him, I had seen him—felt him—feel for me too. Cameron and Bill had been best friends. Cameron had been watching over me, protecting me, all these years, as my brother had asked him to do. Didn't that mean something?

No, I answered with all my head and my heart. It didn't mean something. It meant everything. It was as though Bill had had a hand in my destiny, as he always had. If it hadn't been for Bill, I would have been just another rich girl obsessed with money and with other people who had money. If it hadn't been for Bill, I wouldn't have been me. Sending Cameron to me was Bill's way of giving us his blessing.

My destiny—I could feel it—was to be with Cameron. This was where I belonged. For the first time in my life, I knew where I was supposed to be. I was more *me* with Cameron than I had ever been since Bill died.

Cameron loved me. I was sure of it.

But then there was all the other evidence that I couldn't refute, either: he was a killer, a drug dealer, a crime boss, an expert pretender. Frances, Griff, and even Roach had warned me about him. Though I couldn't deny any of these things, none of them changed my mind. There were two sides to Cameron—the real side was the one who took my hand and answered my incessant questions about his secret life while I tried to avoid watching the movie he had picked up just for me. The real Cameron was the one who kissed me in the darkness, the one who sat on my bed and admitted that he loved me ... and had loved me for a very long time.

The final blow—Cameron's decision to end my life—could have been attributed to Spider and Carly's cunning abilities to sway him.

No. Cameron was stronger than they were. He was simply appeasing them, for now, until he could find a way out for us.

Perhaps I was in denial about Cameron, about what he was capable of. I loved him, and he loved me ... but I still needed proof that I hadn't just imagined it all, that I wasn't going crazy.

When I got downstairs, I didn't see Cameron right away, but I did see Carly and Spider as they walked by. I ducked into the kitchen, out of their way.

Carly stopped. "Feeling better?"

I needed time. I needed to find the right words, ones that would give me enough time to save myself. Was I feeling better? Was I feeling the same? Or was I feeling worse? I could feel anxiety rising inside me. This feeling only served to jumble my thoughts, blur my focus.

I gave her a slight smile and stuffed a handful of animal crackers in my mouth. Then I grabbed a bag of Oreos that had been left on the counter and went to the table.

When Cameron walked through the patio doors, I kept still on my chair. His dark eyes automatically came to find mine, and he slowed his pace. Catching himself, he quickly looked away, picked up his pace again, walking through the house and out the front entrance. Carly and Spider followed him out, and I heard the front door shut behind them. In that brief moment, I knew what I had to do. I immediately started planning over the bag of Oreos.

Rocco hobbled over from the couch and grabbed himself a chair to help me with my meal. "What's the matter with you?" he asked with an accusatory tone.

"Nothing. Why?"

"You're staring at the wall. Smiling by yourself for no reason."

I shrugged, removed the smile, and shoved a cookie into my mouth. I thought I was going to hurl, but at least I wasn't going crazy—not anymore.

"I did a bunch of homework while you were loafing around," he announced. "I'm having trouble with the math homework, though."

I would have offered to help him, but math was my worst subject—I had always found it unsettling that, no matter what I did or how I calculated a problem, there could only be one right answer in the end.

"I was thinking that we could do a bunch of the work when the rest of them leave," he continued when I didn't put anything forward. "That way, next time they go, my foot will be better, and I'll be able to go with them again."

I wondered if he had discussed any of this with his brother.

"When are they leaving?"

"Tomorrow morning," he said dejectedly. "With most of the guards still down with the flu, it'll be pretty quiet around here."

The plan was quickly taking shape.

By the time the diminished troops started pouring in for supper, Rocco and I had dug clean through a second box of cereal, and the Oreos had vanished. The minute I got up, I regretted gobbling so much food in one sitting. I lay on the couch and spent the better part of an hour focusing on not hurling Cap'n Crunch. Rocco enjoyed his second supper with Tiny, Spider, and Carly; Cameron didn't come back for the rest of the evening. When eight o'clock rolled around, Rocco was opening a bag of chips for his midevening snack. I'd had enough of the gorging marathon by then and excused myself to go up to bed.

I went to work as soon as I got into Cameron's room. With Cameron and the rest of the high-rankers gone and most of the guards out of commission, there was no better opportunity for me to sneak away in the night. I found an old green duffle bag back in the almost-empty closet and started packing. The bag looked bigger than it was; I barely emptied three drawers and the bag was already full. I still had two drawers to go, plus all my stuff that littered the bathroom.

I had two options: I could run away on foot and try to get to the road, as Griff had planned, or I could try to steal one of my brother's cars, try to drive it without crashing, try to drive fast enough to elude the flying bullets … As far as I could see, I had only one option, even if I didn't take any pleasure in the idea of running through the woods by myself in the dark.

I packed and repacked and realized I had no idea what I would even need to camp out in the wilderness, how long it would take me to get to the road, or what I would do when I actually made it to the road. Once again, my cushy upbringing had come back to bite me … I was full of excuses. I didn't want to go, but I couldn't stay, either. Maybe I could convince him, change his mind, make him see what I saw. But what if I couldn't convince him? I dragged the duffle bag to the patio door and hid it behind the heavy curtain. And then I went to the small desk, found a working pen, and pulled out a piece of paper.

"Cameron," I scribbled. "I love you. I do believe you when you say that you love me. That's why I have to go. If you do this, you'll be changed forever. I can't let that happen." I took a breath, gulped, and finished. "I wish things could have been different. I promise to come find you someday, when things are better. Please don't worry. Love, Emmy."

I didn't want to risk leaving the letter out until I was ready to leave. I grabbed the *Rumble Fish* book from under my pillow, took the *Rumble Fish* movie off the shelf, and folded them into a pair of jeans along with the letter. I packed the jeans on top of my stuff in the duffle bag.

Spider would keep his word to Cameron—of this I was sure. I just hoped that he wouldn't come for me that night.

I spent the night listening for any sound that he was coming. Trying to keep myself awake, I sat in front of the TV with the sound barely audible. I jumped when the front door squeaked open shortly after two o'clock in the morning. When I heard the clatter of dishes and cupboard doors in the kitchen, I relaxed.

A few minutes later, Meatball came scratching at my door. In an almost imperceptible voice, Cameron ordered him downstairs—several times. Finally he had to come upstairs to get the dog. Sitting there, knowing that Cameron was so close, with just a door between us, knowing that I wouldn't see him again, it was very hard for me not to run to him. I could convince him. Or at least try to. I could get him to change his mind. But what if I couldn't? What if he wasn't ready to hear me out, ready for me to talk some sense into him?

Then he would know that I knew. And it would be too late for any plans.

I had to stay in place, for both our sakes.

When dawn broke, I watched Carly and Spider sleepily trudge out of the pool house with their bags. By five o'clock, the troops had left the compound, and I finally went to bed. I could have left right then, but I knew that with the journey I had ahead of me, I needed the rest, and I needed more time to make sure the coast was clear—and just a little more time with Rocco.

I was sad when I figured out that Meatball wouldn't be coming back, begging to be let in. He had gone with the rest of them. I wouldn't get the chance to say good-bye.

Knowing that this was my last day at the Farm, I didn't sleep for very long. Instead I went downstairs to wait for Rocco to get up. How could it be that the kid would turn out to be my best friend in the whole world?

I would miss Rocco so much. I felt like I was leaving my family behind.

My efforts to spend as much time as possible with Rocco were somewhat wasted; he didn't get up until well past noon. He lumbered into the living room, grunted, and crashed on the other couch. We slept until midafternoon. I told myself that at least he spent his last hours with me doing one of his favorite things: sleeping. As for his other favorite thing—eating—I commemorated by making a really big lasagna. We sat at the table. He wolfed down most of the lasagna; I ate without appetite.

"You know you can come visit me any time," I told him, spearing my cold lasagna.

He squinted over his fork. "I already do."

"I don't mean upstairs. I don't mean here ... I mean when I go back to Callister. Someday." As I said this I realized that I wouldn't be able to go back to the city, or back to my former life.

"Okay?" Rocco watched me.

I dropped the subject. I was giving myself away, getting emotional. He was getting suspicious.

The night pushed forward, and I became more apprehensive about leaving. I had to remind myself several times that I had no other choice. It was time to go—before it was too late.

I had decided that I would follow Griff's lead and sneak out of my room in the middle of the night by climbing down the two levels of balconies—strolling out the front door would have been a lot easier but a little too obvious, even with so few guards. Climbing down without breaking my neck was as far as my plan went.

I waited for Rocco to go to bed, but after having slept all day, he was going to be up for a while. I closed my eyes to rest before the big escape.

CHAPTER TWENTY

TERRORIZED

I heard fireworks.

Rocco was on his feet before I even opened my eyes. He ran to the front door just as the off-duty day guards who had been unwinding in the basement bolted past him and ordered him to deadbolt the door behind them. Rocco did as he was told and limped back to the living room, his face white with terror. He had a cell phone to his ear.

"Cam ..." he half-yelled, out of breath, "We have a big problem. The house is being attacked."

I heard a voice on the phone calmly responding, but I couldn't make out what was being said.

"I don't know who or how many!" Rocco answered. "It's dark out!"

A fresh round of gunfire exploded in the distance and seemed to be moving closer quickly. The voice on the other line was now speaking rapidly.

"I'm not running, Cameron. I'm not a coward. I'll stay and fight with the guards," Rocco said.

Cameron was screaming, cursing on the line. Rocco peeled the phone away from his ear and handed it to me. "Here," he said, "Cameron wants to talk to you."

269

I picked up the phone, "Camer—"

Cameron didn't give me a chance to greet him. "Emmy … go with Rocco. Get out of the house. Run for the woods." He was panicked. I could hear commotion behind him. Spider was barking orders, and people were yelling and shuffling rapidly.

Rocco had tottered to the cabinet and pulled a handgun out of the drawer. He handed it to me. Steady thuds could be heard at the front door.

"Oh god!" I breathed into the phone. "Cameron, they're at the door. I think they're trying to knock it down."

Cameron swore successively and then pleaded, "Emmy, get out—" and the line went dead. I looked at the phone and handed it over to Rocco.

He examined it. "Battery's almost dead. I forgot to charge it," he confessed, putting the useless phone back in his pocket. He started to rush me toward the patio door, but I resisted.

"You need to get out of here, Em."

"I'm not going without you." I grabbed Rocco by both arms. "We run together. Cameron said—"

Rocco shook me off. "Run? Em, I can barely walk! I would just slow you down. Besides, I'm not going to let them take my brother's house without a fight."

"This is no time for you to prove your toughness to your brother—"

There was a loud snap at the front door—the door frame was giving in to the attack. "Can't you just listen to me for once? I'm not going with you, and I'll be dead if something does happen to you because Cameron will kill me himself." Rocco seemed to be getting calmer while I was getting closer to losing my mind.

"Rocco, I am not leaving without you! Please …"

Crack! The doorframe had finally given in. I jumped. Rocco swore. He looked around the room and, with all his might, pushed me into the farthest corner of the living room, where there was a large wicker chest. He opened it, threw the blankets that were inside it on the couch, and forced me inside. As he closed the lid,

I heard loud footsteps rushing toward the living room. Through the weave of the chest, I could see Rocco standing in the middle of the living room, his arms crossed.

A heavyset man in black body armor led an equally armored troop into the living room. With his finger on the trigger of his automatic weapon, he glanced around the room and stopped to stare Rocco down. Rocco didn't flinch.

"Clear!" the leader yelled.

He and the rest of the men slightly relaxed their grips on their weapons, and then the group parted as a lanky, bookish-looking man strolled through them into the room, stopping in front of Rocco. Unlike the sweaty, agitated men backing him, he seemed tranquil, unconcerned. There was something familiar about him. My heart was pumping so fast I was shaking.

"Where's the girl?" he demanded. His voice had a slightly feminine tone.

Rocco cocked his head. "It's Norestrom, isn't it? I've heard a lot about you."

"Where's the girl, mongrel?" Norestrom repeated more forcefully.

"What girl? There aren't any girls here."

Norestrom peered at Rocco through his red-rimmed glasses. "Listen, kid, we know the girl is here. All your men are dead. Now, you can tell us where she is and you'll live, or you can die and we'll still find her. Which one is it?"

Gunfire erupted at the back of the group, and I saw two of Norestrom's men crumple to the ground. Then I saw the body of one of Cameron's guards lying in the archway, rifle fallen by his side, blood pooling around him.

While Norestrom's men were distracted, Rocco cocked his fist and punched Norestrom, who fell back like a rag doll and slid to the floor, his head hitting the ground with a thud. One of his men ran to his side, but Norestrom shoved him away. Disoriented, Norestrom wobbled to a sitting position, his nose bleeding and his glasses shattered on his face.

"Kill him," he said, pinching his nose with two slender fingers. The heavyset man immediately raised his weapon and fired. Rocco fell limp to the floor.

I felt like I'd been knocked out of my body. What I had seen … it couldn't have happened. My vision blurred, but my eyes stayed on Rocco.

Get up!

I willed him to get back up, to fight back, to run.

But he wasn't moving. Red stains soaked the front of his gray T-shirt, and now a puddle of red was spreading around him.

My breath caught in my throat. My skin constricted, like rubber left out in the snow.

I couldn't take my eyes off him.

I couldn't take my eyes off him!

Rocco!

Thick fog had started creeping into my brain, blurring reality.

Norestrom got up and brushed his hands over his khaki pants. "Find her and bring her to me, dead or alive," he said. He thought about it. "Preferably alive."

The men scattered, leaving Norestrom behind in the living room. He approached Rocco and kicked his lifeless body. Satisfied, Norestrom bent over him and searched his pockets. He pulled out pieces of my Rocco's world: screws and a nail, a napkin, a few peanuts, candy wrappers, and the cell phone.

Norestrom flipped open the phone and quickly scanned the screen before the battery went completely dead. Then he bellowed, and the heavyset man ran back to him.

"He had time to call them. We don't have much time," Norestrom said. "Get the body out of here and make sure it's the first thing they see when they drive in." The heavyset man jumped and called for assistance.

As his men dragged Rocco out of the living room, leaving a trail behind, Norestrom stood and scanned the pool of blood with a smug smile. When the heavyset man came back and stood with him, Norestrom snarled, "We need to find that girl."

The two of them stomped off through the kitchen doorway, and I heard their footsteps climbing the stairs to Cameron's room, and then the crash of things getting thrown around and broken as the men searched the house.

But the living room was left empty.

I didn't have much time before they would start pulling apart the living room to find me.

In a daze, I opened the lid of the chest, crawled to the patio door, and slid it open. I was an automaton—I had done this before. I crept out into the night and crawled into the dark recess where I had once shared a hidden kiss with Cameron. Then I could hear the men stomping through the living room and kitchen, and I lunged myself over the deck railing, stuffing the pistol in the waistband of my shorts as I heaved my body over. For a moment I clung to the side of the railing, hanging from my fingers; then I dropped to the ground and immediately skittered away from the basement light, flattening myself against the cold brick wall.

The basement patio door slid open, and a man stepped outside and glanced around. My heart pumped frantically as his gaze slowly came closer to me.

Gunfire erupted again, and flashes of light came through the windows of the basement bedrooms. One of the guards, too ill to get up, had surely been found and killed. Norestrom's man rushed back into the house to view the action.

I saw shadows moving violently inside the pool house: Carly's world was now being ripped apart. Soon the men would start searching the grounds for me. With the moon and stars lighting up the landscape, I knew I would be exposed once I moved out of the shadow of the house. Taking one big breath, I darted across the grounds, praying that no one was watching.

I managed to get near the trees without notice.

And then I tripped.

I pushed myself up in the long grass and looked to see what had caught my foot. Staring back at me were dead eyes—one of

Cameron's guards, shot down. An involuntary scream left my lips as I kicked, struggling to get my foot loose.

In the distance, I heard a booming voice from somewhere near the pool house. "She's over here!"

Suddenly it seemed that all of Norestrom's men had left the house and were running in my direction like a pack of hyenas. I struggled free of the dead guard's body and ducked into the woods and kept running, my arms outstretched in the darkness to feel the trees that I could not see. Branches slashed me in the face. I could hear the men's shouts and crashing footsteps all around. I didn't stop.

My shoulder hit an unseen tree limb and I fell backward, my head hitting the hard ground. I struggled to get up but just fell forward onto my hands. My lungs were burning. Black was all I could see. Voices screamed all around me. I slid my body next to a tree trunk and took out the gun. My hands were shaking.

It was cold, and heavier than I had imagined it would be; my hands didn't fit well around the handle. I pointed it in front of me with both trembling hands, resting my elbows on my knees, and curled up into a ball against the tree. I closed my eyes and hoped that the voices would go away. In a half answer to my prayers, the wind picked up through the trees, and the rustling of leaves drowned out some of the voices. But the screaming in my head continued mercilessly.

I was dressed in a T-shirt and shorts, and my bare feet were covered in cold mud. I rocked back and forth, trying to stay warm.

It got much colder. I could feel the chill flow right through me, and my body began shaking uncontrollably. And then I felt nothing. On a few occasions I heard branches snap nearby as the men continued to search for me in the darkness, and I just squeezed my eyes tighter, praying that they would go away.

After what seemed like days of being curled up against the tree, dawn seeped through the woods. I became terribly aware that I was no longer hidden by the darkness, but I could see nothing but thick brush around me—maybe this would be enough to keep me unseen?

But then there were rapid steps and crashing branches. I listened with all my senses and realized that the noises were heading in my direction.

I had been discovered …

Somehow, I always knew that I was going to die alone. Maybe I even knew that I was going to die young—or maybe I had, once upon a time, just wished that I would die young to get it all over with—but I had never thought that in the face of death I would have something, someone to fight for.

As the footsteps moved closer, faster, I stopped my hands from shaking long enough to cock the gun's hammer, as I had seen done in so many movies before.

I could now clearly hear running steps just beyond the brush that had kept me hidden until now. Though my hands were shaking uncontrollably once again, I gripped the gun as tightly as I could. When the leaves to the side of me rustled, I turned, closed my eyes, steadied myself tight against the tree trunk, and pulled the trigger. There was a deafening bang. Pieces of tree bark went flying everywhere.

My ears were ringing, and now more footsteps were running toward me.

I pulled the trigger again. Nothing happened this time. My body was violently convulsing as I pulled the trigger over and over but nothing happened; the gun was stuck or it only had one bullet or I had broken it.

Someone jumped out from the brush, wrapped his arms around me, and tried to pry the gun out of my hands. I struggled, fought back with everything I had left in me.

But I couldn't compete.

The gun was snatched from my hands.

He cupped his hands around my face and forced me to look at him. It was Cameron. His lips were moving rapidly but I couldn't hear anything—just screams in my head, ringing in my ears. His warm lips scorched my freezing skin as he kissed my forehead, my nose, my lips.

The brush next to him moved and I clambered backward. Cameron threw his arms around me, grabbed me in bear hug, as Meatball slunk to me and licked my frozen fingers.

Cameron looked panicked. He was holding me by the shoulders and talking to me, possibly shouting, but I heard and felt nothing. He took out a short-wave radio and hastily spoke into it. With one last, frightened glance at me, he turned his back to me, grabbed my arms, and threw them over his shoulders and around his neck. He hoisted me onto his back and started running.

Meatball was ahead of us and led the way home. We trekked for what seemed like miles. I hadn't realized that I had run so far out into the woods.

Slowly, I started hearing again, starting with Cameron's rapid breaths. I also started feeling the cold through my body. By the time we reached the Farm, my teeth were chattering and my naked feet and fingers were burning.

Cameron carried me toward the house. It was chaos everywhere on the property. Some of the high-rankers were carrying bodies into parked vehicles while others rushed around, surveying the land, looking for an enemy.

"Don't look," Cameron softly warned me as we walked past two guards placing a body in the back of a pickup truck. I concentrated on how good it was to hear Cameron's voice again.

Cameron carried me into the house and immediately up the stairs, not giving me time to think about glancing toward the kitchen doorway. The bedroom was in complete disarray: drawers, my clothes, my stuff were strewn on the floor, the mattress had been flipped off the bed, and my bedside lamp was shattered. Cameron released me and sat me down on the mattress on the floor.

"We need to grab whatever we can and get out of here," he said, taking the clothes on the floor and piling them up by my feet. In a nightmarish haze, I got up and walked over to the curtains. The duffle bag was still hidden there, untouched. I dragged it out a few inches.

Cameron squinted at me for a second.

Then he threw the bag's strap over his shoulder and simultaneously grabbed a blanket from the messy bed. He wrapped the thick blanket around me and picked me up in his arms again. We headed downstairs and out the door. Cameron set me on the passenger seat of his car, kneeled in to put the seat belt around me, and closed the door.

He went to Spider, who was wearily standing by the front stoop, engrossed in a conversation with Tiny. I watched them, and I watched a puffy-eyed Carly walk out of the house with a bag. She threw it in the back of Spider's truck and climbed in.

Cameron, Spider, and Tiny spoke hastily; then they all dispersed. Spider climbed into his truck, his tires spitting rocks as he raced away. Meatball climbed into the back of Cameron's car while Cameron grabbed another T-shirt from his own bag on the backseat. I hadn't noticed until then that his shirt was drenched in blood. Then Cameron and I sped away from the Farm too.

He drove down the gravel road even faster than he had the day we took the Maserati out. When we turned onto the main road, he grabbed my hand. Though I was wrapped in a thick blanket, my teeth hadn't stopped chattering. I stared at the road ahead, semiconscious that Cameron was worriedly glancing at me every other minute.

We drove for hours with neither of us speaking, with me never breaking my stare with the road. Cameron didn't let go of my hand.

Eventually I recognized the Callister city limits, but we continued driving past the city. Cameron finally veered onto a dirt road through a cluster of trees. We arrived at a small log cottage with a sunken front porch. He stopped the car and sighed.

We got out, and Meatball excitedly led us to the door.

Inside, the cottage was simply furnished. There was a small kitchen table with two chairs in the middle of the room, a tiny kitchenette on one side, and a black wood-burning stove on the other. A narrow staircase led to a small, square loft; through the railing I could see a single bed. The bare walls were made of exposed wood. It smelled of Cameron. It all made me feel a little warmer.

Cameron took me by the hand and led me into a minuscule bathroom off the kitchenette. He pulled the blanket off my shoulders, stood me in front of the mirror, and started the shower. I didn't recognize the person who was staring back at me in the mirror. This girl had a horrifying, petrified look to her. There were scratches all over her face, and her hair and skin were filthy and streaked with blood. Her eyes were wild and shocked. *This can't be me,* I told myself.

Cameron's reflection appeared behind mine. He didn't look like himself, either. I noticed that his face was as dirty and scratched as mine; I watched in the mirror while he pulled the leaves and dry brush from my hair.

The steam from the shower started to fog up the mirror. Cameron left the room to grab a towel, and I undressed and entered the shower. For a while I just stood there letting the water burn my skin. I shifted and the water hit my head, and I watched the remaining debris from my hair wash down the drain. Slowly, the feeling came back, inside and out. I could feel the throbbing in my bruised and bloodied legs. I could also feel the fear and the pain that were lingering deep, slowly rising to surface.

I wrapped myself in the towel that Cameron had left for me and walked out to the kitchenette, where he was waiting by the small table.

"Here," he said as he gently handed me a stack of his clothes. "These will keep you warm."

Like a robot, I dressed myself while Cameron took his leave for the shower. The clothes he had given me smelled like him. By the time I was dressed, Cameron was already out of the shower; he'd pulled on a pair of jeans but was still shirtless, and I noticed his tattooed bullet wounds. I could feel my drowned emotions bubbling up.

Keeping a close eye on me, he went to the stove, where the kettle was now boiling, and poured tea into two cups. He walked back, placed the cups on the table, and sat in the chair next to mine.

I picked up the mug, cupped my hands around it, and turned to him. He returned my gaze. When I tried to offer him a reassuring smile, my vision blurred. The cup started to shake in my hands. Cameron took it away and set it on the table.

"Rocco was right there ... I didn't know what to do ... I lost him ..."

And I started to fall.

Cameron lunged out of his chair and wrapped me in his arms as hard sobs surfaced.

I cried until the tea grew cold and the room dark. I cried until my shoulders, my arms, and my lungs ached, long after the tears had dried. Cameron carried me to bed. My head on his chest, his hand on my head, I fell into a dreamless sleep.

****

It was the middle of the night. My throat was throbbing, and Cameron wasn't next to me. The pain in my heart was unbearable. The cottage was quiet, and I could hear the crickets lamenting outside. I heard a chair creak down in the kitchen, and I tiptoed to the edge of the loft. Through the rails I saw Cameron sitting at the table with his head in his hands, his fingers raking his hair, his shoulders shaking. It took me a moment to realize that he was sobbing.

I knew I was witnessing something no one had ever seen. I thought about going down there. But I let Cameron grieve the loss of his little brother in peace.

After a while, the chair pushed away from the table and the wooden stairs groaned. Cameron crawled back into the single bed and lay next to me. Feigning sleep, I exhaled, took his arm, and brought it under my arm to my other shoulder, fitting myself into him. Cameron didn't push me away. He clasped his fingers through mine and pulled me even closer to him. He buried his face in my hair.

Chapter Twenty-One

I Never Said It Was a Good Plan

I had no idea where I was or what time it was when I woke again. Disoriented, I glanced around the barren room, looking for a clock, and suddenly remembered. Disarrayed images of what had happened started filtering through in pieces—gunfire, the wicker chest, the guard's dead eyes, Rocco … I gulped to force down the knot that was growing in my throat, and sat up.

The light from the small downstairs windows told me that the sun was up and Cameron was gone. I climbed down the creaky stairs just as he was walking in the door, grocery bags in hand.

"The corner store didn't have much, but it'll do us for a while," he announced, breathless. He placed the bags on the table and rushed to meet me at the stairs.

He cradled my face in his hands and surveyed it carefully, passing his thumbs over my puffy, scratched cheeks. I forced a cheery smile.

"Mornin'," he whispered, kissing me on the forehead without reserve.

He went to put the groceries away while I worked to get my bearings back. I made my way to the table, tightly holding onto the fallen waistband of my pants and almost tripping on the hems, which were dragging on the floor. Cameron nodded toward the bathroom door. "I brought your bag in if you want to change into your own stuff," he said.

We sat down to breakfast. Even after Cameron's insistence, I couldn't eat anything, but I did manage to drink a glass of milk, which soothed my raw throat. The stillness at the table was making me self-conscious, particularly because Cameron was staring at me intently the whole time. I could tell that something was bothering him. I swallowed the rest of my milk and went to shower again. When I came out of the bathroom, Cameron was sitting on the stairs, waiting for me. Whatever was bothering him hadn't been satisfied.

I took a seat a few stairs below him and began struggling to get my wet locks into a ponytail. Cameron didn't wait another second before scuttling down to sit on the stair behind me, his legs on either side of me, wrapping his arms around my shoulders and pulling me in. Something had changed. His emotions had become … unrestrained. I couldn't explain it. Whatever the reason for the change, the new, uninhibited Cameron disarmed me.

I closed my eyes and let my head fall back.

"Emmy," he murmured into my ear.

"Hmmm …"

"Can I ask you a question?"

"Uh-huh."

"Yesterday, when we went back into the house to pack your stuff and leave, how come you had a bag already packed?"

My eyes shot open. With everything that had happened, I had forgotten about the eavesdropped conversation between Cameron, Carly, and Spider.

"What is it?" he asked when I didn't answer. "Your body just went stiff."

I'd forgotten who I was talking to. "I don't want you to be mad."

"Why would I get angry?" His body had stiffened too. I hesitated to say anything else.

"I promise I won't get mad. Can you please tell me what's going on?"

I was playing with my hands, trying to find a way not to ruin the moment or the change in him.

"Emmy, you're making me nervous—"

"I know you were going to let Spider kill me," I blurted.

"What? What are you talking about?" He sounded genuinely confused. It was easy for me to forget all the bad stuff when I was cocooned in his arms—perhaps it had the same effect on him?

Taking a deep breath, I told Cameron everything I had overheard, word for word, without emotion. All of it seemed like a dream now. As the story progressed, I watched his eyebrows slowly curve up, until deep lines carved his forehead.

He moved down next to me and took my hands between his. "Emmy, no matter what you did or said, no matter how bad things got, that would never happen. No one would ever be able to convince me that getting rid of you was the solution. Not Carly or Spider. Not even you."

"I didn't imagine it," I said quickly, heat building behind my ears.

"What you overheard had nothing to do with you."

"I sneaked around ... I talked to the guards ... I didn't follow orders ..." Was I actually trying to convince him that getting rid of me was a good idea?

"Yes. You did do all of those things. You and Frances have that in common."

He was still holding on to me. When I had determined that he wasn't going to let go, I relaxed and spoke up. "Frances?"

"Spider thinks that Frances has been spying on us and selling our secrets to rival gang members. She sneaks around the farm and asks the guards a lot of strange questions about us, about our business."

"So you ordered her killed? She's a mother! She's my nephew's mother!"

"She's not who you think she is, Emmy. Daniel lives with Frances's mother full-time while Frances lives in a big apartment downtown. She disappears for days at a time. I've been giving Frances's mother money every month just to keep food on their table and a roof over Daniel's head. Frances hemorrhages any money that we give her directly."

Though this slightly changed my perspective on Frances, it didn't make Cameron's decision any easier for me to understand. After seeing my brother grow up motherless, I knew how much a child needed a mother, no matter what she was like.

"Cameron, she's still his mother—"

"Don't worry. I don't think Frances is smart enough to spy on us, to sell us out without getting caught. I was really tired when I agreed to it, but I called the whole thing off the next morning." He leaned in closer. "After spending three nights up, worrying, wondering whether your fever was ever going to break and whether I should give away our hiding place to get a helicopter to take you to a hospital, I was ready to agree to anything by that point. Spider used my weakness to get what he wanted."

"He must have been upset," I said, aware of how close Cameron's face was to mine.

"He's been wanting to get Frances out of our lives for a long time. He hates how she still gets to Carly." He shrugged. "He'll get over it."

After everything that had happened, I needed Cameron more than ever. I considered bringing my face a few inches forward to bridge the gap between us as he continued to shake his head in disbelief. "So how were you planning to run away, exactly?"

I told him about my plan to climb down the balconies and escape through the woods.

He burst into laughter. "You were going to climb down with that huge duffle bag and drag it through the woods with you? The bag weighs more than you do! You have enough clothes in there to last you three weeks … but no food or water. How exactly were you planning to survive out there?"

I could feel my face turning red. "I never said it was a good plan."

"I need to take you camping someday. It'd be a hoot to watch you try to survive without a hot shower or electricity. Anyway, didn't I promise you that I was going to bring you home safely?"

"It was getting hard for me to distinguish between truth and lies."

He grew serious again. "Maybe I haven't always told you everything, but I never lied to you."

"Oh?" It was done in a sort of clumsy way, the way I brought my lips to his. When I quickly leaned in, he jerked sideways and our foreheads nearly smashed together. But I didn't let that dissuade me. I pressed my lips hard against his. Then I forced myself to pull away to see the effect. I could feel the heat of Cameron's gaze, and he was a little winded.

"Does it mean anything to you, or am I still just wasting my time?"

He smiled slyly. "It doesn't mean anything. Just a kiss, nothing else."

I leaned in again. This time he leaned in, too, so that we met in the middle. It was soft, not so clumsy. Then he pulled my face away and held it a few inches from his. "I did lie about that. I wondered for a long time what it would be like … but when I finally kissed you that night, I knew I was in really big trouble. And then I heard about that Griff guy being up in your room, alone with you, and I felt like someone had just stabbed me in the stomach. I panicked. I shouldn't have said what I said."

I understood what Cameron was saying—I had felt exactly the same way when he told me that our kiss meant nothing to him. I winced at the memory but quickly recovered. "Actually, I kissed you," I said. "And next time you feel panicked like that, will you talk to me instead of turning into a jerk?"

"Only the truth from now on."

"Promise?"

"I promise."

I kissed him again. But when I tried to seal the space between our bodies, he seized up and leaned back. "I have to check on Meatball," he announced while my lips were still on his. Then he lunged past me and practically ran to the door, where he stood waiting. He forced a reassuring smile, but the fact that he would hardly look at me confused me.

I went to meet him and tried to mask the ache in my voice. "Where's Meatball?"

He shrugged. "Swimming. That's all he does when we come here."

"Swimming?"

We went outside, walked to the back of the cottage, and followed a dirt path into the woods. Being in the woods reminded me of something I was trying hard to forget. If Cameron hadn't been holding on to my hand, I would have turned around and run.

"How did you find me yesterday? I ran pretty far into the woods." As soon as the question left my lips, the memories started rushing back. I gave an involuntary gulp and concentrated on putting one foot in front of the other.

"Meatball caught your scent by the pool. He started sniffing around and bolted for the woods. I knew he had found you; I ran after him." He lifted my hand to his lips as we continued to make our way through the trees. "You really scared Meatball when you shot at him. I don't think he was expecting that kind of welcome after running all that way. Good thing you have no hand-eye coordination." He paused and then said, more seriously, "I'll have to teach you how to shoot. You should know how to protect yourself better than that."

"Cameron," I said, "I was really far out. He couldn't possibly have followed the scent that far."

"Meatball has spent his whole life learning to follow your scent. Finding you is his favorite game. He hunted you down through a huge crowd of people the first day we met in the projects, remember? You're like his real-life *Where's Waldo.*"

The pathway led to a dock and a pond. Trees and brush came right up to the water's edge, and large lily pads floated on the surface, with pink and yellow flowers attached to their underwater stems. The sun was peering through the break in the trees, and the beam of light glittered on the water. It was magical.

Meatball was swimming around in circles, his head the only thing visible. He looked like a big muskrat. We lay on the dock with our hands crossed over our stomachs, enjoying the sunshine, while he continued his tireless swim.

I looked at the blue sky through the leaves of an overhanging tree. "What is this place, anyway?"

"It's my place," he said with emphasis. "I come here whenever I need to get away and be alone. It's the only place that no one else knows about but Meatball and me—and, well, you too, now."

"Spider and Carly don't know about it?"

"Nope."

I paused, debating whether to ask the next question, which I really wanted to ask. It came out before I had time to dwell on it. "What about Manny? Did you ever bring her here?"

From the corner of my eye, I could see Cameron break into a smile. "No, Emmy. No one." He continued to smile at the sky, and then, after a few minutes, he turned his body toward me, resting his head on his fist.

"Well?" he asked, staring at me with amusement.

"Well, what?"

"I know you've been dying to ask me about Manny. So go ahead. Ask away. Nothing but the truth."

"Do you love her?" As the question came out of my mouth, I realized that it was the same one that she had asked Cameron about me.

"At some point I think I might have liked her a lot, but no, I didn't love her."

"But she spent the night with you? I saw you give her her T-shirt back."

"Yes, she has spent the night."

"More than once?"

Cameron remained silent.

"Nothing but the truth, remember?"

He sighed. "Yes, more than once."

"Were there other girls like her?"

"I never brought anybody else to the Farm," he replied.

His face was near mine. I kissed him. I didn't really think about it; I just did what came instinctively. It was strange for me to want someone so much it hurt. He let me kiss him for a second, but then he withdrew and rolled onto his back, turning his eyes to the sky. I felt like I had just been slapped in the face.

"I don't understand what you're doing, Cameron."

Cameron turned to me, surprised. "What?"

"One minute you're hugging me; the next minute you're running away. I don't understand what you're trying to do."

He sighed. "Emmy, I wish you could see yourself, see what I see, see how beautiful you are. Have you never noticed how everyone turns to watch you enter a room?"

I didn't know how to answer that. Cameron hadn't been there when kids were trying to outdo each other finding new nicknames for me, or when they were taking bets in high school about whether I had red hair ... all over.

He took a breath, reached over, and swept a lingering hair away from my face. "For me, there's no one else but you."

"Then why won't you kiss me?"

His eyes were piercing. "Do you know how hard this is for me? I want to kiss you. I want to wrap my arms around you, never let you go."

"You're making me so confused." This time I let myself roll onto my back in exasperation.

Something blocked my sun. I opened my eyes to see Cameron leaning over me. His face was twisted.

"I thought I lost you," he murmured. "When I got back to the house, when I found Rocco ... Emmy, I started looking for your body too, and when I didn't find you ... I thought for sure they had taken you, which would have been just as bad. I had no idea where to start looking or how I was going to get you back—"

"But you did get me back. You found me."

"I found you," he agreed. "But look what I've done to you. Everything that you've been through, that you've seen ... you would never have had to go through that if it weren't for me. The fact that you're here is pure luck. I'm not going to make this worse for you by making us more complicated. I haven't changed my mind, Emmy. Once this blows over, you're going home." There was no hint of doubt in his voice.

"When?" I asked, my voice quavering.

"I don't know. As soon as it's safe for you."

I left it alone for now, but I wasn't going to give up. Since Cameron had recognized that there was an *us*, I still had hope.

Chapter Twenty-Two

Fitting Pieces Together

I remembered.

Rocco was spread on the ground. I yelled at him to get up, but he refused to move. I was frantic. He was lying on the grass right in front of me, and I bent over, trying to get to him, but someone was holding me back. I fought the hand that was grabbing on to the back of my shirt and turned around to see Norestrom sitting across from me at the picnic table. I was back at the outdoor commons at Callister University. I now knew the name of the man who had joined me during my lunch break all that time ago.

I woke up in a cold sweat; Cameron had already taken hold of me. I was screaming Rocco's name. His face had implanted itself in my brain while I was sleeping, and it wasn't going anywhere this time. Cameron rocked me back and forth as the tears and trembling started up again. But something was different this time. I didn't want to hold it in anymore. After a few minutes, I willed myself to calm down, and I turned to Cameron. He looked sick with worry.

"Emmy, are you—"

"Who's Norestrom?" I asked point-blank, wiping my cheek with the heel of my hand.

He head snapped back. "Why do you ask?"

"Because Norestrom is what Rocco called the man that night."

"Emmy, do you remember everything that happened that night?"

I nodded.

"Do you think you can tell me everything you remember?" he asked cautiously.

I nodded again. I didn't wait for further encouragement; I started my discourse right away. The gunfire in the distance, the phone call with Cameron, the view from the wicker chest ... The words poured out; the tears continued to run down my cheeks, unnoticed. I couldn't stop any of it. Cameron's face remained unchanged. He listened to my every word without question or interruption.

By the time I finished, Cameron was already digging through his jeans, which were draped over the banister. He found his cell phone and pressed one key, and I heard Spider grumble hello on the other end.

"It was Norestrom," Cameron said. "Bring him in."

He then hung up the phone and came back to me while I sobbed every tear that I had left in me. He held me tight. I could tell from the quickness of his breathing and the tenseness of his body that he was furious. But he continued to hold on to me without wavering.

In the morning, I awoke to the sound of his voice coming from outside. I went downstairs and peeked out the window. Cameron was pacing back and forth on the sagging porch, talking rapidly on his cell phone. I could hear him angrily retelling my story to whoever was listening on the other end. He was beside himself, and a string of profanities preceded and followed Norestrom's name.

I took the opportunity to scrub my face and have another hot shower, washing away the last of the grime from my body, as well as my remaining jumbled thoughts. Everything in my head was clear again, and although my heart still felt like it was being squeezed every time I thought of Rocco, I didn't let my brain run away from it anymore. I let myself feel the pain and remember everything as it happened. When I walked out of the bathroom, Cameron was still outside. I couldn't hear his voice anymore, so I went searching for him. He was sitting on the porch swing, glaring into the distance. This time I went over to him. I kissed him on the cheek and wrapped my arms around his neck. Cameron followed my lead and held me in a crushing hug. His body slowly started to relax, and he buried his face in my neck.

After a while, he looked up with his tired, dark eyes. "There's something I need to do today. You'll have to come with me. I can't leave you here alone."

I got breakfast ready while Cameron showered. He came out of the bathroom dressed only in jeans; I couldn't help but ogle as he walked about bare-chested. I'd never liked tattoos— but everything about Cameron, especially his tattoos, made him irresistible. When he caught me staring at him, I quickly glanced away.

"So where are we going?" I asked, obviously trying to change the subject.

"My mother's," he replied, stuffing a piece of toast into his mouth. I couldn't hide my surprise at hearing this.

We drove away from the cottage and back into the city. Cameron drove too fast, and I noticed that as we got closer, his hand started to squeeze mine tighter.

"You need to prepare yourself for this," he said. "My mother can be pretty shocking when you first meet her."

I smiled at him reassuringly. I couldn't imagine any mother being more horrifying than mine.

We pulled into one of Callister's slum districts. It was the middle of the week. The streets were empty except for the men and boys who hung around the corners, eying us as we drove by. Most of the shops were boarded up, and those that were open receded behind steel latticework, with blinking neon lights barely shining through dirty glass. The streets were lined with garbage bags and empty cardboard boxes that had been broken down and stacked by the side of the road. Bottles and other litter were strewn along the sidewalks and at the foot of the boarded-up buildings.

As I looked ahead, I could feel Cameron anxiously glancing at me, watching for any sign of revolt. I remained unchanged and continued to survey the scene.

We turned onto one of the side streets and were met with row upon row of low-income housing. Most of the yards were completely paved; the houses that were fortunate enough to have green patches out front had, for the most part, knee-high weeds growing around damaged furniture, old couches, and other forgotten possessions. I watched an old woman stroll slowly along the sidewalk, pulling a disagreeable-looking cat behind her with a leash. There was one of those in every neighborhood.

Cameron pulled up in front of a semidetached house and turned off the engine. He sat silently for a few seconds, uncomfortably staring ahead.

"Is this your mother's house?" I asked, breaking the silence.

"Yep."

"So this is where you grew up," I mused, glancing over at the house. It was faced with red brick and had an aluminum door with a ripped screen and cracked window in front of a windowless brown door. The porch roof looked like it was going to come crashing down on the cement stoop at any second. The front yard was littered with mismatched chairs, broken and lying on their sides, and bottles were strewn throughout the overgrown grass.

"No. The place my mom and I lived in was a lot worse than this," he said. "The city had it torn down a couple years ago."

Cameron's eyes jumped from me to the front door.

"Well," I said, "are we going in, or are we just going to sit here?"

Cameron sighed, let go of my hand, and stepped out of the Audi. I met him on the sidewalk, where he quickly picked up my hand again. Together we made our way up the front walk, stepping over trash, and finally came to a stop at the front door. With a deep breath and a last, anxious glance at me, Cameron knocked on the door. We could hear the muffled noise of a television from inside. When no one came, he knocked again.

We waited for a minute, but still nothing happened. Cameron heaved another sigh, screeched open the aluminum door, and pushed on the windowless front door. He peered inside first and, with his hand protectively on the small of my back, guided me in.

The smell of mold and tobacco hit my nose as soon as I walked in, but I didn't allow myself to react. There were hoards of junk piled in the hallway and on the stairs leading to a second story. The pink wallpaper in the foyer was yellowed and peeling off in spots, and the dirty, greenish carpet was speckled with cigarette burns. I jumped when a cat leaped up from behind a pile of laundry on the floor.

Cameron put his arm around my shoulders. I could see that he was embarrassed to have me there. I smiled my most supportive smile at him, but I wasn't sure if he bought it.

We walked into the living room, where two little girls and a boy were sitting side by side on the couch, watching cartoons. They looked so tiny on that big couch. One of the blond girls had mad knots in her hair. Their bare feet were dirty, and their eyes looked almost wild as they watched us walk in. I noticed that the little boy had Cameron's dark eyes.

"Where's your mother?" Cameron asked them abruptly.

The bigger of the little girls pointed toward a doorway, expressionless.

We continued past them and walked into the kitchen, where a cloud of cigarette smoke hung in the air. Half the cupboard doors were either hanging from one hinge or missing altogether. Dishes were stacked in and around the sink, and dirty pots sat on the encrusted stove and counters. The floor crunched under our shoes.

A lady was sitting alone at the kitchen table with a large plastic glass half-full of beer in front of her, two empty beer bottles next to that, and a cigarette burning in an overflowing ashtray. She lifted her head and peered at Cameron as we walked in. The sound of the television in the background was met by the dripping of the kitchen faucet. We quietly stood there while the lady took a puff of her cigarette, looking lost in thought.

She sneered when she finally recognized Cameron. "What the hell are you doing here?" she croaked at him. "And who the hell are you?" she said, turning to me.

"Mom, this is Emmy ... Emily,'" he corrected himself nervously. I smiled at her.

"You brought a girl with you. That's a first." With her cigarette hanging on her bottom lip, she got up and walked over to us. She put her hand on my shoulder, directing me to sit at the table. "It must be pretty serious for my boy to bring you here. He's usually too proud to introduce me to any of his friends—apparently he's too good for his own mother."

She took her seat again, and Cameron yanked out a chair for himself.

"Can I get you kids anything to eat?" she asked sweetly.

"No, we're fine," Cameron quickly answered for the both of us.

Her hair was shoulder-length, crimped, and blonde—though from the overgrowth at her scalp, I guessed that her natural hair color was likely closer to Cameron's dark locks. She was wearing a tight, sleeveless V-neck that showed off her ample cleavage. Unfortunately, it also emphasized the beer gut that hung over her skin-tight jeans. Her blue eye shadow drew attention to her beautiful dark eyes, and almost all the cigarette butts in the ashtray still had traces of her bright-red lipstick. Her skin was translucent, like tissue paper.

We sat in silence while Cameron's mother gulped down the other half of her beer, staring at me over the rim of her glass. "You're too skinny and you're very pale. You need to put some makeup on, but I doubt there's anything you can do to make that hair color any better. Have you tried to dye it? The lady next door sells wigs—they're made from real horse hair. I can get you a good price."

I could feel the blood rushing to my cheeks.

Cameron scowled. "I didn't come here so that you can insult my girlfriend. I came here to talk to you about Rocco."

"Rocco?" she asked between puffs. "Where is that little bastard?" She leaned across the table. "You know that ungrateful child left me alone with no good-byes or anything. I was worried sick and almost called the police till Cammy called me a couple weeks later to tell me that Rocco was with him." Cameron rolled his eyes as his mother turned to him. "Seems all of my sons eventually leave me to fend for myself."

We sat in uncomfortable silence again. Cameron's mother got up to pull another bottle of beer out of the fridge. Cameron was shaking his leg, nervous, mentally preparing himself.

"You came to talk to me about Rocco, so talk," his mother said, holding her cigarette in one hand and taking a swig from the bottle with the other.

Cameron cleared his throat and looked at his interlaced hands on the table. "Rocco was ... he's dead."

His mother immediately looked up and glanced from Cameron to me. The tears welled up in my eyes, and the knot in my throat inflated. I had to look away.

"What?" she asked, the cigarette continuing to burn, suddenly forgotten, between her fingers.

"He was killed a few days ago," Cameron said, his voice quavering.

His mother stood and started pacing around the kitchen and shaking her head. I could hear her mumbling and swearing under her breath. Finally she stopped and winced at Cameron.

"You're just a pariah," she rasped. "I didn't put up a fight or make the police bring Rocco back to me when I found out he was with you because he looked up to you so much. You come here with your expensive car and your little girlfriend and you think that this makes you better than the rest of us. All your money did was get my little Rocco killed. You're nothing but a bastard, just like your father. You ruined my life, and now you've ruined my baby Rocco's life. I curse the day you were born."

I watched Cameron. My fists and my jaw were clenched. He was very calm, as though he had expected this reaction. He got up and dug into his pocket, pulling out a large stack of hundred-dollar bills.

"Someone will contact you with the funeral details," he said as he placed the money on the table. "Make sure some of this goes to getting food for those kids." He walked over to me and gently pulled my chair out to help me up. As we exited the kitchen, I saw Cameron's mother snatch the money from the table and stuff it down her shirt.

Neither of us spoke in the car. Cameron's eyes stared vacantly at the road as we sped down the street. We passed a streetlight, and instead of turning onto the road that we had come in on, Cameron kept driving and turned down a narrow alleyway instead. There was barely an inch between the car's side mirrors and the warehouse walls flanking the alleyway. He continued to drive dangerously fast until we got to the end, where the string of warehouses stopped and the alley opened up into a makeshift pier of gravel and rocks overlooking the Callister River.

Cameron unfastened his seat belt and dashed out of the car. He stuck his hands in his pockets and stiffly leaned back against the hood. I stepped out, climbed up on the hood, and wrapped my arms around him. His body was rigid, and he was breathing short, angry breaths. When I pulled in closer, I felt his muscles slowly relax.

"I used to come here a lot when I was a kid and needed to get away from my mom," he said.

I glanced around. We were in a bay in a commercial part of the river. Factories and smokestacks bordered the shores, and large barges carrying steel and crates floated back and forth across the harbor. A dead fish drifted among the rocks in the mud-brown water near our feet.

"Lovely," I remarked.

"I didn't have much to work with back then." Cameron turned around to face me. "So, you met my mother. What did you think?"

I smiled sheepishly. "She's lovely too, Cammy."

He shuddered. "Please don't ever call me that. I hate it."

I leaned in and kissed him lightly, so as not to frighten him away.

We lay on the hood of the car and listened to the sound of horns from the opposite shore. I thought about Rocco and finally understood why he had been so desperate to make a life away from his mother. Another thought occurred to me, and I turned to Cameron.

"That night, when those men came in, Norestrom kept asking Rocco where I was. They were looking for me."

"Uh-huh," Cameron replied cautiously.

"That wasn't the first time I met him."

"Who? Norestrom?"

I nodded and told him about the day Norestrom joined me at the picnic table on school grounds. Cameron stood up abruptly and walked to the edge of the water, swearing under his breath.

"I need you to tell me," I pleaded, "did Rocco get killed because of me?"

Cameron turned around to face me. "He didn't get killed because of you. Rocco got killed because of one man's greed."

"I don't understand what that has to do with me," I said.

Cameron sat down on the hood in front of me and pulled on my legs, sliding me closer to him. "Before your brother and I started the business, a guy named Shield already had almost all of the underground market. He controlled shipments, sales, business dealings, and all the money that came with it. He had connections everywhere, and the gang leaders let him control everything because they were afraid of him and his connections. When your brother, Spider, and I came in and started making contacts with the gang leaders, they joined forces with us instead. Even though Bill was a pretty smooth negotiator, the gang leaders didn't need much convincing—none of them trusted Shield, and they had been looking for a way out. The business thrived under our management. The gang leaders were happy, and Shield lost everything but the small business he ran from his own turf. He tried to threaten us and the other leaders with his connections, but with all of the leaders peacefully united, there was nothing that Shield could do."

"What does this have to do with me?"

"Shield feels that we stole the business from him and that we should have to pay him for that. After Bill died, he appealed to the leaders, asking that Bill's money be given to him. The leaders just laughed in his face. Now Shield is coming after you for that money."

"I don't have any money, Cameron. My parents stopped sending me money after they got sick of me sending it back to them."

Cameron raised his eyebrows. "I never understood that. Why do you choose to make life harder on yourself when your parents' money opens doors for you that are closed to the rest of the world? You could do anything you want with their money to support you."

"I can do anything I want with my parents' money, as long as what I choose to do is what they want me to do." Cameron looked confused. I shook my head, flustered. "Point is, I have no money, and this Shield guy is wasting his time."

"Actually, you do. You have Bill's inheritance, which is pretty generous, I might add."

"I think I would have remembered if Bill had left me anything. He didn't."

Cameron slid off the hood of the car and turned around to face me. Then he reached over and put his hand down the front of my shirt. I stood frozen in place. He pulled his hand out with the angel pendant Bill had given me clasped between two fingers.

I laughed, shaking off some of the nervousness that had lingered after his touch. "I hate to break this to you, Cameron, but that pendant is worth a few hundred dollars at best. I don't think Shield will be satisfied if I pawn it and give him the money."

"Look more closely. What do you see?"

I humored him and looked down. There was nothing unusual about it, although it was beautiful to me. An angel standing on a pedestal, with a ruby in the middle. I shrugged.

"Look closer." He held the pendant upside down so that I was looking at the bottom of the pedestal.

I squinted. "Numbers."

"They're not just numbers; they're bank account numbers. Before he died, Bill set up offshore bank accounts in the Cayman Islands, and he made me promise that I would move all his money into them if something ever happened to him. I kept that promise too," Cameron said, winking.

"Why didn't this Shield person just send one of his dumb goons to come grab the necklace from me?"

"Because they have no idea that the information they're looking for has been hanging around your neck for years, and until they saw me with you, they had no idea you even had the money. They must have assumed that Carly, Spider, and I had kept it for ourselves."

"What does seeing you with me have to do with it?"

"When you moved to Callister, I started keeping an eye on you when you ran through the projects because it was easier for me to stay hidden from you and keep anyone from guessing why I was there. It was a good way for me to make sure you got through the roughest part of town without any problems." He shook his head. "I still don't understand why you had to run through the projects when you could have just gone to visit Bill's grave and turned back around. There are better places, safer places to run. Plus you were running the same route almost every day, at almost the same time. Your appearance was predictable. You were making it easy on anyone who was looking to cause you trouble. It's like you have a death wish."

What was he expecting me to say? That he was right?

"So you were in the projects, waiting for me to run by," I said. "Then what?"

"Meatball is almost always with me when I go check on you. You're familiar to him. When he saw you running that day, he got excited and ran off after you before I could grab hold of his leash."

"And then we met."

"And then we officially met."

"And you came back. The next day," I remembered fondly.

299

His lips stretched thin. "I've done a lot of dumb things in my life, but going back to you was probably one of the dumbest moves I've ever made."

"Thanks."

"It was, Emmy," he insisted darkly. "I didn't know it at the time, but Shield had been sporadically sending some of his guys to keep an eye on me in case the money showed up. If I had left you alone, not gone back again, I don't think they would have known anything was up other than my stupid dog attacking some girl. They probably wouldn't have thought twice about you and just kept following me around."

"Why *did* you come back?"

"I broke your Walkman. I saw an opportunity to bring you back from the Dark Ages."

"That's it?"

He held my gaze. "I just wanted to talk to you. One more time. One last time. I'd been watching you for so long. Having imaginary conversations with you. Having you there, talking back to me, it was surreal."

"And? How was the real thing?"

He smirked. "You were a lot more argumentative in real life than you were in my head."

"But you came back. Two days in a row. Actually, you came back three days in a row, though you were with Spider on the third day," I said, cringing a little at the feel of Spider's name on my lips.

"After the second day, after I gave you the iPod, I spotted one of Shield's guys. I ran after him, but he got away. I knew he'd be back."

Things suddenly started to make sense. "The runner? The one from the cemetery?" He had come out of the cemetery shortly after I had.

He nodded somberly. "He's the worst of his kind. He wouldn't have just kidnapped you—he would have done a lot nastier things to you before he took you to Shield. When I heard him say in the cemetery what he had planned to do to you, it drove me over the edge … I completely lost it."

I remembered that night in the cemetery, the rage on Cameron's face as he shot the man repeatedly.

"Shield must have sent Norestrom to try to get information about you," he reasoned.

"How is Norestrom related to Shield?"

"Norestrom is Shield's right-hand man, kind of like Spider is mine."

"But I didn't tell Norestrom anything."

"It wouldn't have mattered. I think they already suspected who you might be because of your hair. I guess someone must have told them that Bill had a little sister with flaming red hair." Normally I would have been slightly offended by that description, but Cameron had an affectionate smile on his face, so I let him get away with it—this time. "That's why they planted a trap to see if it was really you. But I didn't catch on in time."

"What trap?"

"We normally paid some local gang kid to keep Bill's grave site clean. But the bastards threw garbage around Bill's grave right before you came through. Of course, you couldn't resist cleaning up the mess, could you?" he teased. "When you stopped, they knew without a doubt who you were, and we had to stop Shield's man from coming after you or running back to Shield with more information. Spider and I grabbed him just as he was running out of the cemetery after you."

"Did Spider know who I was?"

"He knew that Bill had a little sister, but that's it." Cameron passed his fingers through his hair. "Believe me, it wasn't a pretty conversation when I had to admit to Spider that I'd been secretly watching over you and that, because of that, we would have to kill one of Shield's top guys, possibly starting an all-out gang war."

"You must have gotten in a lot of trouble because of me," I mused guiltily.

"None of this was your fault, Emmy," he said. "I tried to keep everything as quiet as possible so that no one would know about you. That's why I brought Rocco along to keep watch—and, well, you know how that turned out." He looked off into the distance. "When we got back to the Farm, I held an emergency meeting with all the leaders and gave them my version of events before Shield got to them. I let them vote on my fate. They all hate Shield, so I got a unanimous vote of support right away."

"What was your version, exactly?"

"Strictly what they needed to know—that Shield was still trying to go after the money, even after he'd been told by all the leaders that it didn't belong to him, and that the financial controller of Bill's estate had been targeted."

I threw my hands up in the air. "Because why else would you be interested in me?"

"As far as they knew, I was just making sure that my money was safe."

I recalled Cameron's cold conversation about me with Manny. "And that you had taken care of the insignificant girl who had witnessed everything." I couldn't hide the hurt in my voice.

Cameron turned back to me and cupped my face in his hands. "Emmy, if I told them the truth about my feelings for you, the word would get out really quickly, and you would become a target not just because of your money, but because they would know they could control me if they had you."

He pressed his lips against mine—but then he stopped and pulled away.

"Why can't you just kill Shield?" I asked, frustration coloring my tone.

Cameron didn't seem shocked by the fact that I had just suggested that he kill another human being. "I wish I could get rid of him that easily, but he's got too many connections. When someone like that goes missing or turns up dead, people start asking questions and pry into our stuff. Anyway, any decision like that needs to be made by all the leaders, not just me. And they would never risk attention from the feds just so that I can protect the girl that I love."

He pulled me in, lopping his arm around my shoulder, and we walked back to the car.

He took my hand as we drove away, but he didn't kiss me again.

Chapter Twenty-Three

Normal?

Rocco's face came back to haunt my dreams. I woke up, but there were no tears or cold sweats this time—just an immense sense of loss. The room was almost completely dark, with the only light coming from the moonlight that shone through the cottage's small windows. I knew that Cameron was still asleep—his heavy breathing was tickling the back of my neck. I turned without a sound to make sure that he was really there, and not just something else that my mind had made up.

He was there.

I watched him for a while and tried to breathe as quietly as possible. I was afraid of waking him up. This was the only time that I could look at him as much as I wanted to without having to look away. I watched his chest rise and fall, his fists still clenched, ready while he slept.

But Cameron's alarm system was much more sensitive than mine. His eyes snapped open as though he could hear my stare. "What's wrong?" he gasped. He sat up, threw a glance around the room, and then looked back at me, his hand hovering over the gun that he kept on his nightstand.

My heart was so full; if I tried to speak, I feared it might explode. A force pulled me up and edged me closer to him.

"Are you okay?" he asked, his voice calmer now.

He brushed my arm. I wondered if I was really awake. I looked him in the eyes.

He pushed my hair away from my face, one strand at a time, brushing my shoulder, letting the hair cascade over it. I brought my hand to his, resting mine against it, the fire inside me burning so fiercely that keeping still was torture.

Cameron let his thumb come to my lips, sweeping it across them. His hand was calloused, worn. "Emmy, I love you. You know that, right?"

"I do." I had been waiting too long—a lifetime—for him. If he rejected me again, I knew I couldn't bear it. I kissed his thumb. Then I kissed the palm of his hand. He shut his eyes.

I pulled up on my knees so that we were the same height now. I leaned in, took his face in my hands, and kissed him.

He hugged me to him, lifting me so that my legs were around him, so that I was looking down on him and he was looking up. His muscles were taut, powerful. I kissed him again, but with more force. Then I pulled my T-shirt over my head. He stared fixedly at me, his gaze burning.

He picked me up, his hands cupping my buttocks. He laid me down and laid himself down on top of me.

I could smell every inch of his skin, hear his every breath, and feel every part of him that touched my skin, as though he and I together could make time stand still.

****

The gray light of dawn woke me up. I had a smile on my face. I had imagined this moment—what it would be like to be with him in that way. Turned out the real thing was a million times better.

It was as though my skin were brand-new, as though I had finally fully awakened. As though, with Cameron, I belonged in this body. I wanted to shout. I wanted to run outside in my underwear. I wanted to do it again, over and over.

It was still very early; not even the birds were up. The cottage was so quiet that I thought I could hear Cameron blinking. He was awake too. I turned around. His cheeks were blotched red, but not in a good way, not like mine. He was glaring at the ceiling.

"Was I that bad?" I joked, though I was afraid of the answer.

He startled out of whatever dark corner of his mind he had been in. "I love you," he said.

"I love you too," I said shakily, carefully, waiting for the other shoe to drop.

"I took advantage of you."

Huh? I was pretty sure that I had attacked him. "Then can you do it again? Because I'm starting to get cold over here," I said, confused. I had meant that in every sense of the word. His odd mood was making me shiver.

Cameron searched my face with worry, looking for evidence of whatever crime he thought he had committed. "Are you okay? Did it hurt?"

He was too close for me to try to lie. "A little. At first. It was wonderful."

But he wasn't really listening to me. "I shouldn't have let this happen. I really messed things up."

"If you're planning on telling me that I was just another one of your mistakes, don't bother. I'd rather live in ignorance of it."

"No, you don't understand. That's just it. Everything is different because I love you. Now I was your first on top of that. I don't think I could have screwed this up any more than I already have."

"I'm sorry I didn't let some frat boy mount me before I got here," I mumbled heatedly.

"That's not funny."

"I'm not laughing."

His eyes turned back to the ceiling. "I warned myself that this might happen if we were alone together for too long. I definitely set myself up to fail this time."

"You're acting like you were the only one there making the decision. As far I remember, I was around for the whole thing too. Cameron, I wanted this. I made up my own mind a long time ago."

"Emmy, I'm worried that we won't be able to go back to the way things used to be."

"Good."

"You're being impossible about this," he argued.

"Why would I want things to go back to the way thing were? Until a few minutes ago, I was smiling so much my cheek muscles were burning." I turned my face away.

Cameron enveloped me in his naked arms. "I'm sorry. I completely ruined the moment, as usual. I just don't know how to fix this."

"You can start by not talking about this anymore."

"No, I mean I don't know what we're going to do when we have to go back out there. We can't stay hidden here forever."

I struggled out of his arms and glared at him. "Why do you overthink everything? Can't you just turn your brain off, even for a little while? It works for me all the time."

He chuckled. "I don't think I can do that. My brain has had too many years of practice at constant juggling."

I leaned toward him and kissed his cheek. "How about now? Still juggling?"

He locked eyes with mine. "Still juggling—a mile a minute."

I kissed him on the lips. "And now?"

"Uh-huh," he said, his voice rasping slightly.

I shrugged and proceeded to get up. He pulled me back into bed before my toes ever touched the floor.

Whatever dilemma was raging inside him would be pushed aside, for a while. I was grateful for this respite, even if it would be short-lived.

****

In the late morning, Cameron grudgingly got up to let an impatient Meatball outside. His cell phone started ringing as soon as he got back into bed. He nuzzled in close to me and sighed.

After a minute of incessant ringing, the phone went quiet. Then the ringing started up again.

Cameron didn't move.

"Um, are you going to get that?"

"No," he said sleepily.

The ringing eventually stopped ... and started again a few minutes later.

He huffed, whipped the blankets off in annoyance, and stomped toward his jeans. He dug his cell phone out, looked at it, threw it back in his pocket, and rushed back to bed, closing his eyes.

I waited.

Not a word from him.

The suspense was killing me. "Do you have to call anyone back?"

"I turned it off so it'll stop bugging us," he said.

"Won't you get in trouble for doing that?" I asked ingenuously, avoiding the real question.

"I'm the boss, remember? If I don't want to pick up the phone, I don't have to."

"Oh."

Cameron chuckled and finally quenched my curiosity. "It was Spider, no big deal. Whatever's going on, he'll have to handle it himself."

"Where is he?"

"Don't know. Somewhere with Carly, I suppose. They're doing the same thing we are."

I raised my eyebrows.

"Okay, maybe not exactly what we're doing. I meant that they're hiding out, too. Everybody is. We have a rat somewhere. Nobody's safe until we figure out who the traitor is."

"What makes you think someone sold you out?"

"Someone told Shield where you were, when we'd leave for the city, and that half our guards were out of commission because of the flu. It was all a little too convenient for him to decide to attack that night. Somebody from the inside warned him."

"You have doubts about Spider and Carly," I said matter-of-factly.

"No, of course not." Cameron looked confused. "Why would you say that?"

"They're hiding from us; we're hiding from them. Why would we need to hide from them unless you suspected them or they suspected you?"

He smiled sheepishly. "I was looking for an excuse to be alone with you, for once. This was as good of an excuse as I was going to get. I told Spider that you needed some quiet time to recover."

"He bought that!"

"Not at all, but I wasn't asking for his permission, either."

I thought about what Frances had told me about Spider trying to take over the business after my brother died. "Do you like being the boss?"

He looked at me curiously. "I don't know. Never really thought about it." He pondered for a moment and then said, "Most of the time, it's just a pain. Everyone wants you to make all the decisions so that they have someone to blame if something goes wrong."

"Why doesn't Spider just do it, then?"

"I wish he would. He did do it for a little while, after Bill died. But the bosses decided that I was going to manage everything, and we had to go with what they wanted. If they don't like or trust the big boss, everything falls apart really quickly and the turf wars start up again." Cameron was rolling a lock of my hair around his finger. "It doesn't matter much because Spider doesn't want to be the big boss, anyway."

"Seems to me he would love that kind of power," I mumbled.

"You're under a lot more scrutiny when you're the boss," Cameron said. "Whatever decision you make is made for the good of the business, no matter what. You can't have any weaknesses that could affect your ability to manage the business and make the right decision. For some bosses, it's things like drug addictions or gambling. For Spider, it's Carly. He knows Carly is his weakness— if he had to choose, he would put her before the business, which would be bad for all of us. The bosses only care about the money that goes into their pockets. Anything that threatens their bottom line would get all of us killed."

I looked away and asked, "Wouldn't your relationship with Manny have put you at risk of making bad decisions?"

"If she had meant anything to me, and if the bosses had found out, then it could have been an issue. But none of that happened. It never will. The leaders don't care what you do in your spare time as long as it doesn't affect your judgment."

"Have you ever had any weaknesses, then?"

"Nope. Never. And I don't plan on it," he said coolly.

I stared at him. He laughed and pulled me into his arms.

"My addiction to you is definitely a catastrophic weakness."

"Oh dear! What are you going to do?"

His expression turned serious for a second. "I haven't figured that part out yet. Right now I'm planning to just keep you here as my prisoner. We'll pretend that the rest of the world doesn't exist and that no one cares that I love you."

My heart flipped. That sounded like the best plan I had ever heard. "So, Sherlock, do you have any suspects in mind as potential traitors?"

"Could be anyone. We have a lot of people who work for us."

One shady character came to my mind. "What about Roach?"

"There's no way."

"You seem pretty sure about that."

"You think I would let him live after what he did to you?" he asked, his voice bitter. "He was gone before he could betray us."

It wasn't that I was sad to hear that there was one less maniac like Roach roaming the earth. What stunned me, however, was the fact that a man—another living, breathing human being, flawed or not, with a past and a family and friends—had lost his life and that I didn't really flinch at the idea.

Had I simply become desensitized to the violence that was a regular part of my life now, or was I changing? I didn't know.

"Cameron, can you try not to kill anyone else on my behalf? No one will want to come close to me anymore if they think that one wrong glance in my direction will land them on the chopping block."

"Good. No one should come near you anyway," he said and looked at me intently, "He was dead no matter what, Emmy. I can't have an animal like that in my crew. He was too much of a liability." He brushed my hair aside and started to kiss my neck.

"What's it like doing what you do?"

"What do you mean?" he asked, his voice like velvet.

"I mean having to make decisions like you did about Roach, having to act like a different person."

"I don't know. I guess I've been doing it for so long that I don't really notice a difference. How do I act?"

"You're just different. You don't smile, you don't laugh, you become distant—and sometimes you're, well, scary." I felt my face go red.

His brow furrowed. "I forget sometimes that what I do is scary to normal people like you."

"I've never heard anyone call me normal."

He gave a halfhearted chuckle, then eyed me. "Are you scared of me now?"

I looked into his brown eyes. My face was still burning, my fingers were still tingling, and my heart had still not regained its normal pace since I attacked him the night before. "I'm terrified," I answered truthfully.

****

When I got out of the shower, he was sitting at the kitchen table, engulfed in the paperwork strewn in front of him and mumbling into his phone. I ate my cereal and listened as he ticked off numbers to Spider. "Forty, ten, eighty …" They didn't seem like big numbers, but I expected that several zeros probably followed the double digits.

Cameron grinned when he caught me peeking at his papers. I couldn't make anything out anyway. I found it odd that they would have any kind of records; I didn't know much about criminal enterprises, but I had watched enough TV to know that leaving any kind of evidence behind was a really bad idea.

"Aren't you afraid that those papers are going to fall into the wrong hands?" I asked when he finally got off the phone.

He slid the papers over the table to me. "You can look if you want."

Though the papers were now right in front of me, I still couldn't make out anything. All I could see were jumbled letters, numbers, and symbols—nothing that made any sense.

"We have an encryption system," he explained. "Carly came up with it. Every letter and symbol means something else."

"Wouldn't someone eventually figure it out if you gave them enough time? Like the FBI?"

He shrugged. "Sure they would. But we take extra precautions, like changing the code every couple of weeks and only writing down what we absolutely need to. Once we're done with the paperwork, we destroy it right away."

"So how do you keep track of everything if you don't keep any records?"

He smiled deviously and tapped his head with one finger. "I've got everything I need in here."

One smile from Cameron and I had already forgotten what I ate for breakfast a few minutes ago.

I pushed the papers back over the table. "I guess it's back to work today." I wasn't even trying to mask the sadness in my voice.

"If I don't get some work done soon, Spider will have a heart attack."

"You got in trouble for playing hooky?" I teased.

"Yeah, Spider was pretty upset. He thought something had had happened to us." He grinned. "But I just blamed it on you, so we're good."

"Thanks."

With no TV and nowhere to go, I wondered what I was going to do to occupy my time. It occurred to me that I would have to be alone, the idea of which suddenly made me hyperventilate.

"How long are you going to be gone this time?" My voice cracked slightly, but I tried to keep calm and brave for Cameron's sake.

"A day, if we leave within the next five minutes."

"We?"

"I'm not going to leave you here alone. You're coming with me."

"Where are we going?"

"I have to go see one of my distributors and check on the new shipment."

"Drug dealers?" All of a sudden, the thought of staying alone for a day seemed like a better alternative.

"Distributors."

"Cameron, I don't think it's a very good idea."

"I have no choice," he said. "I don't know how long it'll take for things to settle down. The business can't wait any longer."

"What do I have to do?"

"You have to be scary like me for a day." He looked pleased at the thought.

"I don't think I could pull that off."

"Actually, you're already really good at it," he said dismally. "Pretend that I'm standing in front of you after you just overheard me tell Manny that I don't love you—because that reaction was pretty scary ... except without the crying ... and don't start ripping your clothes off just to prove your point. I don't think it'll have the same effect on them."

I blushed at the memory. "I was feverish. I wasn't myself."

"Right." I thought I saw him roll his eyes as he turned to put the papers away. "You'd better get dressed. We need to get going if we want to be back at a decent time."

I looked down at my shorts and T-shirt. "I forgot to pack my cocktail dress. I didn't realize that drug dealers were so formal."

"Distributors," he said again. "You'll be cold if you don't get changed."

It was early August. Even though it was still early in the morning, the cottage was already steaming from the sun's rays.

He headed over to my duffle bag and grabbed the pair of jeans that was on top. When he took them out, they unrolled and out fell the book, the movie, and the letter I had written him. He pitched the jeans to me and picked up the letter. While I anxiously got re-dressed, he carefully unfolded it, read it, and reread it. Then he folded the paper several times until it was the size of a credit card, slid it into the front pocket of his jeans, and took possession of it. When he returned to me, his smile seemed worried but genuine.

We walked out together.

Cameron's crooked smile made me think that he was up to something. This suspicion only grew as I started walking toward the Audi.

"We're not taking the car," he finally announced when I pulled on the door handle.

He handed me a backpack, walked to the toolshed next to the cottage, and opened the door. My heart dived.

Chapter Twenty-Four

A New Calling

As Cameron rolled the fluorescent-green Ninja race bike out of the shed, statistics for motorcycle accidents ran through my brain.

He went back into the shed and returned with a plastic bag. He rifled through it, took out a vanity plate, and matched it to a driver's license.

"So, who are you today?" I teased, although my brain was now recalling statistics for fatal motorcycle accidents.

I picked up the card while he screwed the plate to the back of the bike. "Melvin Longhorn from New York," I announced. "It suits you."

Cameron chuckled and handed me what appeared to be a child-sized black helmet. "It's what I wore when I got my first bike. It should fit your little head."

"Remind me again why we're not taking the car?"

"I don't use anything that can be traced back to me when I'm working. You never know who's watching. Besides," he said with a broad smile, "this is a lot more fun."

Fun wasn't one of the words that had been floating through my brain.

I squeezed my head into the helmet. My cheeks were compressed so much that my lips were forced into a fish pucker.

Cameron laughed and took advantage of my incapacitated state to steal a kiss. "Last one for a while," he reminded me.

I would have nodded but I was afraid the heavy helmet would knock me off balance.

He climbed onto the bike, and I got on behind him.

We zipped down the gravel driveway, leaving Meatball to eat his breakfast on the porch. I kept my eyes shut while flying pebbles stung my face. It wasn't until we reached the pebble-free road and I was still getting stung that I realized that the pebbles were actually bugs kamikazeing against my exposed skin. I made a point of keeping my mouth shut after that.

Cameron skillfully weaved in and out of traffic. At some point he complained that he couldn't breathe, and I was forced to relax my death grip around his torso. Eventually I even opened my eyes and watched the scenery whoosh by.

We drove along the outskirts of the city and made our way down a country road that snaked beside the Callister River, which divided the state of New York and the province of Ontario, serving as a natural border between the United States and Canada. Although some freshwater trickled down from the Canadian mountains into the Callister, it was fed primarily with salt water from the Atlantic that poured in at its basin. Because of its proximity to the ocean and its practically bottomless depths, the river was almost always congested with commercial schooners that motored back and forth from one country to the other and then back into the ocean.

Little by little, the evergreens turned into cornfields and farmland. There was something exhilarating about being open to the elements and about holding on to Cameron for dear life. After a couple of hours, Cameron turned onto a farm road. My hips, legs, and arms were starting to cramp up, and I had to close my eyes as rows of corn whipped past us hypnotically. When we finally came to a stop and I opened my eyes again, what I saw was not what I had expected to see.

There, in the middle of a field, stood a slanted wooden barn ... and nothing else. There were no ten-foot-high electric fences, goons with automatic weapons, or man-eating dogs—just an old barn, barely big enough to fit a tractor. And there was a lot of corn around us. My first experience with the drug world was, so far, extremely disappointing.

When I got off the bike and tried to put my full weight on my frozen legs, I almost fell on my face.

"Ready?" Cameron whispered anxiously. I wasn't sure if he was asking me or himself.

I yanked the helmet off my head—it was like sucking a strawberry through a straw—and struggled to put the escaped hair locks back into my ponytail.

"Leave your hair down," he commanded.

"I hate having my hair down."

"That's the point. It'll force you out of your comfort zone. Make you look like you're on edge."

Like most things Cameron said, this didn't make immediate sense to me; however, I didn't think that now was the right time to argue with him about my follicle-related insecurities. I grudgingly obeyed and pulled my flattened helmet-hair out of its comfort zone. Cameron gave me a quick once-over. I thought for sure I detected a hidden smile in his eyes, and I couldn't help but suspect I'd been duped.

With a quick nod, he indicated that it was time. I watched his face expertly turn to stone, and he stepped away from me as though I no longer existed. Even though I knew it was just an act, it still stung.

Cameron coolly walked toward the barn, and I not-so-coolly followed not-so-closely behind him. He opened the door, and a shadow moved somewhere inside. I anxiously waited for my eyes to adjust to the barn's dark interior as we stepped over the threshold.

"Ginger!"

My heart leaped. I never thought that I—or anyone—would hear that voice again.

"Geez, you're a sight for sore eyes," Griff told me. I could finally see him; he had jumped off the table he was sitting on and was grinning from ear to ear as he strode toward me, ignoring Cameron.

Cameron turned and glanced at me just as Griff walked past him. From the sour look on his face, I knew that he was, one, extremely jealous, and two, warning me to stay in character. With extreme difficulty, I glanced away from Griff and kept moving with Cameron.

It was painful to watch Griff wince at the snub.

"Open the hatch," Cameron said impatiently.

"Yes, sir," Griff bitterly obeyed. He walked to a pile of hay that was loosely strewn in the middle of the wood-planked floor and pitchforked it to the side, revealing a square trapdoor. He pulled on a cord and the door opened, revealing stairs that led down into the dark.

Cameron walked past Griff and started climbing down the stairs.

Griff shifted uncomfortably, deliberating. Then he called after Cameron, "I heard what happened to your brother." His tone was soft, genuine. "I'm sorry for your loss. He was a really great kid."

Cameron paused; his jaw dropped a bit. "Thank you." His still-harsh tone did not betray him.

I began climbing down after Cameron, waiting until I was sure he was out of sight before quickly turning to Griff. I smiled at him, only for a moment. The effect was instantaneous—Griff's face lit up.

The hatch closed above us.

We were in a hole in the ground; it felt like a grave. It smelled musty. The floor and walls were beaten earth. I could still see a bit of light seeping through the floorboards above us. And then a light came on: a single light bulb was hanging from floorboards. Then another light came on a few feet ahead, where I saw that someone had dug a passageway that sloped down underground. Cameron and I followed it, descending until we could no longer see the floorboards above us and we were completely surrounded by earth and rocks. At the end of the passage there was a grate. When Cameron pulled it open, I realized it was a mineshaft elevator.

We got in. Cameron closed the grate, pressed a yellow button, and we went down. A million questions were speeding through my head—most involving Griff's new job location. It took every bit of my self-control to resist the urge to ask questions. As if he could sense my fraying composure, Cameron cleared his throat to get my attention and shot a quick look above us. There was a glass globe mounted overhead, an "eye in the sky," similar to what you would find in a Vegas casino.

We were being watched.

My ears kept popping, and I had to swallow repeatedly to prevent the pressure in my skull from forcing my brain through my nose.

When the elevator door opened, two men stood to greet us. The man in front was tall and sturdy. From the wrinkles that were starting to line his olive skin, I guessed that he was in his midthirties. His demeanor was grave. His black hair and dark facial features only enhanced the severity of his appearance.

The man who stood behind him was older—much older. Although he had similarly dark coloring, he was shrunken by two or three inches, and his face was leathery and worn. His hair was gray except for a few black strands, and it went straight down to his elbows, like dead straw. His tired eyes twinkled—and stayed on me from the moment we stepped out of the elevator.

"New bodyguard?" asked the younger man with a grimace.

Cameron didn't flinch. "I brought my accountant."

I almost choked, and I hoped with every fiber of my being that I wouldn't be asked to display my math skills.

"You haven't seen the need to bring an accountant before. Why now?" the man continued to probe.

"Things change," Cameron said plainly. And then, in a haughty tone, he said, "I'm a busy man, Hawk. If you don't want to talk business, I'll take my business elsewhere. I don't like to waste my time."

While Cameron and Hawk stared each other down, the older man continued to look intently at me—maybe waiting for me to make a mistake. I was trying hard to ignore his stare and keep my face expressionless. But I could feel the corner of my mouth starting to twitch as the muscles in my face began surrendering to the exertion. I'd had no idea that being purposefully uptight was so much work.

Hawk finally acquiesced and hesitantly turned so we could follow him and his older counterpart. They led us through a pearl-white marble tunnel. Because of the narrowness of the tunnel, Cameron and I were forced to walk shoulder to shoulder, which made it even more difficult for me to ignore him. I focused on looking ahead.

Unlike the cave-like tunnel under the barn, this winding tunnel was sparkling clean and outfitted with silver sconces on the walls and expensive-looking cameras on the ceiling. Every few feet, we awkwardly brushed past armed guards who would look me over as we passed by.

Hawk and the older man continued to move ahead of us. I could hear their echoed voices as they started conversing in French. Though the two men's dialects were decidedly different, with a little concentration I could understand most of what they were saying. My mother had grown up in Marseille and was a proud Frenchwoman. Of the few childhood memories I had of my mother, almost all of them included her correcting my French.

Suddenly aware that I had been intently staring at the back of the men's heads, I averted my eyes just as Hawk anxiously glanced back. Fortunately he didn't notice, or at least he didn't appear to. He turned back to his partner, and I continued to eavesdrop with my eyes on my feet.

"Why the hell would they bring a girl like that here?" Hawk was saying. "The crows are hiding something, Pop. I can feel it."

"I don't know about the boy, but I think you are right about the girl. She is without a doubt hiding something," croaked the old man.

"Like what?" Hawk asked nervously.

"I'm not sure yet, but I sense something distinctive in her."

"Do you think she could hurt us?"

"How much harm could one young girl do?" the old man said pensively, as though talking to himself.

"I don't know. There's definitely something strange about her," Hawk continued.

"There's something strange with all the crows, son," said the old man. He chuckled hoarsely. "At least the girl is easier on the eyes than the unpleasant baldheaded one they call Spider."

Hawk groaned in annoyance. "What should we do?"

The old man paused before answering. "Call the guards. Tell them to be on high alert. We'll see where this goes."

Hawk took out his shortwave radio, and his uneasy voice reverberated within the marble tunnel through the radios that were holstered on the belts of the tunnel guards. While I was growing nervous, Cameron remained unchanged. I doubted that he had understood any of the men's discussion, and I wished that I could warn him. But I knew that if I could so easily hear the men ahead of us, they would just as easily hear me if I spoke.

I remained silent.

A skunk-like smell had started to seep into the tunnel. I understood the source as we stepped out of the passageway and into a large greenhouse. Fluorescent lights were hanging low from the ceiling: artificial sunlight. People in white coats were moving about the room, tending to large marijuana plants. Lined up against the walls were more armed guards, all of whom were glaring in our direction—now on high alert.

Cameron and Hawk met up and walked ahead between the tables, while the old man joined me behind. Cameron scrutinized the plants and frowned in disapproval. Their color, their size, and their quality were, apparently, unsuitable. This, of course, sent Hawk into an uproar, and the two businessmen commenced arguing over proper pricing of the crops. While I fixed my attention on the argument, I could feel the old man studying my every move.

Eventually, Cameron and Hawk agreed on a price that neither seemed pleased with. I was relieved when we continued to move forward; my nose was starting to get stuffy from the flowering plants. The old man rejoined Hawk ahead of us, and Cameron was back at my side, continuing to artfully ignore me.

Hawk turned to the old man and spoke in French, his face red and sweating. "That insulting … How dare he attack the quality of our work? We have been growing for generations, before that kid was even born."

The old man was calm. "You know as well as I do that it's a bad crop. The boy is smart, and he's a good businessman. You shouldn't be severe with him for doing his job."

Hawk huffed. "Well, whatever his reasons, I'll make sure to give him the worst of all of the plants. Maybe next time he'll think twice about insulting us."

The old man quickly peeked back and caught me looking at him. I looked away and felt my cheeks burning. He only smiled and kept walking.

We passed the endless tables of plants and headed into another marble tunnel. Large vents over our heads were churning out fresh air. I gratefully took several deep breaths.

I could see the old man's mouth moving, but I couldn't hear what he was saying because of the noise from the vents. This was the opportunity I had been waiting for. When I was certain that the men weren't watching, I turned to Cameron with urgency, unsure how long I would have before they noticed us talking.

"They think that I'm hiding something … They don't trust us … They put the guards on high alert …You're right, the crop is bad … The Hawk guy is planning on giving you all the worst plants … Oh, and why do they keep calling you 'crow'?" I finished, out of breath.

Cameron looked at me, puzzled, and then his expression quickly turned to fury. He pushed me behind him so quickly, so fiercely, that I almost fell to the floor. Hawk, who had come running in my direction, looked violent, his apparent rage equal to Cameron's.

"What game are you playing at? You brought the girl so that you could spy on us?" Hawk screamed. I had been tricked into thinking they couldn't overhear me. Obviously, Hawk and the old man had heard everything.

Cameron shoved Hawk backward. "Step away. Now." His voice was sharp, leaving no doubt that he would kill if pushed to it.

The old man stepped between the two and urged them to calm down. He then turned to me with an excited smile.

"I knew I recognized those green eyes," he said in French. "You looked like you understood what we were saying, but I had to be sure. There aren't many people in these parts who speak French. Your brother Billy was the only one I knew outside our tribe."

The old man started to move toward me, but Cameron barred him with an outstretched arm and looked at me, absolute confusion on his face.

I translated in a hurry. "He knows I'm Bill's sister." That was the gist of it, anyway.

Cameron continued to stand his ground, glancing from me to the old man, trying to figure out what to do. In my mind, there were only two options: fight through an army of armed guards and try to escape without too many bullet wounds, or let the defenseless old man approach me. Deciding for both of us, I held Cameron's gaze and tugged his arm down. He let me by with great reluctance. The old man gleefully looped his arm around mine. Cameron flinched.

"In Manuuk tribal legends," he explained in French as we moved ahead of Cameron and Hawk and continued to wind our way through the vented tunnel, "crows are powerful spirits that move between the worlds of the living and the dead. They are highly intelligent creatures. They learn and adapt quickly."

"Crows are also greedy and tricky," Hawk added bitterly— in English, for Cameron's benefit—although the effect was lost on him, as this was the only part of the conversation he had understood.

"Yes, crows are mischievous," the old man continued. "They like to play tricks on us, but they are also extremely loyal to their kind. When a crow is struggling, it will seek out its kind to survive. They take care of each other like a family, blood ties or not. Your brother and this one," he said, pointing to an oblivious Cameron, "were a lot like the crows of my tribe's legends when I first met them."

We arrived at another elevator, and the four of us squeezed in. Hawk pulled the elevator grid closed.

"I'm Emily," I blurted out. Cameron looked like he was going to jump out of his skin.

"Your brother called you Emmy, yes?" the old man asked, his gaze inquisitive, persistent.

I figured that I wouldn't be able to lie to him, so I chose not to. "When I was young."

"And you're not young anymore," he said, grinning. Apparently this was funny to him. "I'm Jerry, but call me Pops."

The elevator motor hummed. Pops still had his arm around mine. He patted my hand as though he could feel my heart beating a mile a minute. His skin was cold and rubbery, and I could smell pipe tobacco off his clothes. I usually didn't like to be touched by strange old men.

We stepped out of the elevator into a darkened grotto. The rock walls and ceiling were glistening with dripping water, and a stream gushed along one of the walls, from one side of the grotto to the other. The room was dimly lit by lanterns that had been clumsily hung on the walls. I couldn't see my feet in the darkness and had to rely on the old man to guide me to a small bench next to the rushing stream. We sat down as Cameron and Hawk silently stood behind us. Armed men standing against the walls completed the scene. We waited. For what, I didn't know.

"I was really sorry when I heard your brother passed on. He was a good kid. Much too young to die." Pops was sincere.

"Thank you," I said in English.

The water bubbled. It was too dark, I couldn't see, so I leaned in for a closer look. A big fish suddenly surfaced, and I screamed, almost falling over the bench. Cameron caught me before I busted my skull open on the rock floor. Everyone laughed except me. Cameron chuckled, but only a bit. The men quickly went to work as more fish broke the surface. Pops and I watched from the sidelines as, one by one, the huge fish were pulled from the water by the gunmen and gutted—guts in the form of plastic bags fell out.

"Look real, don't they?" Pops said proudly. I nodded, still in shock.

"They're just robots covered in latex," he explained.

"Where do they come from?"

"From everywhere—boats, submarines, neighboring states, Canada. This batch came from a German boat two miles off the East Coast."

"Aren't you afraid that they'll get seized? Or fished?"

"Hasn't happened yet." He seemed amused by my questions. "They can't be traced back to us, anyway."

A volcano of profanities erupted between Hawk and Cameron, who had resumed their earlier argument over the market value of the merchandise. Echoed curses bounced off the rock walls.

"Are they always like this?" I asked loudly.

"This is the most well-behaved I've ever seen them," Pops said. "By this point, I usually have to order them to put their guns away, or get one of the guards to pull them apart. Both as stubborn as mules."

Pops caught Cameron nervously glancing over at me for the hundredth time. I quickly distracted him.

"What was my brother like?"

The smile on his face told me he knew it was a diversion, but he went along with it anyway. "Your brother was just a boy when I first met him," he said. "One day he showed up unannounced and demanded to speak to me. The first thing he said to me: you need to change your alliances. I didn't know what to make of this kid.

He was either a fool or pretty brave for strolling in here like that. I decided to listen to him. Well-spoken kid. Made a good case. He convinced me. Been doing business with these crows since."

I thought of my brother, tried to imagine him as a businessman, as a drug-dealing businessman.

Pops's voice brought me back to reality. "This one, on the other hand," he said, nodding in Cameron's direction, "was very young. Too young to be in this business. Your brother relied on him quite a bit. The boy's smart, but I always thought it was more than a kid like that could handle."

Pops eyed me, waiting for my reaction; he didn't need to wait long for me to falter. Cameron glanced to check on me again, and our eyes locked for a split second. I tried to signal—motionlessly—that I was okay. I was starting to recognize subtle changes in Cameron's demeanor: he was definitely angry with me. I would have to deal with that later. I had bigger fish to fry for now.

It seemed to please the old man to watch us silently communicating. "He's a quiet young fellow," he remarked. "Impossible to read. He seems lost, as if he's already in the spirit world ... We don't like to do business with crows who don't have any roots in this world. But he's a good businessman and has always been fair to us. I'm glad to see that he's human after all." The old man's smile was telling.

I didn't feel threatened by Pops, but that didn't mean I wanted to gossip with him about my relationship with Cameron—even if I had understood anything about our relationship.

"So what, exactly, is in those plastic bags?" I blurted out.

Pops didn't draw back at my insolence. "What do you think?"

"Heroin? Cocaine?"

"What if it is? What do you think about that?" he asked me.

I'm fine with it, seemed like the appropriate response. The truth was, as much as I loved Cameron, what he did for a living did bother me. It didn't lessen my love for him in any way; I had been able to tuck this small, disturbing detail in a locked compartment inside my head.

"It just seems awful to think that these drugs might end up in the hands of kids." I tried to put it nicely.

"I don't sell to kids," he quickly replied, his brow furrowing.

"But you can't control what happens to … the product once it leaves here," I said, almost apologetically. "I mean, at some point, some street thug will try to push the drugs on kids."

Pops crossed his arms over his belly and crossed one leg over the other. "Kids don't decide to start taking drugs because of some pusher they don't know on the street. They're convinced by peer pressure, by family and friends. You know, children are more likely to start by looking through their parents' medicine cabinets for drugs that won't cost them anything."

It sounded a little rehearsed. I quickly realized that Pops was looking for a sparring partner, and I didn't know if I could deliver. I wished that I had paid better attention in my high school political science class when we debated the issue.

"Yes, but drugs lead to violence."

"Violence in the media is the leading cause of violence. Illegal drugs might cause bad people to do bad things, but so do alcohol and licit drugs."

"But drugs do increase crime." I had no idea if they did, but the argument definitely sounded good.

"Most drug crimes relate to the sale of drugs. If selling drugs weren't illegal, we would free up the court system and jails."

Pops waited with delight for my next claim.

I searched for something, anything. "Drugs are just really bad for you. People can die if they take drugs."

"People do all kinds of things that are bad for them, like eating fast food and smoking," he responded with satisfaction. "You know heart disease is the leading cause of death in America? More people die from fast food and cigarettes than they do from anything else."

Meanwhile, Cameron and Hawk looked like they were about to come to blows. Whatever Cameron said had set Hawk off on another vulgar dissertation, and they were angrily facing off. I looked at Pops to intervene, but he just smiled at me.

"My son has a hot temper," he explained. "He doesn't trust the crows. Though … I think his opinion may change about this one after today." He winked at me, and then he glanced back at the businessmen and stood up. "I'm afraid there isn't much that I will be able to do with the one they call Spider. There's something false about that boy."

Pops made his way to the barking men and calmly put his hand on his son's shoulder. "Give him what he wants, Hawk," he ordered in English.

Hawk looked incredulous. "What? Why would I do that?"

"Because I said so," Pops answered with authority.

Cameron was just as surprised as his sparring partner, but he took advantage. "And the plants?" he asked Pops, glancing at me from the corner of his eye.

"Only the best ones."

Cameron and Hawk stood there. I imagined that their jaws would have been agape if they had been capable of showing surprise. Everyone in the grotto had gone silent at this development; all I could hear was the swishing of the stream.

Pops broke the tension and turned to Cameron. "If there is nothing else, then I suggest you take this young girl home. I'm afraid I have taken enough of her time, and she will soon grow tired of me."

Arm in arm, Pops and I made our way back through the underground maze, with Cameron and Hawk now quietly, reflectively in tow. I could feel Cameron's stare. We walked through the stinky greenhouse, and I permitted myself to make a casual comment.

"Your electricity bills must be insane."

"Hidden solar panels on the surface," Pops replied with a smile.

We left Hawk and Pops at the elevator doors, but not before Pops whispered in my ear, "I hope we will see you again, young Emily."

I didn't look at Cameron's face as we stood in the elevator. I already knew that I was in really big trouble. We headed back where we had come from and met Griff at the top of the trapdoor stairs.

"Have a good day, sir. And madam," Griff added with emphasis, bowing low and grinning.

Cameron walked quickly, his shoulders tense and erect. I genially grinned back at Griff before sprinting to meet up with Cameron at the motorcycle. He handed me my helmet without looking at me. I snuggled in behind him on the bike, but the trick didn't work its magic this time. He remained on edge as we sped off in a cloud of dust.

Chapter Twenty-Five

Broken

We rode without a word, and I was conflicted: distressed that Cameron was angry with me, yet happy—even a little smug—that I had pulled off my first business meeting with distributors without getting us killed.

We pulled into a small parking lot where an old school bus had been converted into a fast-food stand. It was midafternoon, and I was starving. I decided the aroma of greasy fries was the best thing I had ever smelled. Cameron barely looked at me while we waited in line. The extent of our conversation was limited to "What do you want to eat?" and "Veggie burger with extra fries." Cameron asked for mayo for my fries. I didn't need to say anything.

I followed him around the back of the converted bus and through a cluster of trees. I could hear crashing water as we neared the end of the trail. Fifty feet above ground, a waterfall plunged in an almost perfect line down the face of the rock into a gurgling pool. People had sporadically spread out among the trees and grass to picnic and take in the breathtaking scene. Cameron dug a blanket out of the backpack and unfolded it on a tiny patch of grass, as though he had been there before. We were mostly hidden in the brush.

While he ate and brooded, I pulled my hair back into a ponytail. This caused Cameron to smile, which he tried to hide from me. I wasn't sure exactly what I had done to make him angry. I did know that nothing about the meeting had gone according to his plans, and that I didn't do anything I was supposed to do—like stay quiet.

With a bit of food in my belly and Cameron's mood seemingly improved, I figured I would get it over with, whatever was bugging him.

"You're angry with me." I was really good at stating the obvious.

"Uh-huh." Cameron was lying on his back with his legs crossed one over the other.

Apparently I was supposed to guess what I had done wrong—which I wanted to do as much as a serial killer wished to confess every crime he had ever committed to the rookie cop who had just stopped him because of a broken taillight.

"Can you tell me why?" I finally asked.

"Things could have gone really wrong in there."

"But they didn't," I replied.

"They *could* have," he reiterated. "I had no idea what was going on."

"Welcome to my world," I mumbled, spearing my straw though the plastic lid of my cup.

Cameron half-smiled. "Emmy, when I don't know what's going on and can't understand what you're saying, I can't react."

"You don't have any faith in me."

"It has nothing to do with my faith in you and everything to do with my mistrust of them. These people aren't angels. This isn't a game. As far as I knew, the old man was threatening to put a knife to your throat as soon as I wasn't looking."

"He never threatened me."

"I had no way of knowing that."

"Considering the circumstances, I think I made the right decision." I was convinced of this.

Cameron rolled his eyes at my cockiness. "I should have known that you'd be able to charm yourself out of trouble. Must be in your genes."

I wasn't sure whether he meant that I had charmed myself out of trouble with the distributors or with him. It didn't matter in the end. I took his change in demeanor as a signal that I was on my way to being forgiven. I decided to swoop in for the kill and snuggled up against him. He didn't recoil.

"I got you everything you wanted, didn't I?" I said with a sigh.

"Yes, Emmy," he conceded, also with a sigh. "You made me a lot of money today. But it's just money. I would have preferred it much more if you had just kept your distance from them."

Nearby, something moved in the trees. Cameron abruptly pushed me off and sprang up. A couple of little kids came crashing through the brush and disappeared again.

He lay back down on the blanket. If I hadn't been aware of his paranoia, I would have been insulted by his apparent fear of being seen in public with me.

I propped myself up on my elbows and looked at Cameron.

"What's going to happen when things settle down?" I asked.

"What do you mean?"

"What happens to me when the danger is gone?"

"You go home," he said instinctively. He hadn't changed his mind, after everything.

I tried to keep it cool. "And then what?"

"And then nothing. You go back and live happily ever after," he said, refusing to look at me.

"What about us?" I realized my voice was shaking.

Cameron was silent.

"I could just stay with you," I offered cautiously.

He laughed, but his tone was tight. "Em, you get yourself in more trouble when you're bored. Do you really think you could just stay home and wait around for me while I go to work? I mean, don't get me wrong, it's a nice fantasy, but we already tried that and it didn't work."

I was flustered. "I could go to work with you. Turns out I'm pretty good at it. You said so yourself."

"Absolutely not! I won't allow it."

"Why not? Carly does it."

"Carly can't do anything else! You …" He took a breath to calm himself. "You have a life, school, a family, friends. And you would be much more at risk than Carly because of my position."

"I'll take my chances," I grumbled.

"Well, I'm not willing to take any chances. Not with you." His voice was icy. "Besides, it's not just up to me. You become a risk to the whole organization if you get caught by rivals. The leaders would have our heads before they let any of that happen."

"So promise them that you won't do anything if something does happen to me. That you'll let me die if I'm dumb enough to get caught."

Cameron stared at me vacantly. "That's the stupidest thing I ever heard. Don't ever say that again." He briskly stood and started packing up. "We need to go before it starts getting dark."

I did what I was told and then struggled to keep up with him as he stomped back to the bike.

It started raining about an hour from home. By the time we drove up the gravel driveway, it was dark, we were soaked, and Meatball was anxiously sitting by the cottage door, waiting to get out of the rain. Cameron immediately got a fire burning in the cast-iron stove; then he was on his cell phone, dictating numbers to Spider. He smiled at me on occasion, particularly when he repeated the day's purchase prices. He was keeping busy, throwing paperwork into the fire as he went through the numbers one by one with Spider, and then making supper for the both of us while he replayed the day's events over the phone. He stayed on the phone the whole time we were eating, talking about what I assumed was business, although I didn't understand any of it. Eventually his phone died and he reluctantly hung up. He insisted that I sit or, even better, go to bed, while he did the dishes.

I didn't want to believe it. But as I continued to watch him, while he tried his best to pretend that everything was okay, I felt something familiar creeping within me—a dull ache in my heart, like the stitches of an old wound were coming undone.

Before long, things inside me were shattering, falling to pieces.

It was the look on his face that gave him away. I had seen it played out in front me a thousand times. It was the look Bill had given me the last time I saw him. It was my mother's pressed smile the day she had come for a surprise visit in Callister, just before she came up with an excuse for why she needed to leave, quickly. It was the avoidance of eye contact by the inconsequential boys when they were getting annoyed with my lack of affection.

Cameron was getting ready to leave me. I wanted to latch on to him, hard, so that we would never be separated. At the same time, I wanted to run away so that, perhaps, I wouldn't feel the pain when he found a way to let me go.

Whoever said love hurts was wrong. Love is excruciating, especially when you can feel it slipping through your fingers and there is nothing you can do about it. What it would feel like when love was lost … I wouldn't survive that. I closed my eyes, willing the tears to stay hidden behind my eyelids and focusing on breathing in and out instead of on the pain in my heart.

Cameron finished the dishes and turned off the tiny kitchen light. With the only light coming from the shimmering flames shining through the square of the stove window, my tears were safely out of sight.

"We should get some sleep. It's been a long day," he said with an exaggerated yawn and stretch of the arms.

It didn't matter that the tears blurred my vision; I wouldn't be able to see anything anyway. But Cameron turned and caught my arm as we climbed up the stairs.

"Emmy, what's wrong?" he asked, bewildered.

He reached a hand out. I whacked it away. "You're going to leave me no matter what I do, aren't you? I won't go back without you, Cameron. I can't. You're all I have."

He wrapped his arms around me, pinning my arms to my sides. "Em, I'm not going anywhere. We'll make it work, I promise. Whatever it takes."

Then he let me go and lifted my shaking chin. He looked into my eyes for a moment, sadness swelling in his dark features. "I never knew you were this broken."

"Only when you're not there," I confessed.

"You'll probably die if you stay with me."

"Then I'm dead either way, because I won't survive without you."

There was nothing he could say that would convince me that being without him was the better option.

He sighed and shook his head. "Whatever I do just makes everything harder. Worse for you."

It was in the flickering light of the fire that I noticed that familiar sparkle in his eyes, and suddenly I understood. The rush to get everything done, the fake yawn, the attempt to get me into bed, early ... Cameron was right. I was broken. Probably beyond repair. But in that moment, and all those other moments—when it was just us, and especially when he looked at me like that, smoldering, as if I were all he needed—I didn't feel broken. I was like a shattered coffee mug that had been superglued back together; with him, I couldn't feel the cracks.

I latched on to him. He kissed me and carried me to bed. The other stuff—life—was left behind for another night.

Chapter Twenty-Six

Deadly Risky Business

Cameron was sitting on the edge of the bed. The day had come, the one we had both been dreading. Today was Rocco's funeral. Cameron had tried to avoid it as long as possible, hoping to wait until they found the rat—or at least until things got a little better. But it couldn't be put off any longer: Rocco needed to be put to rest, and we needed to move forward. The way that Cameron was hunched over, his shoulders carrying the guilt of his little brother's death—this day was going to be difficult, agonizing for him.

In a movement that had become ours, I scrambled behind him and wrapped my arms around his shoulders. There we sat, mentally preparing for what lay ahead, becoming one skin once again.

Dressed in black, we ascended the loft stairs and walked outside to the car. Cameron had shaved his growing beard. I had missed his face, but now I also missed the stubble. He was wearing a suit and a tie, looking handsomer than ever. I'd managed to find a wrinkled skirt that I had never worn and black flip-flops to match. My duffle bag options were limited.

As we drove away, Cameron's hand was squeezing mine so tight that my fingertips were going numb.

"Tell me what you and the old man talked about back at the distribution plant." His voice was unsteady, and his eyes never left the road in front of him.

I was content to provide his distraction. "His name is Jerry, but he likes to be called Pops," I started. While I gabbed, Cameron listened—or looked like he was listening. Perhaps he just needed the noise. Although his hand never left mine, his grip loosened after a while—and I was able to feel my fingertips again. I told him everything, even shared Pops's perception of Cameron, but I left out the comment about his initial, negative impression. I knew it would hurt Cameron too much.

Cameron was particularly interested to hear about our debate over the pros and cons of drugs.

"Does it bother you what I do?" he asked.

I couldn't lie to him, but I also didn't want to tell him the truth. "It's not … ideal," I said, treading very carefully.

"It's okay for you to be bothered by it," he said quickly. "In fact, you should be bothered by it. It would be abnormal for you to think it was okay."

Cameron paused in hopes of an answer, but I just shrugged my shoulders and remained silent. I wasn't about to fall for that one: the "it's okay for you to tell me the truth as long as it's what I want to hear" trap.

"The old man whispered something to you as we left," he continued with curiosity. "What did he say?"

"Pops," I corrected. "He said that he hoped to see me again."

"Absolutely not!"

"I know. But you asked, so I told you."

Cameron glanced at me—I was sulking—and quietly chuckled. After getting a small taste of Cameron's work, I was still convinced that I could do some of what Cameron did. But I could not fathom what it would be like to make those other decisions. My mind turned to Griff.

"How did Griff end up working for Pops?" I kept my eyes on the road, tried to keep my voice as unconcerned as possible.

"I needed to get rid of him, and they needed a guard. They owed me a favor anyway," he explained. Then he eyed me. "You thought I had him taken care of, didn't you? Even after I told you I didn't."

"The thought crossed my mind," I admitted. I looked at him, trying to decipher his mood. He didn't look upset.

"I wouldn't lie to you," he reminded me.

"But you were also really upset the night he was caught climbing down from my room. Maybe even a bit jealous?" I raised an eyebrow, testing.

"Maybe a lot jealous." He smiled, embarrassed. "But I knew it would hurt you too much if I did anything to him."

"Would you have had him killed if it weren't for me?"

Cameron just glanced over at me, then turned his eyes back to the road. A chill went up my spine. I didn't want to think about the alternate ending and needed to change the atmosphere.

"You're rich, right?" I blurted, trying to shock Cameron. From the look on his face, it worked. "Where does all the money go?"

"Lots of places."

"Like?"

Cameron looked uncomfortable but, with a deep sigh, went along with it. "Like stocks, bonds, property. I have a bunch of bank accounts in different places around the world."

"So … you don't just bury the money under the mattress like they do in movies?"

He laughed. "Actually, I do have some money buried in different spots, but none under the mattress."

His answers only made me more curious. "Don't people get suspicious when you walk into a bank with a stack of cash?"

Cameron looked at me like I was from another planet. "I never actually walk into a bank, Emmy. Everything is done electronically. I carry very little cash on me." I could tell from his tone that this answer was supposed to explain everything. But I didn't understand. Somehow I couldn't see drug users using their bank cards to buy whatever it was they bought.

Cameron searched my face; he must have found complete confusion there. He pulled over to the side of the road and turned to me. He was procrastinating, mostly for his own purposes, I guessed.

"Aren't we going to be late?" I asked.

"They won't start without us," he said. "You want to know how it works, don't you?"

I nodded, and I could feel my cheeks getting warm.

"When we get the product," he started, "it's divided among all the leaders. They distribute it within their gangs, and it's subdivided several times like that until it actually hits the streets. When it's sold, the money is passed by the dealers through small businesses that deposit the money into their bank accounts. Sometimes dealers will also open bank accounts in their friends' and families' names and deposit small amounts there too. Where the money goes from there gets really complicated—property, shares, and other stuff gets bought and sold. The money changes hands so many times that by the time it gets to us, it's virtually impossible to trace back to the product."

"Aren't you afraid of getting caught?"

He looked away. "I'll be killed before I ever get caught."

I instantly regretted asking the question.

We pulled back onto the road. Cameron didn't volunteer any more information, and I definitely didn't ask any more questions. Blissful ignorance would have been better on that last point.

The church was located off of a country road in the middle of nowhere. When we drove into the parking lot, there were only a few cars there.

"Are we too early or too late?" I wondered.

"These kinds of events have to be kept intimate so as not to attract too much attention," he said.

The church building was small and simple, with a white exterior and broken brick pathway. Mature trees surrounded the lot, which was flanked by a perfectly manicured cemetery. It was a beautiful summer day. Somehow this church, this day, was just right for our last good-byes to Rocco. Numbness protectively swelled inside me before the tears could rise.

I was surprised to feel Cameron grab my hand as we walked up to the handful of people who had gathered outside the door, some of whom, like Tiny, I recognized as high-ranking guards from the Farm. Most of their names escaped me in that moment.

Everyone respectfully acknowledged Cameron right away and side-eyed me with curiosity as we passed them, hand in hand, and entered the church. Once we stepped over the threshold, the guards followed us, and my fingers began going numb again from Cameron's squeeze. I clenched my teeth, trying to keep cool for the both of us.

The inside of the church was bigger than I'd thought it was going to be. There were two rows of about thirty pews. Blue and white flowers overflowed in the middle aisle and at the front of the church, where Rocco's framed picture smiled at us from among the petals. I had to look away. Cameron avoided looking ahead, too. There was quiet music coming from somewhere.

Carly and Spider slowly walked up to us from between the pews. Spider somberly shook Cameron's hand. Carly's eyes were bloodshot and puffy.

"Everything looks great, Carly. Thank you for making all the arrangements," Cameron said softly, affectionately, putting his hand on her shoulder, as my brother had often done with me.

Carly smiled weakly back at us but seemed at a loss for words. She slipped her arm through mine as Cameron and Spider led us to our seats in the back of the church. We slid into the bench—Carly and I sat next to each other, and Cameron and Spider flanked us protectively. Silence fell among us, each of us lost in thought, trying to make sense of something that was senseless.

The church was practically empty except for the front pew. I recognized one bleached-blonde head as Cameron's mother. She was sobbing loudly while simultaneously yelling at three children who were running back and forth between the benches. It all seemed surreal.

And then Spider suddenly shot up from his seat and glared toward the aisle. "What's she doing here?"

Carly, Cameron, and I turned our heads and followed his gaze. Frances had made her way up the aisle and was awkwardly standing by the bench in front of us. Carly tugged at Spider's sleeve and forced him to sit back down.

"I invited her," she half-whispered. And then, in answer to our dismayed expressions, she added, "Rocco really liked Frances. He would have wanted her to be here with us." I remembered how Rocco had mooned after Frances that day at the Farm.

Frances continued to glance at us uneasily until Cameron finally motioned to her to sit down. She slid into the bench in front of us and stared ahead while Spider huffed and Carly threw him a disapproving eye. I felt terrible for Frances; I remembered what it was like to be the outsider who wanted nothing else but to be accepted by them. Like Cameron, I didn't think that Frances could ever have been responsible for Rocco's death, and I wondered if Carly had started to feel that way, too. Rocco's death seemed to have rendered unimportant the bad blood of the past.

A big man in big robes walked to the front of the church. He had a crew cut, and despite his size he looked lost in his robes. He was young, really young—as though puberty had forgotten about him. He seemed too young to be a deacon or a pastor or a priest, or whatever he was.

The man in the big robes commenced his sermon. Though he spoke English, I had no idea what he was talking about. Chapters, verses, commandments—these were as cryptic to me as Cameron's business documents.

I was trying to be strong for Cameron and managed to gulp most of my tears back down. But it was becoming more and more difficult as I was forced to sit there with no distraction from my thoughts. There was something haunting about the large man-child's voice ... and I was being forced back into the wicker chest. I could hear the angel voice whispering in my ear. I watched Rocco falling to the ground. The scenes replayed relentlessly in my mind.

It came to me in a rush: not only was Rocco gone, but he wasn't coming back. His picture at the front of the church had become just another image of a boy who would never grow up. Brewing inside me was an intense hatred for the men who had taken his life. I wanted them dead, but first I wanted them to pay, to suffer for what they had done. I was not a vengeful person; yet I felt strongly that they should be tortured. The tears were now gushing down—I couldn't stop them anymore. They were tears of pain and anger, the kind that burned my skin as they slid down my cheeks and into my lap. Without looking at me, Cameron clasped his fingers in mine and brought my hand onto his lap, squeezing. My attempt at being his strong counterpart had failed, miserably. Once again, Cameron had to take care of me.

While the big man who was lost in his robes broke out into a ritualistic hymn, one of the guards had tiptoed down the aisle and stopped at Spider's side. He whispered something in Spider's ear and waited while Spider leaned over Carly and me and addressed Cameron in a murmur.

"Shield's boys are here. They want to talk about a truce and a merger. They say there's a lot of money attached to this deal."

Cameron swore under his breath as he turned to Spider to spit his words. "I'm at my brother's funeral. Whatever they want can wait till tomorrow."

The pastor cleared his throat and pursed his lips. All went quiet. He commenced his sermon.

Spider jutted his chin and, with a nod of the head, motioned to the guard to follow the boss's orders. The guard hurried out of the church but returned a few minutes later. Whatever he whispered in Spider's ear made Spider's face go hard and his brow furrow.

"They came here without Shield knowing. They want to change their alliance and work for us. They're willing to take Shield down themselves to make this happen." Spider looked at Cameron, waiting for a response, but Cameron remained silent and continued to stare ahead. His cheeks were flushed with anger. Spider spoke a little louder. "Cameron?"

Someone in front shushed us, and the pastor raised an eyebrow in our direction.

"I heard you," Cameron skewered back. He tapped his foot and considered. He turned to Carly. "How much money would we be talking about?"

Carly turned her eyes to the ceiling as she calculated invisible numbers in the air. "I don't know," she whispered. "It depends on what kind of merger they're proposing. I need more details before I can give you a figure on a reasonable settlement." She pondered a few more seconds and then looked back at Cameron. "If we make this deal, it would give us control over all the northeastern factions. Might even bring peace—end the war. That would be worth a lot for the bosses. This could be the break we were looking for to make them forget about everything else that's happened." Carly quickly glanced at me as she said this.

Cameron went quiet again and vacantly stared ahead. I could see that his mind was running full speed.

But Spider was growing impatient again.

"We don't have a lot of time," he said in a low voice. "There are over thirty of them out there. They're armed. We can't stall them much longer." He leaned in toward Cameron, his worried voice now audible only to the four of us. "Cameron, if we don't go talk to them, they're not going to let us live to tell Shield about their betrayal. We don't have enough men to cover us."

Cameron turned and quickly whispered something to Tiny, who was sitting behind him. Hushed shuffling ensued on the bench behind us, and Tiny produced two shortwave radios that he handed to Cameron. Cameron turned to me. He looked ill.

"Take this," he said, handing me one of the radios. He latched the other one onto his belt. "You call me if there's anything. I'm going to be right outside the door."

I could hear the click of weapons being cocked as the guards slowly filtered into the aisle. At Spider's low command, they hid their readied weapons under their shirts, tucking them into the waistbands of their pants, and waited for Cameron.

He looked at me for a long minute and then turned his eyes to Frances. With an urgent whisper, he called her name. She jumped and turned around. She looked terrified. I figured that I must have looked much the same way.

Cameron motioned to Frances to sit by me; she immediately obliged. As she moved toward us, Cameron turned back to me, his eyes unyielding. He leaned in. "I'm right outside," he repeated, though I didn't know if this reassurance had been for my benefit or his own. He forcefully kissed me on the forehead. Frances gave me a warm smile as she spied us, but her eyes looked sad.

Cameron walked to the lineup of guards, who quickly encircled him in a protective cocoon. When I saw Carly leave with the rest of them, I wanted to yell at Cameron, demand that he take me with him, but I knew that now wasn't the time and that his mind had already been made up. Nothing I could say would change it. I had nothing to bring to the table. The only thing I was good at was distracting Cameron and getting him in more trouble. I forlornly watched them leave.

The deacon, who had been frowning throughout Cameron's debate, abruptly stopped talking as they departed. When they were finally gone, he heaved a sigh and resumed his sermon.

I was a tumbleweed of emotions—terrified that Cameron was out there; devastated by the loss of Rocco; angry that I had been left out, again; and perplexed about why Cameron would ever want to make a deal with those who might have contributed to his brother's death. As if she sensed my need, Frances slid closer to me and took my hand. She seemed pleased at having been given a purpose. *Even she was assigned a job,* I silently griped. I then smiled to myself. Rocco and I had so much in common.

During my reverie, someone had slid onto the bench behind us.

"Emily," a hoarse voice whispered.

I turned around and hardly believed what I was seeing. He was older now—deep wrinkles mapped his forehead, and his blond hair had grayed at the sides, as if he had grown wings.

Chapter Twenty-Seven

Old Emily

"Uncle Victor?"

He wasn't really my uncle. Not by blood, anyway. He was my brother's uncle, but I had always called him Uncle Victor, and even though I was kind of an adult now, it seemed weird (and maybe a bit disrespectful) to say his name without the word *uncle* preceding it.

"What are you doing here?" I asked—almost accused—him.

He was nervously glancing around the church, and his voice was hurried. "I'm here to get you out."

"How did you find me?" Even *I* didn't know where I was.

"Your parents—" He jumped as one of the rambunctious children at the front of the church dropped or threw a book or a Bible on the floor. "It's a long story. We need to leave now."

"What? No, I'm not leaving," I said, louder than I intended.

The deacon stopped his sermon. And then, with a look of annoyance, he continued.

Victor was beside himself. "What do you mean you're not leaving? I'm risking my badge to come rescue you!"

"There's nothing to rescue me from. I want to stay here."

He grabbed my shoulder as he leaned in and hurriedly whispered, "Kid, in about five minutes the DEA is going to come storming through here and shoot anyone who gets in their way. They won't ask any questions first. If you're lucky, they'll just arrest you, but I won't be able to help you then."

Frances looked like someone had just sucker-punched her. "They'll take Daniel away from me if I get arrested," she whispered, distracted. Her face was pale and terrified as she stared at me. "Em, I can't get arrested. I'll lose my little boy."

Victor looked at both of us and sighed impatiently.

"I'll take her too," he conceded, "but we have to leave now."

"Take Frances with you," I said firmly. "I'm not leaving. They can arrest me if they want. I don't care."

"I promised your mother I would get you out of here unscathed. If I come back without you, she'll have my head and my badge. Either you both come, or we all get arrested or killed."

Frances's eyes were pleading with me. My thoughts were a mess—express decision making was not my forte. I looked toward the door through which Cameron had exited, hoping that if I stared at it hard enough, he would walk back in. He didn't ... but I knew how to make him come back.

Without glancing down, I pressed on the red button of the shortwave radio and guilelessly turned to Victor. "Let me talk to them," I said, hoping my voice was just loud enough for Cameron to hear me, but not loud enough to arouse Victor's suspicion.

"Who?" Victor looked confused.

"The FBI ... or the DEA," I almost yelled, and then I composed myself. "I'll tell them the truth. That I'm fine. There's no need for them to come here."

I was a horrible actress, but fortunately, from behind the bench, Victor couldn't see the radio I was holding. This I was sure of. What I hadn't planned on was a naive Frances curiously looking down at my hands—and Victor following her gaze. I thought the pulsating vein on his forehead was going to burst.

"What the hell are you doing? I could go to jail for coming here, and you're warning them?" he shouted as he knocked the radio out of my hands. It went crashing to the floor, and now everyone in the church was looking back at us. Cameron's mother noticed our presence for the first time.

I was thinking, readjusting my strategy, when there was a loud pop outside.

The stained-glass window at the front of the church exploded, and the deacon fell to his knees, covering his face to shield himself from the shards of glass that had come flying down around him like a lethal blizzard.

Then gunfire erupted outside, and everyone at the front of the church was screaming.

"Everybody get down!" Victor yelled with authority. He adeptly jumped over the bench. "Emily, keep your head down and don't stop running." He grabbed me by the shoulder of my shirt and forced me to run with him. Frances had grabbed my other hand and followed us out a side door of the church.

Outside, an empty white sedan was waiting. Victor forced me into the passenger seat, ordered Frances to get in the back, and climbed into the driver's seat. As he sped away on the cemetery road, I was frantically glancing back, trying to locate Cameron. I couldn't see anyone, but I could still hear bursts of gunfire from the other side of the church. My heart was thumping so hard that my vision was thumping with it, causing the passing graves to pulsate like neon signs in video store windows. I was trying to talk, to yell, but I couldn't catch my breath.

We turned onto a dirt road, and Victor slid the car into high gear.

"Turn back," I finally shouted, using up the miniscule amount of air that I had managed to accumulate.

"There's nothing you can do for them now," he said coldly.

My cheeks were wet. I could hear Frances whimpering in the back.

Victor looked over at me, and his face faintly softened. "If it'll make you feel better, I promise to bring you to the DEA as soon as your parents see that you're okay. You can tell the police whatever you want them to hear. I won't interfere."

That didn't make me feel any better. I had abandoned Cameron on one of the worst days of his life. Talking to the police would never change that. Maybe my warning had come soon enough, I tried to tell myself; maybe he had been able to escape on time. But then there was all that gunfire … All of a sudden I found myself actually hoping that he had been arrested; the mere possibility of the other alternative made me want to throw up. I put my head between my knees, willing myself to keep the vomit down and focus on how I was going to help Cameron.

First I needed to know how much they knew. The police. Victor. My parents.

I felt betrayed by my parents. They had decided to act like parents, to care what happened to me, *now*? For the first time I was where I belonged, and they were pulling me right back to the world I detested. My parents had money. They had connections. I knew this. I knew they had probably used their powerful influence and added it to Victor's connections to find out where I was and come get me. Why? So I wouldn't embarrass them. So they could nip this whole thing in the bud before it became known that was frolicking with drug dealers. I wanted to rip the dashboard off the car.

The car came to a stop. I looked up. Victor had pulled up to the sidewalk. We were in a small town outside the city. The town appeared to consist of a stop sign, four corners, and a cluster of tiny houses with big yards—the kind of place nice parents wanted their nice children to grow up in.

Victor peered at Frances through the rear-view mirror. "There's a convenience store around the corner. The bus comes every hour on the hour. It'll take you back to the city."

Frances looked embarrassed. "I dropped my purse in the church. I don't have any money."

Victor exhaled loudly and then aggressively dug out his wallet, removed all his cash, and thrust it at her. It was a lot more than she needed for a bus ride. As soon as she stepped onto the sidewalk and closed the door, Victor sped off.

"Where are we going?" I asked.

"My place," he said. "Your parents are waiting there."

I had no idea where Uncle Victor even lived, though we had lived in the same area for over a year now.

We turned a corner and came to a stop sign. (I had been wrong about this town—apparently there were two stop signs.) Victor impatiently tapped on his steering wheel as a man slowly crossed the street in front of us. The man was wearing a suit that was two sizes too big for him, and he walked with a strut. I couldn't see his face, but I was on high alert. Not just because he didn't fit in this town for nice people—but because he was purposefully avoiding eye contact.

Please keep walking, I thought. He was taking a ridiculous amount of time to cross the street. Or was I just imagining that he was? Time seemed to stop; I started to shake … I knew.

But what I didn't know was that he had just been a diversion. The back doors opened, and I yelled … didn't I? An arm grabbed me from behind and held my body against the seat while a burlap sack was thrown over my head. I couldn't breathe, and I started flailing, scratching the skin off the arm that was suffocating me. Something pricked my neck. There was a rush of warmth. My heartbeat slowed. Was I still breathing? There was a gurgled moan in my throat, and then nothingness.

Surely I was dead. My eyes were open—I had to feel them with my fingers to confirm this. Yes, they were open. But I couldn't see a thing.

I groaned, but the sound that came out was not my own. It was the sound that a sixty-year-old chain-smoker would make. My head was pounding against my skull. My clothes were drenched with what I assumed was my own sweat. Spit had leaked out of the corner of my mouth and dried on my cheek.

I was lying on something soft.

Now there was a slit of bright light a few feet ahead of me. Good. I wasn't blind.

I struggled to turn my body on its side—everything was numb. I was a marionette, with my brain pulling on strings to make my body move. I rolled onto the ground with a thump. There was carpet, but it was rough and cheap, the kind that was sold by the acre. I could feel the coldness of the cement seeping through it. I was suddenly thankful for the numbness—the tumble would have hurt, otherwise.

It took a few minutes for my eyes to adjust to the light. Then I dragged myself across the floor toward it. My breathing was shallow, and my elbows were too weak to hold me up; I had to slump to my side, with my cheek against the smelly carpet. All I could hear were the cymbals that were crashing between my ears.

There was nothing to see through the slit under the door but a white wall and an expanse of more bargain-basement carpet. I willed myself back onto my elbows and used the door to hold my weight while I struggled to sit up. The blood rushed from my head. With my back against the door, I took a dozen deep breaths, inhaling and exhaling the nausea away, while clumsily groping above me for a door handle. I hit something cold, tried to turn it—the door was locked. I was focusing on breathing … but the panic was slowly setting in. I needed to move. Crawling on my hands and knees, I slid my hand against the wall and felt my way around. Wherever I was, there wasn't much to it: a square room, maybe ten by ten feet, with a bed—nothing else.

The room was so hot. There was no exit. I was having difficulty breathing, and I was sweating through my clothes. I started to dry heave and finally threw up on the floor. I rested my head on my wobbly knees.

I must have fallen asleep or passed out. When I awoke, I was curled up in a ball on the cold floor. Someone had opened the door and pulled the string that hung from the ceiling to turn on the single light bulb. It was still swinging back and forth when I looked up. The light hurt my eyes, but a bit of air had filtered in from the open door.

A man stood in front of me, staring, with his arms crossed and his legs spread in a guarded stance. His head was shaved to the skin, and he wore a pistol in a holster across his chest—like a soldier awaiting his marching orders.

"There's a bed right next to you. You don't need to sleep on the floor," he said, his voice robotic.

I sat up tentatively, rested my elbows on my knees, and held my head in my hands. My lips were quivering uncontrollably.

"Eat," the man commanded. He kicked over a tray of food that was on the floor: a juice box and what appeared to be a bologna sandwich. The nausea hit me again. I brought my trembling hands to my mouth.

"I'm a vegetarian," I said through my fingers. A lie.

"Eat the bread then," he grunted impatiently. "It's the only thing that will make the nausea go away."

"What did you inject me with?"

"Just a mild sedative."

I pulled my right hand away from my mouth and held it flat in front of my face. It was still trembling, more than a mild sedative should make me tremble. I scowled at him. He didn't flinch. I noticed the scratch marks on his arms. This made me grin—at least I had gotten a piece of him.

"You're Shield, right?" I asked with a matter-of-fact tone.

"I'm not leaving here until you eat." His stare was unremitting.

"Where's my uncle?"

He looked at me strangely. "You mean the guy who was in the car with you?"

I stared in response.

"He's fine. Now eat."

I couldn't tell if he was lying, but I assumed he was.

"I want to see him," I said with difficulty. The room was spinning, and a bead of sweat was forming on my forehead.

"Eat," he commanded again.

"I'm not … eating till I … see … my … uncle." I leaned over and threw up.

The soldier-man swore. The walls of the room shook as he slammed the door behind him. I heard the lock on the doorknob click. His footsteps echoed down the hall and eventually faded into silence.

Afraid of passing out in my own vomit, I climbed onto the dirty mattress, turned to my side, and pulled my knees into my chest.

****

The door burst open. The light bulb was still on; I had no idea how long I had been out. The soldier-man was holding Uncle Victor by the collar and, looking frustrated and impatient, pushed him into the room. The door slammed and locked as he exited again, leaving Victor and me alone.

Victor ran to my side and held me at arms' length. "You look terrible, kid," he said, inspecting my face.

"I'm so sorry I brought you into this, Uncle Victor."

"Did they hurt you?"

"I think I'm okay. They drugged me. You?"

"I'm fine," he said distractedly. He looked down at the tray on the floor and grimaced. "Is this what they brought you to eat?"

He picked up the tray, stuck the straw in the juice box, and handed it to me. "Here," he said, "you need some liquids." While I drank, he investigated the sandwich, smelling it first and then pulling it apart. Satisfied, he ripped the bread into pieces and handed them to me one by one, as though I were a child, or a bird.

"Have you eaten?" I asked.

"I'm fine. I don't need to eat."

I glanced over at him. He did look fine. Probably a lot better than me.

"Do you know where we are?" he asked. I was just about to ask him the same question. At least he had been outside the room.

I shrugged my shoulders. "No, but I have a good idea who's behind this."

He searched my face. "Who?"

I lowered my voice so that it was barely audible. "This guy named Shield. A sleazeball drug dealer."

"Drug dealer? How do you know that?" Victor sounded alarmed.

I realized how much life had changed for me in a matter of a few months. The old Emily would never have known about drug dealers named Shield.

"Cam ... the people I was with told me."

"What else did they tell you?"

I hesitated. Cameron had told me things in confidence—and he definitely would not have wanted me to share any of these things with a police officer, even if he was my almost-uncle.

Victor, sensing my uncertainty, leaned in. "Emily, I need to know everything if I'm going to get us out of here."

I knew he was right, but I decided to keep Cameron out of it. "Bill had gotten himself involved in drug trafficking. Shield thinks that Bill stole his business. He's after me because he wants the money that Bill left behind when he died."

"You think all this is about money?"

"I know this is about money."

Victor seemed interested by this. "Where's the money?"

I couldn't see how to tell Victor about the money without bringing Cameron into the picture. I had to improvise. "I don't really know; I haven't seen any." This was technically the truth— numbers on a pendant were all I had seen.

Victor looked a little disappointed but continued, "What about the people you were with?"

"They had nothing to do with us being here." I said this too quickly.

He raised an eyebrow. "How involved were you with these people, Emily?"

The way he was blankly staring at me made me feel like I was in his interrogation room back at the police station. I could feel the beads of sweat building on my brow again.

"Barely knew them," I lied.

"Were they involved in drugs?"

"I don't know. We never talked about that." Another lie.

"Come on! You can do better than that!" He wasn't whispering anymore: he was the interrogator. I was the criminal.

"Uncle Victor, I don't know what you're asking me. You would know more than I would from talking with the DEA." I could feel the tears welling up.

His face went pale. "I'm sorry. I didn't mean to upset you. Yes, you're right. I do know what they're capable of. I was just afraid of what they might have put you through. That's all."

"They're not bad people."

"How can you say that? They're lowlifes. Thugs. Mere children." His voice rose so quickly that I was taken aback.

He paused, composed himself. "These people have no class, Emily. Not like you and me. We're from a different world." He reached over and stroked my cheek with his thumb. "You look so much like Isabelle."

It was the way that, unlike mine, his head did not have one hair out of place and his clothes looked freshly ironed. And it was how he looked right through me, as though he saw someone else, that made something flicker at the bottom of my gut.

"How was my mother when you saw her?"

He gave me a sad smile. "She was very worried about you. She cried when she found out that those thugs had taken you."

My mother wasn't the crying type; it ruined her makeup. "How did you know I was missing?"

"Your mother called me after she had been to your place. All your stuff was gone, and you weren't there."

My mom would never go to my place unless she was dragged kicking and screaming, and she would definitely have no idea where my stuff was, or what my belongings would even look like. "How long have you been looking for me?"

"A few months now."

Nope, she was still in France—and barely thinking about me. My dear Uncle Victor was lying through his yellowing teeth.

Cameron had told me that Shield could not be killed because of his connections, because someone like him could not turn up dead or go missing without too many questions being asked—as would be the case with a police officer. I then understood that Shield was just a nickname for the police badge that he used to shield his crimes.

I glared back at my uncle Victor, who had abused our family ties to lure me away from Cameron. His answers had all been wrong, although he didn't know it because he'd never had contact with either of my parents. It all made sense to me now. I could see how my brother had gotten into this mess in the first place: His uncle's influence. His uncle's power.

I felt the tears building up. I cleared my throat in an effort to keep them at bay and not arouse his suspicion that the game was up.

"How are we going to get out of here?" My croaking voice betrayed me.

Shield's eyes twinkled. His hand had moved to the top of my head, and he began stroking my hair. "Did you know that I saw Isabelle first? Before your father even knew that she existed?"

I was shaking. He smiled.

"We were all at the same party. One of those work parties that your father used to drag my sister to. Isabelle came through the door, and all eyes were on her. She was a stunning woman. Still is. But out of all those people, she smiled at me first." His face then turned grim. "Back then, your father had a lot more money than me. I was just a beat cop. I couldn't compete. But things are different now."

He snapped out of his daydream and winked at me. A chill went down my spine. I yanked his hand away. The tears were rolling down my cheeks, but my glare was unyielding.

"You're still a cop," I reminded him sharply.

"Yes," he said, as if his treachery had been a major feat. "And you'll make me rich again."

I knew the minute I admitted to having access to the money, I would no longer be of use to him. "I don't have my brother's money."

His fists clenched. "That money was my money, not Bill's. It should have been given back to me when he died. I taught Bill the business, treated him like my own son. We were going to take it over. Together. Then that ungrateful bastard stole it all from me and joined forces with those classless bastards. Bill owed me a lot more than the dollars he left behind."

He took a few breaths, and then smiled a tight-lipped smile. "But none of that matters now. With you here, I will get all that back, and more. We'll do great things together."

"I'm not doing anything with you," I spat back.

"I thought you had a penchant for drug dealers! No? Well, seems they like you a lot." He laughed, shaking his head. "We can use this to our advantage. With the pull you have over that boy, we'll control the leaders, the distributors, the shipments, everything. Though I wish I had stuck around to see you blossom into your mother before that boy ever got a chance to pull you in. We could have been much further along by now."

He reached over to stroke my cheek.

The nausea was coming back. I got up and, turning my back to him, glanced around the room, looking for a way out or a weapon. Apart from a plastic tray and a juice box, I didn't have much to work with. I walked to the wall and turned around, sliding my back down the cold surface and sitting on the floor with my knees curled into my chest.

For the first time, I noticed that Victor had a gun tucked into the back of his pants. I felt like an idiot for having missed that earlier—but there was no time for beating myself up. Something that he'd said had piqued my interest.

"So he's alive then." My voice was steady and uninterested, as I had heard Cameron's sound so often.

"Who? That Cameron boy? Yes, he's fine." He searched my face. I was a statue, although my insides were churning at the sound of Cameron's name being attached to the word *fine*.

Victor's stare was smoldering. I needed to keep him talking ... and away from me.

"What do I need to do for our partnership to work?" I asked with a businesslike tone.

He puffed his chest. "Well, by now I'm sure the kid has figured out that I won and that I have you. We'll let him think about that for a few days, then start the negotiations for sending you back. It'll take a while to convince the leaders to let me take control again, so I'll control the business behind Cameron until the change in management is made official."

"What if the bosses don't agree to you taking over?"

"You'll make sure that Cameron does a good job at convincing them when I send you back to him."

My heart leaped at the thought of seeing Cameron again, but I kept my expression unchanged. "What's in it for me?"

He chuckled. "The apple doesn't fall far from the tree. I'm impressed, kiddo. I thought you'd gone soft on me. But your parents taught you well, I see. People like us have to stick together." The fact that he was putting me in the same basket as him and my parents made me want to scream. "Once I gain full control again and get rid of the boy, you and I can live happily ever after together."

The partnership was starting to sound more like a one-sided business deal—he would get to lead the underworld, and I would get to live and become his Isabelle-lookalike concubine.

I inhaled sharply as Victor walked over to me and, pulling me up by the shoulders, made me stand in front of him. With his rough hands, he drew my face into his, whispered my mother's name, and forced his leathery lips against mine. But I couldn't kiss him back. My lips automatically squeezed together, shutting him out. Victor pulled away and eyed me, his jaw clenched.

"Kiss me," he ordered as he tried to kiss me again. No luck—my lips would not cooperate. I was quickly losing his trust and had to think of some way to get myself away from him.

"I need to use the bathroom," I said.

He gave me a blank look, his lips upturned. He walked to the door and knocked three times. The lock clicked and the door opened. Soldier-man peered in.

"Escort the young lady to the bathroom," Victor commanded.

"I really don't need an escort. I think I'm old enough now to find the bathroom by myself." My voice oozed like honey.

"Yes, you're certainly not a child anymore," he said, and then added as he gently rubbed my arm, "Humor me and let Mickey walk you to the bathroom."

Mickey the soldier-man and I walked down a white hallway to a wide open-space—a warehouse, I realized. Cheap carpet and sheetrock came to an end and were replaced by concrete floor and cinderblock walls. The empty warehouse was dimly lit, with daylight coming in from the dirty, frosted windows set high up in the walls. There were armed guards standing by the exits, and more guards were playing cards, using empty boxes as their game table. Our footsteps echoed as we made our way to the bathroom. The picture on the door indicated that it was a men's bathroom. I glanced along the cement wall—no women's bathroom. Mickey confirmed my suspicion when he opened the door.

"Get out," he ordered a guard who was standing by the urinal. The guard quickly zipped up and rushed out.

The bathroom was everything I expected a men's bathroom to be—disgustingly dirty and smelling of urine, among other things. Mickey followed me in while I fled into one of the stalls. There was no point in asking for time alone to think—this was all the privacy that I was going get. Up to that point, I'd had a faint hope that the bathroom would have had a window and that I would be able to distract soldier-man away long enough to escape. That was what usually happened in the movies, right? But there were no windows—just yellowing subway tile and someone's recommendations for whom to call for a good time. If Victor had his way, my name would soon be added to the stall's wall of shame.

I was out of options, and I had to prepare myself for what I would have to do next. I turned my eyes to the stained concrete ceiling and I prayed.

There was a bang on the bathroom stall. "Hurry up!"

I wiped my cheeks, put on a smile.

I couldn't look at myself in the splattered mirror. I was too afraid of who I might find staring back; for the next while, I would have to be anybody else but me. I splashed water on my face and rinsed my mouth out, as I had pledged to do. When we walked out of the bathroom, my teeth were tightly clenched into a smile, and I was breathing short, shallow breaths—just enough to keep me standing. In my head I was signing a tune from *The Sound of Music* to keep myself from crying.

Doe, a deer, a female deer. We walked past the staring card players.

Ray, a drop of golden sun. We reached the threshold of ugly carpet.

Me, a name, I call myself. We were back in the office that had been converted into my prison—where Victor was eagerly waiting. As he approached me, he ordered Mickey to close the door and give us some privacy. My only means of escape slammed behind me, taking the cheery show tune with it. There was nothing in my head now but inescapable fear. I wished that Victor would turn off the light bulb. This, I thought, would make it easier for me to imagine that I was anywhere but here.

Victor was smiling benevolently. I was shaking uncontrollably.

"You don't have to be scared. I won't hurt you," he whispered as he wrapped his hand around my ponytail, pulling my head back, forcing me to look up at him. He looked like a much older, wrinkly version of my brother. This realization only made things worse. I knew that I wouldn't be able, under any pretense of willingness or otherwise, to go through with it.

His face was coming closer to mine.

"Uncle Victor," I pleaded.

That made him smile. "I'm not really your uncle. You know that, right? This would be wrong if we were actually related. But we're not. So, it's okay. Just relax."

Julie Hockley

He pressed his lips against mine, but I didn't respond.

His smile was fading.

"Kiss me back," he ordered.

I started sobbing. "I'll do whatever you want me to do, but not this."

"You're just a tease, aren't you? You think I'm going to let you go back to that boy without some kind of assurance that you'll do what I tell you to do? You'll be mine before I send you back to finish the job."

He shoved me up to the wall and held his hand at my throat while trying to push his tongue into my mouth.

I was paralyzed with fear. My lips remained sealed. He pressed his hand against my throat harder this time, until my mouth finally gasped open for air. He kissed me, and I continued to struggle. His free hand was everywhere on my face, in my hair, but as it started inching down my neck and closer to my chest, I panicked. Instinctively, I kneed him between the legs. The effect was immediate. He fell onto his knees, grabbing hold of himself. But he was on his feet again, enraged, within half a second. He stormed toward me, pulling his fist back. I closed my eyes and waited for the blow.

Chapter Twenty-Eight

Giving Up

When I awoke, I was lying against the wall with my limbs sprawling in all directions. I struggled into a seated position; my face was pulsating with pain. I brushed my fingers against it and felt dried blood under my nose and a hardening, fist-sized sphere of heat that took up most of my cheek. There was something salty, blood, against my teeth. I was otherwise intact—and grateful for that much. I had escaped Victor, but for how long? I crawled back into my defensive ball and rested my aching head on my knees.

My eyes hadn't been dry for long when Mickey slid a tray of food over to me with his foot. I didn't look up. He closed the door and left me alone again.

This time my meal consisted of processed cheese slapped between two pieces of bread, and two juice boxes—I had moved up in the world. I got to my feet and started pacing about the room. I stopped in front of the door, and—ridiculously hopeless—I tried the doorknob ... because once upon a time in Cameron's apartment, the door was unlocked.

"Don't even think about it, girl," came a cold voice from the other side. "The door is locked, and I'm right here waiting for you if it isn't."

I decided to break the code of silence. "Mickey, is that you?" I whispered.

I heard him shifting about, but no answer.

"Mickey, you need to help me get out of here. He's going to kill me." After more silence, I added, "There's a lot of money attached to it if you help me escape."

"Eat your food and shut up," Mickey finally answered.

I had no allies here. I finished my juice box, picked at the bread, and sat on the bed, listening for footsteps.

I didn't have to wait too long. A fresh-faced, clean-shaven Victor walked through the door and sat on the bed.

"Feeling better now?"

I glared.

He looked over my face. "I wouldn't have had to do that if you had behaved."

Nothing but silence from me.

"I brought you some clean clothes," he said. "You can have a shower, too. Would you like that?"

I didn't want anything that he would give me, but I also needed to buy some time. I nodded—and cringed when I saw that my concurrence had pleased him.

Mickey escorted me back to the men's bathroom. I'd noticed him wince slightly as he saw my face when I first walked out of the room. I wondered if I would be able to use this, his humanity, to my advantage.

One of the stalls had been converted into a shower, although from the look of the yellowed floor tile, it seemed that it was also used as an extra urinal. While Mickey stood on the other side of the stall, I got undressed and hung my clothes over the door. I turned on the water, as hot as it would go, and stood under a lukewarm shower. In less than a minute, the water started getting cold.

When I turned around, I saw a pink sundress hanging next to the dirty clothes that I had thrown over the door. I grumbled, grabbing my black frocks. Mickey chuckled when I walked out.

"Pink not your color?"

I went to stand by the sink.

There was a knock on the door, and one of the guards stepped into the bathroom. He handed a bag of ice to Mickey; Mickey handed it to me.

"It'll make the swelling go down," he said.

I glared at him, took the pittance, marched to the shower, emptied the bag on the tile floor, and handed him the empty bag. Then I spun on my heels and walked myself back to my cell, slamming the door behind me. The cold shower had reenergized me, and I sat on the mattress, determined to plot my revenge or my escape, whichever came first. But when I heard the click of the door lock after Mickey caught up with me, I knew I had nothing else. So I waited for Victor.

Hours seemed to roll by in the cardboard box of a room, and Victor never came. The warehouse went deadly quiet; perhaps it was nighttime now. Eventually, I crawled onto the bed, fell asleep, and rebooted. There were no nightmares while I slept—I was already in one.

I heard the light click off and woke up.

Victor was staring at me in the dark. I shot up and curled my body to the wall, getting as far away from him as I could. In the shadows, Victor smiled his sickening smile and moved to the bed, sitting next me.

"You're so beautiful." I felt his hand graze my hair, pushing it away from my face, as Cameron had lovingly done before him. "Lie down."

I didn't move, hypnotized by my fear.

"Lie down," he shouted. I yelped with fright.

Victor got up and pulled on the light cord. I closed my eyes as the light came on.

Victor climbed on top of me. He started kissing me and didn't care this time that I wasn't kissing back. His breath smelled like alcohol or mouthwash. It made me sick to my stomach.

His kisses became more forceful, and his hands more aggressive. I started to struggle. He grabbed my wrists and with one hand held them over my head. I started kicking and screaming. He put his hand over my mouth and held me down with the weight of his body.

"If you don't behave, I'll have you serve your time in one of my whorehouses. Or maybe I'll just kill you. I don't need you to be alive to make that boy lose control." He stared me down. "Now, will you behave?"

I nodded yes. As soon as he let go of my mouth, I spit in his face. "Go ahead and kill me, then, because I will never do what you want me to do. I won't betray him no matter what you do to me."

He slapped me across my already bruised cheek.

I continued trying to twist away from him, but this only seemed to egg him on. His breathing became excited. He started fumbling with his belt buckle; I started kicking and screaming as hard as I could. I managed to free one of my hands and I scratched his face. He yelled, slapped me across the face again.

The door burst open. When Victor looked up, I used the momentary distraction to struggle away from him and run to cower into a corner of the room.

Mickey was in the doorway.

"I said to stay away," Victor screamed at him.

Mickey quickly eyed me and turned to Victor. "I'm sorry, sir. I heard you shout. I thought—"

"You thought nothing. Get out of here and don't come back in!"

Mickey eyed me again. "Sir, there's someone here to see you."

I heard short footsteps, and a man I recognized as Rocco's killer walked through the door. It took everything I had not to jump at Norestrom's throat and choke him. But from the look of his face, it appeared that someone had beaten me to it. One of his eyes was swollen shut, his nose was bloody and crooked, and he was missing several teeth.

"What happened to you?" Victor asked him.

"I got caught by one of Spider's boys. They tried to beat the location out of me. But I didn't tell them a thing and escaped before they could kill me."

Victor half-smiled, glanced back at me, and said absentmindedly, "Well, it's good to have you back, son. We'll need you around for the takeover. Go get cleaned up and make sure that the young lady and I get our privacy."

"Sure, Shield." Norestrom had a smug look on his face as he turned to soldier-man. "Think you can manage to follow those orders, Mickey? Or do I have to draw you a picture?"

Mickey looked furious but nodded his head. The men walked out and locked the door behind them; they gave us our privacy. Victor immediately stood up and swaggered toward me as though he had already won. I got up and met him with my fists up. I threw a punch that fanned him. He found this hilarious.

"You and your brother have always been fighters. I never understood what you were so angry about. Bill, I guess, had reason to be upset, what with your father leaving my sister like that. Can't blame your father, though. Your mother was quite the catch." He laughed again. "Poor Billy. He came to me thinking he would find an ally against his father. But my sister was nothing but a weak-minded woman. I was ashamed to be related to her. She didn't deserve to have her honor defended by me or Bill."

Victor pulled my fists down and brought his smiling face to mine. "Are you still a virgin?"

"No. Cameron already took care of that," I said spitefully.

His smile disappeared, but that gave me little comfort. He grabbed me by the shoulders and dragged me to the bed while my arms flailed. He quickly resumed his position on top of me and proceeded to fumble with his belt buckle. I thrashed about while he loosened his pants, and I wished that I had found pants to wear to the funeral instead of a skirt—at least it would have delayed him a bit more. As Victor struggled with me and his pants, I felt something cold fall close to my thigh. Suddenly, everything changed for me. I grew calmer and stopped struggling, which mildly pleased Victor.

"There. Now that's more like it," he said softly. His grasp on my hands loosened as he took advantage of my change in humor to pull down his pants. I jerked my hand free and grabbed the revolver that had slid next to my thigh. I brought it to his head.

With the feel of a cold barrel against his skull, I had Victor's full and undivided attention. But he just laughed.

"You even know how to use that thing?"

I pulled back the lever, removed any doubt. He flinched when it clicked next to his skin; his eyes widened.

"Get off me," I ordered.

He clumsily rolled off the bed and stood in front of me in his underwear, with his arms up and his pants around his ankles.

"Just relax," he said, holding out his hands. "Don't do anything foolish. One scream from me and twenty guards will come running in here."

"And you'll be dead," I added, standing up. "Turn around." I put the gun to the back of his head and walked him to the door; he was a lot taller than I was, so I had to walk on my tiptoes to keep the gun pressed to his head. Not trusting him to give the right signal, I reached my free hand around him and knocked on the door three times. After a few seconds, I heard someone fumble with the lock and open the door.

Mickey reached for his gun when he saw Victor with his hands laced behind his head and me peering from behind him.

"Don't even think about it—you touch that thing and your boss is dead!" I yelled, surprised by the force of my own voice. I was completely calm. I ordered Mickey to remove his gun from its holster—slowly, using the opposite hand (I saw that in a movie once)—and hand it to me. He complied, chuckling softly. Equipped with two guns, I ordered Mickey to walk ahead of us with his hands up. Victor followed Mickey, hopping and tripping over his downed pants, and I followed Victor.

With the two large men in front of me, I couldn't see anything ahead. I looked at the floor and saw that we had reached the end of the carpet and were entering the warehouse.

I heard hushed voices as we walked in.

"What's going on here?" Victor exclaimed.

I tried to peek around him, but Mickey was blocking my view.

"Mickey, get down," I ordered.

Mickey got down on his knees with his fingers still behind his head. Victor did the same, without my order. The view finally opened up, and my knees almost buckled under me. I was trying to confirm what I thought I'd seen, but my vision was blurred with tears, and I couldn't wipe them away because my hands were still holding the two revolvers.

"Emmy!" There was relief in that voice—a voice I knew better than any other.

I heard hurried footsteps and then saw Mickey and Victor brought to the floor by a group of large figures. I couldn't move beyond the uncontrollable trembling of my hands. My legs were as stiff as boards now, and my head was swimming.

I was still pointing the guns ahead of me, and Cameron's guards were cowering from my trembling aim as they tried to drag Mickey and Victor off. But I was looking at Cameron, who was standing next to me.

"We got them. It's okay," he said softly in my ear as he tugged my arms down and took the weapons away from me. He wrapped me in his arms, and I started weeping. I was bringing my hands to my eyes, trying to keep up with the tears so that I could see his face.

He was laughing, happy and sad at the same time. "I came to save you," he said, "but I guess you didn't need me to save you after all."

I wanted to tell him that I did need him, always, but nothing but tears came out. I gave up trying and brought my face to his and kissed him, grimacing when his lips brushed the cut on my mouth. Cameron pulled me away and glanced over my face, passing his hand over my lip and bruised cheek. His faint smile was replaced with anger.

Cameron lunged for Victor, spinning him around, straddling him, and punching him in the face over and over again. Victor

367

cowered in a ball, covering his bloodied face with his hands. Spider came running up behind them, yelling.

"Cameron, stop! You're going to kill him!"

"Good!" Cameron yelled back.

At Spider's command, the guards pulled Cameron off Victor; it took four of them to finally pull him away. Spider made them drag Victor out from Cameron's sight while a seething Cameron watched from the sidelines. I rushed to him and threw my arms around his neck. "I'm fine," I whispered over and over, holding on.

Cameron calmed down after a while and crushed me in his arms.

"How did you find me?" I asked, trying to wiggle away enough to look at him.

He looked twenty years older. "The guards caught Norestrom a couple days before Rocco's funeral," he said. "We were going to sell him back in pieces to Shield for what he did to my brother, but when you went missing, I tried to beat the location out of him ... before we killed him. He wouldn't talk fast enough, so I let him escape, knowing that he would be stupid enough to come find Shield and lead us to you."

His eyes were locked on mine, but mine started tearing up again. "Cameron, I didn't mean to abandon you at the church. Uncle Victor convinced me to go with him. They started shooting outside. The window exploded. I thought—"

"One of Shield's men shot at the church window when he heard you warn me through the radio. They weren't shooting at us; they couldn't. If they had killed us in an ambush like that, the leaders would have hunted all of them down. It took us a little while to figure out that they were shooting at anything *but* us ... they were warning Shield. I should have known it was a trap and never left you. I completely screwed up."

He held me and then pushed me away from him, holding my shoulders in his hands. "I had no idea Shield was your uncle. If I had, I would have warned you."

"He was my brother's uncle." I really didn't feel like explaining my family history right then, but Cameron didn't push for more.

"That explains a lot, like where Bill got all his ideas and his extreme dislike for Shield," he said, "though I wished Bill had told me."

I smiled up at him and he gently kissed me, on the good side of my mouth.

When we turned around, the warehouse was practically empty except for Spider and Tiny, who were standing by Victor. Tiny was holding Victor up by the shoulders while Spider was waving his finger at Victor and speaking to him in a low voice. Victor looked terrified.

We made our way toward them. Victor glared at me, and I glared back.

"Let him go, Tiny," said Spider, who had his back to us.

"What?" Cameron yelled out. "Tiny, keep hold of him."

Tiny held on to Victor and looked confusedly from Spider to Cameron.

"We're letting him go, Cameron," Spider said as he turned to face us.

"After everything he's done? No, he's a dead man."

"We're letting him go, Cameron," Spider repeated with more force.

Cameron dragged Spider away from us, and in a whispered argument, they decided Victor's fate. I watched Cameron's face turn pale in the midst of the debate; after a while, Spider was doing all the talking, and Cameron was listening, his head bent in defeat.

"Let him go," Cameron said dejectedly to Tiny when they had returned. He was ashen. I swallowed hard.

Tiny held on to Victor for a few seconds to see if Cameron was going to change his mind. When he didn't, Tiny let Victor go. Victor's knees buckled under him and he fell backward onto the ground; then he scrambled up and rushed out of the warehouse. Spider shot a meaningful glance at Cameron and me, and then he turned and walked out with Tiny at his side.

"Why are you letting him go?" I asked accusingly as I turned to Cameron. What I saw in Cameron scared me more than anything Shield ever could have done to me … there were tears in Cameron's eyes.

"Cameron …" I lost my breath.

He grabbed me in a hug and whispered, "Emmy, you need to run. Now."

I pushed him away. "What? No. I'm not going anywhere without you."

I could see that he was in agony. Pain had carved deep fissures in his forehead.

"Tell me what's going on. Right now," I demanded and bit my lip, trying not to cry, trying to fight the sense of dread that was swarming in.

"Please," he said. "You need to go. Don't look back. I love you."

I took a step toward him, reaching out. He stepped back and turned his face away from me.

"Cameron, don't. You're scaring me." I wasn't just scared; I was petrified. "Tell me what's going on. Please." Before he could react, I lunged into his arms and latched my arms around his neck. I heard him sigh, and he held me for a few seconds. Footsteps came from behind us. He unhooked my arms and pushed me away. I followed his frightened gaze. Spider and Tiny were standing a few feet away.

Spider had his gun pointed at us.

"What's going on?" I asked, my voice shaking with the rest of my body.

Spider was staring coldly at Cameron. "You said your good-byes. Now we finish this."

Cameron turned to Tiny. "Get her out of here."

Tiny nodded and started walking toward me.

I pleaded to Spider. "Please don't do this, Spider. We'll leave. You can have it all, and you'll never have to see us again. You don't need to do this. Please …"

Spider kept his eyes on Cameron. Tiny grabbed me from behind and started dragging me away.

"Do something!" I screamed through my tears at Cameron. "Don't let them do this. Please!"

Cameron glanced at me with pain-filled eyes, and then he took a breath, his jaw tightened, and he looked away. His face became expertly impassive as he stared back at Spider's gun, waiting.

I was in a nightmare. I needed to wake up. But the throbbing in my chest was too real for this to be a dream.

Just as Tiny dragged me, kicking and screaming, to the door, the first shot rang out. I watched in horror as Cameron fell to the ground. Tiny jumped too and momentarily let go of me.

I ran back to Cameron and crouched on the ground, putting myself between him and Spider's gun. I looked down. The shoulder of Cameron's shirt was already soaked through with blood. His eyes found me, but they were dull. Life was sapping from him and dragging me with it.

"Get out of here, Emmy," he said too calmly, as though he didn't feel the gushing wound in his shoulder.

"I won't let him do this to you. I'm not leaving you. Why are you letting them do this?"

"I have no other choice," he said. "It has to end this way."

"I won't say good-bye to you," I insisted. "You can fight. Why aren't you fighting?" I was furious that he was giving up so easily. "Don't let him win, Cameron."

I could feel him fading. I put one hand over his wound and with the other turned his face, forcing him to acknowledge me. Tears were burning my cheeks.

"I love you," I told him in a desperate whisper. My eyes homed in on his, but he squeezed his eyes shut. It, love, was no longer enough.

Cameron pulled my hands away and yelled, "Get her out of here!"

Tiny came back, this time picking me up off the ground, throwing me over his shoulder, and hurriedly carrying me out of the building.

The last time I saw Cameron, he was staring at the ceiling. A tear had rolled out of the corner of his eye.

I was still screaming and crying uncontrollably when Tiny finally set me down outside. He wiped the sweat off his forehead and held on to me with one arm while I continued to fight him off.

"There's nothing you can do, Emmy," Carly's shaking voice said. She was standing next to us outside.

There were three more gunshots from inside the warehouse, and then all was quiet.

Carly put her hands to her face. I lost myself and fell to my knees.

CHAPTER TWENTY-NINE

THE ONE WHO HOLDS THE GUN

At that moment, when the last gunshot rang out, I felt Cameron leave me. I snapped, like a wishbone. Cameron was the lucky part that was broken off; left behind was the unlucky part, just hollow bone, sucked dry. I wanted to be dead. And in a way, I already was.

My face was damp. My hair was sticking to my cheeks. I was still screaming, wailing. But inside I felt and heard nothing. My voice was not mine. In my head, everything had gone silent and black, a dark hole that I would never crawl out of. The old Emily had gone down with Cameron; what emerged from the hole was some sinister thing.

When I looked up, when the Shadow-of-Emily looked up, I saw Carly. She was staring at me, her eyes puffy and terrified. She had reason to be scared—I was going to kill her, and the rest of them. Hate and vengeance had spread through my veins, my heart, my brain, my skin. Like a cancer.

I lunged for Carly. Tiny held me back with difficulty. Carly stood still, in a stupor. I was the caged animal waiting for any opportunity to attack, and she was the prey standing by the bars, entranced.

"How could you do this?" The voice that escaped my mouth was hard and violent. "How could you betray him like that?"

Carly was pale. She was shaking through her tears. "It wasn't my decision. I didn't want it to happen. Not like this."

"Spider worships you. One word from you and he would have changed his mind!"

She started sobbing, and I hated her more for it. She had no right to cry for Cameron. She had caused his death. I wanted her to suffer.

"Is that what you did to my brother? You had him killed when he found someone else? Someone who was prettier and nicer than you? He fell in love with Frances, and you and Spider couldn't control him anymore, so you had him put down like a sick dog."

Carly's face turned to despair. "Emmy, please don't—"

"Don't call me that! You have no right!"

Spider—the man who had been holding the gun—had calmly made his way back to us. He glanced at Carly, who was sobbing uncontrollably, and angrily turned to me. "Carly had nothing to do with this. None of this is her fault."

Adrenaline surged through my body, and I lunged forward, evading Tiny's grasp. My fist connected with Spider's face, and he stumbled back from the blow. I managed to throw another punch, though with less force, before Tiny grabbed me by the shoulders and lifted me from the ground. I kicked my legs, and one of them caught Spider, clipping his shoulder. He swore. Carly stood by his side, between us, in a panic.

"Put her in the car!" he said to Tiny.

While I continued to fight off Tiny, Spider turned to Carly, pinching his bleeding nose and circling his injured shoulder. "Go back inside. Make sure the mess is completely cleaned up." They glanced at each other for a half second, and Carly made her way back into the warehouse. In the meantime, Tiny had called for reinforcements, and three men forced me into the back of a black car. I was made to sit in the middle, with my seat belt tightly strapped to my waist as extra security, while Tiny and another guard flanked me. Spider sat up front in the passenger seat, and the third guard jumped into the driver's seat.

"I want to see Cameron," I demanded, wiping my never-ending tears.

"You're in no position to be making any requests," Spider said nasally, his head leaned back on the seat and a bloody Kleenex stuffed up his nose.

He was right. I was squeezed into the seat between two very large, armed men who were nervously watching my every move. I had no energy left to fight them off—the adrenaline had boiled out of me.

We peeled away from the warehouse, which apparently was somewhere in an industrial zone outside Callister. There were gravel pits where rusty, abandoned bulldozers sat, half-submerged. We were speeding dangerously on an uneven, sandy road; the shocks threatened to sever every time we hit a fissure, and the car was kicking up so much dust that we were enclosed in our own fog. I turned back toward the warehouse, where I imagined Cameron's body still lying on the cold cement floor, but I could see nothing but a cloud of brown dirt. My throat was collapsing into itself, squeezing the air out from each end like a trash compactor. I could barely breathe—but then again, breathing seemed overrated, just another luxury that I didn't want.

"Where are you taking me?" I managed to croak.

No response.

"Where are you taking me?" I asked again, with more force.

"Shut up," Spider said with irritation. He had removed the tissue from his nostril, and his nose started gushing blood again.

"Are you going to kill me?"

"Can't you keep your mouth shut for two seconds?"

"I don't care if you kill me."

Spider swore. "If you don't shut up I will kill you, with my bare hands, in this car. Keep quiet."

I started sobbing. I wanted it to be over.

He sighed. "I won't kill you, all right?"

"Why not?" I asked him, looking for a different answer.

"Because I can't kill people like you without other people like you noticing," he said angrily.

Spider's words hit me like a gunshot through the heart. Cameron had died, while I cruelly had to outlive him for no reason other than the circumstances I had been born into, which had put me in a different world than his. Yet Spider, who belonged in no one's world, was still sitting there, alive and mostly unharmed.

Hate boiled in my veins.

"You must be happy now that Cameron's out of your way," I said.

Spider fleetingly turned and glared at me before turning his eyes back to the road ahead of him without offering a response. The car was stiflingly quiet.

I had a captive audience, so I continued, "Looks like there's no one else left but you to take over the reins. How convenient: first my brother, now Cameron. How many people do you have to kill before you figure out that you're not smart enough to lead anything or anyone?"

Spider's jaw tensed as he clenched his teeth together. He was trying to ignore me, but I knew that he was listening to every word. I was on a path to self-destruction—if he wasn't planning on killing me, I would make him change his mind or make him regret his decision to let me live.

"What you did won't change a thing. You'll never be anything like Cameron or my brother. You're just another power-hungry street thug with more gunpowder than brains." My tone was acidic.

Spider's lips were stretched thin. "You've got a pretty big mouth for a little girl stuck in a car with four guys who aren't afraid to use their guns."

"I'm not afraid of you." There was nothing else that Spider could do to me that would change this. "I won't let you control me like you did Cameron."

Spider huffed crossly. "Control Cameron? No one controlled Cameron except for you. You're a parasite. If it wasn't for you, none of this would have happened. Things started going wrong from the day you got here. You took Cameron's focus away—and the business started suffering because of it. If we hadn't done this, you would have gotten all of us killed."

"We?" I asked incredulously. "I only saw one person holding the gun."

Spider turned and pointed his finger at me. "You didn't see a thing. And if you know what's good for you, you'll keep your mouth shut and stay the hell away from us. Or I swear to God, I will hunt you down and squeeze the life out of you myself—rich girl or not. I'll take your whole prissy family down too if I have to. None of this ever happened. Forget we ever existed."

I wasn't scared. There was a hole in Spider's plan, and I was happy to bring it to his attention. "What am I supposed to do when Victor comes knocking at my door? Pretend I've never seen him before?"

"I don't care what you do," he spat back coldly. "Besides, Shield won't come back. You're no longer useful to him now that Cameron ..." He didn't finish his sentence.

I looked at him carefully. I had noticed something change in his face as he said this. He was hiding something.

"You and Victor were in on this the whole time," I said.

When Spider uneasily shifted in his seat and turned his face as far away from me as possible, I knew I was on the right track. I thought back to the day in the church, when Spider finally convinced Cameron to leave me behind. That had provided Victor the perfect opportunity to take me.

The Shadow-of-Emily pounced. "You were setting Cameron up to fail. You needed evidence of his weakness as a leader so you could take him out without getting in trouble with the others. That was your plan, wasn't it? To force him to come after me and show that he was a risk because of me? That's why you let Victor go today."

Spider chuckled nervously but refused to look at me. "You don't know a thing, girl. That's the stupidest thing I've ever heard. Cameron was becoming a risk, but it had nothing to do with me and everything to do with you. We had to recruit other gang factions because you were stupid enough to get yourself caught by Shield. With half our guys dead, it was the only way that we would be able to overtake Shield's guards and get you out." After a moment, he added, "As far as I know, you and Shield were the ones who were playing all of us. He was your uncle, not mine. I had nothing to do with Shield."

I was far from convinced. Spider would have been ecstatic to have Cameron show his weakness by going to other gangs and plead for their help in order to save a girl. This would have only enhanced Spider's chances of getting Cameron out of the picture and taking his place at the head of the table without too much objection from the leaders. I glared at the back of Spider's head.

"I'm going to kill you," I promised. The coldness in my voice left no doubt that I meant this with every fiber of my being.

Spider didn't look back. "I'd like to see you try."

It took me a while to realize that the car was stopped; the driver had pulled up next to the uneven sidewalk in front of my house. I had no idea how I had gotten there; everything was a blur up to that point. But looking at my house was like the nightmare had suddenly merged with reality, or at least the reality of the old Emily.

The new being connected with the familiar only heightened the pain: Cameron hadn't been just a dream. He had been a real person whom I loved and who had, inexplicably, loved me. Now he was gone because of love, because of me. I was the one who was supposed to die. Not him. There was no waking up from that nightmarish feeling of pain and utter desperation.

Tiny slid down the seat, grabbed my arm, and dragged me out of the car. The breeze as I stepped outside chilled me to the bone; my face, hair, and clothes were still drenched with tears.

Spider opened his door and peered at me without getting out of his seat. "We'll have your things delivered to you," he said in a businesslike manner, as though nothing had ever happened. "Keep your mouth shut and stay away from us."

I had expected him to threaten me, maybe drag his index finger across his throat or mimic pointing a gun at his head and pulling the trigger. But there was none of that. They left without another glance. I stood on the sidewalk shivering, watching them drive away.

Chapter Thirty

Passing on the Crazy Torch

It was a while before I could muster up the courage to walk up the path that led to the house. Almost an entire summer had gone by since I left, and it looked as if I had never gone. For the longest time, I was a statue on the sidewalk, afraid of what I was going to find ahead. After being plucked out of my former life and thrown into someone else's reality, after making that reality mine, going back to normal was an impossible option. Though I still had no idea what normal meant.

There was an old lady in our neighborhood who spent her days pushing her rickety walker forward while mumbling to herself, making her rounds around the same block. She did this every day, like clockwork. She had become a local legend with my roommates; rumors about her past were conjured up over beer and pizza. The best story was the one where she hunted for stray cats and hid them under her flowered muumuu. She would take them home and train them for the day when she would take over the neighborhood, first sending them back into the world to await her hissed orders. The sleeper-cell cats got fat off our garbage in the meantime.

As I stood frozen on the sidewalk, the crazy lady passed by, and she looked at me like I was the crazy one. She wasn't far off target. I wondered what rumors would surface to account for my madness. Whatever the stories, I was sure my red hair would make them all the more imaginative. The lady's glance at my expense had been meaningful but swift; she went back to her babbling and pretended I was never there. People in these parts were inclined to keep to themselves, lest they be dragged into their neighbors' misery. They had enough troubles of their own.

By the time I decided to move forward, the lady had already inched her way down the street and disappeared around the corner. Holding my breath with dread, I turned the doorknob and pushed on the front door, almost wishing that it would be locked. It wasn't.

Walking into the house felt like walking into a sarcophagus. The dusty curtains were pulled shut, casting eerie shadows on the mismatched furniture, and the air was stifling. The house was as dead as I felt—and that was a slight comfort to me. When I heard the sound of kids playing somewhere outside, I slammed the door behind me, shutting out all signs of life.

I stood in the darkened entryway, unsure whether I was going to fall down crying, start screaming at the top of my lungs, or both. I did neither. The only thing I wanted to do was get Victor's spit off my skin, as if his touch had left behind his microscopic bugs that would find refuge within my pores. I robotically went upstairs to draw a bath, not even bothering to touch the cold-water faucet. I would burn him off me.

The bathroom quickly filled with steam. Water droplets from the rolling vapor attached themselves to all surfaces, like the first snowfall of the season. I was now free to roam about the bathroom without fear of catching a glimpse of myself in the fogged mirror. I got undressed, and that's when I spotted it: all the blood. My hands and forearms were covered in Cameron's blood from when I had grabbed on to him, begging him to fight for us. My knees were also covered in blood.

My hands shaking, I hurriedly took off my clothes and stepped into the tub before I could fall apart. I sat in the water, barely feeling the burn against my skin. I was careful to tuck my knees into my chest so that my hands and knees stayed out of the water. The red stains on my skin were a reminder of everything I had lost.

I was rocking back and forth, numb, staring at the palms of my hands while tears washed my face.

This, his blood, was all I had left of him.

With every muscle resisting my brain's orders, I struggled to bring my knees down into the water. I was sobbing, deep convulsing sobs. I brought my arms and hands down next and watched his blood swirl in a haze, dissipating into my bathwater. I lay down and ducked my head underwater, silencing my cries.

Finally, my skin pruned and a towel wrapped around my body, I zombie-walked to my bedroom. As I stood dazed in the doorway, it took me a few minutes to realize that my room was completely empty: apart from the sheets on my bed, there was no trace of me left. I remembered that my stuff was somewhere out there being hastily packed up, so that nothing of me would remain behind as evidence of my dream and nightmare.

I yanked the curtain closed and walked away. It would take me a while before I would be able to go in there again. I rummaged through my roommate Cassie's room. Midway through the last school year, Cassie had decided that she was a vampire. Of the few clothes that she had left behind, all were black—good enough for walking around in my coffin.

Dressed for mourning, I went downstairs, turned on the TV, and lay on the couch. I hid under the blanket that I had dragged off of Cassie's bed and closed my eyes. I would stay in that spot, waiting for someone to come identify the body.

The pain had localized to my right hand, which had crunched when my fist connected with Spider's face. I'd spent my time watching the two middle fingers slowly grow black and blue until I couldn't bend them anymore. By the second morning, they were so swollen that the inflammation was starting to spread to the other fingers. All I wanted to do was sleep and forget. But the throbbing was keeping me up now. Grudgingly, I used some of Cassie's pale Goth makeup to cover up the nasty bruises that Victor had left on my cheek and neck, and I headed for the school medical clinic.

The x-rays confirmed that one finger was dislocated and the other had a hairline fracture.

"How did this happen?" the doctor asked, scanning my face over the edge of his glasses as if he could see my bruises through the pound of makeup.

"Kickboxing," I said without flinching. I had planned my excuse ahead of time.

"Hmmm," he said, disbelief coloring his tone. "One more day and gangrene would have set in."

He grabbed hold of my dislocated finger and, without warning, snapped it back into place. It didn't hurt as much as I would have thought, but the awful sound of bones cracking into place brought a wave of nausea. I pushed the doctor away just in time to puke in his garbage can. He rushed out of the room. A first-year medical student came to finish the work.

Though I had to sit still while the nervous student wedged— tried to wedge—my throbbing fingers into metal loops, at least there were no more questions. He needed to focus all his attention on his patient ... his first patient ever, apparently. He would probably remember this for the rest of his life—and I would try very hard to forget.

I trudged back to the house, looking down, avoiding eye contact with the people I passed on the street—as if these strangers knew everything, as if they were judging me for having survived Cameron. My pace quickened with every person who walked by. When I got back to the house, I almost slammed into Tiny on the walkway. He ignored me and went back to the truck for more boxes.

Carly was standing by Spider's truck, directing foot traffic. She warily walked over to me and pulled me to the side so that the guards could finish their job and get out of there.

"How are you?" she asked, her eyes scanning my face. The concern in her voice almost seemed genuine.

I glared back and squeezed my unbroken hand into a fist, but a booming bark woke me from the shadows. Meatball was pulling at his leash, which had been tied to one of the pillars of the front porch. The sight of him made me start crying. I was amazed that I had any tears left in me—everything else inside me had seemed to run dry.

"We brought Meatball. He should be with you," she said softly.

I wiped my cheeks with my shirtsleeve. Carly noticed my taped-up fingers. "Your hand! Is it broken?"

"It was worth it."

She pressed her lips together. "I don't know what you said to Spider in the car, but he was raging mad when he got back. I've never seen him so upset before. He looked like—"

"What? Like he was going to kill someone?"

Carly stood frozen, as though I had just slapped her in the face.

Tiny and the rest of the guards had finished carrying in my bins and were waiting for her by the truck.

"You can go now," I said bitterly.

She jumped, suddenly awake. "No, I can't. I have something for you." She pulled a folded piece of paper from the back pocket of her jeans and handed it to me. I unfolded it, and a business card fell out. Scribbled on the lined paper were some forty rows of jumbled letters, numbers, and dashes.

I looked up with a blank expression.

"That's all of them. Cameron's bank account numbers," she said with confidence. "There's a lot of cash too, but it'll take me a bit more time to get everything to you." I was seeing red, but she didn't notice and pointed to the card on the ground. "That's got our accountant's contact information. The accounts are everywhere around the world. It can get complicated. The accountant will help you get the money out. You can trust him."

If my two fingers hadn't been tangled in metal, I would have torn the piece of paper to shreds. But I settled for throwing it back in her face. She adeptly caught it.

"I don't want your blood money."

Tiny had started making his way to us as my temperature rose, but Carly stopped him with an outstretched hand. "It's not blood money, Emmy. Cameron ... would have wanted you to have this. You need the money."

"I don't need or want anything from you." My glare was meant to be intimidating, but the effect was lost with my angry tears.

"Em, please just take the money." Carly tried to give me the piece of paper again, but I knocked her hand away.

"You think that giving me money will make any of this better." I was sobbing now. "You betrayed him, Carly, all of you did. You were his only family. He trusted you. But like everyone else in his life, you turned your backs on him the minute he showed he was human. I loved him and he loved me. You destroyed that."

Carly's lips were quivering, but the lingering tears never fell. "Don't kid yourself, Emmy; I won't ever forgive myself for letting this happen. I'll have to live with this for the rest of my life."

Her gaze lingered on my face for a long second; I could see the pain in her eyes. "When Bill died, I thought I was going to die," she said. "Even after all the lies, I didn't want to live without him. But eventually, things started to get a little brighter again." Carly gently touched my arm, and I let her. "I know you hate my guts and don't believe a word I say, but things will get better for you too. I promise. Life goes on. You need to move on with it." She forced a smile and then turned to walk away. The tears had finally broken through.

I realized that Carly and I now had more in common than ever—with Bill and Cameron dead, we both had lost a brother and the love of our lives. We had both lost Rocco's light. We had lost so much. But, in that moment, I felt sorrier for Carly than I did for myself. For the rest of her life, she would be stuck with Spider and with the guilt of Cameron's death. For some of this, I pitied her.

Carly turned and walked back to the truck, "Keep yourself safe, Emmy," she called, without looking back. "And please, stay out of trouble." She climbed into the truck.

"I'm worried about you, Carly," I blurted out after her.

She turned. Her head tilted to the side. "You're worried about me?"

"Spider is dangerous. He'll stop at nothing to get what he wants."

This made her break into a smile. "I'm a survivor, Em. You don't need to worry about me. Just take care of yourself."

She closed the passenger door, and they all drove away. I wiped my face with my arm.

I walked over to my new roommate and looped my arms around his thick, furry neck. He struggled to get out of my bear hug and lick my face. After a few minutes, I sighed, released him from the porch post, and led us into our new lives.

****

How do you know when you're There? I had once wondered. Maybe you're lucky enough to notice the moment it's happening to you. Maybe you're able to block out all the other stuff that is, in the end, just background noise. But, most often, you don't know you were There until you lose it, or until it gets taken away from you. Only when you look back can you clearly see that time when all the pieces of you finally fit together to make you your whole self. Like one of those jumbo puzzles that take up your kitchen table: the pieces are just cardboard shapes with colors splashed on them, and they don't make sense until you fit them together. When you put the last piece into place and you have a complete picture, that's when you're There.

My life before Cameron was a jumbled mess: some pieces fit together, while others, like Bill's death, didn't fit at all. The day I met Cameron, the pieces started to take shape. The night he kissed me was when the last piece snapped into place.

But Cameron took that last piece with him, and a black hole was all that was left in its stead. How do you recover from that? How do you survive? You don't, I resolved; there's no coming back from that permanent void left inside of you.

I would become a shell, going through the motions without emotion, like a robot, while the rest of me was wherever Cameron was.

In a few days, my roommates would return, and school—the cycle—would start again. I vowed that I would play the part of the calm sane girl until the moment arose when I could execute vengeance on the people who took Rocco and Cameron away from me. Then, perhaps, I could find Cameron again, in death.

EPILOGUE

I was the kid who crawled out of the womb ready to fight, fists up and everything. I lay on the bed reminding myself of this while I breathed through the pain. But bullet wounds were nothing compared to the hole that had been blown through my heart, leaving a big, bleeding empty space. There was nothing Dr. Lorne could do to fix that hole. No amount of stitches would put her back in there to fill the space she had vacated.

No, people like me weren't built to deal with matters of the heart. Hell, as far as the outside world was concerned, a guy like me didn't have a heart to start with. I'd lived my life trying to prove them right—until recently.

How do you fight something you can't see? I asked myself. *How do you get rid of the guy who's messing with your business, when that guy is you?*

You turn the gun on yourself. It's the only way to sever the human from the gangster.

"Looks like the bullet went right through," Dr. Lorne announced. He was holding an x-ray up to the fluorescent ceiling light. We equipped him with a full ER in his house a few years ago—everything he needed to patch us up, including an x-ray machine. It was worth every penny. We kept him busy.

After Spider shot me in the shoulder, I let Carly drag me to Dr. Lorne's place. This was more for her benefit than for mine; if Carly doesn't have someone or something to worry about, she goes nuts. Dr. Lorne was the best in his field—Harvard Med, one of the top surgeons in the country—and he'd thrown it all away to follow his true passion: booze. But the best thing about Dr. Lorne was that he sobered up quick, took cash, and kept his mouth shut.

"You're a lucky man," he said.

I didn't feel lucky. Actually, I was jinxed. But I knew what he meant, and there was nothing lucky about it. Spider was a straight shot, even with his eyes closed and an arm tied behind his back. This had been methodically planned.

Twenty stitches later and I was good as new—well, my shoulder was, anyway.

Dr. Lorne took out his magic bag of pills, which we also supplied him with, and handed me two yellow ones. I grabbed the bag and took two more. Drugs are great that way: they fix everything that hurts, inside and out. The good doctor was in no position to judge me on this. He left me the bag and walked out.

Carly, who had been whimpering on a wooden chair in the corner while the doctor did his job, spoke up. "I don't think I can do this, Cameron. You should have seen Emmy when she heard the shots. It was ... horrible."

"I didn't need to see her, Carly. I heard her," I said dryly. I knew this day had been hard on Carly. I had heard some of the things Emmy was yelling at her. So had Spider—he'd looked like he was going to explode. But Carly understood what Emmy was going through; she'd been there herself a few years ago. She didn't hold Emmy's spiteful words against her, and I loved her more for it. But I also didn't need Carly to remind me of this day, either. When I heard Emmy's howls outside, it was like someone was stabbing me with a screwdriver. It was too hard to bear, more excruciating than I would have ever thought possible. Knowing that I was causing her all that pain ... I had never felt more pain than at that moment.

After Spider fired the last shots in the air, I had begged him to finish me. "Don't be stupid," he had answered abruptly, and then he quickly turned around and left. I had already glimpsed the tears in his eyes.

Spider couldn't kill me. No one could, unless the leaders decided. With me dead, no matter what Spider and Carly did, they would be next. The leaders left no room for witnesses, no room for revenge. There was no way that Spider was going to let that happen to Carly. And there was no way that I would let that happen to either of them. As annoying as they were sometimes, they were my brother and sister—blood ties or not.

"Why can't we forget all of this and bring her back?" Carly said, teary-eyed. "I promise to watch her like a hawk. Nothing will happen to her again. I should never have let you and Spider go through with this in the first place." She paused, no doubt remembering how that conversation had gone. "I wish you had listened to me when I told you and Spider that you were making a really big mistake."

"It's done, Carly. Deal with it," I sighed. There had been a moment when Emmy looked at me in the warehouse—like she was being tortured, like I was killing her—and I thought about forgetting about our plan and keeping her with me forever. But that could never happen. I couldn't keep Emmy caged up like an animal, like the rest of us. She was too beautiful, too free for that. Even if I could lock her up behind three-foot-thick cement walls, ten feet below the ground—a thought that had crossed my mind more than once—someone would eventually find her. Even if Shield weren't around anymore—and I was still determined to make that happen for good without getting the rest of us killed— there were a thousand others behind him who would readily take his place. As long as I was alive, Emmy would not be safe. I couldn't die yet, but I also couldn't fight off all the thugs that filled the underworld. Emmy had to be forced to stay away from me. And the only way that we could make that happen was to convince her that I was gone for good, force her to let me go and move on.

For a long second, Carly scanned my face the way I imagined a mother would. I already knew what she was thinking. "Cameron, you won't make it through this. I've seen the way you are with her. You're not the same anymore. You can't just go back to the way things were. This whole thing is going to kill you ... both of you."

"Drop it, Carly." I closed my eyes. The stupid pills were taking forever to work their magic.

I heard her sigh and get up. She took a few steps and stopped. "You were nuts to put those two together without me there to supervise," she mumbled. I forced a smile. Spider was as fond of Emmy as she was of him; it was a match made in hell. But apart from Carly, there was no one else in the world I trusted more than Spider to bring my girl home safely. Still, a shiver went down my spine as I wondered how the chit-chat in the car was going.

Carly headed out the door.

"Do me a favor?" I called out to her.

"Anything."

"Get my money to Emmy," I said, and added before she asked, "All of it."

"That's a lot of money."

"Please?"

"You know she won't take it, Cameron."

"You can convince anybody to do anything. It's your specialty."

"I'm losing my touch," she said sourly, and left.

Silence grew around me. I knew I needed to be thinking about how I was going to explain to the leaders everything that had happened in that warehouse, how I would explain all the favors that we owed, how I would keep our heads off the chopping block. My mind had to go back to being completely focused on the business again.

But all I could see in my head was Emmy's bruised, tear-stained face as she knelt by my side, begging me to stay. Instead, I had forced her to watch me let her go.

She's better equipped to deal with this than me, I told myself over and over. She'll forget about me, move on, get married, have a couple kids, and live till she's a hundred years old. No bullets will ever touch her skin. Emmy will survive me.

The fact that I wouldn't survive her didn't matter. I had already lost my kid brother. I wasn't about to lose her too. Knowing that Emmy was out there safe, living her life, even if it was without me, was enough.

It had to be.

Acknowledgments

I would like to thank my mom and dad for encouraging (i.e., bribing) me to read as a child.

I would also like to thank France, Jen, Jess, and Laura, my book club girls (a.k.a. the Baby Club and the Super Fatty Dessert Club). Asking them to proofread and critique my first manuscript was a tremendous favor, particularly when none of us have much time to ourselves anymore.

Thank you to the iUniverse team for your professionalism and timeliness. *Crow's Row* needed such a team!

A big thank you to my iUniverse editors, Elizabeth Day and Allison Gorman. There were times when I would read their comments and want to scream or hurt them a little. But I didn't, because I knew they were right, every time. This is painful for me to admit, so I'll move on.

To Allison Holen: Thank you for getting even more excited than me about designing the cover for the series. And for being patient.

To Alan Bower: Thank you for believing in me. Thank you for helping me feel proud to put my name on this book. You inspire me to keep writing (and editing) and better my craft.

And, finally, to the fans of Cameron and Emily: Here we are. Second edition of *Crow's Row*. I never thought I would be writing this. Surreal, really. I was able to do it because of you and your constant support. Thank you for your patience!

CPSIA information can be obtained at www.ICGtesting.com
Printed in the USA
LVOW06s0800300314

379408LV00001B/1/P